Aristotle and Poetic Justice

Margaret Doody teaches at the University of Notre Dame where she is the John and Barbara Glynn Family Professor of Literature. She is the author of a number of books including *The True Story of the Novel*, and is currently writing a book on Venice, as well as the new Aristotle book.

Also by Margaret Doody

Aristotle Detective

MAGARET DOODY

Aristotle and Poetic Justice

'Αριστοτέλης καὶ Στέφανος
An Aristotle and Stephanos Novel

ARROW

Published by Arrow Books in 2003

1 3 5 7 9 10 8 6 4 2

First published in the United Kingdom in 2002 by Century

Arrow Books
The Random House Group Limited
20 Vauxhall Bridge Road, London SW1V 2SA

Random House Australia (Pty) Limited
20 Alfred Street, Milsons Point, Sydney,
New South Wales 2061, Australia

Random House New Zealand Limited
18 Poland Road, Glenfield,
Auckland 10, New Zealand

Random House (Pty) Limited
Endulini, 5a Jubilee Road, Parktown 2193, South Africa

The Random House Group Limited Reg No 954009

www.randomhouse.co.uk

A CIP catalogue record for this book
is available from the British Library

Papers used by Random House
are natural, recyclable products made from wood grown in sustainable forests. The manufacturing processes conform to the environmental regulations of the country of origin

ISBN 0 09 943558 6

Typeset by SX Composing DTP, Rayleigh, Essex
Printed and bound in Great Britain by
Bookmarque Ltd, Croydon, Surrey

To the memory of two Georges:

George Parkin Grant (1918–1988), who taught philosophy at Dalhousie University in the long ago.
He spoke to me of Plato and my world changed.

and

George Forrest (W.G. G. Forrest, 1925–1997)
Fellow in Ancient History, Wadham College (1951–1977)
Wykeham Professor of Ancient History, New College, Oxford (1977–1992)
He shared his deep knowledge and vital love of Greece with all who came within his orbit. I am grateful for his generous enthusiasm, and for his sense of humour, as well as for his encouragement of my Aristotle on his first appearance.

List of Characters

INHABITANTS OF ATHENS

Stephanos, son of Nikiarkhos: citizen of Athens, age 25; former student and now friend of Aristotle

Eunike, daughter of Diogeiton: Stephanos' mother

Theodoros: Stephanos' young brother, nearly 10 years old

Dametas and Tamia: Stephanos' steward and his wife

Aristotle, son of Nikomakhos: philosopher, age 56; a man from Makedonia living in Athens, head of the Lykeion

Pythias: Aristotle's wife

Pythias the younger: Aristotle's young daughter, age between 5 and 6

Theophrastos: scholar, age 40; Aristotle's right-hand man at the Lykeion

Euphranor: little boy, best friend of Theodoros

Sophrine: Euphranor's sister, age 3

Kleiophoros: an important citizen but good natured, optimistic and anxious to be useful

'SILVER MEN'

Glaukon: freckle-faced citizen, silversmith and shrewd dealer

Ammonios: stout and well-to-do citizen; a major brothel-owner, now developing an interest in silver

Pataikos: middle-aged citizen, friend of Ammonios

Polemon: young man (age 19) of good family; ephebe doing military service; second cousin to Ammonios

FAMILY AND DESCENDANTS OF DEMODIKOS

1. Pherekrates: chief of the Silver Men, recently defunct

   Anthia: daughter of Pherekrates, age nearly 16; an heiress since death of her brother Demodikos; niece of Lysippos and temporarily under his care

   Kallirrhoe: slave of Anthia, age 17; a young woman of Ephesos known for her beauty

2. Lysippos: silversmith, brother of Pherekrates and a chief heir, now richest of the Silver Men

   Hegeso: Lysippos' sickly wife

   Straton: Lysippos' handsome second son, age 22; musical with a passion for flute-girls as well as for horses and chariots

   Gorgias: Lysippos' first son, age 23; missing in action after Battle of Issos

   Myrrhine: Lysippos' daughter, age 18; rumoured to be not quite right in the head

3. Timotheos, brother of Pherekrates and Lysippos, childless widower, philosophic and unworldly

PERSONS ENCOUNTERED ON JOURNEY

Menandros: a little boy with a sense of humour

Smikrenes: old farmer in deme of Eleusis; surly, does not like strangers

Philomela, daughter of Smikrenes: aged 15; possesses grey-green eyes and a sense of justice

Geta: Philomela's old nurse and house-servant to Smikrenes' family

Argos: Smikrenes' mangy house-dog

Anaxagoras: a goatherd

Lykidas: a shepherd

Diphilos: young bridegroom at a rural wedding

Korydon: surpassingly beautiful slave, age 19, in love with Kallirrhoe; formerly citizen of Ephesos who fought against Alexander's forces

CITIZENS AND VISITORS IN DELPHI AND ENVIRONS

Widow of Argos: assertive pilgrim with her own ideal project in mind

'Kleobis' and 'Biton': sons of the widow of Argos, on their first trip away from home

Diokles: Aristotle's old friend and proxenos; rich man of importance in Delphi

Haimon: keeper of brothel 'Haimon's Haven' in Kirrha

Plouta: his wife

Tita: Egyptian prostitute in Haimon's Haven

The Pythia: widow who acts as the voice of the Oracle of Apollo

Tomb-maker: pilgrim who has come to consult the Oracle

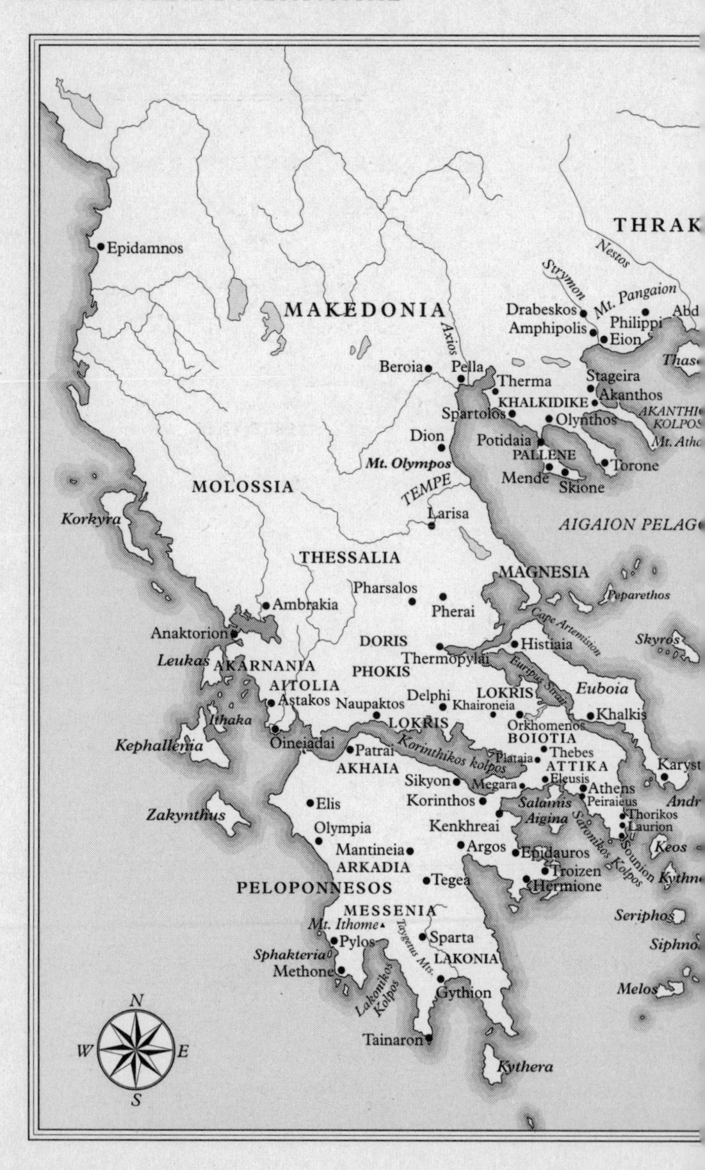
THRAK
Nestos
Strymon
Mt. Pangaion
Epidamnos
MAKEDONIA
Axios
Drabeskos
Amphipolis
Philippi
Eion
Beroia
Pella
Therma
Stageira
Akanthos
KHALKIDIKE
Spartolos
Olynthos
Dion
Potidaia
PALLENE
Mt. Olympos
Torone
Mende
Skione
MOLOSSIA
TEMPE
Korkyra
Larisa
AIGAION PELAG
THESSALIA
MAGNESIA
Pharsalos
Peparethos
Ambrakia
Pherai
Cape Artemision
Anaktorion
DORIS
Histiaia
Skyros
Thermopylai
Leukas
AKARNANIA
PHOKIS
Euripus Strait
AITOLIA
Euboia
Astakos
Naupaktos
Delphi
LOKRIS
Khaironeia
Khalkis
Ithaka
LOKRIS
Orkhomenos
Kephallenia
Oineiadai
BOIOTIA
Patrai
Korinthikos kolpos
Thebes
Plataia
AKHAIA
ATTIKA
Karyst
Eleusis
Sikyon
Megara
Athens
Korinthos
Salamis
Peiraieus
Elis
Zakynthus
Aigina
Thorikos
Olympia
Kenkhreai
Laurion
Saronikos Kolpos
Sounion
Mantineia
Argos
Epidauros
Keos
ARKADIA
Troizen
PELOPONNESOS
Tegea
Hermione
MESSENIA
Seriphos
Mt. Ithome
Taygetus Mts.
Sparta
Pylos
Sphakteria
LAKONIA
Methone
Lakonikos Kolpos
Gythion
Melos
N
W
E
S
Tainaron
Kythera

0 50 100 miles
0 500 1000 stadia
PONTIKON PELAGOS
Bosporos
Byzantion
Khalkedon
Hebros
PROPONTIS
Sangarios
Doriskos
Hellespontos
Kardia
Aigospotami
Sestos
Lampsakos
Abydos
Imbros
Granikos
Kyzikos
Daskylion
BITHYNIA
Kynos Sema
Troia
MYSIA
Tenedos
Sigeion
Antandros
Assos
Adramyttion
Adramyttenos Kolpos
Methymna
Lesbos
Eressos
Mitylene
Pergamon
Arginussai
Phokaia
Kyme
Hermos
Sardis
PHRYGIA
Khios
Erythrai
Klazomenai
Teos
LYDIA
Kaystros
Ephesos
Tralles
Maiandros
IGAION PELAGOS
Samos
Mt. Mykale
Magnesia
Priene
Ikaria
IKARION PELAGOS
Mykonos
Miletos
Didyma
KARIA
Patmos
SPORADES
Leros
Naxos
Halikarnassos
Kos
Knidos
YKLADES
Telemissos
Phaselis
Eurymedon
LYKIA
Xanthos
Thera
Rhodos
Lindos
Khelidoniai

Plan of Delphi
Sacred Precinct and Environs

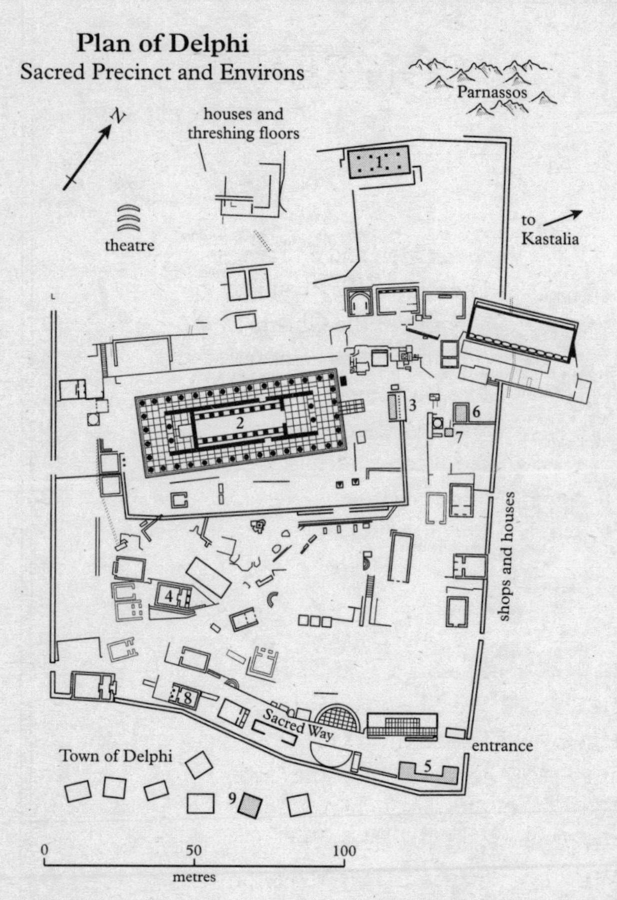

Key

1. Leskhe of the Knidians
2. Temple of Apollo
3. Altar of Apollo
4. Treasury of the Athenians
5. Monument of the Spartan Admirals
6. Chariot of Helios
7. Tripod of Plataia
8. Treasury of the Siphnians
9. House of Diokles

CONTENTS

I	Silver Men and an Heiress	1
II	The Flower Festival and the Night of the Ghosts	27
III	Goblins and Disappearances	48
IV	The Ill-Tempered Man	75
V	Man in a Landscape	97
VI	Rural Interludes	114
VII	Into the Hills	138
VIII	The Slave's Tale	158
IX	Fire and Water	173
X	Delphi	188
XI	The Silver Singer	204
XII	The Brothel at Kirrha	226
XIII	The Beautiful Girl	249
XIV	The Hanged Girl	270
XV	The Elektra of the Cave	288
XVI	The Oracle of Apollo	310
XVII	The Murderer	322
XVIII	Justice and an Abductor	340
XIX	Silver, Gold and Virtue	358
XX	Aristotle's Poetics	381

I

Silver Men and an Heiress

Inspire me, O waters of the Kastalian spring, that I may speak well-omened words. Hear me, O Muses who dwell by the Spring of Hippokrene, Thalia and Melpomene, and speak through me that I may relate in fitting manner my surprising tale. It is a tale of wrongs done to well-born maidens, of murder and rescue, of silver mines and ghosts and wanderings by the way. In the wanderings my own life was changed, and to my surprise a marriage came in view. Let me make clear the truth, even as my master Aristotle made truth appear. Let me render him due honour. And may I also honour the great Oracle at Delphi. Apollo be praised.

Perhaps I should start with the day I first encountered the circle of citizens I still think of as 'the Silver Men'. That was on the tenth day of Anthesterion – a cool month, but it is also the beginning of spring. The eleventh day of

Anthesterion brings us the Flower Festival, the Anthesteria. It is the time of beginning for new shoots and buds when we celebrate the return of Dionysos after the deathly suspension of winter, when the generous god of wine is absent. It is in that month of first flowers, and in that festival time, strangely enough, that we also celebrate accursed Orestes' visit to Athens, doing strange honour to the unfortunate young man who had been doomed to avenge his father's death by killing his mother. Pursued by the Furies for his matricide, Orestes was tried in Athens and at last freed of blood-guilt by the decree of Phoibos Apollo. I remember when someone first told me the tale of Orestes, and what a chill it gave me as a child, and how I wondered if he did not feel badly about killing his mother even after the court said he was free of blame. Of course I was thinking of my own dear mother, not the wicked queen, and I did not then understand the story, a subject of celebrated poems and dramas. At the Anthesteria also we celebrate the youngest children of Athens, those who have reached the age of three and are thus safely out of infancy and likely to thrive. But we also remember the dead, those who have gone before, and whose spirits may walk among us on the Night of the Ghosts. And along with them perhaps mischievous spirits, like goblins and harpies. So, all in all, the Anthesteria seems a strange festival to foreigners, combining blood-guilt and mirth, wine and familial murder, Dionysos and Hades, children and ghosts.

My tale certainly has to do with the three-day festival itself in that year when Aristophanes (the less important one) was arkhon – the spring when Alexander was making himself master of Persia, just after he had captured Persepolis and taken the treasure of one hundred and twenty thousand talents of silver.

I, Stephanos of Athens, had recovered from the trial of my cousin Philemon in the previous year. My cousin had returned to Athens, and our family affairs were in better order. It was the troubles of another and much wealthier Athenian family that were to touch my life at the time of the Flower Festival, and to send Aristotle and myself unexpectedly bound on a springtime journey, as you shall hear. But to make all clear, I should go back to the day before the holiday began.

I remember that day with its Silver Men very clearly. I went up to the Agora to register a land rental; I was letting most of the farm outside Athens to a country citizen, at a good rent. My new tenant farmer was a citizen, and had some connections in Athens, so I was happy to be seen with him. In the Agora, the official buildings were crowded. The Council was busily drafting a bill to be put to the Assembly. Interested citizens as well as hangers-on were pressing round the Tholos, that democratic circular building where the fifty prytaneis, elected by lot so there are five from each of the ten tribes, dine daily at public expense when presiding over public business. Today also the Board of Public Contracts, the Poletai, were about to announce the names of those who had won the leases of some very pretty silver mines in Laurion. This always aroused great interest; nobody dislikes the chance to mine silver. Except, of course, the wretched slaves who must dig the precious stuff out of the ground.

The land in the region of Laurion is pitted with mine-shafts, and dotted about with mills and ore washeries where the silver ore is separated from lead. The good ore must be taken to furnaces to be transformed into pure refined silver. Towns like Thorikos had flourished on all this activity, but most of the really rich producers of silver enjoy life in the city of Athens.

It was the wealth of the silver mines – which belong to Athens – that permitted Perikles in the old days to beautify our city with so many wonderful buildings. True, the mining had lapsed during a long period, and not only in the wars between Sparta and Athens, when the Spartans invaded and took over the diggings and the slaves. For a time afterwards, the coinage had been largely bronze, with a little gold; some coins were only copper with a thin coat of silver that wore off easily. Later, when Athens recovered control of Laurion, the beautiful silver coins returned. Our mines had prospered since that time, and greatly expanded. Everyone with a concession had to pay a sum to the government for the right to undertake the work; a man working on a new mine had to pay to the city the twenty-fourth part of the proceeds. But there were strong advantages. There was the tempting possibility of immediate wealth – and at this time also a valuable concession, the permission not to pay war-tax on the proceeds. That seemed an odd thing, as we were supposed to be proud of paying taxes. Athenian taxes are publicly voted on, and we had recently been urged by highly respected leaders to strengthen Athens. As a further inducement to go in for silver mining, a silver man was exempted from certain public services to the state. A mine-owner wouldn't have to use part of his proceeds in liturgies usually expected of the wealthy, like producing plays for the Great Dionysia or fitting out a warship. Liturgies give a man honour, but they are expensive. If this exemption from taxation, this *ateleia*, was meant to encourage investors in mining, it succeeded. For there were evidently enough people who didn't care about garnering civic honours but did care for the immediate wealth and the tax exemptions, judging from the many bidders now putting in for the Laurion concessions.

I was not one of the rich citizens who could bid for such contracts, of course. But I took more interest in public affairs than I had done in my youth; now that I was a responsible citizen it seemed likely that I would soon be serving on a public committee. Every man over twenty-five years old takes his turn, and I would be twenty-five this spring.

After my new tenant and I had transacted our business, we paused by the bronze statues of the Ten Heroes to read the public notices set out on the white boards. There were drafts of bills which were to come before the Council, and the usual list of impending lawsuits – civil suits of the kind that keep jurors in pay. 'Arkhilaos brings Epikrates before the court on the charge of removing his landmark' and so on. One older notice was still standing: 'Glaukon brings Pherekrates before the court on the charge of selling silver at false weight.' This was a serious charge enough, but the notice was sadly out of date, for Pherekrates of the deme of Kydathenaion had been dead and in his grave for over a week. As a dead man can't be brought before a court, the suit would have to be altered. The dead man's inheritor would have to be brought to answer the charge. Altering the suit would take time – less satisfactory to the accuser. I pointed this out to my tenant, who, coming from a country deme, was not so well versed as I in affairs of the city. But he had heard of the rich Pherekrates.

Pherekrates had begun life as a silversmith, like his father Demodikos before him. The father had died prosperous, having accumulated land and slaves. Even though this wealth had been divided among three sons, Pherekrates had been able to profit by his beginnings, and to triple his property in the first ten years. Before he died, he had acquired property in Peiraieus, and in Athmonon; he was the owner of two merchant vessels, and of a small ancillary factory in the west of Athens as well as the factory in his own deme. He still continued to make a good income from that original concern, where silver was melted and worked, and jewellery and silver-bronze statues created. This impressive business he shared with his equally successful brother Lysippos. If we were all as rich as Pherekrates our troubles would be few – not that Pherekrates was to be envied now, since he had died in his bed and departed this life and these factories.

After we had read over the notices, I treated my tenant to a drink and some food, to seal our bargain. We were lingering, hoping to meet his guest-friend and distant kinsman, Kleiophoros, when the latter was finished with business for the day. I earnestly hoped for this introduction to Kleiophoros. I really needed to make connections in the city and re-establish our family. Just this morning, my own mother had asked, 'Why don't you know important people?' My mother, Eunike, daughter of Diogeiton, was descended from great men of the founding tribe of the Erekhtheidai, and had brought some land with her dowry. Though she lived in modest retirement as the widow of a well-born citizen, she daily had sufficient occasion to observe in our domestic life the fact that we lived in no splendid manner. I did not give dinner-parties, nor did high-born or rich men come to visit me to take wine in the main room of our house. Now, Kleiophoros was an important person, an official in the city, and he had good connections with men who were, if not distinguished by good birth, exceedingly well-to-do like Pherekrates (now departed) and Lysippos. Fortunately my tenant took this day as a holiday, and was not impatient.

We wandered through the Agora and around the Akropolis for a while. I was able to point out to him the site where the new stadium would be, after we peered across at the construction work upon the Hill of the Pnyx, the rocky hill where the Assembly of the people always met; the renovation of the Assembly building had been going on for at least ten years now. Athens was currently under construction. Since the energetic and incorruptible Lykourgos had been controller of finances, Athens looked more important and prosperous than ever. Lykourgos' taxation system had doubled the state revenue, and, as well as reorganising the military system and creating and outfitting warships, he had certainly gone in for building the city so it would shine in splendour in the eyes of the peoples of the earth. New golden statues of victory glistened on the Parthenon. Our new temple of Apollo shone brightly in the Agora. Having seen enough of these sights, my tenant and I eventually wandered into the Poikile, the Painted Colonnade, to hear the news.

'Stephanos – how pleasant to see you!' A tall stout man clapped me vigorously on the shoulder. It was Ammonios, well-to-do citizen and merchant. Since I and my family had emerged into a clearer light (after my cousin's trial) many people had become more friendly to me. At least they recognised me. The prosperous like prosperity. It may be that Ammonios thought that now I was twenty-five I would soon hold some office of importance, perhaps as one of the *sitophylakes*, the Grain Guardians, as my father had once been. That might not be as pleasant as of yore; there were rumours of shortages, and even though Alexander had just taken Egypt, so rich in grain, there were anxieties about grain supplies since we had to import so much. As far as public office was concerned, it would be better to be one of those in charge of the *Emporion*, the market area all about the harbour. I might rise to such a position – ultimately – if I could only raise my family's circumstances. We were not as badly off as in recent years after my father's death, when we were shackled by debts and then by the infamous charge of murder against my cousin, and the ensuing trial. But at present everything seemed static. Nothing I could do seemed to make any striking improvement. I introduced my tenant to the Athenian merchant, and Ammonios clapped him on the shoulder likewise.

'And how are you, Stephanos? But I needn't ask. Had some lively girls, lately, eh?' He nudged my ribs. 'If you want a change, I could introduce you to something agreeable. A little poppet who'd entertain you royally, if you know what I mean. I tell you as a friend,' he added, 'not in the way of business, ha! ha!'

The stout man's friendliness was not to my liking, although many found it agreeable enough. Indeed, some found it more than agreeable. Ammonios, a widower, would invite friends (and acquaintances whom he desired to impress) home to try out a new boy cup-bearer or a musical slave-girl with notable accomplishments. An important part of his business concerned a smart brothel in Peiraieus; to this, once his friends had used her, each notable cup-bearer or flute-player would eventually be sent.

'And here's Polemon,' exclaimed Ammonios, hailing him. 'Fresh from new conquests, no doubt.' The young man did not look over-eager to join us, but greeted us politely. Polemon was a graceful youth, blue-eyed with locks of curling brown hair. His beard, like his manhood, was just beginning. Although at the age of nearly twenty he was doing his military service, he still seemed shy, if stronger and more sunburned than of yore. Polemon's vivid youthfulness made even me feel my age, while beside him my rural citizen looked countrified and heavy-footed, and Ammonios obese and coarse-grained. Polemon harmonised well with the great mural behind him, the painting of the Athenians arrayed against the Spartans. Flabby Ammonios before this picture of ancient glory looked like a satire on the age.

'Well, well,' said Ammonios gravely. 'You know Stephanos, son of Nikiarkhos? Polemon is a sort of cousin of mine,' he explained to me. Polemon blushed, and glared at Ammonios. 'Second cousin,' he muttered. (I had not realised they were related – they certainly did not look alike. Would Polemon ever become so richly endowed with chins?)

'Well, my cousin Polemon the ephebe, he's got to go among the girls, now he's got a beard, and has entered the military. No more boyish fun. That's so, isn't it, Polemon? Still at your exercises, my lad? Going to fight for

Alexander if he'll let you? And how are the night manoeuvres going?'

Ammonios chuckled, and looked at the other wall with its painting of Theseus and his men fighting the Amazons. 'Now there's the kind of war I should prefer. Well, we don't get everything we want, 'tis true. Though I once knew a strange girl who would – but mustn't babble. How is my cousin, your honoured father?'

'My father is very well,' said Polemon formally. 'He is of course grieved at the death of his friend Pherekrates.'

'Yes, oh, yes. A friend and neighbour. Saw your father at the funeral. Very sad, old Pherekrates popping off like that. Lying alone – bad for the health. Too bad, and him so rich. I hear he had nearly six hundred slaves working in his diggings at Laurion – almost as good as rich Kallias of yore, or his son. How some people do get on! Six hundred slaves dig-digging away, and him lying on a bed trying to dig up another breath. Poor old silversmith!'

'He was a very respectable man,' said Polemon, a trifle frostily. 'There's nothing wrong with mining,' he added. 'The wealth of mines has made Athens great in the past. Wasn't it Themistokles or somebody who had two hundred warships built from the proceeds?'

'No need to persuade *me*, my civic-minded cousin, of the value of our silver mines – Athens' "treasury in the earth" as one of those old dramatists had it. But you see all his silver didn't save Pherekrates from going underground himself. And now the great question is – who will get all that money? Hey? What's to become of the little Anthia, now she's an heiress? Can you tell me that?'

Polemon's face lost its look of forced deference. His muscles tightened, but he replied civilly, 'Anthia is under the guardianship of her uncle Lysippos. Doubtless he will marry her off suitably. Actually, they – he promised her to *me*.'

Ammonios laughed. 'Suitably indeed! If you can make them keep to it. You're over-young for marriage. Or Lysippos will marry her himself, *suitably*. It's an old Athenian law – that the man nearest of kin is entitled to marry an heiress. Have you thought of that?'

Polemon looked shocked. 'But – he's *old* – and he already has a wife.'

'True. In a manner of speaking. But everyone knows that Hegeso is sickly and ailing. Can you really call that having a wife, now? I admit, she gave Lysippos two sons, and although he could divorce her, she is the daughter of a well-born man, who would be bound to take offence if there were any mention of divorce. But, as to being old, Lysippos is no older than myself. And *I* am still in service.'

'Surely,' I said, 'the custom is rather that the guardian marries the heiress if her estate is *small*, so that she will be provided for. Otherwise, it would be necessary for her father's brother to endow her from his own estate. But there is no problem of that kind here. Lysippos is so rich that the girl can be married to someone befitting her station. A man of good family, even without great wealth – someone who will look after her properly.' I faintly hoped that someone might remark upon my fitness for that post, but nobody did.

'Hmm. The little poppet will bed well enough, with whoever comes to her door. But – money's money.' Ammonios' restless eye swept over the crowds. 'Don't whet your appetite for little Anthia too soon, Polemon my friend. My guess is that Lysippos will marry her off to

Straton, his second son. His *only* son now. Keep the money in the family and make everyone happy. Don't *you* think everyone can be happy, Polemon?'

Ammonios looked down at the young man, smiling merrily, grey eyes sparkling. Polemon blushed again, rather from anger than from modesty. 'Surely,' he protested, 'the honour of a man's word should be respected. Straton might not wish this marriage, but even if he does . . . If her father Pherekrates had already betrothed his daughter to someone else –'

'That's with last week's dinner. Gone to the shithouse.' Ammonios spoke curtly; the smile had vanished from his eyes. 'A guardian must do what he thinks fit. Whoever marries her will have the chinks. No use in whining. You mark my words, Straton, son of Lysippos, will soon be couching with the wealthy Anthia.'

Ammonios laughed, but not merrily, a sound like a hammer striking metal. Then the big man summoned the twinkle back to his eyes, and he added with emphatic joviality, 'Four legs in a bed. Many a good game can be played in a bed, isn't it so, Polemon?'

'Sir! How can you!' protested Polemon, blushing hotly. But Ammonios proceeded unmoved.

'Not like taking a widow with a hump, either. The little Anthia's as pretty as a picture. I saw her in the Procession last year. Wouldn't mind her myself. Gold hair, fine figure, not yet sixteen. Now there's a poppet, there's a plum –'

'She is a lady,' said Polemon angrily. 'She is the well-bred daughter of a citizen of Athens. Gentle virgins should not be spoken of in that manner.'

'Only my talk, my dear boy,' said Ammonios, refusing to be offended. He threw his arm about young Polemon's shoulders – like a friend, but also like a person of authority restraining someone. Ammonios' small grey eyes, partly hidden among their creases, showed little humour. I wondered if he had been truly offended by his young relative's protest and I realised that I should not care to see Ammonios really angry. Up until that moment I had thought of him simply as an ageing lecher. As if sensing my thoughts, Ammonios at once became lighter and full of smiles. He gave his young relative a merry tap on the shoulder. 'And *marriage* – hmm – marriage is not a garden of delights, when all's said and done. The prettiest wives will fade. They take to puking while they're breeding, and scolding the servants. More pleasure in my flute-girl, after all.'

Polemon turned on his heel, mumbling a farewell, and strode away. Ammonios laughed.

'That young lad has fine hopes of his own, of leading home a pretty bride under a rain of figs and silver coins. Their fathers are – were – neighbours, even friends. But I fear it will be beyond Polemon's father's power to give his son this toy. Lysippos won't let the lady escape from his own household. *That* family didn't get their wealth by inattention. My father knew old Pherekrates' father – he'd pick up a hemi-obol from a dung heap, even in his warmest days.'

'It is sad,' I remarked without sorrow, 'that the departed Pherekrates left no real heir. Wasn't there a son once?'

'A sad story. There *was* a son once. Died, seven years ago, at Khaironia, when Athens and Thebes fought together against – well, you know how it was, doubtless. The son and heir, young fellow in his military service, sent home in a jar. That's why there's no real heir for Pherekrates, only the girl.'

'Yes, I see,' I said. 'A sad fate.' I had been nearly old enough to fight myself in that war against King Philip of Makedon and his victorious son Alexander, who had led the Makedonian cavalry himself in that very battle. No one in Athens liked to mention that war or that defeat unnecessarily nowadays. Athens, like almost every other Greek state, resisted no more but was really ruled by Philip's great son, Alexander.

'That's war for you,' said Ammonios. 'You leave the city like a hero, sword flashing, horses stamping, very fine – and come back in a jar, like potted dates. Not but what that's better than the fate of Lysippos' elder son. You know Lysippos' son, Straton, Stephanos. A very fine fellow, and a good singer. Loves music – oho! He had a favourite mistress who was a really fine instrumentalist. His flute-girl – I've got her in my brothel now. If you see Straton, tell him Lalage sends greetings from Peiraieus.'

'I do know Straton,' I admitted.

'But I don't think you knew his brother. Poor Gorgias. They do seem to have ill luck with sons, that family. He went off to wars a few years ago, like your cousin Philemon who gave your family such a lot of trouble. Off to the war went young Gorgias, following Alexander – and died. Declared missing in action in one of the skirmishes after the battle of Issos town. Bones lie in foreign land, somewhere. Not even a jarful sent home. Not so much as a spot of soot to remember him by. Sad, isn't it? We're all here today and gone tomorrow. That's why I say, take your pleasure while you can.' Ammonios nudged me lightly, and laughed again.

The man seemed in a jolly gossiping humour enough. Yet I had thought all the time he was talking to us that Ammonios was really only filling in time, waiting for someone else. He seemed restless, and his eyes constantly left us to search the scene. A sudden bustle roused the porch, with new arrivals and louder conversations.

One man detached himself and made his way through the throng to Ammonios. This man, a friend of Ammonios and partner in some of his enterprises, barely acknowledged myself and my companion as he pushed brusquely up to the stout man. One could see from his face that he did not bring happy tidings.

'The contracts have been declared,' he said. 'We're not among them. Lysippos has obtained the same contract his brother used to have – *and* one of his own. And of course the benefit of the *ateleia*. It's outrageous!'

'But predictable, my good Pataikos.' Ammonios was scowling, but he shrugged elaborately as if to display his indifference to all.

'Well,' his friend declared, 'at one time a man could get into this honeypot with two or three slaves, but now the big men keep the best of the game in their own hands. They know there's a good time coming. When you think how that devil Alexander is going to need silver – and silver coins – to pay for troops and supplies!'

'Hush,' said Ammonios. 'Alexander has his fill of riches. He is swimming in the silver of Persepolis, at this moment.'

'But that silver may stay in the East, both for the cost of conquest and for handy bribes to leading men of the Persians' empire.'

'True,' interjected Ammonios. 'Not all those in the

Persian empire cared for the Persian yoke, and many regions would change allegiance rather than resisting if it were made worth their while.'

'Just so,' Pataikos continued heatedly. 'Alexander can conquer part of Asia and buy out the rest. Alexander can *always* use silver. Hunger and thirst after silver will grow with what it feeds on! After all, Egypt, however rich in wheat, is not a home for silver. And what Mint but our Athenian one will Alexander want? Who makes better coins than Athens? Lysippos can eat silver fruit all day long. And as for that upstart Glaukon – the lowborn silversmith, whose grandfather crawled up from the back alleys of Peiraieus! – Glaukon has a better concession than he had before. As for the others –'

Ammonios stopped him, with a wave of his hand. 'Say no more,' he said heartily. 'It all goes as we expected.' He turned to us, smiling. 'My friend Pataikos thought we ought to make a bid for the game's sake. But we had no real expectation of winning. We shall happily be spared the cost of importing wood to shore up old tunnels in Laurion. As you see, I didn't even trouble to go to the Council Chambers today.'

The fat man laughed, and gave his friend a slap on the back; this seemed to be Ammonios' panacea for all ills. 'It gives us an excuse to drink deep even before the Festival begins – to console ourselves. And I have a new girl I simply must show you. There are mines better than silver.' He turned to us. 'I know you will excuse myself and my friend. I have promised him we shall dine. But remember, Stephanos, my advice about the poppet. It's bad for the health to lie alone. Take care of your health, and let the world take care of itself.'

I was not sorry to see the departure of this lascivious merchant. His vulgar conversation with us had been designed only to fill in the time. I had the humbling impression that Ammonios thought it best to talk to unimportant people while waiting for his news, and that the news itself had not been such a slight disappointment as he made out.

'If the meeting is over, let us go and look for your guest-friend Kleiophoros,' I suggested to my new tenant. I hoped that Kleiophoros might be found in the neighbourhood of the successful bidders, especially Lysippos. I had a definite desire to become the friend of a man who had an heiress in his gift. (And so important a man: my mother would surely approve, although even Lysippos was not quite as well-born as she would have preferred in her Athenian heart.) After all, I thought, if Lysippos was going to throw over Polemon as a potential son-in-law, might I not try to gain the prize? I was equally well-born, and somewhat older than Polemon, who was really much too young to marry . . .

I cogitated in this manner as we strolled past the Porch of Zeus, making our way through the crowds coming in the other direction, and overhearing various remarks about the shipping bill and the mine contracts. When we arrived at the Tholos it was almost empty, but Kleiophoros and some others were still sitting there, going over documents in that calm round building. I was in luck. One of the men in that round room that smelt of dinners was Lysippos.

Good-natured Kleiophoros greeted us both cordially.

'Have you heard? Up to our knees in silver this morning. Such a busy session we are having. And here it is spring – or nearly – already. With a good harvest this year, Athens should prosper. Lykourgos has raised taxes, it's true, but he's brought a lot of new business into the city.' Kleiophoros always looked on the bright side, and life treated him well.

'How is my friend Aristotle?' he continued. 'I've not seen him lately. Do you know . . . ? Permit me to introduce Stephanos, son of Nikiarkhos, to the honoured citizen Lysippos. Lysippos has a new contract; we were just going over the agreement. Of course we in the Council know Lysippos very well for his excellent work in the Mint.'

Lysippos (brother of Pherekrates deceased) was certainly well known to me by sight. Of course, I was known to him since he had been on the jury at Philemon's trial, but we were not personally acquainted. After what I had heard that morning, I looked upon him with attention. Lysippos, the rich silver merchant. Lysippos, father of Straton (extant) and of Gorgias (deceased). Lysippos, now the chief Silver Man.

Lysippos who was all these things was a fine-looking man, not yet fifty years of age. He was impressively broad, in a way that would have made a shorter or less upright man look stubby, and he had fine dark brown hair and a beautiful beard, attractively touched with grey – or perhaps I ought in his case to say silver. He was dressed simply, but wore one ornament about his arm, a plain and narrow (if beautifully chased and polished) bracelet of his own make and metal.

This wealthy man addressed me in a polite and agreeable fashion, refreshing after Ammonios' familiarity. Lysippos spoke like an educated man, and his deep voice was pleasant; I remembered that Lysippos, like his son, had some youthful reputation as a singer.

'Indeed, Stephanos, it is a pleasure. I am acquainted with the philosopher Aristotle, and from him I have heard fine things of you. He is my very good friend.'

'Yes, it is agreeable to talk of philosophy now and then, isn't it?' said Kleiophoros. 'Though we men of business cannot always find the time. When I'm working on the Council, or when the ships go out, I assure you I don't have a minute's peace for days on end. And when one hasn't time . . .' he sighed happily and turned to speak to my tenant, leaving Lysippos and myself to our own devices.

'I hear,' I said, trying to think of a businesslike topic that would interest such a man, 'that there will be difficulties with trade and shipping this year. Because of Alexander's war. And more pirates.'

'Perhaps,' said Lysippos. 'But look on the bright side – now Alexander has taken Egypt, we shall have Egyptian grain. The best! Business doesn't look too bad.' He smiled, in self-deprecation. 'There you are now – we men of business like to persuade ourselves that business is the only thing in the world. I persuade myself so, much of the time. But at some moments I don't believe it, so there's hope for me yet. Assuredly I cannot account myself a philosopher. Nor even a true guardian, the kind Plato talks about in his *Republic*. But a secondary guardian, one of the helpers? A good dog for a ruling shepherd?' He laughed gently, with his eyes, not guffawing in Ammonios' loud fashion. I decided I liked Lysippos.

'I know your son Straton,' I volunteered.

'Straton, yes. A fine boy, my son – a fine *man*, I ought

to say – but he's always at the games. He has a passion for horses and chariots. I complain as a father ought, but I'm really proud of him. Your father would be very proud of you, Stephanos. I'm pleased to see Nikiarkhos has such a worthy successor.'

I was spared the embarrassment of answering, for a shadow fell upon the bench where we were sitting, a shadow even in that dull hall with its grey-brown stone walls.

'Lysippos, my friend, do introduce me.'

'Most happy,' said Lysippos, rising courteously. 'Glaukon, this is Stephanos, son of Nikiarkhos.'

This was the Glaukon who had won a silver contract. Another Silver Man. I knew him by reputation: he or his factory made some of the best and most costly pans and ewers in Athens. His father had been in the tinkering trade, and had made a modest success of it, but his son's success had been startling. Glaukon the silversmith was rumoured to be nearly as well-to-do as Lysippos himself.

Lysippos' family was ancient Athenian, even if the man's grandfather had not been wealthy at birth. Glaukon's family was not noble at all. This clutch of scrawny blue-eyed people had come up from Peiraieus – and, as some said, from the gods knew where. Glaukon was a thin man, with flat lank yellow hair that seemed to have faded annually in the summer sun of each of his thirty-three years. He wore a fine khiton, but his arms were stringy with muscles and lavishly freckled. There was something comical in his appearance, largely because of his pale hair, the freckles about his round blue eyes and his slightly twisted nose. One expected him to say something funny, like the comic slave in a play.

'How do you do?' said Glaukon solemnly. 'It is indeed a pleasure.' He spoke gravely and slowly, hesitating as if afraid something wrong would come out if he didn't take care of his words. After every sentence he sighed, as if speech were a rather sad craft. If he knew about his comic appearance, he was determined to contradict it.

'My congratulations, my dear Lysippos, on renewing Pherekrates' contract. I know how much it means to you.'

'My congratulations to yourself. I might add that I know how much it means to *you*.'

There was a slight pause. One of Glaukon's shoulders jerked slightly, as if he were getting rid of an insect, but he continued to gaze solemnly and unwinkingly at us both through eyes defended by sandy lashes.

'Our friendship,' he said, 'means much to me, Lysippos. Despite that temporary difference with Pherekrates. I meant to wish you joy of the Festival. Could we not meet during the second day for –'

'The very thing,' said Lysippos. 'Just what I was going to say to *you*. And to you, Stephanos. Will you not both join me on the twelfth day of the month for the Feast of the Wine Jugs? I have already invited the philosopher Aristotle. And Ammonios, with his kinsman Polemon. What of yourself, Kleiophoros? And your friend here?'

My tenant explained that he had to go home, and Kleiophoros said that he was engaged elsewhere for the feast. 'And,' he added with impressive self-pity, 'I shall have to give over feasting early, for I am deputed to stay on duty here at the Tholos on the thirteenth day – the day and night of the Pots. Defending our public weal, and guarding the city. Public office has its inconveniences. Pity me, having to spend such a night all alone here – or nearly.'

'The tax on grandeur, Kleiophoros. You will have a number of the prytaneis with you. Somebody has to be on duty every night in case of emergency, although emergency seems hardly likely on the last night of the Anthesteria. Departing spirits will surely not be ill-mannered enough to interfere with our Tholos. Mournful Orestes or vengeful ghosts or mischievous goblins, they will all leave *you* alone.'

'True enough,' said Kleiophoros, 'but there are some jolly games one could play at home. And the servants tell old stories. I prefer being at home on festival days.'

Our arrangements having been made for the hour of dining, Lysippos and I parted company. I was flattered to be invited to the home of such a wealthy and important man – although it must be admitted that an invitation to the Feast of the Wine Jugs is the cheapest invitation a man can offer during the whole year, since the guests bring their own food and drink.

Kleiophoros, his guest-friend, and I went off together, Kleiophoros grumbling happily about the pressure of work until he turned to discussing the friends we had just left.

'Glaukon's a good fellow, isn't he? And it's a pleasure to see how harmoniously he and Lysippos get along now. Glaukon is a rival of Lysippos, but only in business. Some say that there is bad blood between them, but I don't see any of it. A good thing if Glaukon were to drop that lawsuit against Lysippos' brother. Poor Pherekrates – gone now. Of course, Lysippos wishes it, but I think Glaukon wants to make peace, too. You know, *I* believe they're considering going into partnership. Mark my words. Favouring winds may be blowing Glaukon a fine lady with a bagful of dowry. Good way to bring a partner into the family.'

'Do you mean that Glaukon is to marry the heiress? Pherekrates' daughter?'

'No – no. Didn't Pherekrates arrange his daughter's betrothal to some boy? I was thinking of Lysippos' own child. His only daughter, Myrrhine. He will have to marry her off well, won't he? What could be more suitable?'

'Myrrhine? Yes, I'd forgotten that he had a daughter.' My thoughts wandered a little on the subject of marriage. In former days my father had tried to arrange an advantageous match for me, though at the time I was over-young according to Athenian custom for marriage, and the girl at the time only thirteen. My father had rather desperately hoped for some money advantage by arranging an alliance with Kallimakhos. Even now, I still hadn't made up my mind whether to marry Kallimakhos' girl or not. The arrangements had been made before my father's death revealed our financial difficulties; Kallimakhos had then drawn back, when our family was menaced with severe trouble and disgrace. Nowadays the man took pains to be agreeable, but I was not at all sure whether I wanted to deal with him and his daughter again. It would be a trifle awkward to withdraw, absolutely and openly – but Kallimakhos deserved no better. I should probably look about me for another good alliance. Now, Lysippos' daughter should have bagfuls of dowry, and if Lysippos and I were to become friends . . . It is not indecorous for a young man to be ambitious in his marriage –

Kleiophoros interrupted my reverie.

'Yes, an only daughter. Not many children, poor

Lysippos. Only three: Straton, Gorgias, Myrrhine. Lost one of them. Mind you, there are odd reports of the daughter. Some think – not that I should be indiscreet, but between ourselves – some think that she's *not quite right* in her intellects.'

My heart sank, but lifted again at his next words.

'That being the case, Lysippos is going to be good to the son-in-law who will take this poor girl off his hands. He has other things to worry him, too,' Kleiophoros went on. 'There's Lysippos' poor brother, Timotheos. Never did anything. Even with a third of his father's wealth for an inheritance! Never bestirred himself. He trained in the family business, as a boy, and they hoped he would take over the bronze statues, and the carving, or at least supervise these. But he was inattentive. When he grew up he refused to pursue the trade. He's a good inoffensive creature enough, but idle. His brothers loved music and poetry and they sang in the festivals when they were young – Lysippos sang works of his own composing. But Timotheos could never be brought to sing in public. A poet, so they say, but we do not hear his compositions. Shy, a very shy man, a dreamer from boyhood.'

'What of his wife and children?'

'Oh, Timotheos married once years ago – can't remember the woman's father's name. His wife died in childbirth. No children, and he has never troubled to try again. Just like him – takes no trouble. Everyone likes him, of course, but he never does anything to improve himself. Why, his brothers have to tell him to have his sandals mended.'

'Perhaps,' I suggested, 'Timotheos doesn't feel any need to improve his lot. After all, his inheritance must have left him comfortably off. Perhaps he doesn't see the necessity of doing, or getting, anything more.'

'Ah, you should be a philosopher. And Timotheos too. Not that he would have stirred himself to teach like Speusippos or Aristotle. Yes, really, Timotheos is quite the philosopher. He's not shy of talking under the colonnades. He'll talk your head off, if he's in the vein. All about the Good and the Beautiful, and that sort of thing. Likes a bit of argument, but never loses his temper. Not at all *pushing*, if you know what I mean. Marriage gives a man more ambition, more sharpness. Sokrates himself might not have been so famous for arguing if he had not been married.'

'When are *you* going to get married?' my tenant asked me.

'I don't know,' I said. 'There's plenty of time. I haven't made up my mind yet.'

'Ah!' Kleiophoros laughed. 'Too much thinking about it isn't always the best way. Of course, you're on the young side for marriage. Everyone's saying you won't marry Kallimakhos' daughter now. But I tell you what you should do. Go and consult the Oracle at Delphi. There will be famous doings at Delphi this spring, now the new temple is to be consecrated at last. I shouldn't mind seeing it all myself, but,' he heaved a sigh of happy complaint, 'business won't let me stir.'

I made my way home, thinking proudly of Lysippos' invitation, and musing on the connections between all these Silver Men while trying to keep them straight in my mind: Pherekrates, deceased, who had left only a daughter, golden-haired Anthia, and money to go with her; Lysippos, the amiable and deep-voiced uncle to this unseen heiress. And then there was the rival silversmith, Glaukon the sandy-eyed. And also Timotheos, Lysippos' brother, who refused to bother with the business. And Lysippos' son, handsome young Straton. Surely Straton would be the heir to everything now, including the heiress? And strange Myrrhine, the Silver Man's daughter. There seemed no need for these rich Silver Men to keep everything in the family.

II

The Flower Festival and the Night of the Ghosts

The first day of the holiday came, the day of the opening of wine-jars. My vineyards were small, but at least they bore grapes. My wine had been brought into Athens by Dametas and Tamia, my steward and his wife, who were to enjoy a holiday in the city. With others, I took jugs of the new wine to the shrine of Dionysos in the Marshes – that shrine where one can sometimes hear the frogs croaking, as Aristophanes points out in his Dionysos-play. Nowadays the marshes have been built over and there are fewer frogs. We vine owners offered our new wine, properly tempered, to the god, and prayed that the drinking of the vintage would be beneficial to us. I prayed heartily – and I had reason, for the previous years had been full of sadness and vexation. The wine was good to my taste, and I felt happy. Everyone was merry as we wished each other health and fortune.

The next day, the twelfth of Anthesterion, was of

course the main day of celebration. My little brother, Theodoros, awoke me very early, so excited was he, and anxious to get his present. I gave him at once his little wine jug, his *khoes*; I had commissioned a good jug with a carefully painted scene on it – of little boys playing ball – and Theodoros was highly pleased. When we set off to see the Procession, he held the jug tightly in his hand.

The streets were thronged with people waiting for Dionysos to appear in his ship-chariot. Everywhere there was the babble and laughter of children, for the Flower Festival is especially good to children, and this is their day. The very little ones who have passed safely out of infancy are given their first *khoes*, and also special garlands. Everywhere one looked there were tiny heads crowned with the new flowers of spring – violets, scyllas, and anemones.

Theodoros bustled me along and gave directions: he insisted we stand by his friend Euphranor, and his family. Or rather, the adults were to stand patiently, while the little boys dashed back and forth into the cleared road. Euphranor and Theodoros attended the same small school – one of those where little boys are taught their letters – and I heard a good deal about Theodoros' friend. Euphranor had a little sister, Sophrine, a charming three-year-old.

'Can't see,' complained Sophrine, but her father hoisted her up to his shoulder, and we all pressed forward; we could hear the music at a distance.

'Good day, Stephanos. Greetings of the Festival.' I turned around and saw the middle-aged man with ruddy hair and quick bright eyes who spoke to me. Aristotle, the philosopher, my former teacher and now, I hoped, my friend. Aristotle might indeed have been counted among the important people I knew, but he was a Makedonian, not an Athenian citizen, and thus not at all what my mother meant. As Aristotle was a foreign resident, a *metoikos*, the law prevented him from inheriting Plato's Academy, even though he was Plato's favourite pupil. An alien could own no property in Athens town or its rural demes. Aristotle had set up a school of his own, in rented premises outside the city walls, beyond the unfinished Temple of Zeus and the stadium. His school was referred to as 'the Lykeion', like the area itself, near a shrine of Apollo the Wolf-god, Apollo Lykeios, protector against wolves. Now that Makedonia had become so powerful, the Makedonian teacher was seen with more favour by some – but not by all.

I had once been a student in Aristotle's Lykeion, but certainly not one of the most shining of students. I had regretfully had to leave when my father's financial affairs became troublesome. Later, I turned to Aristotle for help when I did not know where else to turn in time of trouble. I owed him a debt of gratitude for his assistance to me and my family at a time when we were pressed by sinister events. He not only helped me, but taught me how to get out of difficulty by searching for the truth. Subsequently, we had been together when other people's circumstances had needed Aristotle's clear perception and dedication to truth.

Aristotle was now getting on in years; his bald spot was getting bigger, and his hair, once of a sparkling ruddiness, was going grey. But he held a small girl-child by the hand – his daughter, not a grandchild. He and the much younger spouse to whom he had long been married had produced a child late in his life.

'We too needed a good place to view from. Up you go.' Aristotle raised his little girl to his shoulder. Pythias, his daughter, was clutching a small *khoes*. She was a solemn, delicately built child of some five years or six, with a slightly dark olive skin. I thought it likely she was a reflection of her foreign mother, Pythias. Aristotle's wife had been the niece or daughter – or, some said, concubine – of Hermias, ruler of Atarneus and Assos on the coast of Asia. Aristotle had stayed long at Assos in the years before he returned to Athens; when he came back he had this strange wife with him. Hermias himself had been captured by the Persians, who accused him of being a traitor to them in the interests of the Greeks. The wretched Hermias had been sentenced to death on the *tympanon*, the death meted out by Greek law itself for traitors and foreigners. One fine day he was taken out of the city of Assos, stapled to a plank and left to die. Not a very pleasant connection for the family, one would have thought. Of course no men of Athens and very few women had seen Aristotle's exotic woman. Aristotle had no son.

Little Sophrine did not seem very interested in the other child, although the two were parallel in their exalted stations. She was, however, attracted to Aristotle. 'I have f'owbers on my head,' she said to him conversationally.

'I see the ship!' cried little Pythias. The music marched up the street, and the Procession wound its way, led by the happy god. Dionysos rode in his ship on wheels, the ship's mast wreathed with ivy leaves. The Procession came near and passed with a sound of music. Following the god's ship were the train of white animals, and the young men, the celebrants. The music sounded, an insistent rhythm, and through it, the people of the

Procession, those on foot and those on chariots, shouted to us, in the exchange of traditional insults.

'Stephanos, your vines are feeble – your growth is small!'

'O fat-bellied Mikon, why do you serve your friends nettle soup!'

'Straton, your Lalage is Ammonios' whore! Had her myself last night!'

'Herakleides, when will your wife bear fruit again?'

It was the adults who exchanged shouts; the children were wide-eyed and quiet, as the music throbbed, intoxicating as wine. Then the train – the god, the leafy ship, white sacrifices and white-robed golden youths – vanished towards the Marshes and the shrine, and the music became faint to our ears.

'Oh-h,' said Theodoros, 'I wish they would do it again.'

'No,' said Aristotle. 'That's what a procession is. Something that goes by once.'

'There's always next year,' I remarked.

'That's not the same,' said Theodoros.

'No, it isn't,' Aristotle agreed. 'He's quite right. You will be different – the people in it will be different. Every festival is the same as before, but always different. And you don't tire of it, for there is never too much. That's the dramatic principle of the thing.'

'Good day. Are you still at your lectures, Aristotle?' said a teasing voice. It was Straton, Lysippos' son, who had come up to us. Aristotle chuckled and swung Pythias down from her perch.

'I fear so,' he said. 'Philosophers will philosophise about an eggshell. It's a habit. Though not a habit that has infected yourself, my good Straton.'

Seeing nothing else to do save laugh, Straton did so, looking at me as if he and I shared in amusement at a prized eccentric. I felt annoyed at this, although certainly Aristotle with his white festival robe somewhat rumpled, his hair tossed by the little girl's handling and by the wind, did not look quite the impressive master of the Lykeion. Straton, in contrast, was in a robe of the most handsome and expensive weave. It set off his strong figure, gleaming skin and dark hair to advantage. Like his father, he wore a plain silver loop about one muscular and suntanned arm.

Straton was a big carefree man, the sort of person who always seems in control of all around him, even in childhood. I remembered how when Aristotle and I were investigating an incident at Arkhandros' school, we had seen his name written up on the wall of the changing-room, amid other juvenile inscriptions: 'Straton is beautiful.' Straton had been my junior in the Lykeion when I was a student. Famous for his keen interest in horses, he was also known for good nature and generosity. He would always treat friends and never seemed short of money. He had a reputation as a singer, and, like his father, had competed in festivals, though latterly he had been more interested in games and races. He would naturally inherit his father's business, since his brother Gorgias was dead. Straton had already been brought into the concern. Unlike his idle uncle, Timotheos the philosophic, he spent part of his time working. It seemed strange in a way; it was easier to imagine him leading an army than hunched up with a little hammer, or supervising shipments.

'It is good to see you, Stephanos,' said Straton

expansively. 'It is always pleasant to see family parties at this sort of festival. Rumour has it that you will marry soon. Is that right?'

'Perhaps,' I said. 'And yourself? But I heard that you were much taken up with some new mistress.'

'My flute-girl? Oh, that sort of thing is soon over.' He shrugged. 'Marriage is more important, for men like us. Then we'll have some sprigs of our own to bring to the celebrations. Must go – but don't forget, both of you, Father bade me remind you that you are expected at our house tonight.'

He left us, walking away with strong carefree strides. 'I heard,' I said to Aristotle, 'that he will eventually marry the heiress – Pherekrates' daughter – even though she was promised to Polemon.'

'That may be,' said Aristotle. 'I'm sure Straton would see no reason to object.' He looked down at his little Pythias, half sighed, then smiled. 'Come, my little heiress, we must go home to Mother now. Say goodbye to Sophrine.'

But Pythias was shy, although she was the elder of the tiny damsels, and it was Sophrine who took upon herself the ceremonies of leave-taking. 'Goodbye,' she said, waving a chubby hand. Then she put her hand up to her garland and pulled off a violet. 'I give you,' she said, extending it to Aristotle. 'Thank you very much, my lady,' he said seriously, taking the little purple blossom.

Aristotle and I walked off together, accompanied by his daughter and my brother, who could bear parting from Euphranor only by being reminded that they would see each other almost at once at the school party.

'It is encouraging,' said Aristotle, 'to know that one

maiden in Athens finds me appealing. This is a good festival – children and flowers.'

'And the mystic marriage, too,' I reminded him. 'The Basilinna weds the god tonight.'

'Ah,' said Aristotle, 'that old custom shows that the city ruler, the Basileus, who is now just chief arkhon, was in the old days a king – much more like the Pharaoh of Egypt. His wife the Basilinna was his divine consort, and though married to the king also wedded the god on behalf of the people. The Pharaoh's wife used to go through something similar in Egyptian Thebes.'

'Don't you think on these things too much, Aristotle?' I asked. 'Enough that it is an old custom – it has always been so.'

'Ah,' said Aristotle, 'you wish to think that Athens is always the same. But yet, you know, we change, as you can see in reading plays written only a few generations ago. Festival customs preserve the memory of an older day, but nothing is unalterable. Now I must return to the Lykeion where, like your little brother's teacher, I am giving a reception for my pupils and their friends on the day school fees are paid. It seems odd, perhaps, that the festival of the young should be associated with paying their schoolmasters. A paradox.'

'You don't care about money?'

'I like money well enough, but I don't quite like the ceremony of being paid. It sticks in my gullet, somehow. Fortunately, most of the time I dissociate teaching from being paid for it. I wonder what it is like to live by work which exists for you solely as a means to money?'

I laughed. Not only was Aristotle's devotion to knowledge well known but he was comfortably off and many of the older scholars paid their own expenses in order to be allowed to work with him. Aristotle's chief assistant, the scholarly and systematic Theophrastos, certainly must have had some independent means. Aristotle had built on to his rented house, in order to house his numerous and valuable collection of books, and the plants and strange objects that he and Theophrastos and other scholars studied.

'You, O Aristotle, are scarcely what the world thinks of as a schoolmaster, teaching in some dusty barn of a room for a few obols,' I commented. 'Nor even like our anxious friend Arkhandros who has to teach violent little boys not to kill themselves with javelins.'

'No – but some of my students' fathers offer the payment with such an air, as who should say "Take this, my good fellow." Won't you come to my reception at my wolfish school, Stephanos? I have some new plants I could show you: my nephew Kallisthenes has sent them to me from Asia.'

'No,' I said. 'I have to take Theodoros to his schoolmaster's home. A very tame party. But you and I will both be dining at the house of Lysippos. Why do not you meet me at my home, and return there after the dinner is over? Stay the night with me, for you will not be working tomorrow.'

'Thank you. A good notion. It will save any trouble at the city gates and will spare me from having to stumble back home at dawn with the headache. I know what hard-drinking affairs the Silent Dinners always are.'

The rest of the morning I spent at the school party (raucous with the noise of children) and in making calls. There was much visiting, and much drinking throughout the city during the middle of the day, while in the shrine of Dionysos the fourteen elderly priestesses and the Basilinna offered their sacrifices. They prepared for the high drama of the mysterious marriage in the evening, when the Basilinna (though nothing more in private life than the middle-aged wife of the arkhon) would be united with Dionysos. The day rippled past, a day of soft blue sky and west wind; the city gleamed in the new pale sunshine. In the late afternoon I met Aristotle at my house, and we walked off to Lysippos' home, the slaves behind us sweating under the weight of the heavy wine-jars.

'The enemy are pursuing us with heavy arms, and we shall be overtaken,' said Aristotle, looking at the jugs. 'I have already drunk a good deal today. It will not be possible to avoid taking too much this evening. How easy to say "Nothing in Excess" – and how hard to follow when custom is in the case.'

'Yes,' I said comfortably. The drink I had already taken made me jocund and light. 'This is a different sort of day, and it's always right to act according to custom. Very good of Lysippos to invite us.'

'I could argue against your premisses in both statements, Stephanos. Though it is a cavil, I suppose, to remark that hospitality comes cheap at a dinner party where the guests supply their own food and drink. I admit that what always daunts me about this feast is the *silence*. My appetite is for talk. Like the weak men who can't bear to go without a meal, I have an invalid constitution. A privation – I admit, it feels like a privation to be forced to say nothing. I am always amazed that the Athenians, of all people the most talkative, should devise a Silent Dinner! It seems perverse to gather men together over good food and drink so that they may all be quiet in company.'

'You know the reason,' I said. 'This Athenian custom arises from the time of old, when Orestes came to Athens for judgment, still blood-guilty. After all, although it was in just revenge for his father Agamemnon, murdered by Orestes' mother and her lover, Orestes had killed his own mother! The Athenians offered him hospitality, but could not eat or drink with him, for fear of pollution from such a murderer. He brought blood-guilt among them. So they devised this method of entertainment during the time he was there – each man ate and drank his own, and avoided the curse. And so we do yearly, in memory of the time, which was also the time when Apollo and Athena conferred in judgment on the Akropolis. An ancient tradition.'

'But does it not seem strange that this custom should be upheld at a time when we celebrate Dionysos? And that it takes place at the very hour when the Basilinna celebrates the marriage with Dionysos in the Boukoleion? Incidentally, doesn't that indicate that the Boukoleion must have been the home of the original kings of Athens? That sort of tradition interests me. Pieces of unwritten history. As for Orestes – we are surely in no danger from him, poor lad, any more, as his affairs have long been settled. Satisfactory to all parties, or so they say.'

'Be careful,' said I, laughing. 'Ghosts go walking tonight, you know, and Orestes is supposed to be about. If the ghost of Orestes meets any Athenian this night, he is likely to give him sharp blows and buffets.'

'A most unghostly proceeding. Shades ought to have more discretion. Besides, I am a Makedonian, not an

Athenian, so Orestes – who impresses me as a confused but legalistic young man – would be puzzled as to what to do with me.'

'Well, I'm an Athenian, so Orestes is to be respected by me.'

'And Orestes only a poor foreigner, too,' said Aristotle teasingly. 'We're near Lysippos' house already – I say "alas!" The wine has loosened my tongue, and I dread the moment of saying farewell to the sweet sound of words – even ours, Stephanos. I would like to continue talking about Orestes – do you prefer Sophokles to Aiskhylos? Well, on with our garlands. How I wish this were a true symposium.'

It was true that when we crossed the threshold we said farewell to both listening and speaking. Even the slaves were silent. Lysippos gave us our garlands, and, guiding us ceremoniously in dumb-show, took us into the room with couches and tables all ready for the dinner at which guests bring their food. We unpacked our dinners and, at the motion of our host, began to dine. The first cups of wine were drawn from the great jugs which we each had at our elbow.

The eating part of the feast went slowly and ceremoniously. In the silence I had much leisure to look about me, to admire Lysippos' fine room with its wall paintings and its exquisite furniture of carved wood. The house was large and old, older than the family who owned it now. After Lysippos' father had purchased it, various additions and improvements had been made. One could tell that this room had seen many rich dinners. It was slightly embarrassing (it often is at this self-supplying feast) to bring out one's own provisions, doubting whether they did sufficient honour to the occasion. I caught myself wondering if my bread loaves were not as good as those of Polemon and Glaukon, and then wondering if they noticed. Glaukon had brought a whole large cheese; it smelt delicious. Ammonios had treated himself to some dainty pickled fish.

The feast went slowly, no more wine drunk with the food than is usual at any dinner. But at last the eating was over, as the sun began to slope westward. Then the drinking began – serious drinking – and we paced each other in the contest. Slowly my mind unhinged itself from the rest of me, and I began to feel that I was floating in the silence, gazing down upon the others with a kind of ghostly loftiness. Silence sharpens even drunken observation; indeed, at the time one feels one's observation is better than ever. I looked at my companions, tacitly reading them as some men read a book without moving their lips. Fat Ammonios was flushed and important, full of expansive gesture, extending his hands and trying to intimate the jests he could not utter. Polemon, his neighbour and the object of his humorous nudges, seemed to grow pale as the evening progressed, his golden-brown hair shining in the lamplight like a star. Straton, opposite Ammonios and Polemon, seemed to look at the other young man with disdain. As the shadows lifted in the darkening chamber, I fancied I saw the flicker of a sneer cross his face – more than once – but perhaps it was the effect of the wavering light. His father Lysippos at the head of the room waxed large under my wine-filled gaze: like a great statue, square and serene, his splendid head of hair and large beard looking imposing and wise. Lysippos looked more like a sage, it must be admitted, than my friend Aristotle, who seemed to have withdrawn into himself, thinking perhaps in the strings of words he dared not say. But his deep-set blue eyes were still lively and acute and his red hair flashed like the firelight.

Glaukon drank nervously, persistently. He fidgeted with his hands; at one point he awkwardly upset his cup and red wine ran about the floor. Glaukon flushed wine-red himself through his freckles when he saw what he had done. Although the cup had been only one-quarter full when it was upset, he was penalised by being forced to drink two cups in quick succession. He gazed steadily at Lysippos with his round eyes as he drank his penalty measure. There seemed about him some atmosphere of feeling – reproach? suspicion? anger? I had watched him playing with a little knife at dinner and had seen him cut through a boiled egg in its shell with a quick vicious motion. Irritation, probably. But at what?

Opposite nervous Glaukon sat calm Timotheos, Lysippos' brother. This man I did not know. Timotheos was the brother men usually forgot when they talked of Pherekrates and Lysippos. The man who would take no trouble. Timotheos was a slender man, well shaped, of middle age. His hair curled like that of Lysippos, but was of a paler brown and very thin, lying in loose strips across his pallid baldness. His beard too was wispy. His grey eyes, large and far apart, were meditative. Timotheos spent much of the time gazing at the opposite wall, as if ruminating on the painting, or perhaps gazing at an ideal scene. He alone seemed fully happy in the silence, shrugging off the mere presence of other people around him.

Timotheos' movements were unobtrusive, calm and

noiseless. Though he was not in any way awkward, he reminded me in a way of a schoolboy on his best behaviour among a crowd of men. Or, it might equally be said he was like a man among high-spirited assertive boys. Different from the rest, anyway. Perhaps it was because he seemed so out of place beside Lysippos. The dreamer beside the man of action; the man who despised money with the man who made it. Lysippos had all the authority of this family. That is, I reminded myself, he did now that Pherekrates was dead. In this house at this very moment in the women's quarters women would be preparing the morrow's offering to the dead – and sickly Hegeso and strange Myrrhine would be companioned by the beautiful heiress Anthia, recently bereaved of her father. This would be their first Anthesterion Festival without Pherekrates. Lysippos and Timotheos were mourners.

Perhaps they were all remembering their dead on this night when some shades may walk. Perhaps in this family, and in some others in Athens, there were people who half dreaded, half hoped to see some beloved shade returning in a ghostly moment. All the shrines would be freshly decked. In this family that meant the shrine of Pherekrates, and of Pherekrates' son, of Timotheos' wife, and of Lysippos' son Gorgias killed and lost beyond the seas. Every festival sees some absent who were once present. So every festival brings some sadness – and for me too, for this was only the third Anthesterion since my father's death and the first since the death of my aunt Eudoxia. At this recollection I could feel the tears pressing into my eyes. Aristotle looked at me and gave me a reassuring smile. I took another cup, and was my own man again.

The drinking contest progressed in earnest. I was not wild to win, and Aristotle was even less ambitious, but we played our parts valiantly enough. I expected that stout and practised Ammonios would drain his jar first, as he made such steady progress through the first two-thirds of it, but towards the end he became flatulent and thoughtful. Ammonios' belches rippled the silence, though he tried to suppress them. At last we had a winner: to the surprise of everybody, it was Glaukon the rival silversmith who finished first, showing us he had done so by turning up the empty jar. Lysippos politely applauded in dumb-show, and presented the prize of the cake – a large one. Glaukon took it, holding the cake in front of him so it looked like a ludicrous buckler. I heard Aristotle just suppress a low chuckle, and I wanted to laugh outright. Glaukon's garland had slipped over his forehead and dangled on his brows and nose – ridiculous. His face, however, was as set and unsmiling as the face of a statue, with its inartistic and un-statuelike freckles standing out so you could count them like coins.

Everyone looked flushed and bedraggled as we came to the end of the drinking. Many of us were getting up between cups and going out to relieve ourselves. Lamplight shone on sweaty faces and Ammonios was perspiring in large, damp drops. The lamps flickered and were replenished; there was a smell of oil, and a smell of sweat and of wine everywhere. The lights began to reel and show double before my eyes, and the room felt excessively hot. Our garlands were wilting visibly. I was glad when the last of us – meditative and abstemious Timotheos – came serenely to the end of his jar, and we could move.

Led by our unruffled host, we trooped out of the house

into the deep night, carrying our wine-jars with our garlands slung about them. The wind had changed, and had blown away the fine weather. The night was starless and full of a foggy mist with a deep taste of the sea in it. We each took refreshing breaths of the wet air, and set off slithering and stumbling down the streets. Timotheos began a song to Dionysos and the rest of us joined in as we made our way to the shrine of Dionysos in the Marshes. Around us other groups of revellers were going the same way, or returning. I sang loudly, and lurched about in an unaccustomed manner, grabbing Aristotle to steady myself. We seemed a happy band. Rejoicing in the liberation from the bonds of silence, I felt full of enthusiastic liking for everybody.

'I must ask 'em to a party,' I said to Aristotle. 'Ask Lysippos. Good Lysippos. And Ammonios. And Glaukon.'

'Steady,' said Aristotle. 'We've just come from a party, my friend.'

'Other – zympothium,' I insisted. Ahead of me Ammonios belched loudly and said, 'I need a woman!' Straton laughed, and said, 'Don't wake the ghosts!'

Timotheos said, 'There are no ghosts. I thought I saw one once, but it was a mistake.'

'Yes, there are,' said Glaukon. 'Lots of them.'

'Oh, well,' said Straton, 'you've a cake to offer them, haven't you?'

With hoarse remarks like these and snatches of song, we took ourselves to the shrine, where each gave his jug and garland to a priestess as an offering to the god.

'That's better,' said Aristotle. 'The jug seemed to weigh almost as much empty as full. I was afraid I would break it.'

'That would be bad luck,' I said seriously.

'Who talks of *luck*?' asked Timotheos in his serious quiet voice. 'There is no bad luck or good luck. Only Fate.' But this discussion was not destined to proceed.

'I feel sick,' said Ammonios.

'We'll help you home,' said Glaukon. 'Fat men are easily made unwell,' he remarked in a low tone to Straton, who laughed and said, 'The old lecher has exhausted nature. An old worn-out wineskin soon leaks.'

All of us accompanied Ammonios to his home, which was near that of Lysippos and Timotheos. So we saw the statuesque silversmith and his wispy brother home too, and then dispersed and went our several ways. By this time the streets were quite empty; our party had lasted among the longest, and by now there was that coldness and lightening in the air that precedes dawn.

Aristotle and I set off together towards my house. I was still vaguely obsessed with the notion that I must hasten and immediately make preparation for another party. Thus, I went impatiently, unsteadily, and became very vexed when I discovered I had some strange difficulty in walking.

'Someone's poisoned my foot,' I exclaimed to Aristotle, who glanced down at the offending member and asked, 'What's happened to your sandal?'

'Oh,' I said. 'I've lost my sandal. That's it. My left sandal. Feels funny, walking one off, one on. Street's damp.'

'I'll help you find it,' he said in a resigned tone.

Somewhat sobered by examining my toes, I realised that he was fatigued. 'No need,' I said. 'I know now where I lost it – I felt something at the time – just outside

Lysippos' house where I tripped over a stone. I'll go and get it. You go on to my house – the slaves will conduct you.'

'I should come –'

'Nonsense. I'm perfectly all right. And I can hardly get lost in Athens, even at night. Goodbye.'

And I plunged off into the mist, quite confidently. Indeed, my head was clear enough for finding my way about, and my eyes had already had time to accustom themselves to the dark. I had forgotten all about the dangers of ghosts. Cautiously following a wall, and then another, I found myself back soon enough in the area which I sought, at the side of Lysippos' house wall. I felt around for the stone on which I had stumbled. I must have looked strange on my knees groping in the street, had there been anyone to see, but the street seemed to be empty. Gone were the songs of revellers and noise of footsteps.

I imagined I had the place to myself. Suddenly I heard noises close to me, but I could not quite tell where. Words floated in the air, in the mist, disembodied.

'The lock of hair on the shrine – I recognised the colour. Where is my brother? Where is his grave?'

'There is no grave. Only the dead have graves. Look – here is the ring my father gave me, with his seal; you may feel the pattern with your fingers. Do you believe me *now*?'

'O gods! My dear, dear brother! Have you come home at last? You don't know how they treat me!'

'Hush! Be careful. It wasn't a mistake, it was attempted murder.'

'Murder! – The thought had crossed my mind.'

'The gods have brought me back to you.'

'The gods are on our side. But what now? We must have revenge. Oh, if women were only soldiers!'

'Quiet! We haven't the time. Women have been warriors too. You will have your share. We will take revenge together. Say nothing. Pretend to mourn still for my pretended death. When we have won, there will be time to talk and smile.'

'Pretending won't be hard. Feel – I am crying for joy. I shall be a Niobe, stone, but always weeping. What are you going to do?'

'"The word of Apollo is of great power and cannot fail.
His voice, urgent, insistent, drives me to dare this danger."

We shall be righted; we are closing in.'

My limbs had frozen during this recital, but at these last words the very hair on my head rose upright. I felt the terror of the dark bolt of the Underworld, weaponry of the folk buried under the ground. Everything else had seemed strikingly familiar, but now there could be no doubt. I could hardly fail to recognise the last words. My hand, which had unwittingly come upon the sandal during the course of the first speech, seized upon it convulsively, and now I grabbed it up and rushed blindly away, one shoe off and one shoe on, as fast as if I were pursued by the Furies.

'Zeus! Help!' I cried as I ran, and did not stop until I was at a safe distance from the place of the voices. O gods, save me from Orestes! I kept praying – though the gods seemed just as likely to be on Orestes' side. So the legend of Orestes' ghost was a mere story? So Orestes didn't walk – it was only a joke? I knew better. Orestes was abroad. Indeed, matters were worse than generally reported. Popular legend had said nothing of the ghost of Elektra being let loose as well. In life she had never come to Athens. But here she was, no question. It made sense, as she had been so fond of her brother in life. There they were, repeating the famous scene, as the poets had written it – more or less. Perhaps they were condemned to reiterate it from time to time, as Sisyphos in Hades is condemned to roll his stone uphill, over and over again.

I staggered down the streets, getting dizzy as I went. Near our house, I bumped into Aristotle.

'Save yourself from Orestes!' I cried, and pushed past him as I rushed to my front door. The house slave had to help me, for I was giddy and sick. My foot was cold and scraped as well as dirty. I got into bed . . . Shame . . . acting the host's part most improperly. Not feeling well enough. Do no more. The slaves would . . . My room unfamiliar. Spun around every time I tried to open my eyes. I closed them, and went off into uncomfortable dreams, in which an Avenger insisted I was Oidipous and tried to cut off my foot, while Elektra, in rags and carrying a huge jar, kept saying she must have a lock of my hair to make her collection complete before guests came to her party.

III

Goblins and Disappearances

The next day I suffered from a headache. I was dull and quiet – which was not out of keeping with the day itself which was dull and quiet. This last part of the Festival, the Day of the Pots, is a day of ill omen. It is set aside for the spirits of the dead. As no business can be transacted that day – the very sanctuaries being closed to protect them from malign spirits – Aristotle was content to remain at my home, instead of journeying back to the Lykeion in a fog which refused to lift. On that grey day the women were busied with preparing the meal for the dead, boiling up vegetables in the great pot to be offered to Hermes of the Underworld. The living eat little or nothing: it would not be right to participate in the ghosts' meal. A fast day after a feast is easy to bear.

I did not of course tell Aristotle of my encounter of the night before. Indeed, it seemed to myself like a fragment of a dream. When he asked me about the peculiar words I had uttered as I stumbled to my door, I said only that I had suddenly been taken by a foolish fear of Orestes, and indicated that wine was to blame. I was not proud of my conduct. I did not wish the philosopher to think of me as superstitious, like the women and servants who keep the antique customs and believe without questions.

The slaves had painted our doorway with pitch, to hinder the spirits from entering, and the women chewed buckthorn all day for luck. On this day it is lucky for young girls to swing on boughs or special swings made for the occasion, as their swinging drives bad spirits away. But we had no female children in our family or young girl-slaves to do this, so people made a few masks to swing in the trees. Then they all – the slaves, the children, the women of the house (even Mother) – sat about the kitchen regaling each other with the most fearful stories of omens, and revenants, and malicious tricks committed by goblin spirits from the Underworld. Young Theodoros' eyes grew big, and he was frightened to go to bed, despite his age of nearly ten years. The slaves of course enjoy the Anthesteria to the full. I was somewhat embarrassed that Aristotle, my guest for the first time, should see the household in this period of disorder, lest he think we were always so slovenly. Yet he was amused at my account of the kitchen entertainments. At his request I brought Dametas in to repeat his tales to us. He did so with great enthusiasm, pausing at impressive moments and taking up new voices for all the characters.

'Interesting,' said Aristotle, after we had thanked Dametas and dismissed him with gifts. 'How all men naturally delight in imitation. There you see the native origin of all poetry, even the epics of Homer and the dramas of Sophokles. Dametas, you notice, creates character, and speaks in various voices. In its perfection, that is the technique of Homer, who wastes little time speaking for himself, but is always bringing forth characters who say and do things.'

'But of course,' I said in wise deprecation, 'all the material of Dametas' tale is nonsense – the old stuff of ghosts and unnatural things which we hear from nurses and peasants.'

'True,' said Aristotle. 'Yet the marvellous is required in tragedy. And in epic. All narratives should cause wonder in some fashion. But this kind of fireside tale, the sort which endeavours to rouse horror without moral meaning, is admittedly not a high form.' He continued his meditation on the topic, getting up and strolling round the room as was his wont. 'The hearers recognise their own wonder is cheaply bought. Actions should be connected by cause and effect. A good story should *not* be made up of random or improbable incidents. There are improbabilities in Odysseus' being set ashore in Ithaka which would be unbearably absurd in the hands of a worse poet than Homer. If our belief is suddenly strained, we lose that faith in the work as a whole which is, while not the true pleasure of literature, the basis for all its pleasures.'

'Dametas' tales,' I said, 'are mere exercises in the digestive powers of credulity.' I was careful to laugh in a condescending philosophic way. 'If you swallow one improbability after another even the impossible may eventually be gulped down.'

I hoped I had spoken cleverly. I was uneasy about my own credulity, which might still rest in its robust primitive state. I reminded myself never to tell Aristotle about my drunken delusion of hearing Orestes speak out of the fog.

Aristotle pursued a topic which seemed to interest him.

'Even so, we all loved such tales in childhood. It takes time to learn to distinguish between possible and not possible. Tales of kitchen and fireside have in them the living seed of poetic art. They represent action. Things *happen*. There even the meanest story-tellers have the advantage of philosophers, for philosophers only discourse, and do not represent life. In their lectures and in their pages, nothing happens. We talk about qualities. But in life men live by action – by *doing* – not for some static quality. It is finally in our deeds and experience that we are happy or miserable. The spine of life is truly action of some kind or another. A literature consisting of works in which nothing happens – could such a one be imagined – would be the dreariest and worst in the world. You can have a tragedy without much in the way of character, but tragedy is impossible without action. The vulgar taste for stories of events manifests a permanent truth. The taste of children and the commonest people is always partly right.'

'You sound,' I said, teasing, 'as if poets and dramatists were to be preferred above philosophers. I wonder that you don't write plays yourself.'

'You remember the story of the Boiotian who was asked if he could play the flute and answered that he didn't know, he'd never tried? But I fear I am not entitled to that modest assertion. I *have* tried most forms of writing in my life – even dramas – in what I like to call my youth. You may remember that Plato did the same. I wrote two *very* tragic tragedies. Complete failures. I threw in a couple of bloody calamities from time to time. The characters, who all sounded the same, stood about philosophising most tranquilly. I destroyed those scripts, long ago.'

'Oh, what a pity!'

He shook his head. 'Not at all. A benefaction to mankind. And a wise move. No one rummaging through my writings after my death can bring them out to speak against me. I couldn't even make the metres work perfectly. I have written some poems, but I could never write lyric verse anything like as good as Plato's. But some day I must show you my elegiac ode on Hermias.'

The day came to its end, as even long quiet days will. I finished the day in traditional fashion, going around the boundaries of my home and shouting 'Get out, Goblins! The Anthesteria is over!' Little Theodoros echoed me, shouting gleefully 'Get out, Goblins! Go away!' and making shooing-away motions with his hands, as if the spirits were so many hens. It was a relief to see the end of this day. We went to bed early, and I woke up at dawn, happy to see the sunrise through the eastern clouds. The fog had drifted away. Today the sanctuaries would be open, the market would be busy. Life would resume its ordinary course. So I thought.

I had just awakened Aristotle, who was to go home in order to start teaching that afternoon, when I heard a loud knocking at the street door. The slave came to me, saying that citizens Kleiophoros and Lysippos had come wishing to see Aristotle and myself at once, without delay. Scarcely awake, and barely dressed, we went to meet them.

'It's all very well to say "without delay",' said Aristotle, 'but I can't think what the matter can be save a philosophical problem, and a philosophical problem can always wait until a man has washed.'

Kleiophoros and Lysippos did not look like men awaiting the solution of a philosophical problem. They were dishevelled and Lysippos' beautiful beard had not been brushed. They looked pale and anxious, and their feet were splashed, as if they had come hurriedly without picking their way.

'Thanks be to Athena that you are in the city,' said Kleiophoros on seeing Aristotle. 'We heard you were visiting Stephanos here, and were glad, for otherwise we should have had to go all the way to the Lykeion to find you.'

'Good day to you, Stephanos,' said Lysippos, paler but more polite than his companion. 'I am sorry to disturb you at such an early hour, but I need your help and advice, and the help of your guest, so we have taken the liberty –'

'Yes, yes,' said Kleiophoros, '*I* said the only one who could help you in such a delicate matter is Aristotle. I *insisted* we come. Pardon us, but you see, the matter is so distressing for Lysippos here, and ordinary channels won't answer. He got hold of me just as I was leaving the Tholos at the end of my night's vigil.' I wondered fleetingly if Kleiophoros and the others had gone around the Tholos shouting 'Go away, Goblins!' the previous night.

'What precisely is the matter?' asked Aristotle.

'Why, only this – is the door closed?' Kleiophoros lowered his voice. 'The niece of my friend Lysippos – Pherekrates' daughter Anthia – has disappeared! She has been abducted!'

'What? When? Are you sure?' Aristotle turned to Lysippos. 'Are you certain that this is a case of abduction? Might she not have gone to visit some neighbour –'

'Just the sort of thing I said at first,' said Kleiophoros. 'Isn't that so? But no – he'll tell you himself.'

I could see now that Kleiophoros, although perturbed by being aroused early and by bustling about, was not unpleasantly animated by the event and his own importance. That his vigil on the Night of the Pots had produced a real emergency did not displease him. It was Lysippos who was really suffering. He was notably pale, and kept mopping his brow. His eyes seemed tired and strained. In pity for him, I sent for food and drink, and bade my guests be seated. Lysippos dipped a piece of bread in his wine-and-water, and slowly ate it; at length the colour returned to his face, though he still seemed stiff and strained, like a man walking in a dream.

'Anthia has gone. My wife's slave, who acts as housekeeper in our family, went to call her just before dawn this morning. My wife, Hegeso, was not well, and had asked for the girl. Anthia was not in her bed, nor in her room. The bed did not look as if it had been slept in. Anthia's own slave-girl was missing also.'

'When was she last seen?'

'Yesterday in the afternoon. You know what a peculiar kind of day that was: the slaves don't do their proper duties, and there is no family dinner. I sat by myself, reading and working much of the day. I went to bed early, and save for my wife I saw no one. The slaves sat about telling their stories until quite a late hour. My niece was not seen by them; Anthia has a room of her own in the women's quarters, and we all presumed she was there. She summoned no one, for of course she does have her own servant, the slave-girl Kallirrhoe who always attends her.'

'That's a lovely name,' I commented, tempted to laugh. 'Like a water-nymph. It's the name of a stream here in Athens, in fact. Not that it's an altogether clean stream now, though named for its "beautiful flowing". Too good a name for a slave-girl. What did she say when you questioned her?'

'Ah! I am afraid it is impossible to question her. The slave-girl is gone too. Now, you must know Anthia's cousin and her aunt Hegeso did not see her, nor the slaves, after about the mid-afternoon. Nor did they see the slave-girl after that time.'

'Sad weary sort of day, the Day of the Pots,' remarked Kleiophoros. 'She might have wished to be by herself. Mourning her father, and so on.'

'Has she been melancholy? What was Anthia's state of mind?' Aristotle asked sharply.

'No – no. I thought of that,' Lysippos protested. 'She had been sad, yes, but resigned. And she is in good health. She would *not* commit suicide. But there is more to come – I haven't told you all. We searched the house and grounds at once, and carefully. And then I saw footprints in the damp earth by the gate – small prints, like those of two women. As I see it, my niece must have gone with her slave to the courtyard, to the altar of the departed: there was an offering upon it. And she was surprised by some noise at the gate, and went to see. Or someone called to her, and she went.'

'Yes,' said Kleiophoros. '*And* at the very gate itself – I have seen – there were marks of a struggle of some kind. The muddy earth is churned up, as by feet, and a piece of cloth was found on the latch, probably caught by the pitch smeared on the gate. Look.' He nudged Lysippos, who wearily produced a small bit of rag. 'There,' he said. 'Fine linen cloth. I'm sure it was from some part of my niece's robe.'

'Interesting,' said Aristotle. 'You did well to find it. But I am still not satisfied. Are you *sure* there was a struggle? There may have been merely an exit. Accidents do happen to clothes without violence being involved. Forgive me, but might not the girl have run away from her new home? She might well be irrational in her grief. You may find her wandering about Athens.'

'Ah, but you haven't heard the rest,' said Kleiophoros, leaning forward triumphantly, like one who has the answer to all questions. 'The slave next door told us when we made enquiries – discreet, you know – as to whether he had seen anyone go by yesterday evening. Lysippos, as I prompted him, pretended he had been expecting someone and feared he might have missed the house. The slave told him that he had seen a man. A man *walking beside a litter* going around the corner, a little after dusk. You see what that means. A litter is unusual. *Both* girls – Anthia and her slave Kallirrhoe – could be carried off in a litter.'

'I put this reluctantly,' said Aristotle, 'but may the girl not have eloped with some lover?'

'Anthia would never do such a *dishonourable* thing!' Lysippos was indignant. His tired eyes grew bright with anger, and he stood up restlessly. 'No! She is an Athenian girl, gently bred. A *good* girl, an obedient girl. My niece, whom I have known all her life. It is not to be imagined that she would listen to the poisoned falsehood of a seducer. That would be the worst shame of all! No, she has been abducted, poor child, carried off for some man's infamous purpose. Who knows what she may not be suffering at this moment!'

'And the villain, whoever he is,' Kleiophoros continued, more calmly, 'this rascal wretch may think to bed her and wed her by force and thus come into her inheritance from Pherekrates.'

Lysippos groaned, and sat down, holding his head in his hands. 'My poor niece! And a beautiful girl too, with golden hair – enough to tempt any vile – Oh, my poor wretched family! The disgrace!'

'Where is Straton?' asked Aristotle. 'Is not this matter his business too?'

'After a fashion, it is,' admitted Lysippos. 'At least we cannot hope to keep it from him for ever. But Straton went on an errand to the mines at Laurion before dawn on the Day of the Pots – not thinking any harm. The news will take time to reach him. In any case, I fear he is hot-blooded and not discreet – whereas I am old and slow. We need someone discreet and calm and wise to manage this business for us. For if word gets out, we are all undone!'

'You see,' said Kleiophoros with a compassionate glance at his friend, 'the whole family can suffer so terribly. Word of the matter must not get out, or their honour is injured – permanently scarred. The girl herself, even if by some miracle restored unharmed, would *never* be able to get a husband.'

'Therefore you cannot ask your friends to help you,' said Aristotle, 'and so have come to me.'

'Lysippos certainly cannot ask friends and neighbours to help in such an affair. We must do our best to keep the matter quiet – just among ourselves in this room and some of those in Lysippos' household. But we can trust you. You are discreet by reputation, and strong enough to keep lies from flowing. And, favoured by Alexander, you can do what other men cannot.'

'I confide in Kleiophoros, and have entreated his help,' said Lysippos.

'When Lysippos heard what happened he came straight to me at the Tholos. He begs me to take no *official* notice. Let the matter not take air unless it is absolutely necessary. That is, if it turns out disastrously, and all we can do is punish the villain. Lysippos has acted correctly, for I, representing the civic authority, can testify to the truth of the matter, and can show – if matters unfortunately come to the point where the affair must be made public – that he did the right thing in reporting to me. I sent at once to the city gatekeepers, to ask if a litter had gone by. One large enough to serve our villain had gone out at the western gate just before the gate closed last night.'

'Do you have any description of the man with the litter?'

'Not really, unfortunately. Just a man in country garb. Hooded, you know. The gatekeeper didn't make out the face. But a slave at the gate heard the slaves carrying the litter say something about how far it is to Delphi. So there you are! The Abductor is carrying Anthia westwards – to Delphi, to take sanctuary there and be out of our clutches.'

'I see. Very clear, so far.' Aristotle placed his fingertips gently together, judicially. 'You have done much, gentlemen, in a short time. You are already, it seems, on the track of the malefactor. I don't see how I can assist you.'

'But,' said Kleiophoros eagerly, 'this is just the point at

which you can help us, Aristotle. You are wise, and observant and discreet. I have some knowledge of how you assisted Stephanos here over Philemon's case. I said to Lysippos, when he mentioned your name, "If Aristotle will help you, even the most wretched cause is not lost!" And we are come to beg you to follow Anthia and her captor on the Delphi road – to find her and bring her back.'

'That is surely the task of her guardian!'

'Yes . . . but no. Don't you see how difficult it is in this case? How can Lysippos say to friends and business associates "My niece has been taken by some man, and I must rush out and get her back"? The girl's name is ruined! And his own, too. Unbearable disgrace! But if *you* were to go on a journey to Delphi, no one would think anything of it. If you and perhaps Stephanos here journeyed to Delphi in the ordinary way, to consult the Oracle. After all, you are the wisest man in Athens – I said so, didn't I say so, Lysippos, in those very words, "the wisest man in Athens"? So you could certainly do whatever could humanly be done.'

'What exactly have you in mind?' Aristotle asked, a trifle drily.

'Revenge can wait, you see. What we need is to get Anthia back – if possible, untouched – before there is any alarm. Lysippos will authorise you to bargain with the villain, if necessary – that is, if Anthia is intact. It seems a poor hope. But there *is* just the hope that this Abductor might defer his foul purpose. The girl herself might fend him off; the gods might restrain him. If the worst has happened, well, if he is of a rank where marriage might be possible, you, Aristotle, may be able to treat with him for us and arrange for a wedding.'

'Well,' said Aristotle, 'that is not precisely my –'

'Do not refuse us! We would supply horses and pay for your journey, over and above all expenses, and give anything you might need to persuade this Abductor. You see how well it would work. Through you Lysippos would be able to make some stipulations. After all, the legal penalty for seduction is severe. Lysippos would certainly be entitled to *kill* the man, if he caught him in the act. So the villain could be made malleable. *You*, O Aristotle, have authority. You are eloquent. You have influence. This villain would listen to you. You would reason and persuade better than poor Lysippos here, whose spirit is so shaken. And we can trust you to make no mistakes in pursuing or finding the wretch.'

'I am flattered,' said Aristotle, 'but I must beg to be excused. I am not a thief-taker, nor a marriage-broker. Then there is the little matter of the Lykeion – my lectures –'

'Yes, yes, of course,' said Lysippos, wiping his eyes. 'It is asking too much. I should have been so grateful – and so hopeful! But alas! At least, I beg you and Stephanos here to keep the matter a profound secret.'

'Ah, sir,' said Kleiophoros to Aristotle, 'you cannot mean it! Will you not help our friend in his distress? Consider – to whom else can he turn? It is much to ask, certainly, but recompense will be made. And a donation to your school. Though we realise that to such a philosopher as yourself this is no inducement, at least you must permit us to state that you will suffer no financial loss, whatever the success of the expedition. But chiefly we ask *you* as a friend. What man can see through riddles and make the crooked straight as you can? Do not the Makedonian powers count on you to do your part in seeing that good order is maintained in the city?'

Aristotle looked very unsmiling at this. The world thought that he wrote reports regularly to Antipater, Alexander's lieutenant, effectual governor of Makedonia who kept his eye on every city in Greece. Particularly Athens, since the Athenians were not joining in the hue and cry against King Agis of Sparta in Sparta's great conflict with Makedon. I myself had reason, because of the affairs of my own family, to think that Aristotle was indeed on very good terms with Antipater. But this reputation did not sit well with all Athenians, and Aristotle was not fond of having it mentioned. Lysippos must have noticed Aristotle's coldness because he changed the topic, turning towards me.

'And if young Stephanos would go with you to assist you, the journey would not be such a hardship. Stephanos, cannot *you* persuade him?'

I was gratified at this appeal. Certainly this adventure if pursued would give me close and valuable connections with these Silver Men. 'It would certainly be interesting,' I proffered, 'and you know, Aristotle, things mysterious to others are not so to you. Think what a fine time it is to go to Delphi! Delphi will be celebrating the consecration of the new temple – it might be good to see.'

'You think it would be of interest?' said Aristotle. 'Very well, Stephanos. If you add *your* voice to the debate, I must lose the contest. If you wish to engage me in unriddling riddles, I suppose I can humour you. Yes, gentlemen. I shall go, as you ask, and Stephanos will accompany me. But I fear I cannot promise success.'

'Excellent,' said Kleiophoros, his good-humoured eyes

beaming above their pouches. 'And my friend here can supply you both with horses, so you will go quickly on the road. You can start almost at once.'

'Certainly,' said Lysippos, rising. 'My humblest thanks, O Aristotle. But first, I suppose you will not be satisfied unless you inspect my house and grounds, where the crime took place. Oh, the shame of it, the horror! Forgive me; anxiety has made me importunate. We shall need time in which to prepare some mounts for you. And we can hardly expect that Aristotle will leave Athens without going home to the Lykeion first.'

'True,' said Aristotle. 'Let us look, as Lysippos suggests, at the scene. Then I shall go on to the Lykeion, and make arrangements, and you, Stephanos, will return home and do likewise. We shall then return again to Lysippos' house, and make our departure.'

We set forth, through the morning in its mist and heavy dew, accompanying the bustling Kleiophoros and the slow-moving weary Lysippos. After the dull yesterday, when Aristotle and I had had nothing better to do than talk about old stories, my life had suddenly been led to unexpected paths.

'I am delighted to go with you, of course,' I said to Aristotle. 'But – *why* am I going? I mean, what reason can I give to my family – or anyone else – for going to Delphi?'

Aristotle paused and then burst into laughter, slapping me on the back, almost like hearty Ammonios himself.

'Why, there it is, Stephanos – of course! You are going to Delphi to consult the Oracle about your marriage! What a good idea. You have proposed making this journey for some while (you will say) but have had to put it off. Now it is opportune, for I must go to Delphi and we thought we would travel together. I shall say I have official business. I also go to pursue my researches. You know I was there in the days of Philip, just after the Sacred War? I was working on the history of Delphi and the Pythian games then, with my nephew Kallisthenes to help me. Kallisthenes is now with Alexander as his historian, and it will easily be supposed he has written to me asking for certain historical information at Delphi. Friends in Delphi have long expected me to return. But as to you – *everyone* knows your difficulties with Kallimakhos. People will think you're concerned about marriage, and about your financial affairs.'

I blushed. It was a pity that my private affairs should be made a wooden horse in this fashion. Aristotle seemed amused, and better reconciled to the expedition than before.

When we arrived at Lysippos' house, the distraught master of it begged us not to let our purpose be seen openly, nor to talk of it before the slaves. In the eyes of the household, we were to seem like business acquaintances paying a call. So he made us go through the ceremony of arrival and sitting down, as if it were an ordinary visit. The master of the house then took us through the back and into an extensive garden. Aristotle was shown the pitch-smeared gate and sticky latch on which the rag was found; the place of the women's footmarks was silently pointed out to him, as well as the shrine. Lysippos allowed us time to linger and look as unobtrusively as we could. I saw Aristotle measure with his own feet the distance between footprints. Within the house we observed the main doorways. Naturally, we could not peer at any of the rooms in the women's quarters.

'It is a pity that we cannot interview Hegeso and her daughter,' said Aristotle to me in a low voice. But of course it would not be permissible for a man to interview, or even to meet, a gentleman's womenfolk. We did interview one tearful female slave but got nothing out of her; as usual, a slave's testimony was frozen by the natural terror slaves have of the law that dictates a slave must be tortured before giving evidence in any court. The parts of the house that we could see gave us no information. Nothing in the hallways seemed at all remarkable. No one had chalked up intentions of suicide, elopement or seduction on the walls.

At last Lysippos led us to his fine day-chamber and bade us sit again and rest ourselves. He had been watching Aristotle attentively, and he now looked questioningly at the philosopher. Aristotle shook his head. Disappointment, like a fine film, clouded Lysippos' face.

'Well we can't hope everything can be settled at once,' said Kleiophoros for the benefit of the attendant. 'Important business takes time.'

Lysippos left us, to arrange personally for refreshment. After a minute Kleiophoros also left, murmuring apologetically something about a call of nature. We did not have this very fine room to ourselves for long. Someone knocked, saying 'It's only me,' and entered at the same moment, strolling into the room with that mixture of guesthood and ownership found only among relatives. It was Timotheos. He did not seem disconcerted to find his brother was not present.

'Well,' he said. 'Philosophy honours us. Actually, I heard you were here, O Aristotle. You have come about our trouble in this household, is not that so?'

This might have been a good time for us to begin our dissimulations, but Aristotle nodded, evidently thinking it would be useless to try to deceive a member of the family.

'Quite so,' said Timotheos. 'I know all about it. It is good of you, Aristotle, to help us. I am an admirer of your early writings, by the way,' he added unexpectedly. '*For Eudemos on the Soul* is excellent.'

'Thank you,' said Aristotle, drily acknowledging praise of a book he had written nearly twenty years ago.

'But,' Timotheos continued, looking intently at Aristotle, 'do you think philosophy can do anything in the practical world? I – I myself am a lover of the Beautiful, simply.' He held up his right hand, attesting to the truth of his statement, and a plain silver bracelet, the evident twin of that worn by his brother, slid down his arm.

'Your family has given many beautiful things to the world,' said Aristotle politely.

Timotheos frowned, as if he did not care to be reminded of his family's merely mechanical connections.

'This world of metal and ivory – of bricks and mortar and flesh, of business and families. Not the *real* world in Plato's sense, of course – but so very obstructive. I still remember Plato. You were a pupil of Plato once – but now how different from Plato. Strange.' Timotheos looked towards the window as if seeking the light, and raised his voice to an elevated tone:

'"The soul of the true lover, passing beyond particular things, climbs aloft to the highest beauty so that in the end he knows the being of Beauty itself, pure and unmixed, uncontaminated with the flesh and colouring of humanity and that sort of transient and dying stuff.'"

After having thus quoted sonorously – if a trifle roughly – from the Symposium, Timotheus nodded several times, as if applauding himself and Plato together. Then he turned back to the philosopher. 'O Aristotle, how happy you were, to have studied so long with the divine Plato. His favourite student! What would not one give for such a blessing?'

'You do me too much honour,' Aristotle said politely.

'And yet, how strange it seems to me that you are fastened to particulars, the flesh, to transient and dying stuff. How can you not attend to the higher world – the *real* world? But you keep a school. That must be a pleasure to you?'

'Indeed it is.'

'I have often thought I should like to have a school. I know so many of the dialogues of Sokrates by heart, and have meditated on them all my life. I have thoughts of my own that I am anxious to impart before I pass from the world. But in this case of Anthia, I do not know what should or can be done. I simply do not know.'

'I do not know either,' said Aristotle. 'But I believe philosophy is not without resource.'

'Perhaps.' Timotheos sat and fidgeted, looking at his feet. 'It is strange,' he burst out. '*Strange*. That's it. I'm not the practical man of the family – far from it – but I see things occasionally. Even I can see things in front of my nose.' He shook his big head slightly, pushing his wispy hair away from his face as if to allow us to view the member in question.

'Yes?' said Aristotle encouragingly. 'Students of philosophy sometimes see more than other men,' he added.

'Well . . . may I trust you both? You mustn't let anything go further than these four walls. But about my missing niece. I've wondered. You see how my brother is at the moment – dismayed, in a turmoil, which is not his usual way, sirs. But I ask myself, "Why is he not *angry*?" It does not seem like my brother to suffer a wrong so patiently. If someone has stolen my niece, why are we not taking revenge? He doesn't even talk about revenge, not really. And then I ask myself – some other questions.'

'You mean,' I said, 'that *you* think Anthia may have gone willingly?'

Timotheos frowned at me, as if I were a dog with muddy feet that someone had let into the house.

'No, I do not. What a disgrace! – the idea! But,' he turned to Aristotle, 'I ask – and you might ask this of yourself – one question chiefly. This question: *where is Straton?* Why is it not our son and heir who is in hot pursuit of the criminal, bound to rescue his cousin? Who last saw Straton? That's what *I* wonder.'

He rose, hitching his khiton about his lanky form. 'I can't say anything. If ever a man was helpless in the midst of a sea of family troubles, it is I. Nobody tells me anything. But I see what I see. And I don't see at all why you should go on this strange errand without being in possession of as much truth as we can scrape together.'

He turned to go, but at that minute Lysippos entered, accompanied by Kleiophoros. The latter registered his approval at seeing Timotheos.

'Excellent! Brother must stick to brother. You will see

that Lysippos bears up. That's the good thing about families – you're never alone in trouble.'

'Yes, stay, Timotheos,' said Lysippos in his tired voice. 'The gods know I don't wish to be solitary in anxiety.'

'Solitary? Ah, no, of course not.' Timotheos sat down again, if reluctantly.

'As we have seen what we came to see,' said Aristotle, 'there is really no need to stay longer. I must go to the Lykeion. Theophrastos will have to take on the next few weeks' instruction at short notice. Stephanos, you too must go and make ready.'

We said our farewells and departed. Aristotle paused to look at the front gate as he went; this gate seemed innocent. As we started to walk away, however, his eye was caught by something. There was a narrow – a very narrow – slip of muddy ground between the wall and the trodden roadway, some distance beyond the gate.

'Look,' said Aristotle under his breath. And I saw the marks, barely visible, of two feet close to the wall and pointing towards it. I say 'of two feet', but I mean of feet shod in sandals, and not the shape of the whole foot, for only the toe half of either foot was imprinted. 'Come,' said Aristotle, 'let us look at the back again.'

So we walked, going around the corner and following the wall until eventually (Lysippos' grounds were extensive for a city dwelling) we came again to the back gate and explored outside the back wall. By that wall too, but even further from the gate, Aristotle found similar prints, again facing the wall.

'Whoever it was stood on tiptoe on both occasions,' Aristotle muttered. 'Was he trying to see over the wall? Or to talk to someone? Or only to listen?'

'He and not she?'

'Yes – the prints are the size of a man's feet. And what we saw formerly *within* the grounds were certainly prints of women's feet. There are prints of women's feet within the area on the inside of both gates. Oh, well, we haven't really discovered anything they didn't tell us, I suppose. We shall meet again at this mansion at midday. Bring warm clothes for the journey. The weather will be colder once we get into the hills.'

I went home and made my arrangements with what haste I could. I told my mother that I had purposed to go to Delphi to consult the Oracle about my marriage, and was taking advantage of Aristotle's going thither to have company on the way. She accepted this explanation. It is good to be master of a household, for people accept your statements and do what you command. The slaves made me a neat bundle of my travelling clothes. My own slave carried the bundle on my way back to Lysippos' house, but he could not accompany me on the journey, as I would be riding. (Anyway, as our concealed mission demanded haste and secrecy, we should have to do without servants.)

The fact that I would be riding had not meant much to me until I arrived at Lysippos' house again. There I had to wait for Aristotle, which was awkward, as there was nothing to do, save to listen to Lysippos' slaves expressing their opinion that I needed a leather bag for my travelling bundle. They fetched one with loud expressions of concern, and packed my clothes into it, explaining that otherwise the rain would get into my garments, which would also be steeped in the sweat and smell of horses. I could see they thought little of me as a gentleman, and much less as a traveller.

'Going about in damp garments, that would never do,' exclaimed one. 'Get a cough and fever which would carry you off in short order – or an ague which'd rattle your bones like nutshells.'

'It's the sickly season,' another remarked. 'Powerful number of illnesses going about still. Have a care what you eat and drink on the road, sir. Not too much water, remember – nor too much wine. Get cramps, or a gout to the stomach. Some says riding is good for the stomach, but it's rough medicine if you're qualmish.'

'Tell you who's qualmish,' responded his associate with a chuckle, 'and that's citizen Ammonios. Moaning and groaning and clutching his belly since the night of the Silent Dinner, they say. Oh, he's in a bad way – couldn't keep a thing down. Has the cramp from his big toe to his scalp – curls up like a wood-louse in his bed. I hope you've worked off the Festival wine, sir.'

'Hadn't I better put in some ointment?' the other asked me with odious kindness. 'You know how hard riding is on the rump and the sides of the legs, when one hasn't – ahem! – ridden for a little while.'

I fended off their dubious civilities with what I hoped was calm assurance, although this waiting time was almost entirely consumed by my private anxieties about riding a horse. I had attempted riding only once or twice, and knew little about horses. My cousin Philemon, now – he would have enjoyed the chance. I wished heartily that the philosopher and I were going to walk to Delphi.

Aristotle eventually appeared, properly accoutred, with a leather bag, somewhat worn, and a serviceable thick woollen cloak. He apologised for the delay. 'I had to talk to Theophrastos,' he said. That alone was to me sufficient explanation.

It wasn't that Theophrastos was long-winded, he was just anxious to be clear. Once he started on a topic he liked going into detail, and that made him seem prosy. This plain man and rather dull dog – so I then thought of him, when I thought of him at all – was a former pupil of whom Aristotle was very proud. I thought perhaps he was related to Aristotle, but I wasn't sure. Theophrastos had a beautiful clear voice for lecturing, and was deeply devoted to his work and to Aristotle, whom he assisted in classifying things, especially plants. Theophrastos loved making lists. In my mind, that was all he was good for. (I had never cared for Theophrastos, but I was careful not to say this to Aristotle.) For all his beautiful voice, the fellow was never a great orator; he spoke in a fussy, precise way. He was not quick-witted. Theophrastos struck me as the sort of person to whom one has to say everything twice. Yet his memory was retentive. In recent years Theophrastos has written a book of *Characters* which are much admired, but I know these descriptions are almost entirely compilations of Aristotle's own witty remarks, thrown out by-the-by in the course of conversations. These things Theophrastos repeated, memorised and then wrote down in the hope of classifying humanity as he did his horticultural specimens. (He could rarely see a joke, that was his problem.) Still, I had to admit that Theophrastos was admirably conscientious; Aristotle could trust that the school would be sedately run in his own absence.

Once Aristotle had arrived, I thought we would soon be off, but there was yet more delay. Lysippos invited us in, and Kleiophoros gave us formal letters of introduction to the official Athenian representative at Delphi, in case we should need them. Then it turned out that Lysippos had forgotten to give orders to a slave to bring the horses to us, so we had to walk to the stables, some distance from the house. As we went, the slaves repeated for Aristotle's benefit their vivid account of Ammonios' gastric plight. The rest of us talked busily about the horses, the fiction being (for the benefit of slaves and strangers) that Aristotle and I, having occasion to go on a journey, were hiring the animals from Lysippos. This was satisfactory as a deception, but it meant that the whole conversation ran continuously on horses, not allaying my anxieties. When we got to the stables there was all the business of having the creatures bridled, and seeing cloths put on their backs – and then of making them (or trying to make them) stand still while we mounted.

I did not enjoy the first sight of my horse, nor did I enjoy getting on it; the ground seemed an uncomfortable distance away. Nor did I feel much happier once we trotted off, with Kleiophoros, Lysippos and Lysippos' male household earnestly wishing us a prosperous journey. My bag bumped steadily in front of me and I bumped also. I could not understand why the very rich set such store by these beasts, seemingly designed to shake a man to pieces. I had little confidence in the intelligence of my mount, or in that of horses in general. It seemed madness to undertake a journey in such a fashion, instead of trusting to one's own good feet.

One of Lysippos' slaves helped to pilot us along the streets and winding way, until we came to the western gate of the city. At the gate, Aristotle gave the slave something for his trouble, and the man turned back with final instructions to us not to let the beasts drink water while heated, or break their legs in the hills.

Aristotle spoke to the gatekeeper, asking, as travellers do, for any news about the road to Delphi and enquiring if there were others departing from Athens bound in the same direction with whom we might catch up. He elicited little information. A traveller had gone through with a litter carried by two slaves. There were a few other persons, mostly citizens known to be going a short way. Also a shoemaker and his apprentice returning to their village after buying hides in Athens, and an itinerant perfume-seller – but no gentlemen. Aristotle thanked the gatekeeper, gave him a hemi-obol, then remounted his horse. I did the same – with more difficulty. 'At least the litter is something,' I said. 'And if the Abductor is taking two captive girls, certainly he would choose to go west first with his burden, to take advantage of the flat road as far as Eleusis, and then turn north.'

We passed, more or less grandly, through the high gate and left Athens, bound on our strange quest. Our preparations had taken a considerable time, and the westering sun had slipped far down from its midday point. The road ahead seemed long and lonely. I, who had wanted some adventure, who had felt some spring stirring of the blood which made me desire to leave my city and see the world, now felt an uneasy sensation as I saw, over my shoulder, the walls of Athens recede into the distance. I reminded myself that this journey, unlike my last and only other departure from Athens, was not a desperate and difficult venture but a civilised expedition; we were departing in the light of day, and in the manner of rich travellers.

'Well, we're off,' I remarked, not very brightly. 'Here we are on the road to Delphi. How extraordinary. When I think that when I woke up this morning I knew nothing of this!'

'Yes,' said Aristotle. 'We're on the road to Delphi. Why am I – why are we – on the road to Delphi? Chasing some greensick girl who may or may not have gone in this direction, who may or may not have been willing. Kleiophoros is certainly persuasive. Notice how he likes to do business with me – less, I fancy, because of my beauty and grace than because he sees in me the friend of Makedon. Kleiophoros is developing a powerful personality. I wonder if you and I are the only persons whom he has moved to brisk activity.'

'But we didn't get away very quickly,' I remarked.

'No, indeed, Stephanos. Is that something we should take notice of? Much of the delay has emanated from Lysippos. I think of what Timotheos said. Why is Lysippos not *angry*? And where is Straton?'

IV

The Ill-Tempered Man

Although there were few good hours remaining in the day, Aristotle was in hopes that we could make good speed on the first part of our journey, as the road to and past Eleusis is wide and easy. The impediment to speed lay chiefly in my horsemanship, which to say the least was inexpert. Indeed, I spent the rest of that short day learning how to ride. Aristotle, though so elderly, went on horseback without apparent trouble, but of course he had ridden in his younger years. I tried to conceal my sufferings from him – the strain on back and thighs, the soreness – but could not hide the fact that my mount strayed from the road despite my earnest efforts. The mare was imperfectly under my control. Philosophers say one should control the passions as a charioteer or rider masters a horse. Certainly the one is no easier than the other.

But we covered a little ground. As we went we could at first catch sight of the blue sea to our left. We came to the laurel groves where they say a nymph was turned by Apollo into a laurel. By sunset we were very near Eleusis. The great Procession to the Mysteries takes a day to go from Athens to that sacred site of Demeter, though a healthy man walking can do it in half the time. Two horsemen on an empty road could fly along – one would think. This was not the case with us at all. My mount threw me, and I was ready to stop. So we stayed the night at a little inn just outside Eleusis where we ate a slender meal of boiled eggs, figs and flat cakes which we had brought ourselves. Aristotle had thought to bring two bed-rolls with him – just as well, for I had none. The ticking was thin and the floor hard, but we had a roof over our heads, and even a room to ourselves, so we fared handsomely. Soon, Aristotle advised me, we would be in poorer inns with only the bare ground of a courtyard to rest in. Aristotle had guest-friends in Phokis upon whom we could call when we were farther advanced on our journey. He had guest-friends around Eleusis also, but our mission required secrecy. Gossip in Eleusis is gossip in Athens.

The inn's hostess was a kindly soul who offered us wine and set a boy to looking after the horses. Aristotle attempted to gain information about other travellers, but although the woman was loquacious enough we heard of no one answering the description of our quarry. An itinerant perfume-seller had been there, and sold her some perfume, but he had gone on to make a delivery to some great house in Eleusis. Otherwise her house held a rich citizen of Korinthos and his attendants, as well as some Athenians of low degree who made merry in the courtyard about the fire.

'How far do you think the Abductor could have gone by now?' I asked Aristotle when we were alone.

'Still well ahead of us,' Aristotle answered. 'I should guess that we are now as far along as he was at noon today, or even earlier – mid-morning.'

'Then we have hardly made any progress at all!'

'We have done well enough,' said Aristotle, now almost asleep. 'We should start going twice as fast as he, so we should eventually catch up with him – provided we are travelling in the same direction. It's a question of mathematics.'

'What about Akhilleus and the tortoise?' I retorted smartly, but he did not think it worth his while to answer. Indeed, I always have to pause to remember how this remarkable paradox works, so I was glad he did not interrogate me on the subject.

Next morning I awoke late, suffering from pain and stiffness which made me reluctant to arise. We had intended to set out very early, but I had first to buy some ointment from the hostess. With this soothing compound of her own devising I anointed my sore skin before getting on the horse again. At last we were making our way past Eleusis, to the north-west of that remarkable shrine, and we were going into the countryside. Forgetting my pain for a while, I was able to enjoy the beauty of the dawn and the sparkles of light in the drops of heavy dew. The early day was cool – cattle in the fields snorted in clouds of steam – but it was the sort of morning that makes a man rejoice in the happy gift of life. We ate some more dried fruit as we rode, but after a short while the thirst came upon me, as well as a great desire for a wash, and we stopped to consider what to do. There was no other village or town in the area.

'Look,' said I, pointing. 'There in that grove is a shrine to the Nymphs. There must be a spring. Let us go for water.'

'It is on someone's land,' said Aristotle. 'We might ask the farmer who owns it for a drink.'

'But one has to be careful not to beggar one's host,' I reminded him. 'Athenian hospitality is proverbial, and it is well known that if you ask a poor family for a cup of cold water they will feast you and rob themselves of their own dinner, or even beggar themselves of provisions for a week in order to treat you properly. For we Athenians know that Zeus himself is the Protector of the stranger and the wanderer.'

'Well then,' said Aristotle, 'let us hope there may be a prosperous farmer! Even so we shall take nothing beyond the water – or perhaps a cup of goat's milk – however much he presses us. And it is time we set ourselves to asking some questions. After all, we are *hunting* for someone, not just journeying.'

At that moment, we caught sight of a boy playing with a hoop on the dusty road. He was rolling it along, shouting and pretending it was a horse, or a troop of soldiers, or something, as boys will. He caught sight of us too, and gazed at the horses with admiration.

'Friend,' said Aristotle courteously, 'do you know of anyone nearby who might offer travellers the refreshment of a drink of milk? Or of water to wash in?'

'My uncle might,' said the lad. 'I'm visiting him. I don't live here,' he added. '*My* home is in a city deme.'

He spoke with an Athenian accent, and his clothes were nicely made. Evidently this was a well-kept little boy of good family.

'Where does your honoured uncle live?' I asked.

'His house – oh, that's many stadia ahead, down that road there. I came out for a walk on my own.'

'I see. I wonder now,' said Aristotle very confidentially, speaking over the ears of his horse, 'have you seen any other travellers, last night or on your walk this morning? People going in the same direction as ourselves?'

'Well,' said the boy, 'I saw a pedlar. And the neighbours' steward. That's all, I think.'

'Are you sure?' I said. 'You didn't see a man walking beside a litter? Yesterday, if not today.'

I realised I had perhaps said too much, been too eager, but there was no going back on it now. The boy was interested.

'I should have noticed anything like that,' he said with assurance, 'but I tell you what. The only person who's really likely to have seen anything that goes by here is old Smikrenes. That's his place there. His land runs right by the road, and his house and barns aren't far from the highway. Folks here say he never sleeps – well, hardly ever – and he notices everybody.'

'That sounds promising, indeed,' Aristotle said to me. 'We were just thinking of going to this man's house, to beg a drink – so we may as well do so. And perhaps this lad will take us thither and introduce us.'

'Oh,' said the airy lad, 'I can take you to his gate, but I don't *know* him – not to say properly. He and Uncle are neighbours, but they don't *speak* – or not often. Smikrenes doesn't like speaking to folks. He doesn't have anything to do with neighbours unless he's obliged. My uncle says Smikrenes is harder than flint, and meaner than second skimmings. He'd toss a withered olive away rather than give it to a body, Uncle says. Smikrenes hates *everyone.* All the folk around here know that. He quarrelled with his wife – years ago – and she left him and went back to live with her first husband's family, or her father or somebody. So now Smikrenes lives here with his daughter and does all the work himself. Though Uncle says he's rich enough to hire help or buy man-slaves if he could bring himself to part with an obol. He never offers sacrifices or has a neighbour in to a feast.'

'But,' I objected, 'he has a shrine on his property.'

'Two shrines,' said the boy. 'One to the Nymphs – that's in that cave behind the grove – and one to Pan. That's part of the trouble. One shrine would be enough, Smikrenes says, and two are going to ruin him.'

'How does he make that out?'

'You see, people are always coming by and offering sacrifices and having parties, and that means they trample all over his land, and he *hates* that. And some of them send their slaves to ask to borrow pots and pitchers. So it's no wonder he watches the road so carefully! Uncle says Smikrenes always has half an eye on the highway to see if people are coming to offer a sacrifice so he can chase them off. He rips and tears and halloos after them, and threatens to set the dog on them. He doesn't really harm them with the dog, most of the time, because of Pan. But Uncle says Smikrenes scared off two rich women and one merchant's family – *and* their cooks. I wish I'd been there to see,' the boy added wistfully.

'Hmm,' said Aristotle. '*Not* promising. Still, we need scarcely fear that his hospitality would beggar him. And this Smikrenes sounds like an admirable observer for our purposes, if a trifle morose. I've half a mind to try him.'

'Let's do so,' I said recklessly. 'We can speak to him courteously, and we can offer him money if he doesn't practise hospitality.'

The prospect of goat's milk, or of clear fresh water, was most appealing. Also, I thought I should like to be off my horse for a while.

'Very well,' said Aristotle, and the boy, evidently seeing his position as that of captain or pilot, tucked his hoop over his arm with a manly air and walked briskly ahead of us to a dilapidated gate. We dismounted (a procedure I always underwent with some difficulty); after tethering our horses to the outer gateposts, we followed the gossiping boy – all equal now on foot.

The boy led us up a cart track. We passed the house. It had a forlorn air, in contrast to the rich and flourishing quality of the great dung heap beside it, which sent its vapours steaming forth into the clear morning. There were a good number of chickens to be seen, and from somewhere I could hear the sound of pigs – and could smell them too – while on the hill slope I saw both sheep and goats. Smikrenes was evidently not impoverished. His fields seemed in fair condition, despite his unkindness to the Nymphs and imputed discourtesy to the gods in general. The ploughed land gleamed. We walked on, past two or three small fields, and then the boy drew to a halt and pointed.

'There! That's old Smikrenes. In the fallow field, clearing stones away.' We looked at a stooping figure in an old grey cloak, its backside to us, showing like a large boulder against the sloping land.

'I see,' said I, and feeling rather ridiculous, went to the edge of this field and called to the stooping back: 'Sir! O Smikrenes!'

The grey boulder moved and straightened like a tree, then turned, revealing a bushy head and beard. Carefully, the boy drew behind me. No longer in the vanguard, he prudently awaited developments. Aristotle stepped forward and spoke in that well-bred and courteous manner which had found favour in the courts of kings and the groves of philosophers.

'Pardon our intrusion on your ancestral lands and on your kindness, O Smikrenes, but we are travellers from Athens. We wish most humbly to ask you for a cup of cold water from your spring and permission to rest ourselves here for a short space.'

'Eh?' said the man, cupping a hand around one large red ear. His body was tall and thin, his arms and neck scrawny, but face and ears were red, as if sun and wind aroused his blood. 'What's that?'

'Pardon us, O citizen Smikrenes, but we are travellers from Athens and would beg –'

'Blast your eyes!' said the countryman. 'Bless me, if they're not at it again! You would, would you?'

And before we knew what he was about he caught up a greasy clod of earth from his field and threw it at us. It landed on my cloak.

'To Hades with you and your boots too!' he advised. 'There's no getting away from you. *People!* Riff-raff of Athens! Hunt me in my own fields, would you? Be off with you!!' Red-faced Smikrenes caught up another clod. We were obliged to retreat, still facing our unsatisfied enemy who came slowly but steadily after us, hurling the occasional clod as he came. He varied his protests as he advanced.

'If it's not one thing, it's another. *Water* from my own

well! *Cooking pots!* Sacrifices and hot dinners! Go and make your sacrifices on your own land. Do you take this for the market-place? Be off with you! To Hades! By the frogs of Styx, I wish I had the burying of the lot of you!'

We reached the edge of the field (in undignified haste) and turned again to face and expostulate with this unreasonable man.

'Sir, we would only wish to say –'

'Oh, so you wish to say, do you? And *I'd* like to say, when I get the chance. I'd like to say that *I* do for myself. Wish others to do likewise. All I ask is to be *left alone*. This isn't the highway, is it? Where can a man get away from you? If a man wanted to hang himself hereabouts, he couldn't do it in peace. Why will you keep plaguing me, rot your hides!'

'Sir –'

'Shut your face! I ask no favours. I don't need anyone. I've worked this land, man and boy, forty year, and I've not asked no one for so much as a crooked nail. So why can't folk let *me* alone, I'd like to know? I'm an independent man. All I ask is that everyone should *mind his own business*!'

He roared this last phrase as a peroration, his red face angry as a bull's, and stood there, frowning at the edge of his fields, waving his hoe. Evidently he would not be satisfied save by our departure. Meekly we gave the fellow the longed-for sight of our backs, and went down the track. When we turned our heads we could see the disagreeable Smikrenes returning to his field, but going backwards to keep an eye on us, and still waving his hoe.

'Be off!' he shouted as a final farewell.

As we went, slinking foolishly by the house, someone said 'Hiss-st' and we paused. A girl stepped from the house door and towards us, a girl clad in simple grey wool, with a spindle in her hand. The hood which served as a veil had partly slipped from her face, and I could see she was pretty, with grey-green eyes and brown hair with a sheen to it, the colour of ripe acorns. 'Hsst!' she said again, and beckoned to us. We three slipped around to the house door, beyond the midden and out of sight of our furious host of the field.

'I heard you,' she whispered. 'Zeus favours the stranger and the traveller. I will give you the water, and even some milk and perhaps a little cake. But you must be quick about it.' She nodded apprehensively in the direction of the field.

'Thank you, my daughter,' said Aristotle. 'You are kind, and may the gods bless you – but we would not have you trouble yourself.'

'It's not a trouble to *me*,' she said, still whispering. 'You mustn't mind Father. He is a good man, really, but he has had losses. And many troubles to vex him. But I usually try to help travellers – without him knowing anything about it. Then the gods and Nymphs will not forsake us. Besides, it is so lonely here.'

She returned into the house and quickly emerged again, bearing a handsome bronze pitcher. An old woman, evidently a servant anxious to preserve the proprieties, came with her.

'I will not be long,' said the lovely daughter of unlovely Smikrenes. 'He usually wishes me to bring him a drink of water at this time in the morning. I will do so now, so he will be busy while my nurse gives the rest of the water to you, and some barley cakes. Our well is deep, and the water is cool and sweet.'

The woman set out three cups; the girl took one, and the pitcher, and she and the old woman went off to the well, a fountain surrounded by a high stone coping. It stood at a pleasing distance from the dunghill, beyond the house near the grove. We could see it from our position by the house door where we lurked uneasily in the sun, Aristotle and I and the boy, not saying anything. I think even Aristotle felt awkward. Certainly I did. The boy sat hugging his knees, awaiting events with a detached air, as if all had been got up for his entertainment.

'Do you think –' I whispered to Aristotle.

I was interrupted by a sudden clang and two shrieks, followed by loud lamentation from the old servant.

'Oh-h! Deary me! Would you look at that now! Master's fine pitcher is gone down into the water! Oh Pan! *What* will become of us!'

'Hush,' said the girl. 'There's nothing for it but to tell my father. He can fish it out with his hoe. Don't cry, Geta! I'll say I did it.'

The two women rushed off up the fields. We waited where we were, perhaps in part because if we went down to the roadway we now stood an excellent chance of being seen by the angry man on his way to the well. But I know I also stayed so that I could say my farewell to our kind hostess with the acorn hair and grey-green eyes. I felt oddly responsible for the mishap, and anxious for the girl. If the old man started to take his wrath out upon her I knew I could not remain silent – though I had little desire to be in anything like proximity again to our irascible acquaintance.

Surprisingly quickly, considering the distance he had to cover, the master of the house could be heard, coming along and bellowing his imprecations.

'A fine thing! What man alive would ever rear a daughter! Who but a cursed daughter would lose a cursed pitcher down a cursed well? The Nymphs take it! Poseidon confound the blasted well! Isn't a man to ever have a moment's peace to get his own work done?'

We could hear his approach before we saw him and could not resist moving along to the house corner in order to peer at Smikrenes' success in fishing for his pitcher.

We were well rewarded for our curiosity. We saw Smikrenes approach the well and lean over. Very carefully, he thrust his hoe down into the well and evidently clawed the water with it. Then he thrust the hoe in more deeply – and leaned over a little further – and a little further – and then *splash*! Head over heels, in went Smikrenes, neatly into his own well, as if it had been fitted for the purpose.

The two women shrieked. At once we left our hiding place and all three of us, uttering cries, rushed to the well.

'Hush!' I said as I approached. 'Are you all right, sir?' The query seemed inane, for I was certain at that moment that Smikrenes must have been killed.

'Of course I'm not all right, blast your eyes,' said a gruff voice from the depths. Peering in, I could see two beady eyes among wet tangled hair, and two hands holding moss-grown bricks. Smikrenes seemed unhurt.

I drew my head back from gazing into the deep pit, as did Aristotle and the boy. Our eyes met in startled gaze. The boy broke into a fury of laughter, hooting and stamping and waving his arms. All his earlier dignity of manner was broken in fragments of abandoned mirth. We frowned at this graceless and disrespectful infant, but his mirth was infectious, and Aristotle and I found ourselves joining him in helpless laughter.

'That's right,' said the voice from the well bitterly. 'Enjoy yourselves. Don't mind me. I'm just dying of drowning and dampness in here, that's all.'

A frog jumped on to his head, gave a startled 'Brekx-kx' and jumped off again. The boy was overcome with incoherence and hiccups and went away to roll upon the ground. He was temporarily useless. I could have been in the same state, if it had not been for the presence of the anxious women.

'Look here,' I said to the wretch's daughter, 'is there any rope in the barn?'

'Oh, yes, I'll show you,' she replied, and ran off as fleet as Atlanta, with myself following. We found a good coil of stout rope and brought it back. I wound some about my waist and about Aristotle, several times each. At the other end of the rope I made a kind of noose, and dropped this longer end into the well, trying to capture Smikrenes' body. At last it went about his shoulders, and he gingerly withdrew one hand from the well-coping and put his arm through, so he was secure.

'Now,' I said sternly, stifling my temptation to giggle. 'Hold on tightly to the rope, and pull yourself up. And you'd better pray to Pan and the Nymphs. Promise a libation. This is serious work for you.'

'Very well,' he growled at the end of his rope.

'Now – come when I say "heave!" And go slowly. Don't move save when I give the word.'

I said 'heave!' and pulled, and Aristotle pulled. Slowly

Smikrenes heaved up the slippery sides of the well, and I shouted and pulled again, with Aristotle pulling behind me. The man emerged, like a stopper from the bottle – first the bushy head (dripping now) and then the shoulders and the torso; and then, with a last pull, thighs and knees, and I could grab him and bring him to safety.

'There,' I said officiously wringing out his cloak and patting him on the back. 'Now you're all right again.'

He fixed his eyes, beneath their still-drooping shaggy eyebrows, severely upon me.

'Where's my hoe? And my pitcher? I'd like to know?'

'Oh, Father,' the girl protested.

'I'll get them,' I said recklessly, and I climbed hand over hand down the rope and into the well, finding toeholds in the coping where I went, while Aristotle and the girl held the rope. I don't think I would have ventured thus if the girl hadn't been there.

I did find the hoe, which had lodged itself between stones near the surface, and by dint of poking and pulling and lowering myself to the waist in cold well-water I was able to find the pitcher and to coax it back to light – much to my own surprise. It was difficult coming back up with the hoe and the pitcher both, but I managed it.

'There,' I said, handing the gentleman his property.

'It's *dented,*' he said indignantly, looking at the bronze jug.

'Well, and so it might be,' I said, losing patience. 'If you ask me, the Nymphs have been kind to you. You said "Nymphs take it" and they did – and you too. But they've given you back everything. They've played a good joke on you, sir, and I for one don't blame them. You owe them a libation, remember. And now we'll be on our way.'

Aristotle and I had unwound ourselves from the rope, and we turned to go, myself still dripping cold well-water.

'No, Father,' said the girl unexpectedly. 'This isn't right – it isn't decent. We owe these people your life. Suppose this good young man hadn't been here when you fell in? Do you wish him to catch an ague for all his thanks? Before Zeus, we must feed these travellers and offer them shelter and dry their clothes.'

'Well, my Philomela,' said Smikrenes, softening unexpectedly. 'You may be in the right of it. I'm not sorry to be out of that there well, and that's a fact.' (Stifled giggles from the boy, but Aristotle frowned him down.) 'It's true that I owe you hospitality,' Smikrenes continued in tones more rational than any we had heard from him so far, 'and I dare say it wouldn't ruin me once in a way. In my old father's time, things were different. You must pardon my rough manners, friends, but I'm only an old country fellow, and have had much to vex me these past years.'

'Friend,' said Aristotle, touching the sodden Smikrenes lightly on a damp shoulder. 'What man could not say as much? We all have things to vex us. And you are blessed with health and strength, with fair lands and a kind daughter. Praise the gods, and do not use their names for cursing. And consider – let me speak freely as a friend, for you and I are two aged men together – that no man is truly free from all need of his fellows. I too have been at times tempted to despise my kind and live aloof. But to remain alone is not in the nature of mortal men who eat bread.'

'Speaking of bread,' said Smikrenes more cheerfully, 'is there any in the house, Philomela? This exercise has given me as much appetite as if I'd gone a-swimming. And

I dare say these folk could do with a bite. Stir yourself, girl, and see what you can provide. Come into the house, friends, and we will do our best to entertain you.'

And so what would have seemed impossible a little while before truly came to pass, and we were given the shelter of this man's house, offered hot water to wash in, and good country food – bread and olives and goat's cheese – to eat. I was glad of the goat's milk. I could no longer fancy cold water from the well, having had too much of it externally – and I remembered that Smikrenes' old cloak and dungy hoe had been in it. The fair daughter herself dried my own cloak. Though now she had veiled herself and resumed the natural modesty of a well-bred Athenian girl, yet she had to minister to guests herself, as noblewomen did in the heroic age. I had seen her face before it was veiled, and knew her skin was fair, though with a few fine freckles across the nose, like gold dust. She had neat wrists and ankles, and moved gracefully about the kitchen. If she were well treated, and not worried to skin and bone by her surly progenitor and a deal of hard work, she would be as handsome a woman as one needed to set eyes upon.

There was goodness in her mind, too. She was obviously a meek and obedient daughter, yet I admired her for standing up to her father in justice, and for our sake, as she had done. And though her behaviour was as solemn and as becoming as it could be (given the ungentle fact that she was compelled to speak to strange men), still beneath the gravity I thought I could distinguish a flicker of understanding of the boy's impulsive mirth. Probably she had little to laugh at most of the time. The boy had control of himself now, and sat in the house as grave and polite as any gentleman, eating in a mannerly fashion with small bites, and watching us all.

'Look at that misbegotten boy,' growled Smikrenes, good-humouredly. 'Young varmint. Laughing fit to kill, and now sitting there like a juryman, watching us as if two eyes weren't enough.'

'He is an observant young fellow,' Aristotle agreed. 'And it is to be hoped his manners will improve with time.' He looked at the boy with mock severity. 'But, speaking of observation,' he continued. 'We did wish to ask you if you had seen any travellers come this way. There is someone we are . . . are anxious to overtake on the road, if possible.'

The old man scratched his shaggy head. 'Hmm. Yes. Last night at dusk there was a young man – a bit like yourself it may be,' turning to me. 'Athenian by the sound of him. Not going fine, though – rough-dressed with a hood over his face. He spoke to this good-for-nothing here' – nodding at the slavewoman, who snuffled nervously. 'Came snooping about, asking for milk, and for water from the well. Claimed he needed food and drink for friends. I wasn't going to have any strangers about, let alone at nightfall. Robbers, most like. So I whistled for my dog and we soon sent him packing.'

'What did he look like? Can you tell us more about him?'

'Young,' repeated Smikrenes. 'Tall young rascal – one of the sort who do nothing all day, I'd judge. Leastways, we argued a bit and his voice was like gentry, if you understand me. Well built, dark hair. Might be a soldier out of work, so's to speak. There's too many of that kind now, and I don't care for 'em. If he wants food, I told him, better work like an honest man. He was a bit haughty –

and he had a few oaths of his own – but the dog and I took him down a trifle, didn't we, Argos?' The old mangy house-dog thumped his tail. 'Yes, he went off like a good one. He won't bother us no more, I'll be bound.'

'Did you see anyone else?'

'Not much but slaves – locals mostly. And my neighbour up the road here with his old knock-kneed ox. Not many foreigners about this time, saving your presences. But there was that pedlar early this morning. Big chap with a pack. He caught sight of us, and had the bad judgement to ask me to buy perfume and bracelets for the girl here, "against her marriage", he said.' Smikrenes snorted angrily. '*Marriage!* Thing's'll come to a worse pass before she need think of that. Not for a long time yet. I can't spare her. I've seen enough of marriage and marrying. *You* married?' He turned to me, and I shook my head, blushing unaccountably.

'Be warned. Don't do it. Marriage has no survivors. This pedlar was going to a wedding, at a distance. So *he* said anyway. Some fools or other are always getting married. I sent him off in a hurry. We don't buy trumpery here. If the girl wants to scent herself we grow herbs, and there are acorns enough for a necklace. And our cloth's our own. Only fools buy what they don't need – and nowadays with money they don't have.' He caught himself in mid-tirade, and returned to the subject. 'So I reckon that's all the passers-by I've seen. Neighbours often pass of course, but I usually manage to pray they'll go by without me wasting more breath on 'em.'

Aristotle and I made polite comments about his household management, his well-noted financial prudence, and his fair estate. I could see that Aristotle was anxious to leave – and so was I. For the description of the young man with dark hair offered food for speculation, and reason for hurry. Our task was not merely to travel, but to overtake.

We said our ceremonious farewells with some difficulty, for the stubborn and taciturn farmer had waxed talkative in the unwonted pleasure of company. Smikrenes' farewells were loud and long-winded, country fashion. His daughter, Philomela, said a farewell to us modestly bowing at the door. There was a queenly air about this country girl, standing there with her spindle in her hand and the light shining on the vagrant wisps of brown hair; she was like some rustic princess of the time of Alkinoös.

'The day is far advanced,' I remarked to her, for something to say, and as a kind of excuse for taking leave. 'Yes,' she replied. 'The sun shines brightly on your road.' And she gestured with her hand in the direction of the road we were to take. I realised that perhaps she too might wish to travel to the world outside the farm, the fair places which she had never seen.

Once on the road again, Aristotle and I recognised that we were responsible for returning the boy to his uncle's home. The boy himself seemed quite satisfied with his morning's adventure, and the little feast of bread and cheese had not come amiss either. He was even more pleased when Aristotle took him up to ride before him on the horse, and kept up a flow of chatter and comment on places we passed, the condition of the land and the nature of the inhabitants, as well as general remarks.

'I'm going to travel when I get big,' he announced. 'I shall go to Delphi too, before very long, and when I grow up I shall go to Olympia and Epidauros and maybe even to Rhodos.'

'It's not so easy to travel,' I remarked. 'Horses are dear, and roads are long – and how will you ride to Rhodos?'

'I shall go on a *ship*,' he replied, obviously thinking me a fool. 'And it's not to hard to travel. All you have to do is go. I don't know what people stay home for. Even if I were poor, I could be a pedlar. You don't need anything for that – just your feet and a bag. Anybody can do it. But I'd rather be a rich man and travel properly.'

Aristotle looked at the lad attentively. 'There is much truth in what you say. But do you think about an education, my lad? Can you read? Do you want to learn?'

'Oh yes, I can read – some – now. And I will read all the great books and the poems and plays. Then I will write some myself and be famous and get prizes like Euripides.'

'No small ambition in so small a frame,' Aristotle murmured. 'Listen, my good fellow, when you are of age if you think you would like to attend the Lykeion in Athens, just come to me – Aristotle of the Lykeion – and you can be one of our students. Or if I'm not there any longer, go to Theophrastos. I shall tell him about you, and he'll be sure to admit you and give you a good education. You are an observing lad, and quick-witted. You'd do us credit.'

'Oh, thank you. Yes, I will,' said the child politely, not at all overwhelmed by the honour. 'Look, there's Uncle's house. Oh, and there's Auntie.'

He scrambled down and ran towards the woman on the path, who saw him and came quickly towards him.

'Menandros! Where have you been? We were looking for you.'

'Oh – just out,' said the boy.

Aristotle and I hastened to give what explanation we could, emphasising the boy's assistance to us and the harmlessness of the morning's activities. (We left the episode of the well for Menandros himself to describe as he chose.) The woman was mollified, and went with her chattering nephew back to the farmhouse, the boy capering beside her. He was evidently a favourite child, indulged and in no fear of punishment. He turned and waved an airy hand at us and shouted goodbyes as we went on. We had made three friends (of sorts) that morning and said three goodbyes. That is one of the things that make travel fatiguing.

Aristotle and I were glad to be alone at last, so as to talk over the interesting description of a traveller.

'A young man, tall and dark-haired,' I said. 'Aristotle, do you realise who that sounds like? It could be Straton. And when he asked for a drink "for his friends" he could mean the slaves and Anthia and her slave-girl. Then – Straton is the Abductor.'

'Yes,' said Aristotle, 'I thought of that at once. But why should Straton abduct his own cousin? Could he not marry her in the ordinary way? That still puzzles me.'

'Well,' I said hesitantly, 'the young traveller may have been Polemon, of course. I don't know if we can put too much stress on Smikrenes' impression of the colour of the hair, especially as it was getting dark when he saw the young man. Polemon was practically betrothed to Anthia – he would have married her if her father hadn't died before things could be settled. He feels certain he has a claim. If Polemon found he wasn't to have Anthia, he might have run off with her.'

'All true,' said Aristotle, 'but not definite. As you say, we would probably be wrong to cling to the hair colour as a definite sign. Even golden-brown hair like Polemon's might look dark in some circumstances. The most definite thing Smikrenes said really was that the young man reminded him of a soldier. There might have been something military about him. That would be true of Straton, or of Polemon the ephebe. Admittedly, it would also be true of many other men. Ah, well, if we do see Straton, or Polemon, we shall recognise either, because we know them. And if we see any other Athenians who we know might be connected with this case, we shall recognise them likewise. The thing to do is obviously to catch up with *someone*. Do that first, and then find out what has really been happening.'

So we went on, but could not resist thinking of the puzzle still.

V

Man in a Landscape

As we went on, the region became wilder. We left the trim farms of the plains as the road sought its way between hills. We were leaving Attika and slowly approaching Boiotia. In this hill region there are fewer estates and broad-acred farms. The people there cultivate sheep and goats rather than the friendly corn.

We were favoured with good weather at first. At noon when the sun was overhead, we became almost hot and could slip off hoods and heavy cloaks. There were a few clouds, small ones moving quickly and casting purple shadows upon the hillsides, which were austerely dressed still in gorse and buckthorn and dry bracken. The smiling blue sky, the little clouds and the sunlight all spoke of spring, and quick-coming spring urged us on. There comes a time in the turn of the season as winter departs when, even if winter cold and days of rain persist, the earth stirs. And when the sun shines the earth, no longer sullen, gives back the light. So it was now. The brown earth, with a veil of new green grass appearing under the withered growth, gave back the light and filled the air with that first green scent that tells you she means to have rose-filled summer once again.

For several hours after leaving Smikrenes' farm we went on at a good pace, our heads full of speculation and the courage of spring in our veins. It was easy to believe the world was engaged in the arts of peace, to forget the uneasy knowledge that in the south, in distant Arkadia, the troops collected by King Agis of Sparta encamped about Megalopolis were making a last desperate attempt against the indomitable and efficient Antipater. On this day when nature seemed to promise happiness, even our own odd quest seemed not impossible. The sun was beginning to slide down the western slope of the sky when we thought of pausing again to take food and perhaps to consult some villagers in order to ask our perpetual question. The thought came unseasonably. There was nobody around us but goats. We stopped anyway, to relieve nature, shake our stiffened limbs, and to eat the last of our cakes.

'At the next village,' said Aristotle, 'I am going to buy another water-skin. This bottle holds too little.'

'And that little is warm,' I said. 'There are goats enough hereabouts to provide the villagers with a hundred bottles apiece, I should think. Here's a ditch by the roadside, with a trickle of water. Not clean enough, but if we followed it up we might come to a better – a hill stream, perhaps.'

We did as I suggested, leading our horses by the bridles and going on foot along the side of the ditch, trying to find the spring or stream which fed it. But the ditch went on sluggishly, too muddy for our tastes, though the horses were glad of it when we let them drink. We continued our search, moving off the road and up the hill; there seemed to be a sort of path, as if goatherds or goats had trodden through the prickly vegetation. The hill was covered with scrub, with here and there spinneys of tall bushes, hazel mostly, and even some trees sparsely scattered on the hill flank.

'There's a sacred oak,' I remarked, looking at the brave tree spreading its arms to the sky; there were the usual fillets bound round it, offered by local admirers and suppliants. Not far from the oak tree there was a thicket with a small mound beside it, but no spring or stream could I see.

'There's something wrong about that tree,' said Aristotle. 'Look at the carrion crows in it. And why is there a vulture on that mound? Great Athena, come quickly!'

And he was off, as fast as the resistant herbage underfoot would let him pass. At Aristotle's bidding I tied the horses to the tree and then followed him. The crows flew off, and Aristotle scared away the vulture, who circled the tree indignantly and fluttered over our heads. Our horses eyed the birds nervously and whinnied. When I caught up with him Aristotle was already on his knees by the mound, throwing off the dead oak leaves and grass and twigs with which it was covered. I joined him in his work. This strange task did not last long.

Our hands touched – I still shudder to think of it – dead flesh, cold and resistant and clammy through the dry leaves. I pulled out a hand, a man's hand. Very white. A crow shrieked angrily. The vulture stared down at us from the tree and writhed its long neck jealously.

We then made frantic haste to uncover the place where the head should be – and we succeeded. A dead face stared up at us. Very dead. One eye had been plucked out by the competent vulture. But the face was still recognisable. It was the face of Straton.

'So here we find him,' said Aristotle. 'We said we should recognise him if we met him, and it is true. Though he has adopted the last disguise, and is now a stranger to all his friends. Nothing alters a man like dying. Now – how did he die?'

To my horror, Aristotle pushed the body up and began to examine it as if it were a living patient. One-eyed Straton leered at us as he rose, winking with his final unchangeable wink. A small silver coin shot out of his mouth, as if Straton spat out small change.

'It's not hard to see how he died,' said Aristotle. And indeed it wasn't, even to my untrained gaze, for I could see a wide slit in the man's chest, about the length of my fourth finger, and some scattered light-coloured bloodstains in the torn khiton about the wound. There was also the mark of a long knife wound on the man's left shoulder. But Aristotle was behind the corpse, looking at its back. His hands held the top of the shoulders, and the body was inclined off the ground, stiffly and all of a piece, like a plank.

'Not that, Stephanos, I think – look here! Not the wound in the chest – I believe it was this one that did the mischief.' When I moved about I could see that the back had been stabbed deeply, between the shoulder-blades. Quantities of blood had stained the khiton and soaked into the ground.

'Much more blood in the back,' said Aristotle briskly, 'and very little in front. Straton was stabbed in the back, between the ribs and straight through to the heart. Presumably by a large knife or a straight dagger. When he was stabbed in the front, one lung was nicked. So there would have been less blood anyway, and that frothy, as we see by the effect here – light-coloured spattering. Which blow came first?'

'I don't know.' I didn't want to look. 'Does it matter?'

'It might. The blow to the lung came before the stab in the back – the man was still able to bleed copiously at that final forceful thrust that took life away.'

Aristotle was of the tribe of Asklepios and a physician. He could talk about such things without unease. I did not care much for any of this, but I admired his skill. I should at once have assumed that the stab in the chest had killed the man, as seemed more natural. I should have assumed also that the wound in the back – if I had bothered to discover it – was merely the mark of the knife emerging, but Aristotle said that could not be so.

'The wounds aren't aligned that way. Besides, when a man is stabbed, the knife thrusts the flesh *inward* around the wound, while the force of exit pushes the flesh outwards. These are two quite separate in-going stabs. As well as that smaller wound on the shoulder. That third wound bled a little, and dried. The man was living when he felt this, and he lived afterwards. The skin has puffed up slightly about it, and had time to be sore. Only a flesh wound, not made in the same assault as these other two. The last thrust – the stab in the back – killed him. I'm not sure if all three wounds were inflicted by the same implement, or not. Of course, a knife can wiggle about a good deal. Straton has certainly been very much murdered, as it were.'

'Evidently. This is certainly not *suicide*,' I retorted. The philosopher laughed suddenly, a kind of grim chuckle, and let the body slide back on its bed of leaves. The silver bracelet on the corpse's rigid arm gleamed in the glow of the westering sun.

'He died hours ago,' Aristotle added. 'This body is stiff. But it is so very straight. So neat. Did someone straighten out the corpse just after death? There are a good many complications here.'

'The murder of our friend Lysippos' eldest son – the heir of the man we were supposed to help – is a complication, certainly,' I said with conscious irony. 'Especially for Lysippos – not to mention Straton himself.'

'Especially for Lysippos, yes. We will have to tell Straton's father – somehow.'

Reluctantly, but moved by some strange curiosity, I picked up the dead hand. Straton still wore a plain silver bracelet. I remembered that I had seen it on him in life, and that his father Lysippos wore one just like it, as did Timotheos. Whoever had killed Straton had not bothered to steal this piece of valuable metal. The dead arm, strangely flaccid now and white under its tan, was already shrivelling within its silver loop. The cool hand's unresisting fingers were curled around a squashy mass of – something. It made my gorge rise. Hoping not to vomit before Aristotle, I forced myself to look. I recognised the sticky brown mass. The dead hand was clutching dried figs, a substitute for the honey cake or pomegranate offering to the Underworld. I was revolted and yet filled with pity. Looking at this disgusting corpse I was oddly reminded of my own father's funeral.

'Why, Straton has been given a decent burial,' I exclaimed.

'That is a really strange thing,' Aristotle agreed. 'Care has been taken to cover him with earth, too, not just sticks and leaves. *Why* has this corpse been given a proper burial? Who did it? Murderers aren't usually so pious, or so friendly to the victim's soul.'

I was still remembering my father's funeral – the pomegranate, the silver coin to pay for the journey over the dark Underworld river, the sound of earth falling on the still figure in its wrappings. My aunt Eudoxia's laying-out with her favourite honey cake in her hand, her son Philemon scattering trinkets into the grave upon her little body, and then the earth falling round it. Lacking the earth-fall around the body, the uneasy soul cannot cross into the proper abode of the shades. The silver coin that the corpse had spat out – money had been placed in the dead mouth (more than enough) for his fare over the Styx.

'It is strange,' I said. 'The people who see to it that a proper burial takes place are usually relatives.'

Straton had been given burial enough to satisfy the gods and the demons, though not sufficient to keep off the crows.

'We must bury it again,' said Aristotle. (I noticed he first said 'it' and not 'him'.) 'There's no time to lose. Quick, Stephanos, cover him up again, carefully. I don't want either of us to carry the smallest trace of blood. Where's that silver piece?'

He found the coin, and replaced it in that cold mouth. We both muttered prayers and lamentations for the dead as we went about our work of reburial, so as not to undo the work of the original strange funeral. Soon the mound was straight and tidy again. Silver had gone back to the earth from which it came. Aristotle made us look carefully to see if we had left any traces of our presence, beyond the inevitable trampling of grass and ground. As best he could, he erased our footsteps where they had pressed into the earth as we had squatted by the corpse. Then we moved cautiously away from that grim barrow. As we went, we looked for signs of the other person or persons who must have been there before us.

'Our own horses have trampled on some of the marks,' Aristotle frowned. 'And they have left traces of our presence here which we can hardly cancel.' He pointed to the droppings that my mare had let fall. 'Now, look – somebody came this way.' He had found a fresh-made track of broken bushes and trodden herbage leading down to the ditch and the road again.

'There's little enough to be found,' said Aristotle. 'All we can say is that certainly one, perhaps two, persons, presumably but not necessarily men, went down by this track. He – or he and she – they – jumped the ditch, and then blotted out their footprints. There's nothing in the road here by the ditch but scratches and deep scuff-marks. What I don't see are any signs of the litter. The heiress was run away with in a litter. If Straton caught up with it, it must have been set down here somewhere – perhaps on the road, perhaps beside it.'

'The road itself is so much trodden in the middle,' I said, 'while a lot of the ground on the hillside is covered with heather that wouldn't leave much trace. Here is a place where goats have lain down and browsed. A litter might have gone there.'

'True. The place is full of goats who wander about constantly making paths and breaking off twigs. And the road, as you say . . .' He examined it. 'A public highway is so very public. There have been many passers-by. I don't quite see the sort of prints I'd expect to see made by slaves carrying a litter – two sets of prints, fairly heavy, always at the same distance, and one man's footsteps walking over the leader's track. I don't see them, but that doesn't mean slaves carrying a litter didn't go by. Let's retrace our own steps.'

We went back along the way we had come, walking near the road's edge and glaring about. Not very far from where we had first stopped to look at the ditch we came to some footmarks which *might* have been those made by bearers of a litter: two sets of prints, one superimposed on the other and keeping an equal distance. There was a flat heathery place by the roadside where one might imagine something had been set down – but then, many persons might have sat down there, or set down a load of some kind. The footprints of the bearers appeared to stop and not to go on again.

'That only suggests,' said Aristotle, 'that the litter got this far, and went up the hill to the thicket and mound – and then disappeared. It's a great pity we haven't got time to go over the whole hillside. But this is a text we must abandon before we've deciphered it. Let's go back and retrieve the horses. Perhaps we'll find some more traces as we go.'

He was quite right about that. As we went towards the hill, a short distance from the track we had first found and near the road I came upon drops of blood, staining the leaves of weeds that grew in the ditch, and rusting on the pebbles. I should not have found them if I hadn't been looking. It was no wonder we hadn't noticed at all when we first went by.

'That's all we needed to make matters truly complicated,' said Aristotle. '*Whose* blood? When?'

'Perhaps,' I suggested, 'Straton was killed here, and then the body was carried up and out of the way, and hidden.'

'No – no. I don't think he can have been killed here. He must have met his death wound where he was found. Did you not notice all the blood in the earth where we found the corpse? I did not expect to see this blood that we have just discovered. Curious. Was Straton in a fight? Did he attack someone else? Someone who, wounded and irate, later followed him up the hill and murdered him?'

'How do I know?' I asked, not helpfully.

'Do you remember, Stephanos, what Patroklos says when he is dying?'

'This is not a time for Homer,' I retorted.

'But *can* you remember, Stephanos?'

'Well, Patroklos is run through by a spear – Hektor's spear, but only after Patroklos was assaulted by Phoibos Apollo and also struck by Euphorbos. So Patroklos says to Hektor, "You are the third one to kill me." '

'Exactly. "But deadly Fate and the son of Leto slew me/And among men Euphorbos; you are the third one to kill me." So. "The third one to kill me". Suggestive, don't you think?'

'This is no time for poetry.' I felt tired. 'We should get away from this place.'

'True enough, we haven't time to stand here and discuss it. I too have a strong desire to leave this place, no matter how interesting it is and prolific in fateful signs. You notice the blood is not very old, and the grave was freshly made. Someone may come upon us at any moment. It's bad luck to be found near a corpse, as the robber said to the jury.'

We hastened back up the hill to get the horses. As I untied them from the oak tree, I noticed something. One of the fillets bound about the oak tree was still unweathered – a girl's riband, finely woven with a pattern in the weave. It felt fresh and new. I untied it.

'There,' I said to Aristotle. 'That must have been put there today or yesterday. It might have been placed there by Anthia herself. You see that it is not discoloured. It hasn't even been through heavy dews, nor faded by wind and rain.'

Now I myself was doing some finding and interpreting, and I was pleased, for Aristotle was much quicker to read wounds and footprints than I was. His praise of my observation was heartwarming even in this uncanny spot. He decided, however, to replace the fillet on the tree – explaining that he thought it 'bad luck' to carry anything away from the site.

'You don't know,' he said, 'whether having this riband on our persons mightn't be inconvenient at some point. It might tie us (sorry, unintended joke) too closely to the murder. The main thing is that we know it was there – and we shall remember.'

We went down the hill, mounted our horses and paced quickly away from that place made unlovely by violent death. The oak tree looked as graceful as ever, but I could hear the wings of ill-omened birds impatient to resume the feast.

'Now,' said Aristotle, speaking low even though there seemed no one near us. 'We are faced with anxiety and decisions. What should we do now, Stephanos of Athens?'

'I suppose we should turn back to Athens, for someone must tell Lysippos. O wretchedness! What are we to say? "Sir, we had a pleasant ride – didn't find your niece, but we can tell you where her hair-band is. And by the way, your son is dead." '

'Yes. As you say, it is going to be difficult.' Aristotle frowned. The horses paced slowly on.

'I suppose we must look out for the next village and tell them there's a body back in the hill, and a killer at large.'

'But, Stephanos, do you think any village is going to *want* to hear about this? And do you think that once a murder is reported they will let us go on our way? No! We'd be detained – jailed, I shouldn't wonder. We could be returned to Athens to await trial, most likely. Another complication: I'm not sure whether we're in Attika or Boiotia now. But in any case, as the murder was the slaughter of an Athenian, any local authorities will want to rid themselves of all Athenians involved. We'd be bound to be suspected.'

'But when we get back to Athens everyone would *know* we weren't murderers – and we have Kleiophoros and Lysippos –'

'Yes, yes, but even if everything went as smoothly as you say, think of the time this would waste! The real murderer would get away. Not to mention our other little commission of finding the lost lady.'

'Umm,' I nodded. I was more than a little swayed. If I had to go back to Lysippos with the horrible news, farewell to any faint hope of winning the Silver Man's daughter.

'I'd rather not rely on anybody else just at present,' Aristotle continued. 'Athens is distant. And how do we know that it wasn't *intended* that we should come upon the body – or for it to be found when we were nearby – precisely so we could be the ones first accused of this murder? Did Lysippos wish his own son dead? Who knows if there was a real abduction, after all?'

'Surely, Aristotle, you are unreasonable. Your imagination is too strong! Lysippos is a good father and guardian, an important citizen, a well-born Athenian.'

He shrugged. 'Perhaps all this bloodshed is poisoning my mind. Well, what now?'

'We must wash soon, Aristotle – we have been badly polluted by handling that corpse.'

'Yes, indeed, we will stop and wash. Though we are innocent of blood-guilt, and someone else is carrying about the true and deep pollution of murder with him. No villagers will be glad to welcome a blood-polluted man, let alone an accused murderer. I am not Orestes! The villagers – we talk of this village as if we knew it, here where the only inhabitants seem to be goats! – these people in the next village, whatever it is, might just as well be left out of it.'

I was astonished. 'What, then? Do we just stop at the next village, and change our clothes, and say nothing?'

'The murdered man was not one of the villagers. They have sustained no loss. I take it we neither of us believe that this murder was committed by some local thief. This violent death seems too well tied in with the abduction of Anthia. So – if neither victim nor murderer comes from the next village – if there is one in this waste – that place and its people are free of pollution and blood-guilt. The matter therefore doesn't concern these people at all, and it is best to say nothing about it to them. They're much happier *not* knowing. And they would be most likely to suspect us, not help us search for unknown murderers.'

It seemed unnatural to keep such a piece of news to oneself, but I agreed. We went on in silence after this conversation. The clouds still chased each other lazily over a light blue sky, as the sun neared the horizon. Spring still called in the reddening light. But the whole day seemed changed. I thought of Straton, whom I had seen at the Dionysos Procession, from whom I had parted in my mood of good fellowship after the Silent Dinner. I thought of the trivial exchange between myself and Straton after the Procession of Dionysos: 'We'll have some sprigs of our own to bring to the celebrations.' He had died before he could marry and beget children. Straton would never produce his sprigs. No blossom nor fruit. I kept thinking of that young man who would not see the orchards bloom this year, who had fallen into eternal winter (those dreadful white hands!) at the first stirring of spring. Persephone abhors violets, for she was gathering them when Dis gathered her into his dark hall. Perhaps now Straton's shade remembered bitterly the leaping day and the morning's sun which had made him run towards death.

A village did appear of course, at last. Aristotle and I rode into it at dusk like affable travellers, rich and unconcerned. We were travel-stained and weary, we said (truly enough), and wished to wash, and change, and eat. The people were hospitable, and we had some ado to manage to wash before going into a house, but this we did, out of respect for our innocent hosts. There was a shrine where we offered prayers, and we bought a kid and sacrificed it, so the gods were appeased and we could treat the villagers to a meat dinner. 'When in doubt,' Aristotle whispered to me, 'spend money.' The villagers admired our generosity and courteous behaviour. Aristotle explained that he was on an embassy. We were very well treated and spent a passable night, wrapped in fleecy wool in a good house (not of the richest sort, but clean) where we were offered the best of everything. I was glad that none of those around us could read my mind, or my dreams. Both waking and sleeping there rose into it an image of that ghastly mound and its secret inhabitant. Straton, eating silver, and wearing it. The youngest of the Silver Men. Gone.

Before sleeping, Aristotle found time to write some letters on the wax tablets he carried with him, and in the morning he hired for a good sum a stout young man, completely illiterate (Aristotle had made sure of that), to take his messages all the way to Athens. Aristotle said they were letters on business, and the people had no reason to disbelieve him. I noticed that Aristotle tied up the tablets with careful knots, and he himself accompanied the bearer of his epistles out of the village – obviously to prevent any of the villagers from intercepting them. In this neighbourhood, even in this small place, there were probably one or two persons who could read.

As usual, we wove into our talk some apparently casual queries about other passers-by, but got little good of this – less than I had hoped. Surely, now that we were on the track of a murder, I thought hopefully, we would be favoured by signs and information. Apparently, however, a number of travellers had gone by. The people in this hamlet showered us with detail about persons we cared nothing for and never wished to meet. The villagers noticed their own, while taking a very unobservant view of those they didn't know. Pedlars and shepherds and men in cloaks had passed and repassed, as well as pilgrims going to Delphi. In the matter of the litter we were also disappointed – by a plethora of information. One litter – two – several. All borne by slaves and all with a man walking before or behind. And the conversation became so involved in the bedridden wife of Philokles, a local landowner – 'her that's so twisted up with the rheumatics' – and the litter she had travelled in that it seemed best not to hope further. So again we parted from kind stranger-hosts and set off into a new spring day. But yesterday morning we hadn't carried a heavy secret with us.

'What did you say in your letter to Lysippos?' I asked, once we were beyond the earshot of strangers.

'I said only that I was sorry to announce that Straton was dead, in suspicious circumstances, and that Lysippos would hear from us again when we got to Delphi. I said nothing very specific about the place where the body is to be found. Unkind – but you can't be too careful. The slave who carries the message might be intercepted. It is all too likely someone in this region will come upon the corpse soon enough, but I don't want the people here to connect *us* with it inconveniently soon. In my letter I said also that I would be writing to Antipater – and to the Basileus as well. Which I must do, for my own protection as much as anything. I don't know if you've noticed, Stephanos, but some Athenians don't like Makedonians very much.'

'I had noticed that,' I said drily. 'Lysippos will be terribly distressed.'

Aristotle frowned into the distance. 'Yes. Yes. *How* I wish I could be in two places at once! It's no good asking you to go back to Athens, Stephanos, as I need you here. And it's no good my going back to the city, as I need myself here even more.'

'You wrote two letters. Who was the second one for?' I asked, ignoring these riddles.

'To Theophrastos, naturally. I merely asked him to go at once to Lysippos and offer any help he could in a time of great calamity, as Straton was dead.'

'That was kind of you,' I said.

'Yes, wasn't it? Having Theophrastos there is an advantage – if I cannot be there myself. After all, students of philosophy should aid one another in their studies and searches, shouldn't they? And Theophrastos can tell a hawk from a vulture. He uses his eyes, at all events.'

'Don't mention vultures.'

VI

Rural Interludes

That day was a beautiful day, the sort the gods give sometimes, shining like the smiling valley along which we travelled between frowning hills. It was hard to remember that Straton lay like a secret within a hill. There was sunlight, and the streams sang along the hill slopes, while a flexible breeze touched the small leaves, the shining grass. In the most sheltered cornfields the tips of new green shoots poked through the earth and shone like metal. In the wild pasture, flocks grazed. We looked at all these things as we rode by, trying to cast off the darkness that we carried with our hidden knowledge. It seemed amazing and untrue that Straton could be dead – like something heard in a story, or a dream. The cheerful day was all around us, and the cheerful stirrings of the great earth.

At one hamlet we came upon a struggling procession of very young boys and girls. The tallest of their number carried on a pole the crudely carved figure of a bird decked with a garland. The other children followed, smiling under the uneven garlands which they had made for themselves. They sang in their clear voices, the ancient song:

> She has come, she has come, the swallow
> With summer on her wings;
> To us the happy hours
> And happy years she brings.
>
> Rise up, rise up from your rich house
> To offer fruit and wine;
> Our bird will take the coarse pulse-bread
> Or wheaten cake so fine.

I laughed, looking at that band of bright faces and remembering the years when I myself had taken part in the swallows' welcome.

'It seems rather early in the season for this celebration,' remarked Aristotle. 'I don't know if I have seen a swallow yet. Possibly these enterprising children have got up their procession for the benefit of those passing on the highway.'

The ring of teasing, smiling faces seemed to be daring us to say that it was not swallow-time. 'Perhaps,' said I, 'but the spring seems to be forward this year.'

We could not spare our provisions, but we offered the children a small coin instead, which they took in very good part. Two small boys turned cartwheels to express their elation. As we left, the children stood in ragged file by the road and waved to us until we were nearly out of sight. I could still hear their lilting young voices when they took up their procession again; the melody hovered in the air above the hills like the swallow herself.

The earth seemed to be bursting into activity, as if the children's spell had set every creature stirring. Wild things came out of hiding to look for green shoots, and their presence spurred the hunters. A hare darted down the hill and across our path from left to right, scampering madly to the flat field by the roadside. Then there came another – and behind, in hot pursuit, ran lads and young men, whooping and crying out with the madness of the hunt:

> 'One! A hare! Two Hares! Ohé – Run off, run away!
> So, So, So – to the net!'

Laughing, shouting, running, they passed by us, so nearly under our horses' noses that the animals shied and tried to rear in fright. The running hunters moved so fast they were almost a blur, a confusion of brown-clad bodies and twinkling bare legs. They ran athwart our path and into the brown and green landscape to the point where the net had been fixed. Terrified hares, beaten down from their coverts on the hill, ran madly to their doom. We could see the netting-place on our right as we went, the net of coarse stakes and loosely woven withies. The men at the net shouted, 'Three! Dinner tonight, men! Four!' Where the beaters and net-men took their prey, we saw the movement of clubs. One of the hunters held up the timid creature, its head bloody, blood over its drooping ears, discolouring its fur. The hunters chanted merrily:

'The hare gave me a fur cap,
The hare gave me a meat broth.
Was not that good of the hare, my lads,
To offer clothes and dinner both?'

I was glad that these country folk had their meat. Normally, I would not have been at all averse to hunting, myself. But the idea of something rushing blindly to a bloody doom was not comfortable – at least, not at present.

The next encounter delayed us longer, and it too was not of our seeking. We had been going along in silence through a deserted stretch, the hills on our left getting higher and higher, and only herds and flocks to be seen, when we came by a little spinney and a grassy bank near the side of the road. Two men standing by the hazel trees were arguing heatedly, for we could hear voices raised in anger before we drew beside them.

'I'm *known* as the best, I tell you. Best in my village. The women always ask for me! There's no one of my age – or older – who's half as good.'

'Nonsense. With that little pipe? I could do better any day of any month.'

'Do you think, you goat-headed goatherd, that anyone would prefer you? Your breath itself stinks like a goat. And that poisonous breath soon gives out. I could go on all day and all night, but you soon stop short.'

At this point we drew level with the arguers, who gazed at the sight of fine strangers on horseback. These quarrellers by the roadside were young countrymen, no question. They were both healthy and strong, and wore their dingy long hair in tangles, but there the resemblance ended. One of them was a large brawny fellow with a heavy goatskin over his shoulders. The other was shorter and skinny, with bow legs. A half-grown red beard straggled under a mouth filled with snaggle teeth and topped by a snub nose. This one wore a cloak of woven sheep's wool.

We had no intention of pausing. But the large fellow abruptly said, 'Ho! Halt!' so we stopped.

'I say,' said the large man, evidently not at all abashed by our important appearance. 'We need a judge. You'll do – the older one there' – nodding at Aristotle. 'Be our arbitrator in this case.'

'Oh, no, no thank you,' replied Aristotle, embarrassed. 'Had the woman not best decide?' Like myself, he had already decided what the dispute must be about. Apparently we were wrong.

'Wait. Let me explain,' said the shaggy one in the goatskin. 'We don't need no women. And it ain't a dispute to do with lands or anything the like of that. It's just me (I'm Anaxagoras) and my friend Lykidas the shepherd here want to settle a question about who's the best singer. So we want to have a singing match, and we need a judge. You'll do. Agreed?'

'Won't take long,' said the snub-nosed Lykidas.

'Very well,' said Aristotle. 'But it had better not take long, for this man and I are in a hurry, and have friends waiting for us.' I knew he was thinking it might not do to let these men who waylaid us believe we were solitary travellers without friends in the district. The herdsmen seemed peaceable enough, however, once we acceded to their request.

We dismounted and tied our horses to the trees at a

place where they could crop the fresh grass. Our hosts, the contestants, offered us a place on the grassy bank protected by a hazel thicket, and gave us a skin to put under us to keep us from the damp. They also offered us some bread and cheese (rather sour and musty), which we accepted. 'At least,' Aristotle whispered to me, 'we are given a meal for our pains, which is all to the good. And once this "contest" is over and they calm down, we can ask them some questions about who else has passed by.'

It was really quite pleasant sitting there in the sun which shone on shining hazel and soft grey catkins. Under the thicket bloomed small scyllas, and crocus flowers splendid in saffron. The bank on which we sat harboured violets, both the dog-tooth and the sweet-scented blue. The violets, however Persephone might feel about them, were welcome, since the scent of the two contestants was rather powerful – particularly in the case of the goatherd, whose shaggy rug steamed like a mixture of carrion and sour milk. Aristotle managed tactfully to persuade the contestants to stand in a spot downwind of us. The shepherd and the goatherd took their places as solemn as actors and suddenly bashful as children.

'What is the prize?' asked Aristotle.

'The prize,' said Anaxagoras, 'is a kid from me to him if I lose, and a lamb from him to me if *he* loses – which he will.'

'I say!' said Lykidas. 'No! Not fair. My father'd just about kill me if any of those sheep were missing.'

'Oh, well then,' said Anaxagoras, 'my wooden bowl – it's polished beech, and carved-like – wagered against your set of pipes.'

Anaxagoras took out his own pipe, a single whistle carved out of hazel, and Lykidas produced his finely made set of Pan-pipes. They each wiped off the mouthpieces on their dirt-sodden shirts, made an experimental blow or hoot, and then stood ready.

'Let the one challenged start first,' said Aristotle.

'That's me,' said Anaxagoras the large and goatish, and began:

> 'Come woods, come streams, come heavenly
>   Nymphs,
> If you like music, so do I.
> Then feed my goats and starve his sheep
> Until the earth and seas run dry.'

The next verse was of course the turn of Lykidas, who wrinkled up his snub nose and went at it, playing the melody on his Pan-pipes before he sang:

> 'I do much more than the goatherd knows
> I kissed Alkippé on the hill.
> On the violet bank I twined her close.
> She loved me, and she loves me still.'

Anaxagoras (tooting energetically on his whistle):

> 'Alkippé is a foolish wench.
> I think her kiss not worth a rush.
> And, Lykidas, I'll tell her pa
> What you was doing behind the bush.

'Snubnose my goat, come here I say
And be a husband to his ewe,
For in the bushes or on the hill
That's more than Lykidas can do.'

There was a good deal more. The verses were made up of old phrases flung together and as many personal references as could be managed. Anaxagoras was the more insulting, but not inspired. The contest ended thus:

Lykidas (gracefully):

'The summer comes with the nightingale
And strawberries sweet amid the dew.
Then I shall play, both night and day
On the hill by the brook, with her and not you.
By the breeze and the stars and the soft summer dew.'

Lykidas had ended with an extra flourish on the Pan-pipes, while Anaxagoras, as prophesied earlier in plain prose, had run out of breath.

Aristotle and I clapped, as at a play, and stood up.

'Now, then,' said Anaxagoras, moving towards us. 'Who won?'

'Yes,' said Lykidas, picking up his wild olive shepherd's crook. 'Who won?'

'You were both excellent,' said Aristotle, edging towards his horse (I did the same). 'A real treat,' he said with enthusiasm, untying the horse. 'Such skill, such judgement – such choice metaphor. Such *melody*! One would imagine oneself back in the Golden Age!'

He got on his horse, as I did.

The contestants were not satisfied. Anaxagoras laid a heavy hand on the bridle.

'But – come now. You're the judge. Someone has to *win*. That's the point.'

'Aye,' said Lykidas. 'What do you think we wanted you to be judge for, then?'

'You were both superb, each in his different way,' said Aristotle. 'In all my long life, I've never heard anything like it. But – after much inner debate you understand, and upon serious reflection – I believe I must announce that Lykidas is the winner. In a closely fought contest, you understand.' He urged his horse to start moving.

There could be no doubt at all that Aristotle was right about the winner. Lykidas sang rather well, in a country style, whereas Anaxagoras had a voice like that of a bull frog with a bad cold. It was nearly as painful to hear as to smell him.

'That's all, I think?' inquired Aristotle cheerfully. I was not surprised that he was not going to put any questions to the obnoxious pair – I was quite as anxious to get away. 'Sorry we have to be on our way. Many thanks for your kind hospitality, but my friend and I must get on.'

We trotted off as hastily as we dared, relieved to see that Anaxagoras wasn't going to attack us. As we went off, we distinctly heard the goatish loser say to the gentle shepherd, 'That old man! Why, he's no more idea of music than my backside!' Once again voices were raised in altercation, and before we reached the bend in the road we heard blows. Looking back, we saw brawny Anaxagoras endeavouring to belabour Lykidas, while the winner was neatly dodging his fellow-contestant's long arms and holding him off with the crook.

'So much for arbitration,' said Aristotle.

'Shouldn't we go back and stop them?'

'No. They'll tire soon enough. I don't want to hear any more of their rural strain. That big fellow's voice has given me a pain in the head.'

'The Golden Age, indeed,' said I, laughing. 'What dishonesty, Aristotle! And I thought you were going to ask them about passers-by?'

'Humph. Did it ever occur to you that the Golden Age might have been somewhat – shall I say – tiresome? And these men seem incapable of noticing much but themselves. They remind us, however, that striving for supremacy is a truly human desire.'

We were glad to escape from these irritable rustics. The day was now casting its golden hours behind us and the going was more tiring as we were pacing steadily upwards. We were glad to stop for the night at a little house with clean straw on the floor and good bread and goat cheese. We wrapped ourselves in the sheepskins the people provided to keep the cold out.

The next morning we were on our way again, our mounts pacing upwards in the clean air, through the scent of pine trees. The spring sky shone. The spring world was still bursting into motion, in this space without cities. The road wound into the heights and ahead of us we could see Parnassos, still with a snow crown; about us we could hear the sound of water from the melting of snow and the spring rains. Above us were outcroppings and stony peaks too harsh for habitation. Here and there the remains of rough-built stone watchtowers dotted these rocky heights, a reminder of all the wars in this area – the Sacred Wars, the war against Thebes, and fatal Khaironia. These lookout places were falling into ruin, and the stone was steadily taken away by peasants for building houses, byres and field-walls. Eventually these slight structures would disappear, if no new war called them back into being.

Day gleamed upon the rocks. Streams sang loudly, birds called as they flew. And then we saw an unusual and stirring sight – or rather, heard before we saw. First we heard a distant sound of voices, a trampling, and then close to us came a sharp noise of hooves and a sound like heavy breathing. We turned our heads and saw, nearly upon us, a wild boar. The heavy beast, which must have made an early foray near some village in its search for food, was charging along with the fury of a war horse. The boar's head was held low and its vicious tusks and muzzle were flecked with foam. Our horses were frightened, and reared. The beast's little eyes gave us a fierce red glare as it shot past and raced across the road to the next hill. Behind it came men and boys, some on foot and the leaders on horses, armed with thick-hafted spears. It was like being caught suddenly in the middle of a battle.

The hunt surrounded us, and then it was off, up and athwart the hill. After wheeling about the flank of the hill the panting animal charged down again, happily at a good distance from ourselves. The army of hunters, cavalry and infantry mixed, followed in swift pursuit. Hunter and hunted charged back upon the plain, the sun shining on the metal heads of the boar-spears. We had much ado to quiet our horses – indeed, they took us some distance into the rough land before we persuaded them to go back to the road again. We held them still, letting their frantic breathing quieten, and watching the hunt move away from us across the dull green land.

'Beautiful,' said Aristotle, 'I have seen a painting very like it. It is a great while since I have been in a boar hunt,' he added wistfully. 'The wild pig is becoming more rare here – but in Makedonia, ah, you should see the woods and rocks, and the boar bigger than here and fiercer. In my youth I too have spent many hours in a chase like that. And now I'm an elderly gentleman jogging quietly along the road. Everyone seems to be hunting these days.'

'I should like to go on such a hunt,' I agreed. 'But do not forget, we too are on a chase, of a kind.'

'That is so,' said Aristotle. 'And pursuing the biggest game, the most ferocious. Man the Murderer. But our quarry can not only both hide and run; he can also conceal himself within himself. We do not know who he is when we do see him. The persons we have met have not been much help, have they? They haven't been in a mood or condition to answer questions. Everyone is in motion, like the hunters, or wrapped in his own words, like the singers.'

'Look over there,' I said, pointing. 'There are some who will not run away.' I had sighted a group of festive people in a village that occupied a flat space on the side of the hill some distance away from the road, to our right. A cart track ran to the place.

'It's a wedding party. People at a wedding are hospitable,' I reminded Aristotle. 'The horses can rest and eat also. And someone will have time to answer our questions.'

It was true that the people were hospitable. As soon as we arrived and introduced ourselves we were welcomed and offered food. The couple involved were the son and daughter of the two richest men in the village, the groom's father slightly superior to the father of the bride and showing that superiority in feasting. They should have been married earlier; it was explained to us why they were having the wedding as late as Anthesterion, instead of in cool Gamelion, Marriage Month, in which comes the nuptial anniversary of Zeus and Hera. 'They should've been wed last year,' the groom's uncle explained to me, 'but Diphilos' papa was ill, d'ye see. Creaking and groaning, could hardly walk crabwise. He weren't by no means as up and stirring as he wished, come Gamelion, so Diphilos here had to wait. Zeus and Hera did without him. Ah, well, hunger makes a keen guest. Diphilos will be ready for *his* wedding feast' – and he nudged the handsome broad-faced young man, who reddened.

The celebration had been going on for two days already. The girl's father had already gone through the ceremony of giving consent, and now people were doing their duty by the substantial viands while waiting until dusk when the bride would be carried to her new home. The bridegroom, a good-humoured man, was urging his friends to drink, and the men were urging him, in the traditional terms, to perform his part well in the mysteries of marriage, and prophesying a son before this time next year.

Aristotle and I uttered our congratulations, and sat down in a warm place in the sun to eat and drink. We were treated as guests of honour, which made it difficult to mingle unobtrusively with the people and ask questions. We struck up conversation with those sitting round about us. People were pleased enough to see us; we offered something of a novelty to these Boiotian peasants. But the conversation ran only on a few themes and would not be wrenched out of its track, like a cartwheel on a worn country road. Many times we heard the calculation of the exact wealth of both families. We were told to the last hemi-obol and smallest lamb what the dowry was. The amount of cloth the bride had woven in her fifteen and one-half years was recited for our admiration – we were even shown a tapestry of her making. The groom's exploits in ploughing and wrestling were recited for our especial profit, as if he had been a hero. His proud friends endeavoured to bring him forward.

'How many wrestling matches did you win, Diphilos?'

'Well, now, I dunno.'

'Twelve, that's it,' said his interlocutor, another ruddy-faced man, evidently a close relation. 'And how many hares did you catch in our last hunt?'

'Well, now – some. I dunno as I could rightly say.'

'Six – that's the size of it. And how many sheep in that flock that your father is giving you?'

'Well, I wouldn't like to say, hardly.'

'Fifty,' said his friend, and turned to us triumphantly. 'He's a grand fellow, Diphilos. And even in the city you couldn't find better nor modester manners than that.'

I spoke to an old man with a beard, who sat on a warm stone with a dog at his feet. The old fellow was slowly revolving bread in his toothless mouth, and looked the picture of satisfied tranquillity.

'Have you seen any strangers here, recently?'

'Aye-uh. Oh, yes, I do reckon so.'

'How many? When? What were they like?'

'Well – just now. Two. One old and one younger. And

that's yourselves.' He cackled for a long time at his own wit. I could get no more out of him, and he went off to recount his successful joke to a friend, and catch again the gleam and wonder of his jest. Aristotle fared no better.

'Have you seen a man with a litter come by on the main road any time during the last two days?'

'A what?'

Aristotle patiently repeated his query.

'Nay. Not many of us here have a litter, sir. In fact, come to think of it, nary a one in the place, and that's the truth of it. Must have come from beyond, like – near Thebes. Poor old Thebes.'

These rustics in their village had at least escaped the cruel destruction loosed by the Makedonian kings on that unfortunate city, formerly the capital of Boiotia. Poor battered Thebes, famous in story, once ruled over by ill-fated Oidipous; the city had been standing, proud and flourishing, until nearly six years ago. My own cousin's wife had escaped from the sack of the city amid confusion and carnage. On our journey Aristotle and I had passed the road that led to the great ruin. The sack of Thebes is not something one wishes to discuss with Makedonians. I realised that it might not be very lucky for us if these Boiotians discovered that a Makedonian was among them.

Of course we tried again with our questions, with equal unsuccess. Soon we were told, as a matter of real importance, that the dancing would begin again. Once the singing and dancing started, it was obviously impolite to keep on with questions, and even more rude to depart. The trouble with turning yourself into a wedding guest is that you really are expected to *stay* for the wedding, once you arrive. Not that this was unpleasant. I found myself caught in the dance almost before I knew it, in the long chain of men striking the earth with their feet. The rhythm and motion made me almost drunk with the joy of it; I had not danced for a long time. I wanted to dance. I wanted to forget death.

The women (who had been in the house with the bride) came out and danced and then it was our turn again. Aristotle, despite his protesting joints, was compelled into the chain with gentle force – and there he was, hopping back and forth, spellbound like myself by the dance which moves like the sun and sea and stars, blessing men and earth. The day reeled into dusk and darkness. The time had come.

Torches were lit. The music stopped playing for a space; there was a silence of expectation. Then the door opened and the bride stepped forth from her father's house, pushed with friendly violence by her female companions. There was a sound of weeping and lamentation. The bride, her white apparel shining out in the torchlight, her head covered by the veil and garland, was hauled by the villagers into the chariot – a mule cart fresh-cleaned and decked with greenery for the occasion. The flowers on her bridal crown were fresh, but those on the bridal cart were wilted, as the conveyance had stood by her door all day.

The groom took his place, with friends, to lead the wedding cart to his house. Looking at this clumsy young man, I thought of golden Polemon and how much better he would become the role, if the veiled bride were the heiress Anthia and not this village girl. Polemon still had reason to hope . . . Torches were held high, and falling into the procession we began the nuptial song: 'O Hymen, O Hymenaie!'

Though all these people were strangers to me, I sang as if I'd known the families all my days, as we all straggled joyfully around the houses. The groom's house was in fact such a short distance from the home of the bride that in order to make the procession amount to something we had to go once round the village and then back again. At last the cart stopped in front of the house-door. It was time for the round-faced bridegroom to do his part. Reaching into the cart he grasped the bride and, in the usual struggle, pulled her away from her chariot and shrieking companions, lifting her up and carrying her over his threshold – to a new hearth, new home, new gods. Thus in this rapture the bride, a stranger, is compelled to be one of her new family. This particular bride was stout enough to put up more of a struggle had she wished, and was evidently well content that all should be as it was, for I saw her whisper to the groom and tuck her dress carefully out of the way of the doorpost as they crossed the sill. Then the door shut to as the sacred rites began within – the prayers and the sprinkling with water and the induction to the sacred hearth.

The torches still burned with a glow and the scent of spices. The party established itself just outside the bride's new home, and wine and food were brought out again. The dancing went irresistibly and sleeplessly on. The bride and groom of course were not sleeping either (nor could they have done so with the din outside their doors). We were all waiting for the sign of their successful endeavours. At last that came. A woman (probably the groom's mother) leaned out of the window and waved a sheet triumphantly. We could see it in the light of torches, the bloody mark showing the girl had been a virgin and was one no longer. The marriage was consummated.

'So begins a new family,' said Aristotle. 'I wish them good fortune. The bride seems a fine girl,' he added to one of the villagers.

'Truly said. My own niece. Diphilos has done well. Of course,' this uncle laughed, 'the womenfolk have been at her for this past week, anointing her and combing her hair, so she'd please her husband this night. Why, this morning when that outlandish pedlar came along, what would they do but lay out good money on foreign fripperies? A silver pin, and perfume. Women are always caught by finery. She's gone to her bridal smelling of sweet nard and cassia to her very teeth, like the richest city lady, I'll be bound.'

'A pedlar? A perfume-seller? When was he here?'

'Oh, let me think. About the middle of the day. Gone off now – Thebes direction.'

Aristotle turned to me.

'Well, Stephanos, we must pay our thanks to these fine people. We really ought to be going.'

'Going? In the dark?'

'Hush!' – in a whisper, grimacing at me. 'Yes.'

'Oh, that's right. We must be getting on. We have friends we should meet, a little way down the road.' I said this in a loud tone, feeling pleased with myself for being able to tell a lie so handily.

It wasn't easy to depart. The villagers were bent on making a night of it until sunrise and beyond; we were besieged by hospitable invitations. We accepted a pot of coals, so we could have fire and light along our way.

Aristotle at parting gave the groom's father a small pecuniary present, as an addition to the fortune of the young people.

With the good villagers' kindly wishes still in our ears we rode away from the centre of festivity, past the quiet houses at the edge of the place. As we passed one house I heard a woman's voice, singing. Probably this woman, whoever she was, had assisted at the celebrations among the women, and had come home to work at her spinning and weaving, making up for lost time while husband or father was still at the wedding. Her voice was pleasant as she sang an ancient ballad which came softly and clearly through the night air, like music from the hills or stars. This was the song:

> Love came knocking at my door.
> 'Open then, and let me in!'
> 'Who comes knocking here so late?
> All my dreams you break in twain.'
> *In the darkest midnight hour*
> *Love came knocking at my door.*
>
> 'I am but a little child.
> Here I stand amid the rain.
> Moonless night and I am lost.
> Do not leave me in such pain.'
> *In the darkest midnight hour*
> *Love came knocking at my door.*
>
> Pity stirred within my mind.
> Then I set the lamp alight,
> Drew the bolt and saw the boy,

Child with wings and bow so bright.
In the darkest midnight hour
Love came knocking at my door.

Sate him down beside the hearth.
Warmed his hands between my own.
Softly dried his curling hair,
Till the chill and damp were gone.
In the darkest midnight hour
Love came knocking at my door.

'See my bow,' said he to me,
'Is it slackened by the rain?'
Then he shot me in the heart.
Never felt I such keen pain.
In the darkest midnight hour
Love came knocking at my door.

Laughing aloud the boy arose.
'I am Love. Here see my art.
My bow and I endure all storm;
Evermore will ache your heart.'
In the darkest midnight hour
Love came knocking at my door.

This is the sort of old song the women sing while spinning, young girls and old women sitting in the sun. Tonight it seemed strangely haunting. I found myself humming it as we went down the rutted cart-track to the main road.

The night seemed chilly and dark away from the warmth of the village. Night was fighting against the coming of day, and there was no moon. The sky was still decked with stars, like a thousand lamps, like a thousand eyes. I felt as if we were being watched all the time; I was inclined to look over my shoulder. But no one had come after us from the village, and the indifferent eyes of the heavens looked steadily on, growing paler as the sky became grey with approaching morning.

'It seems an odd thing to do,' I said in rather a grumbling tone, 'to leave a village where we were offered such hospitality to go off in the night, when you can hardly see your hand before your face. Our horses might stumble. Wouldn't we have done better to wait until morning?'

'Yes, Stephanos. You have reason on your side. I may be foolish but I must admit I feel overcome with curiosity to see this perfume-seller. I fear if we waited until morning he would be far ahead of us again. I shall not feel satisfied until we lay eyes upon him.'

'Why do you want to see a pedlar?'

'Because this "perfume seller" seems to be a constant. How often have we heard him mentioned? It may not be the same person each time – but it seems likely that it is. The perfume-seller's presence has left a scent behind – if you'll forgive the joke. It's some kind of trail, after all.'

'He hasn't a litter – nor a girl with him.'

'True. But at the very least he may have seen *something*. To tell you the truth, Stephanos, at the moment I wish for action. We have just seen a girl-bride taken to her home, and we were supposed to be looking for that poor girl Anthia, who may have been ravished – rendered unmarriageable. Or has she been married by unfeigned force in a false wedding? Who knows her fate?

That was our original task. And what have we been doing? Capering about the countryside, listening to ballads and going to a wedding. Even after our discovery of a corpse. For all the world as if we were enjoying a holiday! Spring seems to have rendered us indolent. So I feel suddenly, perhaps rashly, impelled to act. Even if it is only going along this road at a slow pace by starlight.'

'I should have thought you'd wish for sleep.'

'So I do, but not now. I can outwatch you young fellows yet. When we've found the perfume-seller and heard what he has to say, there will be time to rest.'

We went on, the horses going at a slow walk, as the sky became less dark.

'Somewhere ahead of us,' said Aristotle, 'under the mountain, in this gorge, there must be that great cross-roads, the Split where the road from Daulis joins the road to Delphi. One cannot miss it. Then we shall know where we are. Dear, dear, we have come slowly, after all. Vexing. It all comes of sitting too often by the wayside and talking too much.'

'It all comes,' I said decidedly, 'of going on *horses.* These animals are overrated. I could have gone this distance afoot with no trouble, and quicker. The beasts always want water and food and time to piss.'

'And men need none of these things?' said Aristotle, laughing. 'Look now how the dawn comes. Before us must be the crossroads, near that hump of rock.'

'That's the famous crossroads, isn't it?' I said. 'Where Oidipous met Laios. Oidipous went to the Oracle at Delphi, and he was coming back when he met his unknown father, travelling in a chariot, just where these roads meet. A famous murder.'

'That is right,' said Aristotle. 'And Laios was buried there. No sign of chariots – or of litters – now. Pity.'

The dawn sent her first rosy finger of light through the sky, visible to us even in this defile. Above us we could make out the dark ragged forms of the watchtowers broken by war and time. Before us everything moved out of grey mist and slowly took on shape and colour, even in the shadowy gorge. Beyond was the third road, leading to dead and battered Thebes. There was the famous crossroads, a few paces ahead. And there in the middle of the crossroads was a dark huddled shape, which clarified as we looked at it into something ever more visible. A low ridgy hump. A man. Lying down.

We urged our horses forward, but the animals shied as they came near the obstacle, whinnying and backing away in fright. We descended and let the horses wander to the further side of the road, where they went to a patch of dewy grass and began to eat, as if they were avoiding seeing what we were looking at – the dark heap still partly touched by the shrinking shadow of a great outcrop of rock.

I stepped over to the shape. 'Ai! Zeus!' It was the body of a man. The body, sprawled in the middle of the road, lay partly on its stomach, partly on its side, its head pointing towards the roadside and the little drystone cairn which marked the tomb of Laios. The body lay as it must have fallen, indifferently left to the elements. We could not see the face, only the limbs and that broad back and torso covered in a homespun brown woollen tunic. The first rays of the rising sun shone on a long polished wooden shaft protruding from the man's back. Cautiously, I pulled at the shaft.

'Wait! He may not be dead,' said Aristotle. 'Though that seems unlikely. We must see him!' He tugged at one large shoulder, and the face came into view. A dead face. No doubt. The eyes were glazed and protruding. From those blue twisted lips no whisper would tell us anything. Very dead. And, again, the dead man was someone we knew. There on the crossroads, on the very place where Oidipous killed his father, was the body of Ammonios. Where King Laios once lay bleeding lay the stout corpse of the lascivious Athenian merchant and would-be Silver Man. A corpse still slightly warm but never to be truly warm again, though it slept angrily on that crossroads under the rays of the rising sun.

VII

Into the Hills

Aristotle grasped the thick wooden shaft implanted in that broad back, and tried to pull out the weapon – but it would not come. Curiously, there was only a slight staining of blood on the brown homespun around the wooden haft.

'It went very deep,' he said, 'almost right through, I should think. I expect the spear-point is caught amid the rib bones. Not much to be gained by getting it out. It will not ease Ammonios now.'

'What is it – the weapon?'

'A boar-spear. Like the ones the men carried at the boar hunt. A stout weapon, not easily broken – it can kill almost any animal. Truly, they hunt for strange game in the Boiotian hills.'

'Who would want to kill Ammonios? This was not a hunting accident.'

'Certainly not. And what was Ammonios doing here? That I would like to know. Hmph, he smells curiously sweet. Is there anything with him? – any goods or possessions? Can we see anything around the body?'

Glad of an excuse to look away from that corpse, which exuded a strong and unexpectedly delicious scent, I glanced idly at the roadside, near the horses, and my eye lit upon something. I picked it up. It was a broken alabaster bottle – or rather, part of a bottle, only the base and a jagged edging as high as my fingernail.

'Look!' I said. 'This has not been here very long. There is still scented oil in it, quite fresh. Smell!'

'Hmm – yes. Sweet oil of spikenard. Where's the rest of the perfume-seller's goods, I wonder?'

Happy to be moving about and away from the body, I went through a kind of film of sweetened air to inspect the outcrop of rock. I did not really expect to find anything, but behind the rock I came upon the leather pouch of a perfume-seller. It had many little objects in it: bottles and jars; a box of myrrh; sticks of cinnamon; medicines, such as a herbal water that children are given for gripes and men for indigestion. These objects had been packed about with moss, but some phials had got cracked or broken. Liquids had begun to drip and ooze, and mingled in gummy fragrance, as if suggesting immediate burial preparations. Some of these perfumes had indeed got upon the dead man. Had the bottles been broken in the lethal struggle, so that their contents spilled on Ammonios? Or had the pedlar tried his own wares before he died?

'This pouch certainly did not come adrift accidentally during the murder,' said Aristotle, examining the bag and its contents. 'The murderer – presumably – has cut the leather straps which bound it to his victim's waist, after the deed was done. Threw the pack away, but didn't steal.

Odd – those bottles would be worth money. Hmm. Gripe water . . . interesting.'

'There's not much left,' I observed.

'So Ammonios still had gut trouble. Our murderer rummaged. What was he looking for? Ai! I nearly cut myself – look!' From the depths of this bag he drew out and held before me an unsheathed dagger, rusty with nasty stains of dark brown, never made by water.

'That's the weapon we were looking for!' I exclaimed. 'So – Ammonios was Straton's killer?'

'Very strange,' said Aristotle, taking out the moss-packing and looking closely at the bottles. 'This dagger has indeed tasted blood. But it was not put into this pouch *just* after it was stained, or the blood which made these stains on the blade and handle would certainly have discoloured the moss, and left traces on some of the bottles. *Very* curious. Did Ammonios have anything else with him? Let us look once more at the corpse.'

We undertook the unpleasant task again. I could not help the feeling that I was being observed, as if the ruined watchtowers on the heights above were gifted with vision. We dragged our eyes along that suffused face, and the crimson dribble from the peaked nose and distorted lips. Surprisingly, only a little dotting of light-coloured blood stained the front of the dusty tunic.

'You'd expect a great big bloodstain on the front,' I said.

'No,' said Aristotle. 'The spear did not totally pierce the body: it did not emerge through the breast. The spear-shaft still plugs the wound.'

As we bent over him, Ammonios the would-be Silver Man guarded his fragrance. Balmy Eastern odours blended persistently with the sharp frank smell of blood.

'Two weapons. Quite different,' said Aristotle. 'Hmm. I think I will hide the dagger under a stone. The pedlar's bag should be left near the body. I wonder what Ammonios was doing, going about so simply clad, and on foot?'

'Well, *he* can never tell us,' I said drily. 'Now we must get back to the wedding village. We can tell the people – and we can question everyone, especially the slaves, about the perfume-seller. We should send word to Ammonios' relatives. The only one I can remember is Polemon.'

'Oh, Stephanos, don't you see why we cannot do that? The same objections arise as in Straton's case. Worse. As a matter of fact, I believe you and I are in very grave danger of being taken up for *this* murder. All my fault. If only we had remained in the village until morning! Someone else would have discovered this corpse. Ammonios would certainly have waited. Now, we are easily suspected.'

'*We* are?'

'And why not? What more convenient than to blame an outrage on strangers? The Boiotians have no cause to worry about us – or to care much for the perfume-seller, for that matter. All strangers! But they would hate us more than the corpse, thinking we had brought the guilt of murder into their wedding. Murderers and corpses taint the air and displease the gods. We would have brought a curse upon that young couple. It is most likely that these villagers would stone us out of hand. The best we could hope for is that they would get rid of us by sending us to Athens bound and under guard.'

'They will think we were too interested in the perfume-seller,' I acknowledged.

'True. And your excuse at leave-taking, Stephanos – that might take on another colour.'

'I suppose,' I said unhappily, 'they could suspect us of being in a confederacy to murder – you and I with my imaginary "friends" down the road. If we were thought to be brigands, every man's hand would be against us. Any one of these Boiotian peasants might feel he did justice in slaying *us* on the spot, without a hearing – if we were caught.'

It was dreadful that my few thoughtless words could bear so miserable an interpretation. Here we were, Aristotle and I, at this fatal place, enmeshed in dark possibilities. Oidipous solved the riddle of the Sphinx – but how were we to solve this riddle? Looking at the strong limb-like shaft which now grew out of the corpse's back, I found myself thinking, irrelevantly, 'Ammonios now goes on three legs and no legs.' Like Oidipous we might be caught in a trap of our making, the story of a murder connecting us with this fatal crossroads.

'We must go,' I said. 'Let us get away as soon as we can from this terrible place. The day is coming on strongly.' The morning light, not rosy now but golden, was pouring, generous and pitiless, over the corpse at our feet.

We mounted the horses and rode away rapidly from that sight. But care and the shadow of that unburied corpse seemed to follow us. I could not help thinking how visible were our horses' hoofmarks in the dust. It was as if a thin but unbreakable thread connected us with the murdered Ammonios all the length of the road. 'Why don't you know important people?' my mother had suggested. Well, I knew some important corpses. With every pace the thread lengthened but remained as strong as the thread of Lakhesis. Sweat trickled down my spine and I felt nervous, as if someone were watching my retreat. Eyes boring through my back. Turning my head, I glanced back down the road, to see if anyone were pursuing.

Aristotle reined in his horse. 'It's no good, Stephanos – I feel as you do. We have left our footprints near that body, so any observant person would know that two men have been there. Worse – our horses have also left their marks. It will take no extraordinary intelligence to begin enquiry for two men on horseback. No matter how far or how fast we travel we are still implicated in this deed. Before us (presumably) is a murderer. Behind us (possibly) are pursuers who will take *us* for the slayers. We are hopelessly visible. So far our luck has held. But at any time now we will meet other travellers on this road, going in one direction or another. Especially pilgrims going, as we are, to Delphi. They will notice us. If we gallop, we merely increase suspicion. No, the thing to do is to disappear.'

'Disappear? I wish we could. But we can hardly vanish.'

'In effect, we *can* vanish – for a while. There is another way to Delphi, after all. And once we arrive in Delphi, where I have friends and some influence, we shall not be in such danger of being accused of murder, nor of being attached as violent robbers. Let us attempt that other way. We must take to the hills.'

'The hills?'

'Up there.' Aristotle nodded to his left, where the mountain raised its great shoulders. The philosopher gave a slight groan. 'No light task for an old man and his rheumatism, to go wandering up those heights. But you ought to be pleased, Stephanos. You have never thought much of our travelling on horseback – you said we ought to go on foot. Now, you see, you have your way.'

'But –'

'Quickly, let us go. We will take one of our bags, and leave the other on the horse. Take out some clothes – only the most necessary. Sacrifice the rest. I'll leave some of my money in the bag. Fortunately the kind villagers gave us food and fire, and replenished the water-bottle. We'll take all that with us. But it will be short commons for us from now on; we shall have to go like old campaigners. Then – up the hill with us, like two frightened jack-hares!'

We dismounted, and quickly divided our possessions as suggested. Aristotle touched both horses on the flanks, and sent them careening down the road to Daulis. My mare looked back at me as if puzzled, paused to snatch a bite by the roadside, and then moved on again.

'Up we go,' said Aristotle, leading the way to the hill, which now looked formidable. We climbed up, myself weighted by the few clothes we took with us, and Aristotle carrying his firepot.

'Ridiculous,' said Aristotle. 'Like the old men in *Lysistrata*, climbing up the Akropolis laden with firepots.'

Neither of us had much breath for talking – nor was this an expedition of pleasure. Our first concern must be to get as high as we could, and out of sight of the broad if twisting road that led to Delphi. The ascent was unexpectedly trying to my legs, which seemed to have set differently after the days on horseback. Up and up we went, through scratchy heather and bracken and around outcrops of severe stone. Aristotle's breath came in gasps. I had to help him over the last bit, pulling him along. At last we reached a small plateau or shelf, at such a distance from the road that no one could have made us out clearly. We sat down and rested, screened by gorse.

'Rash, very rash,' said Aristotle, when he recovered his breath. 'I dislike being reminded of my age. I'm sorry the baggage is such a nuisance, Stephanos. Perhaps we should have let it all go.'

'I don't understand why you let half of it go,' I said frankly. 'At least, I can see the point of our not having to carry it – but why leave money in the bag on the horse? Why not just hide the extra bag, so we could return for it? And we've lost two valuable horses. I hope Lysippos doesn't make us pay for them.'

'I thought of a story which we might use in a pinch. We could say we were attacked in the dark by robbers who stole our horses and most of our belongings. We could add that we were afraid, so we came into the hills and have been making our way along since *before* the point where the roads meet. With any luck, our horses will stray at random. It will seem the brigands lost their booty when the horses bolted from them. Perhaps these brigands were the same as the murderers of Ammonios. Hard to prove our story isn't true. But I hope we don't have to use it at all.'

'Poor Ammonios,' I said. 'No silver – and now too much perfume which he cannot enjoy.'

'What is this about silver?'

'Well,' I explained, 'the last time I saw Ammonios before the Silent Dinner, he was waiting about in the market-place to hear the results of bids on mines on Laurion. His friend Pataikos came to tell him the bad news. Ammonios didn't get a concession, and seemed disappointed, though he pretended not to be.'

'Interesting.' Aristotle put his chin in his hands, in the thoughtful pose that suited him in his study and looked strange on the cold hillside. 'So Ammonios wished to have his hands in silver too? I wonder why?'

'To get rich,' I said impatiently.

'Well, yes. But the mining is not without risk. And Ammonios doesn't – didn't – have many slaves to put into it; he'd have to rent slaves from another man. All of his slaves are wrapped up in his brothel business. Almost always profitable, but a liability in public life. His friend Pataikos is in that way of business too. Incidentally, I think Pataikos has connections who have land somewhere between here and Daulis, where they keep an establishment of that sort. If we could find that household and question the people, we might learn something. Probably Ammonios spent the night there.'

'But we cannot risk questioning anybody now – especially going out of our way,' I said impatiently.

'No, indeed. So Ammonios was trying to get into silver? I wonder if that has anything to do with why he was killed. If we knew *why*, we might know who the murderer is. Perhaps Ammonios was just trying to clean and polish his connections. But if we think of it, Stephanos, there are other advantages to come out of the silver works. No war-tax on the proceeds, for one thing. That might mean something to a man who had money to push about, perhaps money he would prefer to cloak. Ammonios was at the Silent Dinner in Lysippos' house. Was Ammonios trying to harmonise with the dealers in silver, to sit well with them?'

'Judging by what he said to Polemon, Ammonios may have wished to marry Anthia, daughter of Pherekrates,' I explained. 'Which Polemon took very ill.'

'Polemon did? But now Ammonios is no rival for any marriage. Well, this is no place to sit in discussion. Let us keep from the view of the road – I see a party of pilgrims coming. We are like brigands ourselves, my dear Stephanos. We should be getting on.' He rose and I did too.

'Well, now what do we do? Do you know the direction?'

'Dear me, yes. I'm not as benighted as all that.' Aristotle began to walk on. 'This range of hills – of mountains, rather – leads directly (or as directly as mountains do) to Delphi. From here to Delphi there is a kind of causeway of limestone mountain. We shall be scrambling about the back of Parnassos. There are, I think, a few settlements, but not too many. It should be easy to avoid human beings and keep to the society of goats and sheep only. I hope we can look like a couple of goatherds.'

Aristotle looked most unlike a goatherd, but I thought it better not to point this out.

'We will have to be sparing of our provisions, such as they are,' he added. 'Here there will be no wells or pretty maidens, no weddings or songs to detain us. Hunger will drive us on our way. It may be that we shall go faster than we would have done with the horses, though I am an aged man and rheumatic, not excellent in climbing. Alas! Wisdom must have deserted me. Let us hope she returns – if she was there before. Can you forgive me, Stephanos?'

'There's nothing bad about a walk,' I said stoutly. 'By

putting one foot in front of the other, as the children say, we shall do well enough. Let us go on.'

We started our climb again. Soon, though not without some difficulties, we were able to follow a narrow track near the ridge. This track went gently down into a small valley, and then rose again steeply and rounded another part of the hill.

And that is how we spent our time, slowly following the goat track and going along and up and over hills. We walked near the ridge, but the ridge kept changing, moving to left or right, going higher. There were many little paths, thin and thread-like, criss-crossing. Once, we took the wrong one and had to retrace our way. We had no companions save sheep and goats, the former bleating around us, and the latter jumping with sharp feet among the most inaccessible rocks. At times, huge croppings of limestone walled us in.

We had to be sparing of the contents of the water bag, which was now unpleasantly warm. A cluster of houses appeared in the distance, but Aristotle thought it unwise to trouble anyone with our existence. We had not left the road any too soon. Even as we had rested on the plateau we could see travellers, and now from the heights we occasionally glimpsed people passing back and forth on the road below and to our left. In spite of our difficulties, I was not sorry to be removed from the highway which exposed one to view and trapped one so.

Yet still I had the anxious feeling of being looked at. A pebble rolling down the hill made me start. I said nothing to Aristotle. Later, a cascade of small stones came rattling down, some striking our feet. We drew into the shelter of the hill, fearing a landslide, but the shower of stones soon ended. I was puzzled to think how small stones could come from the very solid rock just above, but put it down to the action of goats' feet higher up.

One bad thing about taking refuge in hills is that you have abandoned yourself to the mercy of the heights. I have no especial love of standing on peaks and gazing downwards – one very naturally thinks of falling. Here, if either of us made a wrong step at the wrong time, he might fall into space as rapidly as Ikaros, or be dashed against the rocky slopes all the way to the bottom. My sense of anxiety I set down to this natural (if not very commendable) fear. I scolded myself for thinking someone was looking at me, when I knew it could not be so.

But in the afternoon, as the shadows lengthened, I saw, as I glanced above at a high spur of the hill, what seemed like a face gazing down at me. A pale face, beardless, a boy's face with an impish look to the mouth and a hood of some rough material thrown back behind the head. I saw it for only an instant, like a Pan-vision, but I saw it – and then the face disappeared behind the rock wall. I walked on in silence, rapidly trying to think. But at last I spoke to my companion.

'Aristotle,' I said in a low voice, wondering whether it was safe to speak aloud in these hills. 'I fear that we are being followed. I saw someone just now, gazing at us. Do you think we are in danger here? Could the murderer have come here – into these hills before us?'

'Possibly. But would the murderer look for us, if we were not looking for him?'

'He doesn't know that, and,' I added in a whisper, 'after a fashion, we *are* searching for him.'

'True enough. But on these heights we can keep an eye now and then on the road, as well as watching for other wanderers in the hills. And, you see, at least we are proceeding on our way. Down on the road if we were taken up by villagers – or assaulted by stout killers – we couldn't even put up a good fight. Here we have a better chance. Interesting it would be, if the murderer were to come out in the open and identify himself to us? But I don't think he will.'

This was not much comfort on a cold hillside with night coming on. The sun had struggled against cloud in the latter part of the day and returned in force only in time for sunset. Night in its advance brought with it a sharp wind from the sea. It was cooler on the heights than in the plain. The mountain cut the sun from us abruptly when the time came, and the hill dipped into cold shadow. We found a shallow cave in the rock and earth – not so much a cave as an opening or burrow with an overhang. Thanks to our firepot, we could light a small fire. I gathered what twigs and dried brambles and leaves I could, so as not to let the covert fire go out. We ate some bread and cheese, and watched the stars, and the big clouds that blew across them. There were more clouds than I liked.

'We must divide the night into watches, as soldiers do,' said Aristotle. 'We can hide the fire behind the stone so no one will notice unless he comes very close. Pity we haven't a dog with us.'

I thought so too when it came time for my watch. The time was lonely and bleak, and I felt stupidly afraid, of what I didn't quite know. Once I thought I heard footsteps a little way above us, but that, I thought, must certainly be a goat. Later I thought I heard, borne on the wind, the sound of talk, and even of laughter. I thought of Pan, that goat-foot god of wild places who drives men into mindless fear. But the sounds, I told myself stoutly, were surely the innocent noise of some shepherds. I was weary, and Aristotle allowed me to sleep long at dawn, until the day was well settled in the sky. It was easier to sleep when blessed day chased away the fears of night.

But this day was not bright like the days before it. The sky had settled down upon us, thick and heavy. Sheets of mist blew about us, confusing the vision. Up here we seemed to touch the clouds, and even to walk through a column of them, like walking through ghosts. At least there was plenty of water from the running of brooks fed with snow at the summits. But everything looked strange. A gorse bush looked like an old woman hunching over to fasten a sandal; a little peak of stone appeared like a goat standing still. On our path I kept seeing figures just ahead of us that vanished in the mist.

We plodded on, as if in a dream. Clouds gathered and hovered over us, black-bellied and threatening. It was not so easy to pick one's way now. Once the path on which we walked was overrun by a snow-fed hill stream. Once a goat came bounding down upon us; it was nearly as startled as we when it struck against us, and skidded, nearly flying over a crag into the air. A little later I heard a voice and a chopping of hooves, and a whole flock of goats came flying down over the path. We crouched by the side of the road, pressed into the face of the hill, but were nearly overturned. I was kicked by a sharp hoof. One frowzy old he-goat came back, furious, and tried to butt at us with his wicked horns. A piece of burning coal from the firepot scared him off.

'It is as if the mountain didn't care much for us,' I said gloomily.

We went on, and always I had that feeling of eyes stabbing my shoulder-blades – a difficult sensation to describe, but one almost as definite as itching.

'Do you think,' I said, 'that the Abductor could have brought Anthia here? A woman could be hidden in these hills – or her body. In that case we'll never find her.'

'She could be here,' said Aristotle. 'She couldn't be brought here in a litter, of course. She might have fled to the heights herself, of her own accord.'

'Then you think it possible she might get free?'

'Improbable, but possible. It did strike me that the killing of Straton and the escape of Anthia might be two sides of the same event – *if* Straton was the Abductor. Did Anthia herself kill him and then flee? But there are difficulties in the way of that interpretation. Certainly, if Anthia is *not* herself the killer of Straton – or in league with that killer – she must be in worse danger than before.'

'We know this is a man who will stop at nothing,' I said, thinking aloud. 'He has already killed two people. Both citizens of Athens. I cannot imagine that the murder of Straton and the murder of Ammonios are not connected.'

'Nor can I. But why should someone kill Straton and then take such pains not only to conceal the corpse but to inter it properly? And why then kill Ammonios and leave so very visible a body? Why is one corpse offered a funeral and the other so callously and even impiously treated? The girl Anthia could hardly thrust a great boar-spear into a strong and active man. Does Anthia have a rescuer, a helper? In that case, both could be hiding in the hills.'

'There's another person, too,' I reminded him. 'What's-her-name – the slave-girl. Kallirrhoe. What could have happened to her?'

'Either she is with Anthia (wherever that is) or she is already murdered also. Or, the slave Kallirrhoe is a confederate in the murders and has been freed by her associate. But we are plaiting ropes of straw! Onward, onward!'

We went on, plodding towards Delphi along the backbone of mountains, under a lowering sky. The day darkened long before sunset, and we were walking through mists again. And always I felt as if someone walked beside us or behind us, like a shadow. At length the clouds gathered and burst. Silver rain marched along from the peak before us, like a column of soldiers. Then it overtook us and pierced us with headlong drops. We had a good view of the storm advancing down into the plain below, before the clouds again cut off our view. Sharp rain fell in a businesslike manner, catching me even through the well-woven himation. It was hard to keep our firepot protected in this downpour.

'We shall have more than enough to drink,' said Aristotle. 'But we must look for shelter.' And we hurried a little across the next piece of the way – a hurry that might have been my undoing. Part of the path was of stone, broken and uneven, on top of a natural earth bridge which ran above a little gully now full of water from the storm. Human hands had once placed some of these stones and shored them up as a good pathway, making a stronger bridge over the gully. Presumably goatherds had thought it right to mend the road a trifle just here. But weather or goats had loosened the stones. I noticed none of this until too late. For I went stepping eagerly along – and placed my foot upon a large flat piece of stone that had been moved from its right place. The flat stone gave way at once, slipping to my left. I was thrown off balance, and pitched sideways. As I landed on a sharp slope, I went on rolling down the hill. Fortunately, I had not pitched head first into the gully as I might easily have done, and broken my neck. I bounced some distance down the hillside, but I was able to grasp with my hands and dig in with my knees. My left arm was useless and painful, but with my right I halted my progress by clutching gorse and other bushes. At last I came to a stop, not too far from the path, though I felt I had gone a great way. I was conscious of great pain in my shoulder. I may have fainted for a short space I suppose, or been light-headed, because I heard roaring noises in my head, and also, curiously, what sounded like laughter through the hissing rain.

Aristotle hastened to me and helped me to my feet. Immediately he was concerned about my shoulder and arm. 'We must find some shelter soon,' he said.

We went on, but not rapidly. I was suddenly and very completely fatigued.

'Ah,' said Aristotle. 'The gods be thanked! There is an old hut near the path – we have just come into a little valley. The place looks deserted. We may go in.'

He guided me to this rough shelter, a low brown hut of twigs and mud and rough stones. The roof was thatched with brush and bracken, weighed down with stones in the corners and the middle. We entered. The place smelt damp enough, but it was a real shelter, with even a kind of flooring made of old cowhide and some dry leaves.

'This is something better than our sleeping-place of

last night,' said Aristotle, trying to be cheerful. 'Good thing we have kept the firepot. Behold – a real fire! Someone has left us a pile of fuel here too. Take off your cloak, Stephanos, and let's see your shoulder.'

I peeled off my wet garments with my right hand, while the left arm hung painful and useless.

'Aha! As I thought –' Aristotle ran his hands down my bones, making me wince and gasp. 'The shoulder is dislocated, certainly. But there is nothing broken, the gods be praised. Take a deep breath, Stephanos. This will certainly hurt – but the pain won't last long.'

He braced himself against the hut wall and planted his foot or knee in my back, grasping my arm and shoulder firmly. There was a shot of pain like a thunderbolt, and I yelled; for the space of a few heartbeats the pain was almost unbearable but then it eased. My shoulder and arm felt grateful to be in the right place again.

'Good,' said Aristotle. 'Why, we are fortunate. We have a good fire. And I shall collect some water and boil it up in this old chipped pot here. You'll feel the better for a warm wash.'

He bustled about, and soon had heated some water that he had collected from puddles outside (a little muddy) in which he bathed my back and aching foot.

'I'm sorry you have to do that,' I apologised. 'If Anthia did come to these barren hills I don't know how she could survive. They wouldn't have food and firepots. She might have the slave-girl Kallirrhoe with her – but what good would two girls be against the elements?'

'You never know what people can put up with,' said Aristotle, starting to wash himself. 'Many's the soldier who has had a worse bivouac,' he announced. I tried to smile, but I fell asleep even before I had taken anything to eat. It was not an easy sleep, but a slumber broken and confused, full of strange dreams and half-wakings. Through all my dreaming and waking I kept hearing in my head the song we had heard when leaving the village after the wedding:

> *'Love came knocking at my door.*
> *Open then and let me in!'*

I tried to remember the words, and they moved in and out of my visions of slumber like a weaver's shuttle. In these dreams I saw Smikrenes' daughter again, walking away across a plain of flowers. Gigantic silver hoops then twirled about this meadow; at first they looked pretty, but then they joined and tried to throw themselves over me. I ran away in fear from this silver chain. After that I was walking alone, and two strangers clothed in brown and their faces hooded were walking beside me, and never would they show their faces. When I tried to turn and look at them they disappeared. Somewhere a goatherd was always playing a pipe and the song he played was *Love came knocking at my door.* I tried to sing that song in my sleep, I believe, and Aristotle, also in his sleep, said 'Hush!' in a cross voice.

Then, I don't know quite why, I woke up. I was fully awake, in this strange earthy room lit by the flickering of our little fire, with Aristotle on the other side of it, under his woollen cloak which steamed gently in the warmth. I stirred on my leaves and old straw. And then I heard a sound. A sound of knocking. Someone was knocking at the door.

Quietly I got up, walked the two steps that made the length of the room, and reached the threshold. I opened the door just a crack. The thin partition creaked and shuddered beneath my hand in the gusty wind. Before me, in the light of our fire within, I could see a figure.

A boy. Almost a child he looked, with naked legs and arms, his face round and beautiful, faintly rosy even in this strange light. His hair, wet as it was, was the colour of rich deep gold, and curled about his head, with the raindrops caught in it glittering and sparkling.

'Who are you?' I said.

'Open up and let me in. I'm so wet and cold,' said he.

VIII

The Slave's Tale

'Come in,' I said slowly, as if I were admitting something dangerous. I motioned the stranger towards our sputtering fire. He sat beside it gracefully, shaking the sparkling water from his hair. He seemed, now that I looked at him in the stronger light, older than he had at first appeared – a youth, not a little boy. He was very self-possessed, with that composure the gods give to some, and which art alone cannot teach. I thought I had better awaken Aristotle.

Aristotle, groaning a little, awakened reluctantly. When his eyes were fully opened he gaped at the youth who seemed to have fallen from the sky into our hovel.

'Ur – Who is this?'

'Don't be frightened,' said the lad graciously. 'I will do you no harm. Indeed, I come asking your assistance – and I wish to assist you. I think we can help each other.'

'Is it day already?'

'It is still the middle of the night, Aristotle. And this

boy here came knocking at the door and asked for shelter.'

'Well,' said Aristotle, 'now he has it, why don't we go back to sleep?'

'I have some wine in my bottle here,' said the young man. 'I wish to take some myself, if you don't mind, but I should be honoured if you would share it with me.'

The night was so chill and the hut so comfortless that the offer was unusually welcome. Aristotle sat up. As for myself, in wondering at the stranger desire of sleep had fled.

'I am sorry we have nothing to offer you except the remains of some barley bread.'

'Thank you, but I want nothing. In fact, *I* have food and drink which I can offer you. You will not be sorry you have let me in, I promise you.' The boy showed us his leather wallet, which contained flat cakes and cheese. 'I think I can help you as much as you can assist me.' He passed his bottle, very graciously, and we all drank. The warmth of the wine gave fresh hardihood to the spirit. So I was not as amazed as I might have been when the youth added calmly, 'You see, I understand the journey on which you are bound. Perhaps I can help you to find what you are seeking.'

'Good Pan! How can you do that? And who are you?' This boy continued to puzzle me. He had a kind of elegance, like one used to good manners. Although what he said, had it come from another mouth, might have seemed impudent, he carried it off gracefully. His voice was melodious and pleasing, the voice of a well-bred person, and he spoke Greek fluently, but there was something odd about the way he pronounced words, not like an Athenian nor yet like a Boiotian.

The boy sighed. 'The answer to your questions is rather a long story. But I know that you seek the slave-girl Kallirrhoe – among other things. But I seek her only. Our fates meet. And as my quest is of something the same nature as yours, I think we should go together.'

'But we know nothing of *you*,' I pointed out. 'What is your name? Where do you come from? Why do you seek this girl?'

'Yes,' said Aristotle. 'And you are not a slave?' Then I too noticed the iron loop about the youth's neck. 'You,' Aristotle continued, 'are a Lydian, by your accent. Why are you here by yourself?'

The lad bowed his head, and sadness came over his face. Despite the iron collar, and the coarse tunic that left arms and legs bare, nothing else about him seemed slave-like. Certainly his manner was not servile.

'Let me explain, gentlemen. For I see you will not let me help you, nor assist me in my quest, unless you know all. So I will tell you – if I may relate what is, as I say, a long tale.'

By this time we were both quite awake. Aristotle, wrapped in his himation, moved towards the fire. I put some more fuel on the sluggish flames, and offered this slave the half of my cloak to use in drying his hair. We all three sat about the little fire, and the slave passed the wineskin again.

'Very well,' said Aristotle. 'It seems we are fated not to have a full night's sleep. The wine is welcome, and long tales are suited to rainy nights. Let us hear this story, boy.'

The strange youth sat up, straightening his back proudly and thrusting out his beardless chin. Seen sideways that well-modelled young head was as firm and arrogant as a face on a golden coin.

'It is true,' he began, 'that through the working of Fate, I am now that wretched thing, a slave, but I was not born to be so. My name is Korydon. I am the son of Aganippos of Ephesos in Lydia. You know of glorious Ephesos? Our famous city is renowned for the great temple of Artemis, the temple which burned down – some say the very night Alexander was born. Certainly Alexander has meant no good for Ephesos. My father was one of the wealthiest men of the place and, with other rich men, ruled the city.'

'An oligarkh,' Aristotle explained in a low tone.

'I was educated as suits a proper Hellene. I can recite the *Iliad*, and read it also. I can tell you every detail of Akhilleus' shield, and describe Odysseus' travels. I know how to make an oration. I can ride a horse and throw a spear, and I was victorious in foot-races. My father loved me much. Would that I knew what has happened to him!' The boy paused for a moment, and then went on.

'My father's best friend was Habrokomes, also wealthy and a general of the garrison. You must know that Ephesos paid tribute to Persia, and her soldiers fought for the Persian king. Hence my woe, and the woe of many, and the sorrows of Kallirrhoe. Habrokomes had three grown sons before his wife gave birth to a daughter, and then he doted upon that daughter as much as any man may upon his child. And with good reason. Kallirrhoe was lovely and good from her cradle. She was born almost two years after me, and we were playmates in childhood. Kallirrhoe was very beautiful, even then. But it is not just her features that make her beautiful, not even her great eyes nor her long eyelashes nor her skin with the texture of roses. Beauty itself looks through her, shining like a flame in a vase. Most people, girls and men, are unhandsome at certain ages and grow into comeliness, but Kallirrhoe never knew a day from babyhood when she wasn't lovely.'

'She must have made a lot of women jealous,' I murmured.

'People started to say that she was Aphrodite herself. When she was scarcely eleven years of age she walked, one summer day, by the seaside, her little feet in the foam, and her unbound hair flowing about her. The very birds seemed to crowd in the air above and cry to her. Villagers came out and seeing her, said to each other, "It is the goddess!" And they gazed until the girl herself was frightened. Kallirrhoe was – she *is* – for surely she must still be in being! – sweet-tempered, generous and good. She is a true and chaste servant of Artemis. Kallirrhoe has loved that goddess with a special love since she was old enough for understanding. She made sacrifices regularly at the new temple. But I wonder if Artemis herself was not jealous of the Aphrodite-power, and hence afflicted her servant Kallirrhoe with ill-fortune, and myself too.

'I, sirs, loved the girl as my special playfellow. We shared every toy. But the time came, as she grew towards womanhood, when of course she must wear the veil and no longer play with a boy child. But when I was nearly fourteen, and she was twelve, I saw her at a festival among the maidens, dancing to Artemis, and she outshone the other maidens as the moon outshines the stars. I knew then that I loved her – that I ached with love for her. At that time I made up a song about her:

When I saw you in the dancing
Kallirrhoe, Kallirrhoe
When I heard you in the singing
Kallirrhoe, Kallirrhoe
When I saw you in the dancing,
Like a sunlit fountain flowing
Flowing, brightly flowing
All my heart danced to you,
And I loved you, Kallirrhoe.

Often I have sung that song to her. And now I know whenever we are near, she will recognise my voice, no matter how foully I am disguised, and know her song.'

'Well,' I said, speaking with more scorn than I felt, 'such love in one so young usually does not last very long. Whatever the customs may be in Ephesos – among friends of the Persians – surely such a love could not come to any good when both of you were at such a tender age?'

The boy gave me a rebuking look. 'No, not *then.* We could not be married then, unhappily. But I told my father, and though he laughed, he was not displeased. Habrokomes was important and well-to-do. He spoke to Habrokomes and they decided that we should marry when of age.'

'Of age!' I snorted. 'In Athens men rarely get married before thirty, and then a girl of twenty-eight or twenty-nine would be *much* too old –'

'Well,' the boy interrupted me, most disrespectfully, 'that's not *our* way. And it would have been a good match on both sides. Oh – but our fortunes have altered since then! My father was wealthy – and hers – and now we neither of us possess anything in the world.

'We were betrothed then. And I *knew* that Kallirrhoe felt love for me too. She made up her own version of my song, and sang back to me. "When I saw you in the dancing, Korydon, Korydon." We – our two selves – made a private promise that neither of us would marry anyone else, tide what might betide. We swore by Artemis. I am to bed with no other woman, as she with no other man. Our love was not consummated. Kallirrhoe is a proper good girl – lady, I mean. But we sealed our promise with a kiss. We met from time to time, under the eye of her old nurse, and exchanged gifts and kissed. I gave her a gold bracelet, purest gold, which she promised to wear for ever, for my sake.'

'Touching, very,' said Aristotle, stretching his arms above his head, and yawning slightly.

'You smile, sirs?' The boy looked at us accusingly. 'You think lightly of our kisses. But this is love. I am a slave now, but if we were slaves together, I could be happier than if I were the Great King and she away from me. But now I have the worst of both, for I am a slave and she too, and Kallirrhoe *is* away from me.'

'But how does it come about that you are a slave?'

'You will hear. Now comes the grievous part of my tale. You know the history of Ephesos – how the cities of the coast and ours among them were besieged by Alexander four years ago? While our city was yet untouched, and preparing for the siege, our fathers took counsel together, and decided that if things started to go badly they would send their children to safety. Then after the battle of Granikos we heard of the defeat of the Persians. The news boded ill for Ephesos, so my father and Habrokomes put us on a boat and sent us to Miletos. The city of Miletos was holding out stoutly, and the Persian fleet was nearby. So we left our parents, and I do not know what happened to either of our fathers.'

He paused, looking broodingly into the fire, and then resumed.

'We – Kallirrhoe and I – arrived in Miletos where we were greeted kindly. But our happiness was mixed and uncertain. For Arbazos, one of the Persians commanding the garrison, became enamoured of Kallirrhoe, young as she was. One day as the warfare grew hotter, this man enticed her into a room where he promised her that she would be safe. He tried to offer her sweetmeats and then to embrace her. But the gods relented, for before Arbazos could pull her down there came a pounding at the door. Alexander's fleet was here, and the walls were bombarded. The Persian left the room and ran down to defend the city. He left Kallirrhoe there, locked in – so he thought. But when his servants left quickly by a door hidden under a tapestry, Kallirrhoe followed. She found herself in a kind of tunnel. It was hard for her to see, but a bombardment sent a huge stone through the wall just ahead of her. So she had light to guide her, and when she came to the rent the stone had made she was able to wriggle out and get free.

'Getting free in this case meant getting into the war. Out of doors the air was dark with missiles. I was there too, for the group that I had been fighting with had given up the wall. I fought well on that day, though I thought I was going to die. I killed three men.'

'Only three?' I said sarcastically.

The boy glared at me. 'It's not as easy as it looks – but I dare say you know that. Your sword gets stuck near the bone. Anyway, I killed two for certain, and the other one I gave a good swipe at. But now it was "save yourselves if you can!" Through the stone-storm, Kallirrhoe and I both made way to the beach where the Milesian soldiers were gathered. The city was collapsing, and the ships and troops of the Makedonians had taken the harbour. Some of our men began to hurl themselves into the sea and swam to a neighbouring little island just off shore. Many a stout man paddled with his hands, lying on his shield. I gave Kallirrhoe my shield, and told her to be off. And a wounded soldier who could go no further gave me his. So we each lay upon a shield and frantically pushed the water with both hands, the way you see children do with a piece of board in the sea. We both reached the island, though many died in the attempt. It was dark, you remember, and stones hurtled into the water. Many were struck while swimming to safety.

'This little island was not a true refuge. But one or two Milesian boats had escaped before Alexander's warships bottled up the harbour. They took off some of those upon the island, and a ship of Miletos took both of us away from that day's danger.'

'And then your friend Kallirrhoe had leisure to tell you her story?' Aristotle queried.

'Your maiden-friend has had a trying time,' I added, 'although she seems unfortunately to have had much acquaintance with soldiers.' I wanted to bring this boy down a peg, to remind him that his story was not of the first importance. He forgot his position too easily. The boy glanced at me suspiciously. I added drily, 'I am glad you came to a good end.'

'Oh, that's not near the end of it,' the boy assured us.

'There are more trials to come. The ship made its way carefully in the darkness, leaving people shrieking and lamenting. We had to keep perfectly silent. There were bodies floating all about the vessel but we dared not pick up those who might still have breath in them. No burial rites for any! The sea got them all. Our ship made her way to Mykale, and then we went on to Halikarnassos, the Persian stronghold and capital of Karia.

'In Halikarnassos for a while we were safe, at least from war but not from the trials of life. We were well received and well treated by the Persian leaders, Orontobates and Memnon –'

'Wonderful names!' I exclaimed. 'Like reading Herodotos. Do continue, lad,' I added graciously, as the boy frowned.

'Orontobates and Memnon, who were great leaders,' he said with emphasis, 'were much occupied in strengthening the city. They had built about it a moat, deep and wide, and, as the city had three fortresses and a strong wall, and also the fleet nearby, it was not expected to give way. So the town was still prosperous, and continued its customary arts and crafts. We were given new clothing, and robes of purple-dyed stuffs for a festival, and personal servants. The governor of the place treated us as pretty children, and indulged us. Nevertheless, there were those who did not see us as children.

'When I was dressed for the festival, and happy in the thought that now I should please my beloved's eyes, the arrows of Love smote the wrong person as well as the right one. A man called Theron, a Greek – though I think partly Phoenician – beheld me. Thereafter he would do nothing but seek me out to converse with me.

This man had been a soldier of Tyre, but he was wounded in war and had settled in the city of Halikarnassos, where he carried on the trade of a goldsmith. He had retired from the wars wounded not only in body but in mind. Theron had greatly loved a young man, a fellow-soldier who had fought by his side and had died in his arms. Ever since that time, although his worldly fortunes seemed well, he had been melancholy and inwardly grieving, until he saw me and felt again the power of Eros.

'He recited my name in poems in the midst of the market-place, he besieged me with gifts and embarrassed me with attentions. My friends in Halikarnassos would have been quite happy for me to take the protection of this man, who was rich, but I had sworn to love only Kallirrhoe my life long. Theron proclaimed his love, but I had to tell him that I loved one alone, and had sworn myself hers only till death. Yet I did not wish to appear discourteous, so I spoke in fair words. Surely no one can be cruel when he sees another suffering the grievous pain of love? Theron showed the greatness of his own heart by understanding me and swearing to be my friend always, and to aid myself and Kallirrhoe both as long as he lived. He kept his word, as you shall hear.

'Kallirrhoe meanwhile had similar sufferings, only worse. The nephew of Memnon, Pharnabazos, fell in love with her, and wanted to take her as a wife, although he had a wife living. Kallirrhoe had no desire to be the concubine of this man. So she swore to him and to others that she had taken a vow to Artemis not to marry until she had completed her fourteenth year, and that in loyalty to the goddess and her father she must keep her vow.

Pharnabazos pitied her youth and friendless state. And Memnon also defended her, saying he stood in place of a father to her. Neither was it lucky to force anyone to break a solemn vow. But he treated the girl as a beautiful girl is treated who is being got ready for marriage.

'Things went on in this vein with us as the city was preparing for war. As you know, war came in good measure. Alexander arrived in the autumn with army and fleet and laid siege. All thoughts of love gave place to battle. Orontobates and Memnon and Pharnabazos led the army and the citizens in fighting. At first things went reasonably well.' The boy suddenly stood up and extended his arm full length.

'Sirs, I must make this part as an oration, for it is a serious history, never yet told in writing.'

'Not quite true,' said Aristotle to me. 'Kallisthenes my nephew has been writing his history as he accompanies Alexander, though certainly it has not been given out yet.'

Korydon took no notice. He looked above our heads as if he could see a great crowd beyond. In his manner of old-fashioned rhetorical dignity we saw him embody and exhibit his claim to be one of the civilised Greeks and not a barbarian.

'This terrible history is worthy of the attention of all mankind. Let men not forget Halikarnassos!'

The boy cleared his throat and then spoke aloud and clearly, gazing sometimes at us and sometimes at the imagined crowd:

'Then the army of Alexander destroyed two towers, but the people of Halikarnassos built a wall overnight, a crescent wall, and from the towers at either end rained stones upon the attackers. The Halikarnassians' attempt to set fire to the Makedonian engines failed, but the Makedonians suffered losses.

'Every day was more alarming than the day before. The city was filled with the groans of the injured, both soldiers and citizenry. Private houses were turned into shelters for the wounded. You often met in the streets processions of litters carried by women and the old – rough litters made of doors or coarse canvas, whereon lay injured men, with here a leg dangling useless and there a face half cut off. Blood dripped and dried in the streets which in peacetime had been filled with gay crowds buying figs and silk and fruit and jewels. Those who had lost their houses near the walls were sheltered in empty shops. Day and night were full of noise; we could hardly sleep for shrieks and the thud of stone and the crash of falling walls. The air was dusty with the powder of broken brick, and all the faces one saw were dusty too.

'The siege lasted only a few days after the crescent wall went up. Alexander himself in his rage took charge of the attack on the new wall. The Persian leaders and the fighting men of Halikarnassos decided upon a desperate measure. They made a determined sortie, rushing out in several separate parties, to take the Makedonians where they least expected it. One division encountered Alexander's men at the breach in the wall, and another party emerged from the Triple Gate. They fired repeatedly – with flaming arrows and torches of tar – at the Makedonian assault machines. But the Makedonians counterattacked almost at once. Javelins flew like hail, and well-aimed stones crushed the soldiers. It became clear our side was losing. Many of us who were defending the city could not retreat in safety, for the way back to the city was choked with the rubble of the wall, with shot stones, and with the bodies of men. The worst loss was at the gates of the town, which some of the citizens shut in cowardly haste for fear of letting the Makedonian enemy in at the heels of the fugitives. This panic was the death of many good soldiers. I was myself at that moment with a party of archers on the wall, observing the battle. It was terrible! We rushed down to try to get the gates open again while there was still time – but too late. Men were forced by their own city to face certain death outside the wall. In this dismal action Halikarnassos lost about one thousand men.

'Orontobates and Memnon realised it wasn't possible to hold out any longer. There remained only the last action of utter desperation: to ensure that Alexander would win no victory over a standing city. Somewhere near midnight the leaders and their men set the armoury on fire, and the wooden defence tower, and the houses near the wall.

'The flames caught and were spread about in the wind. It is a terrible thing to be in a city doomed to fire and the sword. I was in the camp of Orontobates, and knew the plan just as they started to put it into action. Everything was soon in great confusion. The streets were full of people, some wailing for their children, others searching for their goods, most trying to fly, when there was no place of safety left to them. Alexander's men called out to us repeatedly, though it was difficult to make out anything they were saying over the noise. They called on us to quench the fire; they swore whoever set fires would be killed but that all found peaceably in their own homes would be spared.

'I was with the forces when they withdrew without waiting to see the whole city fired. We were retreating to the island stronghold just outside the harbour. But on our way, once we were in our ship I thought of an important question: *Where was Kallirrhoe?*'

IX

Fire and Water

'An important question,' said Aristotle. 'You had not thought to ask it earlier?'

'It does seem careless,' I said, laughing carelessly myself.

'But consider – sirs! – I was fighting! Have *you* ever fought in a war?' He turned to me, his great eyes disrespectfully boring into me. I decided not to answer.

'But certainly' – the boy cast his eyes down – 'it is a great wonder and a miserable shame to me that I had not thought of it before. I shall never understand it, nor forgive myself. But I asked the question again. *Where is Kallirrhoe?* And no one near me could answer. Save Pharnabazos, who turned pale and looked with speaking eyes towards the lost shore. He was gazing at the tower of his own house, opposite to our ship as it was rowed away from the city. That day he had ordered his slaves to lock Kallirrhoe for safety in a room at the top of his tower. "For safety," he said – but as I believe, so that she should not find *me* and we two disappear together. Yet in the anger and hurry of the final awful plan, conceived and executed at short notice, he too had offended against Eros in forgetting his beloved until too late.

'Now the anguish mounted in his eyes, for he saw, as I did, the flames beginning to catch upon his own house and creep towards the tower. And at the window of the tower room stood Kallirrhoe herself. I could see her very clearly, lit by the flames. Her long hair, unbound, blown by the wind, shining in the fire which was about to consume her, and her arms held out to us in entreaty!

'How can I express my horror at that sight? My heart seemed to swell and burst. Darkness closed my eyes. When I awoke to life and misery, lo! Pharnabazos in full armour had already jumped into the water and was madly striving to swim the gap of sea that separated our boat from the shore and the doomed walls. But the heat of the harbour was intense and the smoke and glare made him dizzy and slow, as well as the effort of swimming with his breast-plate on. I too in anguish and impatience then leaped into the water, but one of the soldiers snatched me by the hair and dragged me back into the boat. Then they tied me to the boat's floor so that I might not jump in again. I was unhappy beyond expression. My forgetfulness of an hour is the crime against the gods – against Eros – for which I have had to pay by many miseries to follow. Also, I confess it, sirs, a moment's hesitation, of cowardice, perhaps – for if I had jumped from the boat when Pharnabazos did perhaps I might have succeeded in getting to the shore and sharing my love's sufferings. Yet these things too are ordered by the gods.

'At that time, and for many days after, I could do little

but lament my misery and her awful end. For it seemed to me an addition to the terrors of death that the bravest beauty of the world was lost. No token, not even her corpse, had remained. Though she had died in a manner in my sight, yet by the marvellous cruelty of the gods I was deprived of my last kisses. Instead of marriage torches I had seen a living funeral pyre, and the star of beauty had descended in ashes. Now I no longer had Theron to support me, for he too had disappeared, and I presumed him dead likewise.

'In this state of mind I fled with the remnant of our defenders, while Alexander marched into Halikarnassos and had it partly rebuilt. As you know, he gave it to Queen Ada, who had been deposed by Orontobates. Out of revenge she had sued for help to Alexander. So she ruled as vice-regent of Alexander – though Queen in name – and all of Karia was put under her control. I escaped with the Persian forces and we went on to take the island of Lesbos. I hoped to lose my life in the fighting, now that Kallirrhoe had been taken from me.'

'But you evidently didn't die,' I said crisply, to let the boy know I was not to be won by his histrionics. He made me no reply, so rapt was he by his own narration.

'But now I shall tell you of Kallirrhoe's story – for while I was lamenting her death, she was not dead, but had been saved by the power of the gods and the virtue of my friend Theron. Theron had turned himself into a soldier again, and so was at his post when the fire came. When he saw the leaders forsake his city, he rushed through the streets to his own home. There he took up from the floor two bags in which he had put some of his best ware – gold, and coins, gems and bracelets, and so on. Carrying his wealth under a tattered robe, Theron, at once both poor and rich, made for the tower in which Kallirrhoe was captive. *He* did not forget his promise to myself and to Eros even when I myself was guilty of forgetfulness. He knew where Kallirrhoe had been left, stored like a precious emerald by Pharnabazos.

'Just at the time when we in the boat had seen the fire creep towards her, Theron himself came to the house and up the tower by the back way where the flames had not yet reached. When he broke through the still-locked back gate, he found the last of the household had run off at the outcry of "Fire!" He climbed the stairs, seizing a rope as he went. When he got to the tower the heat was very fierce, but he had the forethought to steep a cloth in water from the courtyard well. This he held over his face while he chopped away with his sword at the locked door of the girl's room. Kallirrhoe heard him; she had already moved away from the window, and was trying again herself to break the door. He told her to lie down to avoid the smoke. She had kept her head, and did this. When he entered the room, flames and smoke whirled in from the window at the draught from the open door. When they started down, the fire had seized the lower part of the stairs. So Theron took the rope and hung it out through a window about halfway down the tower stairs, tying one end of it fast to a column nearby. Once it was fast, he ordered Kallirrhoe to slide down it to safety. She did so, and he likewise, and they rushed across the courtyard. They both got out just in the nick of time, for the tower, all involved in flame and making a noise like a wild beast – as Kallirrhoe says – collapsed just as they got to the smoky street.

'The city was now burning fast. Alexander's men, kept back by the wall of fire, were finding their way in slowly. Their temper was not improved by the heat! The night was like no night at all – lit up with flame and full of cries and skirmishes and seething crowds. Alexander's soldiers killed everyone in their path at the same time as they were trying to put the fire out. His captains called out repeatedly that those found in their houses or remaining quietly by the ruins would be well treated and permitted to live. Theron wisely made no attempt to go to his own house, which would have been burnt anyway. He took instead a winding course through back streets, away from the harbour, where the fire was not as strong. Here he found a deserted house in one of the poorer districts. He and Kallirrhoe remained meekly inside this little house, so when the soldiers came at least the two of them were well treated. They looked like poor people. Theron did not seem wealthy. (He did not display his secret bags of gold!) And Kallirrhoe was so draggled and dishevelled, so ill with weeping and smoke, that she aroused no attention in the soldiers and she and Theron passed as brother and sister.

'So they lived in ruined Halikarnassos, during the first invasion and in the time of reconstruction and the advent of Queen Ada. But by this time Kallirrhoe was her beautiful self again in full splendour, and it was becoming difficult for Theron to resist the unwelcome advances made by natives and strangers, even though the girl kept indoors. So with his useful bag of gold he bought the services of the captain of a small vessel. He and Kallirrhoe took flight on the boat.

'Theron could think of nowhere safe to go save back to

the Persian forces. And so – this was in the spring – they sailed to Lesbos, where Memnon had won all the island save Mitylene. That voyage suited the captain very well, for he had a half-brother in Lesbos, a fisherman. Theron settled near this fisherman, with his "sister" Kallirrhoe.'

The boy, his voice beginning to creak, sat down again on the rough floor and took a drink of the wine.

'Now, I was on the same island of Lesbos, in the household of Memnon while he was conducting war against Mitylene. Memnon cared for me well, but after he had a foothold in Lesbos he would not allow me to take part in warfare any more, saying I was too young. So I had the misery of idleness as well as grief. I cursed the day I had fled alive from burning Halikarnassos. Life in the world seemed tedious now. Pharnabazos looked on me with no friendly eye. He suffered as I did for loss of Kallirrhoe, but that made him no more amiable, for he felt that I had blamed him for my loss of the girl, as he blamed himself, and the sight of me was grievous to his eyes.

'Then one day I heard from a servant that Aphrodite had appeared on the west coast of the island this spring – that some children had seen her, that flowers sprang up where she walked, and that then she vanished. I determined to seek out the shrine of the goddess, and to offer my sorrowful plaint to her.'

Korydon stopped, taking another sup of wine and looking into the fire again, as if there he could see past events. The very room had seemed hotter, even here at midnight, when he described the burning of Halikarnassos. His tale entranced with its description of far places, and of a girl we had never seen. But this strange boy seemed almost to ignore us, except as audience. He was very self-possessed, very full of himself, I thought. He was notably not impressed with us – neither with the great philosopher nor myself. Of course, he could not have known who I was, he had not seen me in Athens, a citizen surrounded by friends, of some importance. He had only seen us in this low hut.

'Oh, do go on, child,' I said, taking a drink of the wine myself and passing the bottle (now much diminished) to Aristotle. 'Spin us some more of your yarn. And you still haven't explained, by the way, how you came to be a slave.'

He sighed. 'That I shall tell in due course. Happiness came back, but too briefly. For I wandered myself through the island to make an offering to Aphrodite. There, I saw the graceful figure of a young woman, like Persephone in a field of flowers. I dropped down in awe before her, and she moved her veil over her face with her hand slightly – and I saw the gold bracelet that I knew. I cried out her name, and she unveiled to me. Looking up, I saw that it was Kallirrhoe! Her own self!

'Oh, sirs, figure our happiness – and how precarious such happiness is in such times of war and destruction. Fearing the attention that Kallirrhoe was getting and the jealous eye of Pharnabazos who might discover her, Theron and Kallirrhoe and I decided to abandon Lesbos and sail off on our own, to find some safe place to live. We set out on a small but seaworthy vessel. But a storm at sea came, and our ship was badly damaged. We were going to go down into that terrible waste of pitiless water!'

'But you didn't. You were obviously rescued,' I pointed out.

'We were glad to see a sail. But the ship that came to

our rescue was a ship of pirates. They took all our belongings and talked first of killing us and then of selling us. The pirate captain, however, was pleased with the gold and gems he had found on Theron. And with more than that. For he found Kallirrhoe much to his taste and said he would have her. Theron and I were tied down on the oar deck. As another sail came into view at that time, the pirate captain bound Kallirrhoe and packed her away for safe keeping. He warned Theron and myself that we could look forward to very little. "You will have supper, not on fish, but with the fishes," was what he said. But then the wind arose, and a swell in the waves, so it was hard to make way through the water. The captain did not like the look of the approaching ship so he ordered us – Theron and me – to row at the oars.'

'A hardy exercise,' I murmured, looking dubiously at the boy's graceful frame.

'I am strong, sir, though I am young. And we thought if we were of real use to the pirate he would be less likely to kill us. But the ship that came up was a ship of war, a well-manned trireme accustomed to sea battles. Its fighting men boarded the pirate vessel and there was combat throughout the ship. Bloodstained water rolled down the decks and under the rowers' benches. After capturing the pirates' fighting men, the invaders took the rowers without a struggle. I cannot but say that we were happier when the fray was ended. You must realise that we were tied to the rowers' bench, so we were defenceless and couldn't move or fight. We expected any minute to be killed by some chance blow.

'They marched all of us before the leader of the invading party. The new captain made a little speech, telling us that he was a Makedonian and that Alexander did not approve of pirates, and that all here would be executed or sold as slaves. Theron and I spoke to him, trying to make him our friend. The Makedonian sailors found Kallirrhoe in the cooking-place, under shelter where the captain had stowed her. She had been tied but was not hurt.

'Theron offered the Makedonian captain his treasure. But the charm of this was gone, for of course the Makedonian crew had discovered Theron's goods among the rest of the pirate hoard, and the sailors were already dividing the booty. The captain was pleased with his haul. He doubted having provisions for everybody, though, so he made no long business of dispatching a good number of the pirate men over the side of the ship. Those he considered properly saleable and untroublesome he kept. He made no offer to Kallirrhoe nor cast any kind of smile upon her.

'When we arrived at Peiraieus the captain kept us confined overnight and the next day took the lot of us to a slave auction, where we were sold separately.

'We tried and *tried* to talk to this man and tell him who we were. We might as well have held our tongues, for our story made a bad impression. The Makedonian captain saw only that we were allies of the Persians – he called us "Persian dogs" and "Mede-lovers". Those were only a few of the nicer things he said. The war against the Persians, as he saw it, gave him the right and duty of selling Kallirrhoe, Theron and myself into slavery. We were good pieces of property, as slaves go. Kallirrhoe and I were young and good-looking, and Theron, though past his first youth, was a craftsman. Well . . . it is not pleasant for a man of good family to tell what happened next, sirs.'

Korydon's eyes flashed, and his hand sought his side, as if feeling for a sword.

'Being sold as a slave – I do not want to describe that in many words. Theron was sold to a silversmith of Korinthos. (Pherekrates of Athens bid for him, but was outdone by the other silversmith.) I was full of fear for Kallirrhoe. But fortunately, on the day of the auction, she was not looking quite her best. After all, she had been seasick and taken by pirates and captured and held as a slave. So she was bought by Pherekrates just as a personal slave for his daughter Anthia. I kept these names in remembrance, so I would know where she was. I was sold to a mere farmer of Boiotia, and so I have remained at his farm, kept at hard work and under surveillance. I had no opportunity to search for Kallirrhoe and no means of escape until now. And *that*, gentlemen, is my life story – and the story of Kallirrhoe, the beautiful maid of Ephesos.'

Korydon paused – as well he might – and drew a deep breath. He then, unbidden and in a most unservile manner, helped himself to the last of the wine. He stared into the fire, without moving. Outside of the hut, the first birds began to sing.

'Well, well,' said Aristotle, eventually. 'A most interesting tale, if something on the long side.' He looked at the boy searchingly, as if he were a new specimen of plant or an unusual piece of pottery. 'Let us go back to the beginning of our meeting. How do you know that we seek this girl? And do you have any idea where she is now?'

'Yes, I do know what you are looking for,' said Korydon

frankly. 'I have been following you for a long while. And I heard you talking.'

'When did you first come upon us? And why didn't you speak to us at once?'

He shrugged. 'A slave is in such an awkward position, sir. It doesn't pay to speak where you're not wanted. You see, I had been sent on an errand by my master. Coming back I passed a hill with an oak tree. And upon the tree among many other rags bound to it, there was a fillet – a girl's riband – and between the fillet and the bark a long thread of hair. Kallirrhoe's hair, I would swear to it!'

'Do you have it with you?' Aristotle asked curiously.

'No,' said the boy drily. 'As it was a kind of prayer, I put it back on another part of the tree. But I knew she must have come that way – from Athens, towards Delphi. So I went along the road trying to see if I could see her anywhere. A shepherd boy told me he had seen a litter pass, so I thought she was probably in it. I walked on the hill above, and saw a litter moving along the road, not far from my home. My master's home, I mean, in Boiotia – no home of mine. So when I saw the litter I started to sing, as loud as I could, our song that you know of. And she – I am sure it was Kallirrhoe, for she sang back for two notes or three, before the voice ceased as if someone stopped her mouth. I was nearly maddened by this, as you can imagine! I raced downhill and along the road after the litter. But then my master and my master's dog – ill luck take them! – came upon me. The dog worried me and pinned me down; then my master laid hold on me and beat me. He said I wasted time, and was trying to run away. So he locked me into the goat shed, after tying my hands. He beat me again and left me for the night, without food or proper bedding – only the straw that his goats lie in. But my courage was increased with the knowledge that Kallirrhoe was so near. I managed to get out of this wooden jail, later, when all was dead night and quiet.'

'What about the dog?' I asked. 'Aren't you forgetting him?'

'I killed the watch-dog by strangling him before he could bark. I also took from the kitchen some food and wine for my journey. The housekeeper thinks she has made everything safe from the slaves, but *I* know otherwise. Then I left.'

'How long ago was this?'

'A couple of days ago. Not long after that I came upon you, just after you left a village. I followed you. And,' he added, 'I saw you two in the dawning when you handled a dead man. And then you left the road. I followed you, up on these heights, until this time.'

'Why didn't you speak to us before this?'

'I was trying to decide. But I heard more of your words together, and I now believe that your search is mine. If you are seeking Anthia, I seek Kallirrhoe. Let me come with you to Delphi.'

I was taken aback by the lad's coolness. 'But,' I objected, 'you are a runaway. We can't just walk off with some other man's slave!'

Korydon flushed and stood up defiantly.

'He *is* a slave, isn't he, Aristotle?' I said. 'It's as plain to see as a tree in a desert. He was a captive in war and legally sold in Peiraieus.'

Aristotle sighed. 'I know, I know. Some maintain that captivity in war is the only true reason for enslaving a person. But others would forbid the purchase as slaves of any free men or women taken captive. It is a topsy-turvy effect that the most noble, the most well-born, might be turned into slaves just because they happen to be taken as prisoners in the disasters of war. But according to this lad's tale, at all events, he was captured first by pirates. Piracy gives no valid right of enslavement.' He put his chin in his hand. 'It's a nice case, I grant –'

'I am not a *case*!' the boy burst out. 'I am *not* a slave and I never intend to be!'

'I thought about it while this boy was talking,' I said. 'He tells a fine tale. But the long and the short of it is, he's a slave. Justice demands that we give the Boiotian back his property.'

'There is something in that,' said Aristotle. 'It is injustice to defraud a man of his slave – *if* the entity in question is a slave. But it would be injustice to ourselves – for several reasons – to abandon our quest and plod back to Boiotia. It would be extremely unjust to Anthia's father and family. After all, this lad can track down the slave-girl, which is probably the same as tracking down Anthia. He is undoubtedly a complication. But . . . for the moment, at least, perhaps we must permit him to accompany us.'

'Well, there's a nice speech!' said the lad, standing as tall as he could and glaring at us both. 'It would perhaps be better for *you* both not to forget that I came upon the two of you with a corpse. You were standing over the body of a big fat man – who for all I know still lies alone at the crossroads for daws to peck at. Who put him there? Once that body is discovered, many would be curious. How exactly did the big man meet his end? Did it take two to kill him?'

There was a short and nasty silence.

'It would seem,' said Aristotle, 'that we are not the only ones to take an interest in corpses. And, my young Korydon, I might ask, how do we know that *you* were not first on the scene? By your own accounting, you have killed men –'

'In war,' Korydon interjected.

'By all means,' said Aristotle, 'let us go to Delphi together. If we can find this Kallirrhoe, she may well provide us with the key that we need. So far, we have been like people trying to open an iron lock with our fingernails. Enough. Let us take some rest now, even though it is day. My old head does not take kindly to the effects of sitting up all night to drink and hear strange stories. Enjoyable as the story is,' he added affably, rolling himself up again in his cloak. 'Tomorrow – nay, today – we go on to Delphi.'

The boy also lay down, on some bracken by the fire. I could not feel easy in his presence. As I had spoken in favour of returning him to his master, he had cause for resentment. My thoughts moved in a dissatisfied drift. I thought about the strange things that happen in war, and about a girl so beautiful that she looked like Aphrodite. I thought of Philomela, unadmired, in the house of her grumbling father. I thought of fighting in battle, and why I hadn't done anything of the kind. Why was I getting mixed up in others' affairs? Somebody else's marriages, somebody else's murders. And this boy, Korydon, so beautiful and eloquent. Who was he, after all? Only a stranger, a foreigner and a slave. He had uttered a threat, hadn't he? Could he *really* have suspected us of the murder of Ammonios? Or . . . Who knew if this boy had not been before us at the crossroads? Was it Love or Death that had come knocking at our door?

X

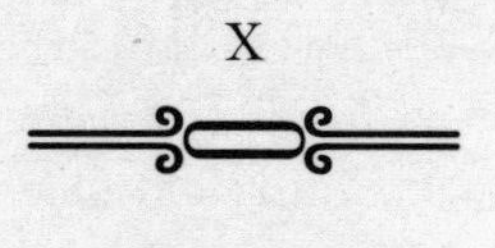

Delphi

When we arose, the storm had dropped and the morning had brought a fresh breeze and cloud-crossed sunshine. A party of three, we set off to make the descent of the great mountain flank. We worked our way around the edges of raw limestone and along the margin where stark stone meets true soil. We had camped not far from a small stony village, the precarious habitation of shepherds and weavers. It is wonderful that people should choose to live in high and lonely places. A baby's first steps might take him tilting into the downward-pulling air.

Winding about the rocks we slowly made our way back to the settled world of men. The soil was thin and full of gravel, but constant terraces of stone held the slopes into little fields. There were slender groves of nut trees, and some olives – even small vineyards, short and brawny vines courageously rooted in the tough ground. It was heartening to see signs of the hands of men, here where the grey rocks reigned over the heights. Big-bellied clouds hung above the mountains, threatening snow even yet to the highest peaks; the grey ridges were striped with purple cloud-shadows. The wind still whistled about our ears. We did not speak much.

I was still attending to my footing when Aristotle suddenly said, 'Look – there is Delphi!'

I looked down and saw the sacred temple, shining and new, freshly painted with bright blue and deep red and gold, and the buildings of its sanctuary. Below that again were the graceful columns of the Tholos of Athena-before-the-Temple. A stroke of sunlight ran across Apollo's temple just at the moment of my first sight of it, and streaked the hill below. The place looked so beautiful that I was full of awe and joy, even before I fully grasped with my mind that the place I looked upon was Delphi. Holy Delphi, the Navel of the earth. This is the centre of the world. Zeus found it out when he sent two eagles from the extremest points of the universe, one from the left and one from the right, and they met in the sky above Delphi. Above me now an eagle hovered in the splendid air, wheeling over the gorge of the Pleistos. I felt it was a good omen.

'Come,' said Aristotle, 'we must go around. Let us go behind the temple by the Leskhe of the Knidians and then take the road into the town. There are such a lot of things to see. If we have leisure, I really want to show you the monument I designed and had put up to Hermias.'

I could see that being back in Delphi cheered him. As we climbed down by a substantial building, he explained, 'This club house is really for Knidians and Delphians, but one of the Delphian hosts will be able to show us the beautiful paintings in it. There is one in particular I'd like you to see, Stephanos.'

'What is that?' I enquired, stumbling along to the path that led by the high brick edifice.

'The portrait of an ass.'

I stared at this insult. Aristotle laughed. 'I meant that for myself, not for you. It is the picture of Hesitation, or Unpreparedness – perhaps of Futility. In Polygnotos' great picture of the Underworld, Oknos sits plaiting a rope of straw, and the ass behind him is eating up the rope as fast as it comes. In our present case, I feel I too weave ropes of straw that go for nothing. Pointlessness. For I have not even a theory that makes sense, and in elaborate delay we spend our time going to weddings and getting lost.'

'What do we do now?' I said once we were on the road.

'Stroll on. Look leisured, seem interested. Let us hope that there are enough pilgrims so that our presence isn't too noticeable. Especially with our young companion here, who may be awkward to explain. I had rather not be known, but I have many friends in Delphi, including my proxenos, an old acquaintance. A problem. I can hardly tell my friends about Lysippos' missing daughter – that would defeat our larger object. We must both remember to watch our tongues.'

'I see *that*,' I retorted. 'And we have a bigger problem. If we pretend that this Korydon is our *own* slave, then we are guilty of slave-theft indeed. Perhaps,' I whispered, 'we could lose him somehow?'

Aristotle only answered, 'Our way lies here,' and took the lead.

'What then?' I enquired, scrambling down after him. 'If

we don't want to braid straw ropes, what are we supposed to do? How are we going to carry on our search?'

'I think,' said Aristotle, 'the best thing to do is to go first to one of the common inns. We won't be able to stay there long, but we may pick up some news. And we should frequent all the common meeting-places. Try to hear any news or useful gossip. We can find out – by discreet listening – if anyone speaks of either murdered man. We should also look about the market-places and small taverns where they hire slave-girls, in case the Ephesian girl is there. In fact,' he added quietly to me, 'it might be as well to allow young Korydon to search on his own. We could follow him without his knowing it.'

I was looking forward to being among people again as we went down past the sanctuary wall and into the little city of Delphi. Delphi is like a village compared with Athens, but compared with the stony villages of the goatherds it is very grand. There are many splendid houses – splendid if you don't mind your house being on the side of a mountain, and that a mountain much given to earthquakes. Forty-three years before, there had been a terrible quake when huge pieces of rock from the mountain were flung on the town and on the very Temple of Apollo, destroying it completely. Poseidon likes to do that kind of thing when he is angry, especially when he is angry at another god. Reconstruction had been going on ever since, delayed by the renewal of the Sacred Wars when the Phokians first, and then the Lokrians had claimed control of the shrine. The last of these Sacred Wars had been brought to an end by the power of Philip of Makedon, who brought his own big wars to Greek cities. Philip subdued the Phokians, razed their strongholds and took their place in the League of Neighbouring Cities.

I did not care to discuss King Philip with Aristotle, although the rule of Philip and his son Alexander had certainly been beneficial on the whole for Delphi, however disastrous elsewhere. Instead, I commented on the rapidity of the repairs. 'It is quite wonderful,' I said, 'that the sanctuary is finished, and the new temple complete. I never thought I would be here for the consecration! And the Oracle.'

'But the Oracle was fully functioning, even during the bad years,' Aristotle reminded me.

'I hope to consult it,' said Korydon earnestly, with an assumption of right that astonished me. He did not seem to notice his own impudence.

As we came closer, we could see that the citizens of Delphi had completed their own reconstruction more rapidly than the temple. The town looked surprisingly prosperous, considering the wars. Neat and handsome houses had little gardens on the slopes, and, in the centre, small tidy squares and market-places offered wares from all over Greece. People come here from everywhere, as pilgrims to pay homage to the great god of the Sun, the god of light, inspirer of music and thought. Some visitors, naturally enough, engage in trading while others, the imprudent ones without sufficient provision for the journey home, are reduced to selling personal goods and ornaments to local shopkeepers.

There were certainly enough people about to make us quite inconspicuous – two travel-worn men and a slave. We slipped off the path into the roadway and joined the throng.

'There are several things I particularly wish to show you,' said Aristotle. 'And one of them is very close at hand now. Come with me.'

We went through the press, sometimes in single file, following Aristotle as he threaded his way through the labyrinth of pathways and streets between handsome monuments. I noticed that he kept his head lowered and his cape over his head so I did likewise, though there was no reason for *me* to fear recognition by Delphian folk.

'There!' said Aristotle. 'The Treasury of Athens!'

I had heard of this splendid Treasury, with its rich store of offerings, most magnificent the spoils which Athens had won from the Persians. Yet the marble building with its many columns was a surprise and a revelation. Behind the fronds of the golden palm tree dedicated to Apollo you could see the spiky prows of the captured Persian warships. I scarcely had time to notice the graceful frieze at the front, I was so eager to read the inscriptions. 'Here I see names familiar to me,' I said, 'citizens of my own city.' The steps, platform and outer walls of the Athenian Treasury were crowded with offerings. Private persons give small statues to Apollo, or whatever they can afford. The poorer sort give pottery. A cup with the figures of Leto and Apollo painted on it caught my attention. Reading it, I saw it was the gift of a woman of Athens whose son had been restored to her after the first eastern expedition of Alexander. I was struck with acute regret that I had not brought an offering in thanks for the safety of my cousin Philemon. He had not only returned safely from exile, but had been delivered from the dreadful charge of murder. Silently I promised the god that I would see to some sort of offering this very year.

'Look at this,' said Aristotle. 'This is what I wanted to show you. The statue given by Lysippos.'

The statue of ivory and rich polished silver was small (about two hands high) but most exquisite. It was the figure of a young man, an Athenian musician and singer who had won a prize. You could see the lips were just about to close fully at the end of his full-throated song. The eyes were still raised, and the lyre remained in his hands as if he had struck his last chord only a second ago. It was Straton. There could be no doubt. Looking at this figure, I had an impression of what Lysippos himself must have looked like when he was a youth – before he went in for business and an important beard. Lest there should be any doubt, an inscription at the base gave the singer's name, and added: 'made and given by Lysippos of Athens, to Apollo'. The sun glinted off the bright metal, touching the hair, the ivory face and hands and the glittering body with an intense and blazing warmth that contrasted with the coolness of the silver and the calm of the lovely singer.

'I did not know Lysippos could do anything as good as that,' I said in admiration. But I felt a deep sadness. Lysippos gave to Apollo this beautiful little statue, the figure of a young man inspired and in pride of life. But Apollo had not spared his son. Lysippos had already lost one son to the war. Now – though the unfortunate father did not yet know it – he had just lost this beautiful son by a foul murder. Never again would Straton's hands hold any instrument, never again would his voice be raised in song or speech.

'You showed me this to rouse me to revenge,' I said to Aristotle. 'You rebuke me because you think I am forgetting Straton.'

He shot me a warning glance, reminding me that Korydon was with us and listening.

'I remind us both,' he said, 'what an excellent silversmith Lysippos is. Now we should go and find a quiet inn somewhere – I know of one. We may have a day to explore Delphi by ourselves before I seek out – as I inevitably must do – my proxenos. A few hours could be very valuable to us.'

We left the last surviving memorial of Straton. Departing from the Treasury of Athens, we became part of the crowd as we tried to make our way towards Aristotle's 'quiet inn'. Nothing else was quiet. There was a great jangle of tongues from a great many people, and we made but slow progress. Abruptly, the street ahead of us was blocked, and we were obliged to halt. The cause of our delay was a stout matron who had seized the cart which, we gathered, she was trying to hire, against all the objections of its owner. She was flanked by two tall drooping youths. These pale lads, at her bidding rather than at their own earnest desire – so it seemed from their looks – had grasped the shafts, and the cart was turned sideways on the roadway (which was not very wide) to the grievance of all who would pass. The two drooping lads joined with deprecatory murmurs in a conversation otherwise being held in bellows and screeches.

'*Visitors!*' shouted the local farmer, owner of the cart. 'Visitors isn't supposed to drive in Delphi! And I need this here cart. You won't be taking it from me, you and these cheese-faces, not if you stays till sunset.'

'Absurd!' screamed the woman, through her veil. 'Kleobis and Biton!' she added unexpectedly.

'Eh?' He was puzzled at this inconsequential remark, as

well he might be. Most people know from nursery or schoolroom the exemplary story of Kleobis and Biton, who harnessed themselves to the chariot of their mother, priestess of Hera, when she could not find horses, and drew her from Argos to the Temple of Hera, a distance of forty-five stadia. The mother prayed, before the family went to sleep in the temple precincts, that the goddess might reward her sons with the best blessing that can be given to men. And in the morning the young men were found dead, having died peacefully in their sleep. The gods have such odd ideas. The Argives of old had dedicated a memorial to the model sons Kleobis and Biton, two great statues in the sanctuary at Delphi. One could only suppose that the lady's anxiety to see these old statues had outrun her reason.

'Kleobis and Biton!' she screamed again to the little farmer, who looked no wiser than before. 'My sons, you idiot!' she explained. 'I've promised the goddess Athena that my sons here – and two better lads you won't find in the world – should harness themselves and drive me in Delphi to the shrine of Athena-before-the-Temple, to do her honour. Just as was done for Hera in the old days. I've been looking forward to it for years. I've been promised long life if they do it. They're model children, my sons – just like Kleobis and Biton, the very image. And Argives to boot. We've all come from Argos. Know that!'

And the determined matron jumped right into the cart. The young men, fiddling nervously with the cart's shafts, looked less than happy with the heroic role into which they had been cast. Decidedly apprehensive, in fact.

The cart-owner spat on the ground, and gave his opinion.

'Rubbish!' he decided. 'Give a nice votive offering, and do your worshipping proper. Give your blessed sons a drink, if they're so good. Let me and my cart be. Treat your cheese-faces to the pleasures of Kirrha, if they're men enough for that work – which they don't look it, let alone hauling heavy loads on an uphill road. We've got enough to do in Delphi without foreigners starting play-acting.'

He gave a great heave, pulled his vehicle completely round and set off, cackling triumphantly, with his unwanted passenger. The disconcerted matron had to jump out again, with no choice but to proceed on foot. She burst into loud lamentation. Her sons awkwardly took an arm each, and tried to console her.

Aristotle laughed aloud. 'Oh, excellent man! Those boys must be grateful to him. They don't seem very cheered by their chance of a divine treat.'

'I hope she never finds a cart in all Delphi,' I added.

'It doesn't do to tempt the gods. Actually, I've wondered about Kleobis and Biton. I think they must have been out of training, or of weak constitution. And these two Argive lads are not in the best condition, are they? Mother's nestlings have grown too fast for their strength.'

Korydon had watched the scene with impatient distaste. 'Vulgar,' was all he said.

The brief delay had its effect upon us, for a man loomed behind us and touched Aristotle on the shoulder.

'My good friend – Aristotle, the philosopher, by all that's wonderful!'

To which Aristotle responded, 'Diokles! My proxenos and my excellent friend!' Aristotle let no hint of regret appear at this meeting (which cut short our unsupervised researches), but cordially embraced the man. His effusiveness was understandable if the man he addressed was his proxenos. Since in a foreign city the stranger must have a sponsor and protector, answerable for him to the civic authorities (and capable of lending him money), it is of the first importance to have a good one.

'Why did you not tell me you were coming? And this is Kallisthenes?'

'No,' explained Aristotle. 'My nephew Kallisthenes cannot be with us at present, greatly as he loves Delphi. He is accompanying Alexander on his way east, as historian of the war against Persia. This is another friend of mine –'

'Another friend? Excellent. But we shall miss Kallisthenes. I long to read his account of the great wars and conquests. Why, Aristotle, I might have passed you on the street, especially with this crowd, but I heard your laugh before I saw you. I hope you were on your way to my home – but if not, you will be staying with me now. You and your friend, and your slave here.'

Aristotle warmly assented, with the ghost of a wink to tell me we must be resigned to our fortunes. Diokles took us each by the elbow, told Korydon to follow close behind, and swept us off down a side street to his house, talking effusively the while.

'I suppose,' he said to Aristotle, 'it's your interest in the Pythian records that brings you here? How you scholars love to look at mouldy records! But you must surely have come to see our great festival, when the temple is consecrated. And do you both come for the Oracle also? Why, what a pity I did not receive your message, for you know how difficult it is to fit in pilgrims' consultations.

But I do not forget my old benefactor – and of course Delphi is another home to you.'

Aristotle had once spent some months in Delphi, seven or eight years ago, before his return to Athens. He had come to Delphi with his nephew Kallisthenes, the ambitious young historian, who at that time burned to write his famous *History of the Sacred War.* In that earlier time, Aristotle had assisted his youthful nephew's researches, and with the young man's help had begun to compile a list of victors of the Pythian Games. Diokles had become his friend and proxenos at that time, as Diokles explained after Aristotle had introduced me properly.

'Any friend of Aristotle is a friend of mine,' he said, beaming. 'I shall be delighted to act as your proxenos too. I have much reason to be grateful to your philosopher, you know. On his former visit, he saved me from a lot of trouble.' The affable Diokles lowered his voice. 'Enemies of my own accused me of being a Phokian malcontent, involved with some of my relatives in bad things – in plotting! Very nasty.'

I could see that it would have been. To be a 'malcontent' at that time meant to be plotting against Philip and Alexander.

'Aristotle spoke up for me – and his credit is good with the Makedonians. Why, he's a Makedonian himself, or as good as. But he also proved that the people said to be my relations were not, which is more than I could have done. He looked into the records and the thing was done in a few days. If he had not helped, I could have lost everything! So I am a friend for ever, and delighted to be his proxenos – and your own, Stephanos of Athens, son of Nikiarkhos.

'*And* as your old proxenos,' said Diokles, turning to Aristotle, 'and not without influence hereabouts these days, I dare say I can help with your arrangements. I feel I can promise you and your friend a visit to the Oracle – and *that* is not as easy as cutting grass, especially just now. The crowds will be here.'

I knew of course that every pilgrim to Delphi needs a sponsor among the citizens of Delphi – even though the number of pilgrims is very great. So the Delphians are kept busy in introducing and guiding and supporting a variety of newcomers. The Delphians naturally wish to exercise some authority over the conduct of the Oracle, as well as to see that the temple worship is properly conducted. When you think about this, it is not really wonderful that citizens of Delphi are well-to-do, considering the necessary gratitude of each and every pilgrim. Diokles, however, did not live by such pickings; he was well-born and rich by inheritance. I felt I was fortunate to have fallen in with an important citizen who would show me as a man of credit and standing. Diokles mentioned his wealth, but not boastfully, and also explained what Aristotle had done for him in days past – all in order to urge me to have no qualms about being his guest.

'It is flattering,' he said happily, 'to have a friend in Aristotle – our first philosopher – and a friend of Alexander, too. May I never forget what I owe him! My family will be most happy, and we will treat you to our own wine. You may not believe it, but these rocky heights produce a good wine – in some years.'

Soon we were ensconced in Diokles' fine house, where we could wash and put on some beautifully clean clothes, and where we were fed with good things, all in great contrast to our previous lodgings. Of course it was hours before I could speak even briefly to Aristotle alone.

'What are we going to do?' I asked. 'It's not so easy now, is it, to go about on our own looking for a slave-girl and a missing heiress?'

'Decidedly not,' said Aristotle. 'It's the penalty for my good looks and general greatness. Here we are, trapped in a respectable home as respectable guests. However, we have the protection of our good host, the wealthy and amiable Diokles – an advantage should anything untoward happen. Like being accused of – of that matter by the crossroads.' He gave a dry chuckle. 'Diokles has already gained me permission to look at the records of the Pythian Games. I start tomorrow. Dear me, and to think I thought originally that the missing heiress was interrupting my work. First I am at work, quietly in Athens, and I find myself pursuing a missing heiress. Very well, I say, I shall pursue this missing heiress – and I find myself back at my studies. There's something cross-grained about this whole case. Something is always being put in place of something else.'

Suddenly Aristotle snapped his fingers. '*Substitution.* That's worth thinking about. And what the man with the cart said – about offering those two languid lads the pleasures of Kirrha. Somehow we must get to Kirrha, the port of Delphi. But I don't see how we can do that before the festival for the opening of the temple. Meanwhile, tomorrow when I am at my labours, you may as well look about the city. Go about the market-place in the morning. Take the boy Korydon with you and don't let him out of your sight. He will be alert to catch any word of the slave-girl abducted with Anthia, but I don't know how much news he would voluntarily share with us. It is very important that you both use your eyes and ears. I am tied while you are free.'

So it was that the next day Aristotle was ushered off in state by important Delphian persons to view the records of the Pythian Games. I was left with the detestable boy. But there was no help for it. Korydon and I went through market-place and side streets, through potters' shops and by fountains – anywhere where there were people, and slaves working. Korydon chose the route of our meanderings, in the hope that he might come upon his Kallirrhoe. It was no use. The town, however, was certainly full of people, now the festival of Apollo was so near. We walked part of the way down the mountain and encountered processions coming up – hundreds of pilgrims and their families, many travelling with complete households.

We looked down the slope and saw the pilgrims coming up the mountain. Those in the distance looked very small. Far below, the white and winding train of folk moved almost continuously along the flat road in the sacred, uncultivated valley, coming from ports where the ships find anchorage. That is the way most visitors come to Delphi – not by the long land road, travelled by Oidipous, myself and Aristotle, but by sea to the coast, and then by road along the valley and up the mountain to the Sacred Way. People from Athens and Megara often come by ship, likewise men of the islands in the East. When the boats reach the thin strip of land holding the mainland and the Peloponnesos together, the ships are put on rollers and the people walk to the other side and start their voyage again. Some passengers are quite seasick when they arrive at Kirrha, and all are weary, but they are glad to see the rocky rise of great Parnassos and to walk on land again. And when they set forth on the road to the Sacred Way, in their clean and sacred garments and singing the hymns, joy has filled their hearts. As Korydon and I watched from above, the voices of pilgrims rose from the plain, singing to unwearied Apollo who helps mortal men, who gives them light.

As I listened to the holy and cheerful note I rejoiced to be in this place, almost forgetting why I had come. Even Korydon became lighter of heart. 'For surely,' he said to me, 'the god is in this place, and in justice the god must help me to find my Kallirrhoe. And it is good that so many men come here, gathering from all the world – it is a place of meeting.'

XI

The Silver Singer

We retraced our steps and went up to the precincts of the sanctuary of Apollo, where pilgrims and strangers are permitted to pay homage and look about them. Here, as arranged, we met Aristotle and Diokles. I made sure that Korydon came too, as I had instruction from Aristotle to keep him under my eye. Diokles was full of enthusiasm, showing me the wonders of the place.

And the place *is* wonderful. I have never seen anything more impressive: even the Akropolis of Athens has not all this rich ornament. We had not gone five paces past the entrance before we were surrounded by statues made by the most noted figure-makers. My heart flowed with pride as I looked upon the great group of thirteen bronze statues – the work of Phidias when young. This shows the Athenian heroes with Athena and Apollo at their side. The statues of the Seven against Thebes offered to Apollo by the Argives are also admirable in their way, and I was interested to see a large model of the Wooden Horse of

Troy set up to commemorate a victory against the Spartans. But, oh – how my breast swelled with anger to see the Spartans' proud monument! They erected so as to dominate the very entrance to the Sacred Way the gigantic statues of their ugly admirals, flaunting their boasted defeat of Athens at the sea-battle of Aigospotami. But that had been seventy-four years ago!

'I *hate* the Spartans,' I said to Aristotle. 'It's all I can do not to go in and deface one of their smug slab-sided admirals. I'd like to take the smile off his face!'

'Many Athenians have felt so,' said Aristotle. 'But how do you think the Spartans felt at seeing the Arkadians, a few years later, put up their own votive statues to commemorate the victory over the Spartans at Leuktra? And in front of the Spartan monument, too! But the Spartans have let this monument against them go unspoiled. Impatience is dishonour to the god. The god is greater than Athens or Sparta or Arkadia. Truly, this is a great wonder of Delphi, that here all Greeks should come as equals, unmolested and under truce.'

'Well,' said Diokles, 'there were the Sacred Wars of course. But things are peaceful now, more or less. And you see how well the sanctuary has been rebuilt after the earthquake, despite the wars. The damaged statues have been buried, and new ones offered. Money has been given from all over Greece for the work – from the rich offerings of great kings to a few obols from poor widow-women in the depth of the country.'

'Yes,' said Aristotle. 'It would seem that the god has been trying to tell us something. Aristophanes in *Lysistrata* suggests that all Greeks should live in harmony and union, as men who worship the same gods.'

Aristotle seemed to be forgetting that he was not, strictly speaking, a Greek himself. Such remarks, especially uttered by a Makedonian, might be taken unkindly by some listeners. To change the subject, I asked Diokles about the earthquake damage, and he responded with minute illustration. Many great works had been destroyed, as well as the temple itself. Beautiful ornaments had gone at that time, including a famous bronze group, statues of horses, chariot and the charioteer, given by one of the tyrants of Syracuse to honour his own son Polyzalos, victor in a chariot-race. This admired piece, 'The Charioteer', which my own grandfather had beheld in his youth, had often been seen by Diokles when a boy. He remembered how these damaged statues, and other injured objects including gold tripods, had been reverently buried in the earth when the site for the new temple was cleared. No votive offering should be taken from its sanctuary and used for secular purpose, as it has been given to the god: to give to the god is to give once and for all. Yet one cannot allow damaged works to remain on view as offerings, for offerings to the god must be perfect – especially offerings to Apollo, god of the beautiful, of perfection and of art. So the very ground we were treading upon, the ground of Delphi, is secretly rich in vanished monuments. The dark earth harbours the brilliant Charioteer, vanished image of vanished Polyzalos, with so many other bright things – gone for ever, never to see the light of day, never again to be seen by the eyes of mortal men. But other fine things remain to delight men and gods, such as the paintings of Polygnotos which are a monument to all painters for the rest of time and the perpetual admiration of posterity.

We threaded Delphi's labyrinth of riches, with leisure to stare and wonder. The celebrated sculpture of the Chariot of the Sun seems to move with its four capering horses. Nearby, I admired the famous gold tripod put up by all the Greek cities who had repelled the Persians, and even more the three intertwining bronze snakes supporting it.

'Once,' Diokles explained, 'Delphi itself was the abode of a powerful snake, Pytho, slain by Apollo. Hence the whole area is called "Pythian" and Apollo's oracle here "the Pythia".'

'And so,' added Aristotle, 'my wife is named "Pythias", showing that Hermias honoured not only Apollo, lord of light, but the great Apollo of Delphi.'

Aristotle was at last able to show me the monument he had put up to Hermias of Atarneos – a whole statue, not in the Athenian section but in the area of shrines and monuments erected by the colonies and eastern islands.

Hermias was something of a mystery to me. All I knew was that Hermias, who was not high-born to begin with, had been a patron of philosophers and had ruled over a tiny state on the coast of Asia somewhere near Lydia, until he was overthrown by the Persians. This ruler was said to be the father (some said uncle) of Aristotle's wife Pythias. A few malicious Athenian tongues said she was neither daughter nor niece but Hermias' former concubine. Others more malicious still maintained he was a eunuch, incapable of enjoying concubines or producing daughters. (Naturally this was not a mystery into which I could enquire by applying to Aristotle for enlightenment.) The statue of Hermias – father or something of Aristotle's wife – showed him as reasonably handsome, if wearing that inert, almost cheerful, grimace so trying on the frozen face of the dead. His figure seemed rather squat and stubby. The plinth of the statue had been neatly carved with a paean in praise of Hermias.

'There it is, my poem,' said Aristotle, proudly and a bit shyly. 'What do you think?'

'Oh, it's very good,' I said, reading it. 'And very moral.' I read aloud:

'"O excellence in virtue, hard to win
For all the labouring race of mortal men,
Object of every search and chase,
Most beautiful of every prize of life.
For your lovely form,
  O Virgin,
  Virgin sweet,
Your beauteous form to gain
It were in Hellas glorious to die
Or to endure sharp unresting pain.

You who instil within the mind, heart, soul,
Such strength undying, more durable than gold,
Dearer than parents' love, sweeter than sleep
. . . So for your form admired
    and deep-desired,
Akhilleus and great Ajax sought the house of Hades.
And for you too the son of Atarneos
  Was widowed of day
  and lost the sun's bright beams,
For love of your dear shape . . ."

'I hadn't thought of virtue like that before,' I said

politely. 'Like a beautiful girl.' But I was really thinking how odd it was that Aristotle should praise this remote and vanquished tyrant. A man whom some called a whoremonger and others a eunuch, a man who had been executed like a common criminal stapled to a plank, killed by the treacherous Persians for treachery – that Aristotle should speak of this notorious failure as one bereft of the light of the sun for the love of that 'lovely form', that 'dear shape'. Aristotle wrote of virtue as Korydon spoke of Kallirrhoe.

Diokles led us back up to the Leskhe of the Knidians, the high brick building at the edge of the sanctuary that we had passed before, when we first came down the mountain. He was empowered to let us in, so we could enjoy Polygnotos' famous works. We sat and rested in this very fine meeting-place and looked at our leisure upon these paintings which retain their freshness after three or four generations of being looked at. The most celebrated picture shows the Fall of Troy. You can see Helen herself, and Nestor talking to Telemakhos; Neoptolemos is still eagerly killing Trojans, though the rest of the Greeks have stopped. (The painting was originally intended to stand above Neoptolemos' tomb.) The Greeks are preparing to sail away, their work completed. The beach is wonderfully done – you can see the pebbles under the waves by the shore. A very fine horse is just beginning to have a roll on the beach, disregarding human action and human grief.

But the most ambitious of the paintings is the large picture with scenes of the Underworld. I saw Orknos and the Ass. Aristotle insisted upon pointing them out to me straight away. But if some parts of this great scene are comic, the greater number are sombre, even grisly. Especially the picture of Eurynomos, a spirit of Hades who eats the flesh of the dead – so men of Delphi believe. This Eurynomos is portrayed with his own flesh blue and black, exactly the colour of flies that buzz about meat in the summer, or the colour of dead meat itself. (It reminded me too much of something hidden under a mound, and what must have happened to it. A man not made of silver, but changing colour and texture. And the vultures? The maggots?) This painting by Polygnotos makes you think a lot about the dead. At one place in the gigantic picture of the Underworld you can see Odysseus talking to the shades. Very much alive, Odysseus stands over the pit, speaking to the dead prophet Tiresias and to his poor mother.

'That's a part of the *Odyssey* I find hard to read,' I remarked to Aristotle, 'when Odysseus tries to throw his arms around his mother and can't – because she's only a shade.'

'I know that episode,' Aristotle said:

> '"Thrice I tried as my heart led me to clasp her in my arms,
> Thrice she drifted away from my arms like a shadow or a dream."

'My own mother,' Aristotle added, somewhat inconsequentially, 'died when I was eight. And my father when I was sixteen.'

We fell silent as we gazed at this lively picture of the Underworld. You can see the River Akheron with fish in it, very shadowy, like the shades of fish. Below, Odysseus

Theseus and Perithoös look helplessly at their useless swords; they are enthroned on rock which has grown about them and you can see they cannot move. Paris – one can tell he is the sort always interested in women, wherever he is – is trying to attract the attention of Penthesileia, the Amazon Queen, who disdains him. Aktaion can be seen with his mother and a deer. Below these sit the ill-fated dead musicians: Orpheus holding a harp and leaning against a willow tree; Pelias, blinded, with his broken lyre. Wretched Marsyas, who challenged Apollo in musicianship, lost the contest and was flayed for his pains, is shown (with his skin back on) still playing on his flute even in Hades.

I wish I could remember all these pictures better, though I hope to see them again. After our rest, we walked back down the path to the area beside the grand temple itself. We saw the very grave of Neoptolemos, by the temple near the great outdoor altar. The Delphians burn offerings to Neoptolemos every year. Some say this son of Akhilleus was murdered by Orestes, but most say he was killed by a priest of Apollo, or by Apollo himself. Very foolishly, this rash son of a rash father was trying to raid the temple of the god. Near to Neoptolemos' grave is the very stone which was given to Kronos by Rhea to prevent him swallowing her last child, the infant Zeus, as he had devoured her other children. So she gave him the stone, wrapped in a cloth, and Kronos vomited it up again and it fell in Delphi. I had always wanted to see it, though I was disappointed when I did. The stone is so small that one wonders how it can have choked a god. But it is highly polished, as every day the people of Delphi pour oil upon it.

So we went about, seeing the marvels of the place, among crowds of other pilgrims. (Travellers don't usually mention this, but it is often so in public places, and one may not see a building or a statue or a painting perfectly because of other people's heads being in the way.)

Delphi was crowded, and full of fine sights. I do remember admiring the Siphnian Treasury, in marble of Paros, a truly old building but very fine. Here the figures of young girls act as columns – a device used later in our own Erekhtheion at Athens. The friezes here show the judgment of Paris – Aphrodite looks just as she would in life – and part of the Trojan War, as well as the battle between Gods and Giants. Everywhere, in fact, one sees famous events celebrated in stone that seems almost to move and breathe. So well carved and painted the stone becomes like living flesh, but more permanent and beautiful. And there are wonderfully painted friezes, frescoes, all showing that the power of poetry is not confined to words. The Treasury of the Athenians has a beautiful frieze of the battle between Theseus and the Amazons. Antiope, very graceful, sinks beneath the onslaught of the hero, and on Theseus' face is a kind of stern pity already changing into love.

'There are also friezes at Epidauros and Olympia of the Gigantomakhia and the battle against the Amazons,' said Aristotle. 'Very popular subjects for large buildings.'

'And paintings, too,' I said, remembering Athens. 'But I suppose it is because large scenes of action with many figures are best suited to such places.'

'Yes. And they also represent the triumph of intelligence over brutish force and wild instinct, which the building itself represents. Now, these friezes are just right, as they are various and intricate yet of a size to be taken in with the eye – just as a good literary plot, while it cannot consist of a tiny episode, must be of a length which memory can retain.'

'But,' objected Diokles, 'does not that mean opinion might differ – and justly? The man with good eyesight can see more of a large and high frieze than a man with weaker eyes. And the man with an extraordinary capacious memory might relish a plot which others couldn't follow.'

'No, no,' said Aristotle. 'That is cavilling, for we are speaking of men with merely normal eyesight – for whom the artist designs his works – and of men with a normal memory. True, men learn more about the arts during the course of time. Polygnotos was a great painter. It was he who introduced transparent drapery, and men who speak. More than that, he created much more expressive faces than any artist before him. But no painter nowadays would create murals so crowded with various figures and actions. Meaning requires unity. If a story is full of mere episodes, then the story is mistakenly planned, and no one should be required to recall such wandering parts.'

'But,' said I, 'there is the case of the *Odyssey*. You yourself say most of that is episodes, and yet everyone likes it.'

'*I* think,' said Korydon, still looking at the frieze of the Amazons, 'that the unity is less important than a good meaning. It is not much of a victory to make war on women! At least, I wouldn't mind making war on Queen Ada – but then, her army would be men, you know. But I would not fight a woman who looked like that!' And he pointed to the graceful Antiope.

Diokles looked repressively at our insolent if handsome slave, but Aristotle only laughed.

'You think the piece is dissonant in effect? It brings together the ideas of love and death in what you feel to be an unpleasant fashion? Console yourself with the story that Theseus married Antiope.'

We had now wandered again by the Athenian Treasury, where we had been yesterday before we encountered the mother of 'Kleobis and Biton', and before meeting Diokles. 'Here, at least,' I said, looking at the Treasury and back at the colonnade housing the spoils which Athens had won from the Persians, 'we see the advantage of right rule and alliances. And citizens standing together against the enemy.' I felt proud to see how handsome and grand the Athenian monuments are, what a commanding spot we had in Delphi. 'And so much rich treasure and great art!' I waved my hand towards it all.

'Yes, indeed,' said Diokles cheerfully. 'If you come along this way, now, you can see the famous stream of Kastalia, the Spring of Apollo.'

'And so we should,' said Aristotle.

'But I want to see some of the Athenian things –' I said, biting off the word 'again'.

'Diokles will think we care for nothing that is not Athenian – when we have all Delphi before us,' said Aristotle.

It struck me that perhaps Aristotle did not want me looking again at the silver singer or talking about Lysippos in front of Diokles. Perhaps he feared I might say too much.

'Oh, well,' I said, turning away with them. 'There is so

much to see, Diokles of Delphi, I can return to this Treasury again tomorrow.' I really did wish to look again at Lysippos' little statue of Straton, even though it was sad. Yet this place certainly did not seem designed for sad thoughts, here at the high centre of the world, in this clear air, with the sense of power all about us. Above temple and sanctuary the two great stone peaks, the Shining Ones, glowed in the afternoon sun, almost as bright as a silver image.

As we followed Diokles through troops of strangers I looked about the crowds constantly, to see if I could catch sight of anyone I knew, or anyone who looked like the girl Anthia or the slave-girl Kallirrhoe as they had been described – but all were strangers. The unknown people looked at us too. At least, many of them looked at Korydon. Heads turned in his direction. I overhead comments on 'that handsome slave-boy', and watched Korydon's ears turn red. It struck me that to go about with the lad was to make ourselves conspicuous.

Diokles, chattering unceasingly and pointing out the sights, was as good as his word, leading us from the sanctuary entrance directly to the stream. The spring of Kastalia gushes out between two rocks, and the water is clear and cool and delicious. This is the site for ritual purification. The Pythia drinks of Kastalia at the fount, and bathes in it in a hidden place, for purification, but everyone may drink from the stream as it bubbles on. I suppose most of the water in Delphi must flow ultimately from this sacred stream which comes so mysteriously through a mountain.

While we were beside this Kastalian fountain, Diokles related to us the story of Kharila, a young girl who, it was said, came to Delphi once in time of famine, and begged for food when it was being distributed.

'She was refused, alas, poor girl,' said Diokles with the impressive paternal sadness people use in relating sad stories that happened centuries ago. 'So in her despair young Kharila came to the grove by the sacred stream, and hanged herself. The people of Delphi were horrified, and the gods rebuked them. So now there is the festival of Kharila, when offerings of bread and lentils are made. And,' he added, 'we of Delphi never again have turned away any stranger or pilgrim who comes in peace, but give food and lodgings to all.'

'Most still pay for food and lodgings, however,' said Aristotle, amused, 'or Delphi would be the poorest of cities. Which is far from the case!' He and Diokles laughed.

Young Korydon paid no attention to this jesting. He was evidently much struck with the tale; his hands clenched and his face was white and tense.

'That is a dreadful story. She *hanged* herself? Poor Kharila! There *must* be more to her story! Perhaps she was attacked by ruffians, and they killed her. Or she was held in captivity until her courage failed. Or she had been raped, and killed herself because of that – which is the greatest cause for a woman to end her own life. Probably she was murdered by a wicked man! For it is no easy matter to hang oneself, surely. I expect she *was* murdered, and the villain escaped.'

He flared at us with a most unmeek demeanour, looking accusingly at Diokles. Our host shrugged in comic amusement at this tiresome slave, and turned aside. I heard him say to Aristotle, 'He's a beautiful boy, but . . .'

Korydon was definitely an embarrassment, especially as he wasn't really our slave anyway. At any moment an infuriated master might be coming after him and suing us for theft. Our 'theft' was indeed quite remarkable. You couldn't call Korydon a common household object.

Next day, still in the charge of Diokles, we went to the festival. There is always rejoicing when the god returns after his three months' absence, but this time was more impressive than usual, for now Apollo's home was newly ready for him at last – after more than forty years. The new and very large statue of gold and ivory was brought in a triumphal car, carried by men and boys and decked with garlands and branches. The statue, which would stay in the *adyton*, the secret recess, was to be carried by chosen men and boys. These favoured ones led the procession after the god himself. Then came other citizens of Delphi, accompanied by special delegations from the cities of the League. Up the Sacred Way to the temple the procession went singing. The temple itself was purified with water and fire and prayers invoking the presence of the god. Then the first sacrifice of the season was offered, upon Lord Apollo's return. The rest of us, the crowd of visitors, were the audience and stood without. Except for the delegates of the League, the Delphic procession is for the citizens alone. Diokles, with what I must imagine was a good deal of manoeuvring, had managed to find good standing places for Aristotle and myself, near the temple wall. Korydon, as our slave, had to stay outside the sanctuary; he would be allowed to enter later.

Even to slaves there were memorials in this place. The very wall against which we stood was covered with writing – the names of slaves freed by Apollo. In Delphi every stone is to be read, and everything has a meaning. Just below the place where we stood that day are two great rough rocks. The first is the one from which the Sybil had prophesied in most ancient days, before Apollo came. The second is the rock whereon Leto herself stood at Apollo's first coming, whence she called to her son to kill the earth-monster, Pytho. These rocks, rough and irregular among the polished stones and ornate buildings, look as if they had come pulled by the gods' hands, up from the depth of earth or down from the topmost point of the universe. It gave me a shiver of awe to see the very rock on which Leto, mother of divine Apollo, stood – and to see it just as we celebrated this year the return of the god himself among us.

Cymbals and flutes made a high crashing music, intoxicating in the blood, a sound combined with the mooing and roaring of the sacrificial beasts. The priest's chant sounded forth, and the choir of boys responded with the ancient song, in voices which echoed from the Shining Ones and filled all Delphi and the gorge of Pleistos with the holy sound. I felt I had come to one of the best moments it is given to mortal men to know.

'Truly,' I said to Aristotle, after a space, 'I am thankful that we have come. I feel life is going to be better somehow. Being in Delphi in the presence of the god at the turn of the year – it is like being inside an everlasting Spring.'

'But,' said Aristotle – and he nodded upwards to the tall column supporting the votive marble Sphinx given by the Naxians – 'we haven't solved our riddle yet.' The Sphinx smiled on. I was disconcertingly reminded of Oidipous, the ill-fated ruler of Thebes, who had sent to Delphi with such unhappy results. I thought of Oidipous' grim crossroads and of Ammonios' stout inert body. (What had happened to it?)

'Perhaps,' said Aristotle, 'the Sphinx's questions are answered by the sayings first inscribed on the temple itself: "Know Thyself" and "Nothing in Excess". Apollo says we are to know ourselves – a very hard command. We know who we are – we think – but we do not know what we may be. And if a man doesn't fully know himself, how can he fully know another? The poets pretend to know, but they fully know only men they themselves create. Tragedy, it is true, usually deals with historical persons, and often with what has manifestly happened. Yet different poets give different accounts of the same persons. Aiskhylos and Euripides created different Elektras, for instance. Who is the real Elektra?'

'Presumably,' said Diokles, who had come to join us, 'the gods know men better than we know ourselves or each other. That is why Apollo, who cares for us, has given us his voice here in Delphi. Because of him the Pythia knows what has passed, is passing, and is to come. The Pythia also knows – through the inspiration of Apollo – a harder thing: the hearts of men. That you know through the true stories of old. Such as the story of Kalonodas Korax, who killed Arkhilokhos the bitter-tongued poet. When Kalonodas later came to Delphi, the prophetess had never seen him before and did not know his name. But as soon as he came to the sacred cell, she shrieked, "Begone, you who have slain the servant of the Muses! Leave the temple, which you defile!" The Pythia knew him for a killer, though his very companions were ignorant of the fact – because the gods know all things. Wherefore Apollo assists us, that we may be wiser.'

'Whether men *do* become wiser is a question,' said Aristotle thoughtfully. 'The poets may be given some credit as mundane prophets, though not without inspiration from Apollo and the Muses. They are most philosophical teachers. For they teach us what men are like, and what they do, what patterns are to be found in human existence. The unforgettable thing about Tragedy – and it is present even in Comedy – is Ignorance. Ignorance reminds us of our true condition. Discovery is most important in the plot of fiction. That is because we know that discovery is important in life. We spend our days coming to know something we didn't know before. Discovery moves us from ignorance to knowledge. Or we move ourselves towards knowledge, perpetually changing and perpetually changed. All memorable stories have in them the divine element of piercing recognition. And recognition usually accompanies a change, a reversal. So in the story you told us of Kalonodas, when he found he was known for what he was. So in the tale of Kharila, when the Delphians realised the meaning of their act, and knew themselves through what they had done.'

'So we may spend our days in being discovered, rather than in making discoveries,' I blurted out. I wished I hadn't said that. Fortunately, Diokles saw it only as a joke, and laughed his jolly laugh.

'Speaking of discoveries,' he said, 'have you, Aristotle, found anything of interest in our records of the Pythian Games?'

'Yes, indeed,' said Aristotle. 'In fact, it would seem to me to be possible to clear up questions of dating and years, so as to rectify the Delphic and Athenian calendars by each other. I think I should like to go to Kirrha for a day, to look at a monument I have heard of. You, Diokles, will be busy tomorrow conducting pilgrims, but Stephanos and I can make the journey together.'

'Well, well,' said Diokles. 'Kirrha? Why not. Though you'll find it a small place compared with Delphi. Now, of course, it will be full of pilgrims and strangers. As it will be a while before you will be able to consult the Oracle, you might as well make the most of your time in these parts. Kirrha certainly has its attractions,' he added jokingly. 'Not just ships and old stones – but the best brothels in Phokis, so they tell me.'

'One never knows when information might come in useful,' murmured Aristotle.

By this time the festival sacrifices were over, and the procession had dispersed. Those who had been kept outside the sanctuary, chiefly slaves and women, were allowed to enter. I went outside the sanctuary walls to find Korydon, who had been pushed far off by the human tide. I told him, as Aristotle had bidden, that we were to go to Kirrha on the morrow, and Korydon nodded impatiently. He was frowning and seemed preoccupied. Crowds of strangers surged about us. It still seemed extraordinary to me that there could be so many people, and that I wouldn't know them. In Athens there are crowds at times, but at home one knows everybody. I heard varieties of spoken Greek – Phokian chiefly, and Boiotian, but also the rough dialect of Sparta, the guttural accents of the south-west Peloponnesos, and the fluting Greek of the islands and of Ionia. I remembered that Anthia would speak pure Attic, and that the slave girl Kallirrhoe would have an accent just like Korydon's.

People pressed and jostled in the congested paths,

good-humouredly on the whole as everyone was in holiday temper. On the way back up the hill towards the gate of the sanctuary, I myself nearly bumped into a little man going in the other direction. This man, who rejoiced in a great brown beard as wide and long as his face, was talking to a friend – his proxenos, presumably – with such passionate earnestness that he didn't watch where he was going. He moved along sideways like a crab, his hand clutching his friend's robe.

'Yes, I quite understand –' the Delphian tried to detach himself – 'but you must wait your turn.'

'I didn't come just to *wait*. My case is urgent! I've come all this way, leaving my tombstones to shift for themselves, for the purpose. Here I am, thirty-five, and I haven't had any yet – and no sign of it! We're not getting any younger.'

'Yes, yes,' said the proxenos again. 'I know your purpose in consulting the Oracle, and I will see –'

'Thirty-five – not a day younger. No children yet! Not even a bastard I can call my own, let alone one by poor Kreusa. And me with a beard that the birds could nest in! And her with a bosom like a pair of lamps! I don't understand it. There's something that's not being done right. Apollo can tell us what it is, and how to fill our cradle – and I'll give him the best goat in Delphi, just for the chance of asking.'

There seemed no doubt as to the purpose of this tomb-maker's visit to Delphi, at all events. It suddenly struck me for the first time that everyone here – or nearly everyone – must have come on some personal mission. Everybody had something to ask the god, either about public matters, such as the founding of a colony, or about his – or even her – private affairs. The road to Delphi was made of hopes and questions. I began to think seriously about my own forthcoming consultation with the Oracle – forthcoming, owing to the enthusiastic assistance of Diokles, Aristotle's proxenos and now mine. An interview with the Pythia was not to be undertaken lightly. I realised that I really *did* want to ask about marriage, now that I would be granted the opportunity.

As we moved on through the crowds of pilgrims somebody bumped into me, and trod on my foot. It was a slender youth, slightly stooped, though nothing of the tallest. His tread was heavy enough. 'Sorry, sir.' The face was pointed, browned with sun and wind, thatched with thick dark hair, though a cloak hid part of his head, as if the weather were colder than it was. It was a young face and not hard-featured, that I caught a glimpse of, but there was something I didn't like about it – something odd, impish or malicious. The black eyes looked both curious and mocking. The youth turned quickly and disappeared among the throng, but I felt uneasy. That face reminded me of something, I could not say what exactly. And the voice reminded me of something equally indefinite. I found myself thinking of Orestes, which was no help. Though it was a curious consideration which Aristotle had raised yesterday. Who was the *real* Elektra? Who was the *real* Orestes? And what had Orestes actually looked like? Probably not excessively good-looking, or the Athenians might not have been so stand-offish.

I hastened to catch up with Korydon. We pushed our way back through the sanctuary gate and up the path to the Athenian Treasury, where Aristotle and Diokles were standing. I stopped to have another reassuring look at my city's monuments and treasures. There they all were – the things I had seen yesterday. The statues, and the Leto cup and the ivory and silver figure –

'Look!' I said, horrified, and pointed. The rich offering of Lysippos was still there. But the singer was sightless: one eye was punched in and darkened, the other removed completely. A great scratch ran along the tinted ivory face, and down the silver body was a deep and ugly gouge. The silver hair and ornaments were scratched also. The silver lyre had been sundered from the hand that held it, and lay useless on the ground, its strings torn.

The figure looked very odd, the gouge over the sightless eye giving it a squinting and raffish look. The deep scratch looked like a scar from the wars. The silver singer now seemed slightly piratical. Metamorphosed, he looked as if he had flung the lyre down in a fit of pique or spite. Nothing had been stolen or taken away, yet the elegant figure had been completely defaced. It was now hurt, like something suffering. Worse still, it was now ridiculous.

Diokles stopped to look, and gasped with dismay. He picked up the image, and we were all shocked to see another deep scratch, or rather a veritable hole or pit, in the ivory back, between the imitated shoulder-blades.

'Dear me! This must be removed at once,' said Diokles. 'I must inform our arkhon, and the Athenian delegation. There must be some enquiry. I beg of you to keep the matter quiet – we do not want visitors upset at the time of the festival when so many are here. Meanwhile, this will have to be disposed of.'

'Couldn't anything be done to repair . . . ?' I began, foolishly.

'No, no!' said Diokles. 'Imperfect offerings must not be exhibited before the god. Once damaged, it is gone for ever. We shall have to bury it. I will take it away to one of the priests in charge.'

He went off, carrying the defaced statue muffled in his cloak, gently and sorrowfully as if he held some sick animal. '*Who* could have done such a thing?' I asked Aristotle in a low voice as we moved away so as not to attract attention to the incident. 'It must have been some of those Spartans, don't you think?'

'No. I don't think this was a political action. Not in that way. Did you notice the position of the wounds on the statue? Significant. Do you not think so?' He looked at me with speaking glance. Of course, Aristotle did not want to speak of Straton's death and corpse in hearing of the Delphians. Nor did I. But I too realised there was something sickeningly familiar about the position of the wounds. I nodded to show I understood.

'Someone must have seen what we saw,' I remarked. 'And – well, copied it.'

'Exactly. An imitation of life. "Life" being not quite the right word in this case.'

'Someone who has come on the same road. Someone not right in the mind, perhaps. Or someone who hates Lysippos. Poor Lysippos! As if he had not sorrows enough. But whoever did this is tempting the wrath of Apollo, and the ill fate of it will fall on his head. That lovely statue is gone – gone for good, away from the sight of men. The silver singer will be lost for ever in the dark ground, like the poor man's own sons.'

XII

The Brothel at Kirrha

The little port of Kirrha is not a great distance from Delphi. The first part of the way to it is almost straight down the mountain. We had been provided with two mules by the kindly Diokles; I thought guiltily of our lost horses. Thus handsomely mounted we rode, with Korydon walking beside us looking distracted and noble despite the mud and dust that settled upon his legs. After the downhill plunge we came to the plain that stretches below Parnassos to the water's edge. This plain, consecrated to Apollo, is not allowed to be cultivated; only bushes and wild olives grow there. Ahead of us we could smell the sea. Once the going got easier, I sent Korydon on ahead, out of earshot. This was my chance for a conversation with Aristotle, the first time we had been alone since we arrived in crowded hospitable Delphi.

'We have done nothing about Anthia,' I reminded the philosopher. 'We have been thinking about Apollo – it is as if we had forgotten our mission. And I have been working out the problem in my mind.'

'A very good way to work on problems,' said Aristotle. 'What is your result?'

'Believing that Anthia was really abducted – and we know from Korydon (pretty well) that we were right about that litter – then it follows that someone other than ourselves was also in pursuit. That would be most likely Straton, coming to avenge and rescue his cousin. The Abductor then killed Straton at that hill and then proceeded on his way.'

'That all makes sense – at least, in some important respects. Continue?'

'The person most likely to abduct Anthia – in hopes of fulfilling the marriage – would be Polemon. Polemon has been trained as a soldier and is in excellent condition. It would be possible for him to kill even young Straton. And Polemon would have the strength of arm to kill Ammonios with the boar-spear thrust at close quarters. But – *why* would Polemon kill Ammonios, who was his own kinsman? The only thing that occurs to me is that Polemon used Ammonios as his agent in some fashion and then fell out with him. Unless Ammonios was simply killed by bandits –'

'No. Don't forget the valuables left with Ammonios. And aren't you forgetting the mysterious burial of Straton?'

'That is something that would make sense only if a relative killed him! And then buried him in proper fashion to atone. There are only a few possibilities, then. It's like some horrible game with but a few pieces to move. Straton was the Abductor and was killed by his kinswoman Anthia. Or –'

'Or?' Aristotle prompted me. 'Or by somebody else?'

'A dreadful thought, Aristotle – I hardly like to express it. But – what if Lysippos were the relative? After killing his own son, he then buried him. That would make Lysippos the Abductor and Straton act as Avenger. Absurd! Impossible anyway – we saw Lysippos the day after Anthia disappeared. No. It would make better sense if Polemon were the Abductor and killed Straton. Then Anthia piously insisted on burying Straton properly, like an Antigone. But – *where* is Anthia?'

'You have been thinking to some purpose,' Aristotle admitted. 'Somewhere in this knot the truth does lie. But I have the feeling that we are missing some pieces of your game. Something that worries me is the mutilation of the silver statue. Whoever did that has much hatred – and presumably not only knows that Straton, the beautiful original of the statue, is dead, but *how* he looked when dead.'

'Yes, we noted the placement of the wounds. But – oh! Then – the murderer is in Delphi!'

'Certainly, that must be so. The murderer is in Delphi – or was there yesterday.'

We were both struck into silence by this idea. Thoughtfully we proceeded past the great walls, built by giants of old time. Soon we beheld the sea close by, ruffling under a light spring breeze.

Kirrha (or as some call it 'new Kirrha', as the old harbour town was razed by Delphi in the first of the Sacred Wars) is a little place curled close round its harbour, something like Peiraieus, though much smaller. The soil above it is of a strange purple-brown colour; tin has been mined in this region from time to time. We went first to the anchorage, attracted by the row of ships bobbing at their ease in the roads. Their passengers were presumably now all in Delphi. A few ship-masters and some sailors were to be seen, but most of the men seemed to have gone off to see Delphi or to taste the pleasures of Kirrha itself.

After a perfunctory glance at the monument he had claimed he wished to see (a stone stele near the anchorage) Aristotle turned back into the winding ways among the white houses clustered about the harbour. I remembered that Orestes, according to some authorities, had stayed in Kirrha for a long time, visiting his friend Strophios the Phokian, father of Pylades. It was during his visit to Kirrha that the unfortunate young man consulted the Oracle and learned of his horrid task, that he must kill not only his mother's paramour but his mother Klytaimnestra herself. I wondered if the house Orestes had stayed in was still standing, and which it was, if so, and whether people would like to dwell in a house which that unfortunate son once lived in.

Kirrha is not a large town, but it has small inns and shops. Most of the shops sell a jumble of things – baskets, skeins, hides, used nails. I saw Aristotle look sharply into the little booths that sold jewels and ornaments, second-hand for the most part. Once I caught him looking intently at a tarnished bracelet hanging on a rusty nail, and nodding – but he said nothing to the shopkeeper, or to myself and Korydon. Taverns were doing a brisk business, and groups of men sat in the cool spring sun. Some of the men were singing strange songs from far away, and the singing was not disagreeable even though the voices were rough.

And then I saw the face of someone I knew. An undoubted Athenian sat outside one of these taverns, by himself, gazing into the distance with those bulging eyes of his, all his dusty freckles unkindly pointed out by the fresh sunshine, as motes of dust show in a sunbeam.

'Glaukon of Athens? This is a happy meeting!' Aristotle sounded unusually warm and friendly. Glaukon raised his dull eyes.

'Well, I didn't expect to see *you*,' he said. Then, to make amends for his ungraciousness, he smiled, but the smile cost him some work. 'Aristotle, and Stephanos – how do you do? I've just arrived. I was not well on the ship, and here I am, recovering.'

A strong man overcome by seasickness, I thought scornfully. (At that time, I had never been to sea.) Aristotle, more sympathetic, became at once the physician.

'Dear, dear! Did you puke a great deal while at sea, then?' Glaukon nodded ruefully. 'Oh, it can be a distressing thing for the head and stomach. Have you stopped being ill now? Is your head clearing?' Glaukon nodded again. 'Try to eat as soon as you can – not too much at a time. An egg, perhaps with a bit of bread. A little wine and water might be good for you. Let us buy you a drink now.'

'Thank you, but no.' Glaukon shook his head feebly.

'You must have taken the *Leda* from Athens. I know the captain –'

'No, no,' said Glaukon. 'I came on another one – over there.' He nodded in the direction of the anchorage.

'Well, we hope to see you in better plight soon,' said Aristotle. 'Have you come to consult the Oracle? Yes?

Well, leave everything to me. I have an excellent proxenos and can make the arrangements and send for you here. Have you friends with you? No? Well, the men of Kirrha are hospitable to strangers, especially to silversmiths like yourself. We must be going. I'm supposed to be looking at monuments – my study of the Pythian records, you know. But we will certainly see you at Delphi, when we consult the Oracle.'

Aristotle bustled away, very cheerfully. I wondered at his being so chattering and officious in his concern for a man who was scarcely a friend, and by no means particularly amiable. The philosopher went quickly down a side street and made a turn so that we were, to my surprise, soon by the harbour again. Once there, Aristotle made enquiries and found the only ships from Athens – the *Leda* and the *Kastor*. The first he ignored, but he managed to find the master of the *Kastor* still on board and engaged him in conversation, asking about the passage home. We were told that the *Kastor* would be leaving in a week, and that she was a good ship.

'You must remember a passenger from Athens this last voyage,' said Aristotle. 'Freckle-faced man with pale hair, name of Glaukon. Monstrously seasick.'

'Never heard of the fellow,' said the master testily. 'Nor saw no one answering that description. As for seasick – there was two women and a slave ill the first morning, but everybody else was as fit as beans.'

Aristotle repeated his praise of the vessel, and sweetened the interview with a small present of money.

'So much for that,' he said to me. 'Seek safety in wood,' he added cryptically. We went on back into Kirrha.

Once you've started meeting people you know, the

process seems to go on for a while, as if things happen in clumps, or in rows like a bed of greens. So it was with us now. We were in a different street from the one in which we had met Glaukon, a wider street with better shops, and ornamental jars outside the tavern doors. We were riding slowly on our reluctant mules past one of these taverns, a large house set back from the road with a courtyard extending from middle to street. The courtyard had vines planted along it, which would be pretty later, and it was unusually crowded with a number of men sitting on benches and drinking. Just on the outer edge of this yard we saw another Athenian acquaintance – in most unusual circumstances. Polemon the ephebe, whom I hadn't seen since the night of the Silent Dinner, was standing at the edge of the tavern yard. Just standing there and – oddly – singing. His clothes were dusty and needed mending, and he himself looked travel-stained and weary, with dust in his golden-brown hair. Yet he still looked handsome and sang lustily, an old hunting-song.

> 'My boar-spear it is mighty
> It's dealt with two today . . .'

The revellers picked up the refrain, between eating fish and talking. Some thumped their pots on a table or bench in time to the music. A shower of little coins rained thinly upon Polemon. At the end of his song he stooped to pick them up – and saw us. He blushed violently.

'Why – what a –' I began.

'Hush!' Polemon said quickly. 'I'll be with you in a minute.'

I could tell from the embarrassed way he looked at us

that he did not desire us to address him by name. We dismounted and stood quietly on the other side of the road until he came over to us.

'Polemon!' I exclaimed. 'What on earth are you doing?' I had lowered my voice, but could not contain my astonishment at the sight of a well-bred young soldier, the pride of a noble house, singing for hemi-obols to a crowd of commonplace strangers in a tavern.

'We know what we are, but we don't know what we may be,' said Aristotle. 'This is a recognition – and a reversal. So, your boar-spear is mighty, is it?'

'Have you any friends with you?' I asked carefully. The reference to the boar-spear reminded me of the grisly death of Ammonios. Polemon might have murdered Straton and Ammonios, and hidden Anthia, his plighted bride (as he would think of her) somewhere in Kirrha. In that case this golden young man would have confederates nearby. Dangerous. Yet we might find Anthia. 'Take us to your lodging – we can talk with you there,' I suggested.

'There isn't any lodging. You see,' said Polemon, still blushing, 'it is so stupid! I set out from Athens on the Day of the Pots. I went on a journey to Delphi because I wanted to see the dedication of the new Temple of Apollo. And the journey has become a nightmare! I lost – I mean, my money, most of it, was lost on the way here.'

'You mean you lost it at a brothel or gaming house?'

Polemon reddened. 'Something like that. And now I have no money, and need to pay to go back by ship. A terrible thing has happened,' he went on, almost in a whisper. 'My – my second cousin was found dead, and the body must be taken home by sea for proper family burial. I need the money for that reason, you see. For transporting the body. I couldn't think of any other way to – to earn it. I've sold my ornaments already.'

'*Whose* body?' demanded Aristotle.

'Ammonios. Dreadful. He was attacked on the road to Delphi. At the Split, where the road turns and divides. The attacker must have robbed him of his clothes, too, and dressed him in coarse garments, like some pedlar. There was a perfume-seller's bag by his body, with perfume and such things in it. Very strange. So bad for the whole family! I was on my way here, to the consecration festival, and found out about the murder as I travelled. People had found the body on the road and put it in an old tower with someone to watch it, while they looked to find who knew it. Of course Ammonios was my responsibility then. One must have justice! But we don't want vile rumours to get out. I didn't know what to do. I took off the strange clothes and threw away the bag of things, so he wouldn't look like a pedlar any more. I didn't want the family to be embarrassed by such a strange discovery, so I've brought the corpse all this way, to Kirrha.'

Aristotle looked at him sharply. 'You're taking a deal of trouble for this citizen,' he observed.

Polemon blushed deeply. 'Ammonios is – was – he was *very* good to me when I was young. We were very close.'

'I see,' said Aristotle. 'Such a faithful attachment does you credit. And you think, if I'm not mistaken, that Ammonios had – let us call them business connections – in Boiotia that you would as soon not have associated with his death?'

Polemon nodded. 'He has – had – associates in the brothels along the way. And sometimes people in those places do strange things –'

'They do. I take it you stayed in one of those places. Proceed with your sad narrative – dilating, if you like, on your experiences as a tavern-singer.'

'It's dreadful! They are so vulgar! But I need money very badly. Here I am in Kirrha, with the corpse, and no money to take it home with. I've had to pay for housing Ammonios while we wait for a ship – I mean, while *I* do.'

'Wouldn't it be better to arrange a cremation here?'

'That's costly, too. Though something will have to be done soon, he's getting so bloated and stinking. But the family in Athens would want to know how he died – and the Basileus too, I should think. The thing is – this was *murder*!'

'Yes, I see. Cremation leaves no trace behind, destroys too many signs. One might suggest,' added Aristotle, 'a box lined with lead, and some strong wine to pickle him in. These might answer.'

'But no captain would want to take *that* aboard,' I objected.

'As an alternative,' said Aristotle, 'perhaps you should inform the arkhons of Kirrha, or rather of Krissos, which has the jurisdiction here. Ask the Basileus to take complete notes of the condition of the body, the nature and site of the wound, and so on. And give your testimony as to the finding of it. Then whatever happens the case can be pursued.' I noticed that Aristotle said nothing at all about our own early viewing of the dead Ammonios or our knowledge of his death.

'If only I knew *who* had done it,' said Polemon. 'But the killers must have come on horseback. *Two* killers. There were prints of hooves near where the body was found, and two horses were found wandering loose in the hills. The people in a village nearby caught one of the animals. Some of the villagers saw the riders – one young, one old. We might trace the murderers through the horses, and the villagers' identification. Meanwhile, I have poor Ammonios' body. And as I said, it's not getting any fresher.'

'Best to throw it into the sea,' I said heartlessly. Polemon gave me a disgusted look.

'You are right, it is a serious matter,' Aristotle said to Polemon. 'I am very sorry. Accept a loan from me – as a friend of the family, and a fellow Athenian? See to it that the body is handled with all proper care and reverence. And buy yourself some new clothes. Why not consult the Oracle about your trouble? Purify yourself from corpse-pollution and come to Delphi. I shall send word to you about a place to stay, and about the arrangement for consulting the Oracle. I will send a message to the ship, the *Kastor*. Do take this now – only as a loan.'

Polemon hesitated, and then, bowing gracefully, took the money that Aristotle held out to him. He took his leave next, and was about to set off. There were cries of indignation from the tavern crowd when they saw Polemon departing. One of the men – and not the smallest of them either – trotted over to us.

'Now then,' he said angrily, grasping Polemon's arm. His other gigantic hand clutched Aristotle by the cloak. 'Don't take our singer away. We'd just got him nicely in tune and set going. He's good for another six songs or so.'

'Sorry,' said Aristotle, trying to draw his garment back from the fellow's clutch. 'You have slaves, surely, and others who will sing to you?'

'Ah, yes – but we're tired of those. And most of them

are otherwise employed at the moment. So many ships in. This is the Brothel of Haimon, d'you see, which some call Haimon's Haven. It's one of the best and busiest in Phokis. Not but what Haimon himself is an Athenian – or he was. And some calls this place the Athenian Treasury. Not so much along of the owner and his wares as because Athenian visitors lay their treasure here.' He laughed. 'You let that fellow stay and sing, and likely there'll be a treat for you in it when we're all done, in the slack time of the afternoon.' He turned to Polemon. 'Sing, boy, sing!'

'That young man is tired,' said Aristotle, 'and he has business to attend to. But I can offer you a fresh singer, for a little while – the slave here, who has a beautiful voice.'

The man looked at Korydon, and slowly grinned. 'To match his face? Come looking for a job to hire him out to, have you? You've come to the right shop. He does look fresher than the other. We'll give you a try, lad. Sing something.'

He dragged Korydon over to the yard. We followed. The other man still kept a grip on Polemon. 'This is dangerous,' I whispered to Aristotle. 'Suppose they want to keep Korydon?' Korydon looked confused and angry. 'He won't like that at all.'

'Sing, boy,' said the insistent man. He thrust a pot of wine mixed with rather muddy water into the slave's hand. 'Cheer up, we're not a funeral party,' he added facetiously, chucking Korydon under the chin. The lad stood grave and immobile – it seemed like taking a liberty with one of the statues of Phidias.

'Sing, now,' said Aristotle, with quiet urgency. 'There's that song you know of, my lad, isn't there? "When I saw you . . ."' He began to hum.

Seeing nothing for it, his face wrathful, but with puzzled eyes fixed on Aristotle, the boy began to sing, quite loudly,

> 'When I saw you in the dancing
> Kallirrhoe, Kallirrhoe . . .'

He hadn't quite got through the first verse when there was a cry from within the house, and a high tear-strained voice began: 'When I saw you –'

The sound was immediately extinguished as if someone had clapped a hand over the singer's mouth.

'She's there!' said Korydon. Throwing down the cheap wine-pot he rushed up towards the door. Aristotle and I ran after, with Polemon just behind us. The four of us managed to get through the door, in a clump or tangle, and past the stout but elderly slave who acted as porter in the entryway. The darkness of indoors puzzled us, however, and the house, which was larger and longer than it looked from outside, seemed a labyrinth of short corridors and small rooms.

'You have to *pay*!' said the irate porter, puffing after us as we dashed from room to room. Korydon with quick instinct – or perhaps just a better sense of direction – took the second passage to the left, which led to the rooms behind the courtyard. Here we were hindered by a woman who emerged from one of the rooms, alerted by the porter's cries. She tried to check us in our headlong if blundering chase, and did manage to catch hold of Korydon. This personage was not an ugly female, if not quite in her first youth. Her eyes were painted like a mask, most weirdly outlined and draped in black, while her hair, uncovered and unbound, hung black as night about her bare shoulders.

'Please, gentlemen,' she said, extending her arms to bar our way, 'one at a time. We take care of you here – very good, very pretty. What for, all the disturbing?' She spoke Greek very oddly; I decided she must be Egyptian. We were obliged to push her along in front of us. As she was no slight matter, and we had qualms about hurting her, this slowed our progress, and she kept a tight grip on Korydon. As we proceeded we could hear, well before we got there, the voices in the room at the end of the corridor, through the half-open door.

'Stop whining, girl!' A man spoke roughly, and the sound of a slap followed. 'Turning customers away – must be mad!'

'I'm sorry,' quavered a young man's voice, rather high. 'Really I am – you said it would be all right.'

'Of course I did.' A woman's voice, angry and sharp. 'She's got to be broken in some time. Be sensible, you slut – you can taste gentlemen. Then you may wear gold – and more and better gold, too. Be a woman. It'll have to be some time – why not today?'

'I will not, I will not!' A girl's voice, high, through tears. 'I beseech you, young man, noble Argive, have pity on me –'

The young man's voice again. 'Sorry to have troubled you –'

This meekness brought forth a stream of invective from the woman. 'Coward! I think you're made of lamb's-wool! If you had done as you should, she'd be quiet enough now. As for you, you curd-faced slut with hair like ink, you'd freeze Priapos himself. Why, I tell you this peevish virginity you make such a work about isn't worth a leftover breakfast. Someone must take it – Haimon himself will – or we'll set the public executioner to you!'

By this time we had arrived at the entrance to the room. I elbowed the Egyptian into the wall, and we pushed through the doorway.

The room was small, and lit only by a little window near the low ceiling. It was hardly suited to accommodate the multitude now in it. Nearest the doorway, with his back to us, stood a tall, bony, pale young man, completely naked. In the centre of the room was a large flabby man, with the benefit of clothes and a big paunch. His fist was raised, and his face – or as much as I could see from a side view – was scowling as ferociously as a heavy beard and flaccid cheeks would permit. Beside him stood a thin woman, evidently not one of the attractions of the place, dressed in dark stuff which did not disguise the pendulous bosom sustaining an array of gold beads and pins. This woman's face was peaked and shrewish, and her little black eyes, squinting under bushy brows, were snapping with rage. The couple were arguing – if that is the word – with someone in the middle of this group.

'Get along, you dogs, and take that Egyptian cow with you!' advised the woman, catching sight of us. 'Throw her on the bed,' she added to her husband or whatever he was.

Then we saw, in the centre of the room, the object of threats and reproaches. A young girl stood there, a tall slender girl dressed in a simple white tunic, but with no ugly iron collar about her neck. Her hair, however, cut short as befits a slave, clung in dark tendrils and exquisite fine curls about her head, rippling as waves that dance at the edge of the shore. Her chin was raised in defiance, her face, sideways to us, clear cut as a statue or a noble carving. She turned slowly towards us, tears pouring from her great eyes, and even the tears were lovely, the shape of pearls. Her hands were raised palm upwards in prayer to the gods high above this low and stinking roof. For all her desolation – and an oddness about her look – she seemed the superior of all those people around her, like a king's daughter. I could see that even the man Haimon, the flabby owner of the Haven or Treasury, seemed reluctant to touch her basely.

'I am of gentle birth,' said the girl, 'and I have vowed to Artemis of Ephesos –'

'What have we to do with Artemis? Or Ephesos?' sneered the man, while the shrewish woman, perhaps irritated by the aspersion on her own birth, screamed, 'Let the gods have her then! Minx! Oh, I would like to kill her with my own hands!' She dived at the girl, making for the throat.

At this moment, before the rest of us could do anything, Korydon, who had at first been squashed between the Egyptian girl and Polemon, took control. He brushed the bitter woman aside, and the thick man too, as if Haimon were made of straw.

'Kallirrhoe!' he cried, clasping the girl in his arms.

'Korydon! The gods have answered me!' The girl looked at him with ecstatic eyes, and promptly fainted. He could not quite hold her up and she sank to the floor.

'Here, watch what you're doing!' protested the naked man, looking concerned. 'Don't hurt her!'

'That fellow has killed her! I demand compensation!' screeched the woman hysterically.

'Of all the interfering lunatics!' the fat man bellowed.

He began to beat Korydon with one hand while trying to pick up Kallirrhoe with the other. Korydon, paying no attention to the fat man's blows, was concerned only for the girl. Aristotle and I came to his aid simultaneously. Aristotle helped him to raise the girl from the floor, and I interrupted the brothel master's flailing. Turning to good use an old gymnasium trick, I quickly secured both his arms behind him and kneed him in the small of the back, lifting him slightly off the ground. This trader in flesh was not in good training, and was quite glad to desist. His female partner screamed and abused us all, while the thin and naked young man, trying ineffectually both to be of use and to find some garment for himself, buzzed about us murmuring concern, like a bee caught indoors. The Egyptian girl stood at the door, anxious not to miss anything, as if we were acting for her entertainment.

'Here,' said Aristotle. 'She's only fainted. Give me some water from the jug there, Polemon – oh, he's gone.' It was true – Polemon had disappeared. 'Girl, get me some wine and some bay leaves. I'm a doctor. Hurry!' The Egyptian, her eyes gaping widely under their thick black decoration, did as she was bidden.

'I'm so sorry,' said the thin young man, who had now found a piece of linen to throw around his body. 'Is there anything I can do?' I recognised him now. One of the sons of the Argive woman, the boys whom I couldn't help thinking of as 'Kleobis and Biton'. 'Kleobis' (or it might perhaps have been 'Biton') looked thoroughly miserable, meek and drooping. His nakedness had shown that, though well equipped, he was nowise ready at present for a bout in Haimon's Haven.

'Get away, you assaulter, you seducer, you villain,

before I murder you!' Korydon growled at this doleful young fellow. But he was too busy chafing the girl's hands to carry out his threat.

'I'm just going,' said doleful Kleobis obediently, 'but I intended no harm at all. Just wanted to see a bit of life. Tell the young lady I am very sorry –'

'Yes, get out, you spiritless puppy, you straw-stuffed worm!' screamed the woman, most venomously. 'But pay up before you go, or I'll set the porter on you!'

The Egyptian returned with the wine and bay leaves. Aristotle crushed the bay leaves under the swooning girl's nose, and gave her wine in little sips. Her eyes were open, and she sighed.

'Throw a pot of water over her?' suggested the Egyptian hopefully. 'Twist her nose good?'

'Tita,' said a voice. 'Tita – where have you gone?' The face that peered around the doorway was the face of 'Biton' (or of course possibly 'Kleobis'). It looked awkwardly roguish and smiled broadly when the boy caught a glimpse of his twin. 'Oh, my brother, you're at it in here, are you? Such fun! Look, Tita, come back –'

'Yes, begone, daughter of a pig,' snapped the mistress of Haimon's Treasury. 'Don't leave customers fidgeting here. Mind you get his money.'

The Egyptian Tita shrugged at the world at large. Then she stepped over to doleful 'Kleobis', threw one arm round him, and took the roguish 'Biton' in the other.

'Come along, mama's poppets,' she said, and swept them away.

'Yes,' said Aristotle, 'it's better not to have so many people crowding round the girl. She needs air. Clear the room, will you?'

'Clear the room, indeed!' Haimon was in a passion. 'Clear the room yourself, old fellow! Who asked for you, Sir Whoever-you-are? We don't need any interfering sons of donkeys here. Pay for the wine and get yourself gone, or I'll give your stomach your teeth for a dinner. *I* am master of this house.'

'My felicitations on what I am sure is a profitable establishment,' Aristotle replied. 'We do not mean to trouble you for long. But I am come for this girl.'

'For the girl, of course!' The woman of snapping eyes and dangling bosom cackled; she rubbed her hands on her knees. A thin smile creased her ill-tempered face. 'Well, sir, a gentleman like yourself – it's an honour and a pleasure, as one might say. But of course the price is high, as you'll understand. Of great worth. Here she is, an untouched rosebud, a very flower in the dew. We have been saving her for a gentleman like yourself. Older men with taste and discernment appreciate rich commodities and you can see her value for yourself. You won't find another like that in all Phokis! And –'

'Indeed,' said Aristotle. 'You labour under a delusion – apart from having a very poor memory. You have just rated her rosebud quality at the price of a leftover breakfast. In any case, I fear you have been misled. The legal complications are considerable, and might be unfortunate for you. You have both put yourselves into some danger.'

'Danger?' Haimon's voice was sharp. 'Hush, wife. What do you mean, stranger? And who are you?'

Aristotle stood in the middle of the room and faced the couple with perfect composure. His face was grave, and he held up his hand with the finger thoughtfully raised, as if he were addressing a lecture audience or a jury.

'I am a rhetorician of Athens. The danger of the girl to you would be grave indeed, if the matter were to come to the law. This maiden is at present the purchased slave of a gentleman of Athens, Lysippos by name. She has been recently stolen. I have been asked to recover her. So you could find yourself in the unhappy position of being accused of theft.'

'There!' said the woman vehemently. 'I said at the time we shouldn't have bought goods from a seller who would not show his face. He came hooded, and at night, I swear, and sent a slave to finish the bargain. But he assured us that it was perfectly valid. He swore by the gods that the wench was his to sell. He needed money in a hurry, seemingly. So – you must see, sir – we are clear of all offence. The girl is ours, honestly come by. I can show you the accounts.'

'Hardly sufficient, I fear,' said Aristotle, shaking his head. 'And if only that were all! The situation is ten times worse than merely that. For there is now reason to dispute whether the girl – she told you she was of *good* family, remember – ought to be a slave at all. Why, should her well-born father come upon you, the pot would come to the boil indeed! For the law looks cross-eyed on those who compass the arrest and illicit imprisonment of a free person. Then – well, the penalty for rape is a fine. The penalty for seduction is death if the male relation catches the seducer at it. Or, if the accused is convicted at a court of law, a heavy fine, or worse. The relations are able to administer whatever punishment they think fitting – within reason –'

'Yes,' I interjected. 'I have heard of such a case, and the

brothers cut off the man's hair, whipped him with nettles and stuffed long radishes up his –'

'But,' said Aristotle, 'there are worse penalties for anyone who procures a free man's daughter against his will for the purpose of seduction or rape by another. The penalty for *that* is death. And assault also is a grave charge, is it not? By Athenian law?' He turned to me as if for advice.

'Yes,' I responded promptly. 'If a man engages in unjustified assault on a free person, his property is in danger. If the charge is made of deliberate wounding, why, the guilty person may have his property confiscated and be exiled.'

'What an array of charges!' said Aristotle. 'Think, O Haimon. False imprisonment – rape – seduction – procuring – assault. Then, about the assault – why, consider. Even if the person *were* a slave, as long as she was the slave of another, you could be found guilty of assault. And the employment of arrogant words and insulting behaviour aggravates the assault, smacking of hubris, which as legally defined permits sentence of death when the accused is found guilty. *Hubris*, my friend Haimon. And do not your insults to myself just now reek of the same quality? You are an Athenian by birth. You know Athenian law allows charges of both seduction and hubris to be brought against the perpetrator not just by the victim or his relations but by any law-loving citizen. Think of it, O Haimon. Stinging nettles – imprisonment – fines – exile – death – radishes! Which are we to choose? It does seem a pity, so many penalties. For as you say, you were in part ignorant. A good rhetorician *might* be able to help you plead your cause . . .'

Haimon blenched under this onslaught. His flabby face was as pale as if he were already in a court of law indeed. His wife began to snivel. Korydon and Kallirrhoe meanwhile sat quietly side by side on the bed, listening. Kallirrhoe began, defiantly, to put up her hair.

I could see that Aristotle had enjoyed his speech-making and was satisfied by the effect.

'But then,' he said, 'there are extenuating circumstances, foolish Haimon. We might be able to help you out. But it must be clear that you cooperated fully *as soon* as you heard that the girl was not legally yours.'

'We haven't hurt you none – just let us alone!' said the woman. 'Let us be as we were, and you can have a bout with the girls. Both of you, free of charge.'

'No, that won't do at all,' said Aristotle. 'Nothing will help but free and glad assistance.'

'Of course there'd be compensation?' said Haimon.

'That would be for the original owner – who is in Athens – to decide,' said Aristotle. 'You are not entitled to any compensation, friend, but I tell you frankly that it will be a good day's work for you to get this girl out of your house.'

'She's a little vixen anyway,' said the woman. 'Some of those foreigners can be a lot of trouble. But I could have the training of her, with a rope's end.'

'Shut up, Plouta,' said Haimon, 'or I'll take a rope's end to *you*. I want to think.'

'If only that were possible!' said Aristotle, in the most civil of tones. 'But action, I fear, is what is required.'

He softened his manner a trifle, offering the paunch-bearer and the shrew a grain of comfort at a time. The burden of his argument was that once they let Kallirrhoe out of their house their troubles would be over. It would be too long to tell how he persuaded the boor and the bawd; he then paid off the pandering toothless porter, and conveyed us out of the brothel.

At last we were out of the place in the free air. We said nothing to each other, all the way out of Kirrha. Aristotle had put Kallirrhoe before him on his own mule, and Korydon walked beside her, gazing on her as if this were the last day eyesight would be granted him.

XIII

The Beautiful Girl

When we were safely by ourselves, going along the road through the plain, Korydon abruptly checked the mule and turned about to face us.

'Sir – Aristotle – does that mean we are free now? What you said to that base fellow?'

'Unfortunately,' said Aristotle, 'I can't say so. You are clever enough to notice that what I said to the brothel keeper was largely conditional and hypothetical – though *he* wasn't meant to notice that. The matter is ambiguous. Truly, as far as the law of Athens is concerned, I believe you are slaves. Though if the father of either of you were to come and pursue the case in court, it would be a different affair. As, however, your fathers would probably now be considered enemies at war with us, at the moment such a course does not seem practicable. I fear you must both remain in my care for the time being, and as mine.'

'That is unjust,' said Korydon hotly. 'We'll run away.'

'I said "in my care",' Aristotle reminded him. 'I don't

need any more slaves – the gods know it. I have three very able man-slaves. I certainly don't think you two would suit my wife and myself. And now I have to keep the girl safely tucked away and unmolested. That presents a real problem. Kallirrhoe, we must see that you remain covered in this cloak, and that your head and face – and as far as possible, your form – remain concealed, at least until I have given you safely over to the women's quarters in the house of Diokles. He is my good friend, and will do you no harm, nor even ask to see you, at my particular request. But I'm afraid you will have to go with your hair unbound again, at least for now.'

Kallirrhoe sighed and began, sadly, to unbind the hair which she had wished to do up as a gentlewoman and not to wear loose and untied as a slave.

'I shall look after both of you,' Aristotle promised. 'And you can help me. I particularly wish to hear Kallirrhoe's story, when she is quite recovered.'

'I'm recovered now,' said Kallirrhoe. 'It is good to get away from that terrible house. I knew the goddess would deliver me from unworthy persons, but I didn't know when. I trust this old man, Korydon, for he has been divinely inspired to rescue me.'

'They fit me with my role in their drama,' murmured Aristotle. 'But, girl, I was not searching for you, but for your mistress, Anthia. Daughter of Pherektrates of Athens. I wish your help in finding out what happened to her.'

'I see.' Kallirrhoe thought for a minute. 'Everything you have said is sensible, sir – what did you say your name is? I quite see that it is not possible for myself and Korydon to go away together just now. How should we get on, with no money? It would be only inviting more troubles. And running off into the wild would not be good for my reputation. Do not fear – I'll make him see reason. Korydon is very good, and very brave, and I love him dearly, but he is not always prudent.'

'I like that,' said Korydon indignantly. 'When I think how you let Pharnabazos capture you in his tower at Halikarnassos, and the agony I suffered –'

'Yes, but *you* didn't rescue me,' said Kallirrhoe pointedly. 'Theron did that. Theron was very wise. I sometimes think neither of us has been very wise, you and I, or things could not have turned out so ill as they have done. Yet it seems this is the fate willed for us by the gods. And, sirs, a great deal may happen to innocent persons in time of war when whole cities lie under cross stars.'

'Yes, yes,' said Aristotle. 'We have heard your story. No need to go through it all again. But we burn to know what happened between the time you were last in Lysippos' house and now. And *what* has happened to Anthia? Is she ravished? Dead? Or has she too been sold?'

'None of these things, as far as I know,' said Kallirrhoe. 'I was Anthia's slave . . .' She frowned distastefully at the word. 'The daughter of Pherekrates is not a bad mistress, though sometimes short-tempered. Her weaving is not as good as it might be, and the taste in patterns curiously simple – but then, we Ephesians have other ways. As you know, Anthia's father Pherekrates died, and we both came to the house of Lysippos in time of sorrow. Anthia was very unhappy. The women were not ill disposed to us, though Hegeso is sickly and complaining.'

'What of their daughter?' I asked, thinking of Lysippos' girl who would be an heiress.

'Oh, Myrrhine – she is a strange being. She talks to

herself half the time – she says that's because there is no one better to talk to. As for the men, I kept well away from *them*. That foolish uncle Timotheos who haunts the house has a way of stroking the servants when he comes upon them. You must realise that Anthia did not know her uncle Lysippos very well, and wasn't too fond of him. Though he seemed kind enough. Well, on the night after the Day of the Pots, after the house had been cleansed of ghosts and goblins, we set out, Anthia and I, to make a sacrifice on the family altar – and someone rushed at us and threw heavy cloths over our heads and bodies and dragged us out of the gate.

'The next thing we knew, we were being carried away in a litter. Some heavy-handed men – low people – reached in and sealed our eyes with gum, and put bandages over them, and stuffed rags down our mouths, and bound our hands. They put raw cloth deep into our mouths, so we couldn't scream. Anthia was sick with the jolting and the cloth, and nearly stifled until she vomited out part of the gag. I tell you, it was no nice matter in a closed litter. The men just laughed and cleaned her up and gagged her again. I was nearly sick myself, but I managed not to be.'

'How long were you in the litter?'

'It was hard to keep account of time. We were weary, and our captors did not feed us much after Anthia's misadventure, so we slept from time to time – there was nothing else to do. We were not going too fast. They hid us for a while: in some barn or stable, from the smell. While waiting for the city gates to open, perhaps. And the times of day became confused. But I think we were in the litter for a night and a day and another night.'

'Did not Anthia have any idea who the abductors were?'

'She did not exactly recognise anybody. But she was very cautious. Anthia is not stupid, and she heard enough to realise they were abducting *her* because she is an heiress. She was very frightened because if somebody *seduced* her she would be in a very bad way. And you know that a woman who is taken by force by a man is often considered as seduced. What would happen after? Either a patched-up and maybe illegal marriage, or the punishment for the seduced woman. Then even if she was allowed to stay alive, she couldn't marry, or go to any ceremonies or processions, or wear any ornaments, and other women could slap her and pull her hair. Anthia couldn't stand that. And she certainly didn't wish to be forced to marry an Abductor. So she decided to escape.'

'Escape? How and when? And how did you know what she was thinking?'

'She whispered a few words to me when we were eating the bread and water provided by the slaves. The slaves fed us several times, but they had to stand away from us while we were eating. I suppose the captor made them do so, lest we should talk with the slaves and persuade them to help us. Later, when she made her escape, Anthia and I freed each other's hands, and changed clothes. But that wasn't until the second day.'

'Are you sure you did not recognise this Abductor? Or get any hints to help identify him?'

'Of course we both tried to find out who it was – but Anthia could not wish to meet him, you know, for that would have been an invitation to seduction. He must have been very nervous, for he was certainly wary. He wore a hood, and was careful not to stand anywhere near us, even though we were not supposed to be able to see anything at all.'

'Curious,' said Aristotle. 'That argues it most probably was somebody Anthia would or could have known – and she would have known, even by sight alone, so few men. He did not want yet to reveal himself. Are you sure *you* saw nothing of him?'

'I did catch a glimpse, but it wasn't much help. He seemed of middle height – just a dark shape, all in a dark cloak. This Abductor spoke with an Athenian accent, but mostly high and squeaky or else in the kind of whisper people have when they are hoarse in the throat. But in the evening – at the end of the first full day of our abduction – he met somebody, and we could hear voices, if faintly, of men talking. They didn't talk as slaves do. Anthia thought she recognised one of the voices then, but wouldn't tell me whose.

'Then the litter-carrying became very jerky. Soon we were taken out – it was dark then, or nearly – and made to walk up a hill. I was really frightened that we were going to be murdered somewhere in the wilds. But we only camped there for the night. The new man and the Abductor talked at a distance from us, after having tied our feet and hands and laying us down like logs. We were partly freed, for the necessary occasion; we were led uphill to do what we had to. The slaves took off our gags again as we gestured that we were going to be sick – and of course they would have to clean up if we were. There was an oak tree near to the place we relieved ourselves. Anthia, who had got most of the gum out of her eye, was able to discern the tree by lifting her eye-band. We made offerings on the oak – she put her fillet there, from her hair, and I gave a lock of my hair.'

'How did you have such a lock?' asked Korydon. 'For that lock was long, as your hair used to be, and now you wear it short.'

'They cut off my hair in Pherekrates' house,' Kallirrhoe frowned. 'But before I was subjected to that wretchedness, I wrenched out some of my own hair as I wore it then – it *was* long, wasn't it? And I put it in a little bag about my neck. I thought it might help prove who I was at some time. People thought it was an amulet, and let it alone. Anyway, I wanted to remember it. But my hair hasn't been cut for some while – and it is growing out now, isn't it?'

'Yes, but that's enough about hair,' I said. 'Go on – what happened after you made offerings to the oak tree?'

'Then we had to go back down the hill. In the dawn, or just before it, the litter was brought again, and we were put in it. Fortunately, the slaves had been drunk in the night and were tired and cross, so there was some delay and distraction. These men didn't want to put the gags on us anyway. Then the master and his friend were cross. The Abductor and the other man took the slaves off to one side to beat them – I suppose so we shouldn't hear what was said, or know that our keepers were beaten and hold them in contempt. So Anthia just bolted.'

'Leaving you in the litter?'

'Yes, but we changed clothes, so I would be her – if you see what I mean. By that time we had learned how to undo each other's bonds. She tied my hands again, just before she went, so I, the "heiress", wouldn't seem to have helped "the slave" get off. And we popped several bags of meal that the slaves carried into the litter, so it wouldn't seem too light. As I say, the slaves were drunk and sleepy, and now they were angry and sore as well. They were less likely to notice any easing of their burden, as they were full of complaints. But Anthia got away – that's all I know about her.'

'When was her escape discovered?' I asked. 'What happened then?'

'We went on a little way after that. The first part of our going was over rough ground, and then we got back on the road. At the first stop the head slave only popped his head in, and I said that my slave-girl was still asleep. I was veiled myself. I tried to sound like Anthia, and I said it wasn't worth waking the girl. So we went on quite a while without the discovery being made.'

'But,' said Korydon, 'you heard me singing to you.'

'Yes – and I started to sing back. But the slave at once prodded me through the litter, with a sharp stick, and said if I didn't stop caterwauling he would knock my teeth down my throat and put his – his *thing* in the hole. So I stopped. I knew he'd find out the other girl wasn't there if he looked into the litter. I was very frightened of being beaten – and of much worse things.' The peculiar slave-girl sighed.

'And,' she added, 'indeed I confess that I began to think your singing, O Korydon, was but some phantasm in my own mind. I was cowardly. But I *do* think it was very good in me, to give Anthia time to get clear, because of course it meant more blame for me later. It wasn't until much later in the morning they found it was just one girl they carried.'

'What then? Were they terribly angry?'

'There was a great deal of cursing, and somebody hit me. Not the Abductor's friend – he had left us at the place of the oak tree. But I cried and screamed and said the slave-girl had run away, and that she was a stupid girl and would be too frightened to say anything of the adventure, as she knew she would not be believed. And that she was terribly frightened of the law, as indeed all slaves are. So they needn't fear her. That seemed satisfactory – for a brief while. The Abductor did not come to look at me closely – he still thought he had the heiress. And I breathed again. But not for long.'

'What then?'

'Still well before the sun was in mid-heaven, my captor and his party met someone – someone he knew, I think – a pedlar. Against my Abductor's protests, this fat pedlar came up to the litter and peered in at me. I saw his big face staring at me, and shrank back, but he had a good look, I suppose. Then he burst out a-laughing, very loud and merry, and he swore to the Abductor that this was not Anthia. I don't know how he knew! The Abductor went off and talked with him. Then the two came back, and one slave was beaten, really hard now. The pedlar and the Abductor laid him down on the ground and beat him with a stick, for letting Anthia escape. The slave was quite ill. The pedlar went away. And then the other slave beat me, when he was ordered to, with a stick also, and I was sick. I vomited. I kept on pretending to be very ill even when I felt better. We had to stop for nearly two days. We stayed hidden behind a grove of trees while the Abductor considered what he must do, and the slave and I recovered from the beatings.

'The Abductor was evidently very frightened. I heard

him say that we must get on, but they must abandon the litter and hide it. The slaves practically carried me between them. At least, they made it look as if I were walking between the two, but hustled me so that my feet hardly touched the ground. I was frightened, for I heard the Abductor say he would "get rid of the girl" at Delphi. He threatened the slaves with great harm if they touched me save at his orders and in his view. They were not even to beat me any more. I think this was not from kindness to me, but the reverse. I think that he feared beating might lead to other thoughts, and that even the crudest love-making might lead to a kind of friendship – a man-slave might aid me after he had to do with me.'

'And yet you came on to Delphi?'

'So we all came to Delphi, in the guise of poor pilgrims – a man with an invalid crippled sister. I heard the Abductor telling this story to some other pilgrims on the road. We were three days in getting there. We went slowly on foot all the way up that steep road. And then the Abductor met someone else and talked with them, and got a mule and threw me over its back. We turned to the road to the coast and next day went down again, all the way to Kirrha, where I was sold to Haimon as you have heard. The dreadful people there gave me that day and the next day to recover my looks – but,' she shuddered, 'they said they would set me "to work" today.'

'How is it,' I asked, 'that on the road to Delphi you did not attract attention and cry out? You could hardly have had bound eyes and a gag going openly on the public road?'

'I still had my eyes bound, and I was veiled heavily. Nobody could see my face, or know that there was a gag between my teeth. When I made noises, they said that was a sign of my illness. Some man asked about me, and I heard one of the slaves explaining that I had weak eyes that couldn't bear the light, and was subject to the falling sickness. They said I was to be taken to Apollo for a cure. But that was the only time a question was really asked. Nobody else noticed me,' she said rather sadly. 'Of course, as I was hooded and veiled and with my eyes bound, nobody would.'

'So,' said Aristotle. 'Is this all the truth? You don't know where Anthia is? She said nothing of where she would go?'

'No. Nor do I know if she is alive or dead. But I think she must be alive. For she is, as I say, not stupid, nor cowardly – though she did leave me in her place. What else could she do? And I was willing to pretend to be her, because I thought I would be better treated as the heiress than if they thought I was only a slave.'

'The oak tree with the fillet,' Aristotle said thoughtfully. 'All that long distance back. She may be roaming anywhere in the wilds.'

'She might have gone back to Athens,' I suggested.

Kallirrhoe shook her head. 'I think not. Who would believe her – that she had been abducted by a strange man for two days, and yet was still marriageable? Would she dare return home to Athens until matters had been set right? No – perhaps she waited and spied upon us to find out if the Abductor was suitable for her to marry. But it is more likely that she fled into the wilds, until she felt safe. Perhaps she hired herself out as a serving-woman, as a weaver or cheese-maker on some small farm until she could send word privately to her family.'

'If she still trusted her family,' Aristotle said, thinking aloud.

'Perhaps she too came to Delphi,' said Korydon.

'Alas!' I said. 'If only we had found Anthia instead of this slave girl, we would have had something to show to comfort the wretched Lysippos.'

'Indeed, although this has been a scene rich in peripeteia and recognition, our lost heiress is still lost,' said Aristotle. 'We should consider Anthia's case from her point of view. It is a good question that Kallirrhoe asks. Who would believe that Anthia could be abducted for two days and still be marriageable? An impossible probable, or probable impossible. You swear you have no idea as to who the Abductor might be?'

'No. Neither of us did. How could Anthia – newly come to Lysippos' house, and kept properly in the women's quarters at home all her life – how could she know a strange man? We both tried to get a look at him, of course, but all we saw was but a dark hooded shape. I tell you, we had to be very careful, for if Anthia looked as if she were interested in the Abductor it could have been fatal to her virginity.'

'Describe what you did see.'

'The Abductor was a man of middle height. And in command of the slaves. He had a man's voice, though high, but that was probably disguise. He must have been rich to afford the slaves and the litter. I tell you, even when he sold me in Kirrha he was careful not to let me see him. After Anthia was gone, when I was alone, I did not try too hard to see him. I felt then that if he thought I would recognise him afterwards, he would kill me.'

'But a voice and nothing more. Well, well. This

Abductor seems an admirably cautious person. Certainly he is not *lustful.* If he had wished to take both girls by force, he had plenty of opportunity. And if he wanted to seduce Anthia, why did he not begin to show love to her right away? Honeyed speeches, gifts and that sort of thing. Strange.'

'Perhaps,' said Kallirrhoe complacently, 'he was not very good-looking. I think that was most likely. So he would wait until he had Anthia safely alone and imprisoned in a house somewhere. He did not *sound* like a handsome person.' She sighed, but in pity rather than sorrow. 'There are so many who are not beautiful. They do not realise that they are blessed! I'm sure I've often wished I were quite ugly, or at least very, very plain.'

'Oh, no!' said Korydon, quite shocked, and the two had a mild argument, which ended with Korydon passionately kissing Kallirrhoe's hand and arm.

We arrived in Delphi late in the afternoon, after a long and toilsome climb up the base of the mountain from Kirrha. Aristotle, with profuse apologies and the vaguest of explanations, was able to place Kallirrhoe in the women's quarters of the house of his good friend Diokles.

'And that is a relief,' Aristotle said to me when we were by ourselves. 'A blessing to have the girl safely out of sight. We hope she will not add to her agitating history. Here surely she will be safe from Persian satraps, pirates and brothel-keepers – for the time being, at any rate.'

For the time being also, Korydon seemed cheerful – ecstatic indeed. Quite different from the melancholy lad he had been. This was almost a pity, for in his jubilant mood he was even more attractive than before. Both men and women could hardly take their eyes from him. Korydon was not as easy to hide as Kallirrhoe.

'I wish I could keep them both in a box,' Aristotle grumbled to me privately. 'Or in separate boxes, rather. Keeping those two apart will not be the least of our troubles. However, I ought not to say such things, thinking of the box that Ammonios now needs. I am a fool! I should have taken a look at the body that Polemon guarded.'

'Whatever for? Ammonios is certainly not going to recover, though the best doctors in all of Greece came together to look at him. Nobody could be more dead. And the corpse would be most unpleasant by this time.'

'But who knows whether what Polemon has *is* the corpse of Ammonios? In these latest episodes in our lives, substitution has run riot. Metaphor. The exchange of one thing for another. The greatest thing of all is to be a master of metaphor. And everything has come in pairs, or seems to – even the two cheese-faced lads at the brothel.'

'Kleobis and Biton,' I agreed, laughing. 'Speaking of being a doctor – what of the health of the girl? And do you think her story was true?'

'There is nothing to contradict it. She has been suffering slightly from lack of food and sleep, as well as from distress. But her constitution is excellent, her breathing sound, and she has digested her supper. About her tale? All she says matches what Korydon has narrated, though Ionians have a more florid manner of description than is usual with us.'

'You know,' I said, 'Korydon greatly exaggerated the beauty of Kallirrhoe. I am disappointed. She is quite dark, and her nose is strangely both too large and too thin. Her eyebrows are thin and too high-arched. She is not really my idea of a first-rate beautiful girl. *I* would imagine golden hair – and eyes like the first violets of spring.'

'You are poetic, Stephanos! I suppose that I should have predicted that you would not find Kallirrhoe beautiful, for you have not lived in Asia as I have done. She is probably partly Persian.'

'Oh, no – a barbarian! How can anyone be Persian? I mean, how can a beautiful person be Persian? Detestable!' I burst out before I could stop myself. Aristotle was looking at me quizzically out of his deep-set eyes – and I suddenly remembered that he had the strange foreign wife whom I had never seen. The outlandish woman, Pythias, daughter or niece (or something) to Hermias of Atarneos. Mother of the little girl Pythias – whom I had seen at the Flower Festival – a child olive-skinned and dark-haired.

'Perhaps I sound intemperate,' I said, in a less heated tone. 'But just the same, how can there be different ideas about the beautiful? All men agree. And the Greeks know about the beautiful: it is one of the things distinguishing them from the barbarians.'

'You may think our young couple barbarians,' Aristotle said calmly. 'And you may be right, even though they both are Greek speakers. Nevertheless, I believe they both are, as they insist, of good birth. They have the aristocratic arrogance which is hard for an untrained impostor to assume. You know, I have maintained that those who are not slavish in nature should not be slaves. What to do with them is a question.'

'You could ask the Oracle,' I said.

'I may ask the Oracle,' Aristotle agreed. 'Our

consultation is in three days' time. But I should more properly ask the Oracle about the heiress, for we are no nearer finding the unfortunate daughter of Lysippos than before. May the gods be kind to Anthia! I feel regret, for, do you know, at one time I had begun to doubt Lysippos' story, even thinking there had been no abduction.'

'We have been wandering in regions of uncertainty,' I said reassuringly. 'You have done all you could. But now we know. Anthia was certainly abducted and escaped, and is roaming around somewhere – it might be anywhere. Poor Lysippos!'

'It is a terrible thing for the daughter of a good family – and we have not prevented it.'

'But . . . Aristotle, did you notice how Polemon ran off from us in the brothel, quite suddenly? Don't you think he was afraid of Kallirrhoe? That she might identify him, perhaps. This certainly strengthens the case against him.'

'It does seem suspicious – but is Polemon rich enough to compass all that had to be done? The Abductor must have a good deal of money.'

'But,' I pointed out, 'Polemon is related to Ammonios, who is – who was – rich enough. And the Abductor met with Ammonios on the road. Perhaps that was by arrangement. Ammonios in his pedlar's disguise was certainly the fat-faced man who looked in on Kallirrhoe.'

'We shall not lose sight of Polemon, never fear. I shall keep up correspondence with him and induce him to come to Delphi to consult the Oracle.'

I tried to persuade Aristotle to go out for a walk, but he felt too weary after yesterday's expedition and said he would do some quiet reading. I was restless – the visit to the brothel had excited me. Despite what I had said to

Aristotle against barbarian women, my thoughts returned over and over again to the Egyptian girl Tita with her dark-rimmed eyes. But, even had Kirrha been closer at hand, I could not wish to encounter Haimon in his Haven again. I stole away to compose myself, walking outside the sacred precincts in the gathering dusk. The air was very cool on the mountain, and a mist arose from the Pleistos below.

I passed by the sacred spring, hearing its cool chattering on the rocks. Thinking myself in solitude, I came to the grove of Kharila, the hanged girl. There I saw a dark figure, thin and hooded, standing under the tree. As I looked, another figure came up to the first one and gave it something, which was put in a basket. This newcomer looked female, not particularly slender, and not young. An old woman, almost certainly one of the more charitable Delphians, giving something to some needy body. The thin shrouded form in its hood then stole noiselessly away. The figure of a woman? Yet it was commanding and solitary, like a man. In the mist this thin form seemed like neither living man nor woman, but aerial, a shade. At the same time, this strange shape reminded me of something else. Something I could not at first trace. And then I remembered the boy who had mockingly brushed into me outside the sanctuary of Apollo. And that recollection aroused other memories – fleeting and formless, like cloud-shadows on the mountains.

Oddly perturbed by an incident which had nothing to do with me, I returned to Diokles' house. There I found Aristotle sitting comfortably alone. He had taken up one of the Pythian scrolls and had become absorbed in it. Once he started reading he always found it difficult not to continue. He greeted me kindly, however, and put down the scroll.

'This is a list of victors in the games in the year we lost to the Spartans,' he said. 'How strange to read the names of those who are long dead and gone.'

'"Long dead and gone",' I repeated. 'Aristotle, do you believe in the story of Kharila?'

Aristotle shrugged. 'It is an old legend – it could be true. It is neither impossible nor improbable that the Delphians, who are like other people, were once unkind to a poor foreign woman.'

'I saw something just now,' I said, 'which made me think of the ghost of Kharila – if such things should be. And that reminded me of something else – something I heard on the Night of the Ghosts.'

I told him, briefly, about the figure I had just seen by the sacred spring in Delphi. And then, somewhat shamefacedly, I told him at last about the weird words I had overheard on that foggy night – so long ago it seemed – in Athens. I explained how I had heard Orestes and Elektra conversing when I was by Lysippos' house.

'I didn't want to tell you, because I thought you'd think me ridiculous, believing in ghosts,' I confessed. 'Like slaves and peasants. And these unseen speakers seemed so ghostly, and so like Orestes and his sister. What they said wasn't the same as any of the tragic poets' scenes,' I added, 'though a lot like them. And at the end I heard words that sounded familiar:

"The word of Apollo is of great power and cannot fail.

His voice, urgent, insistent, drives me to dare this
danger." '

'From Aiskhylos' play. Yes – I see. What else reminded you so strongly of Orestes and Elektra?'

'She said she recognised the colour of hair on a shrine, and told him "You don't know how they treat me," and he said he had no grave, but it was "attempted murder". And she wanted revenge.'

Urged by Aristotle I repeated the conversation in detail, as well as I could remember it. I was ashamed of my belief in these spectres, but Aristotle did not laugh at me. On the contrary, he followed me attentively, saying some of the words over to himself.

' "The word of Apollo is of great power and cannot fail." Yes. No wonder you thought Orestes had returned on his special night. On mature reflection, are you certain that you did *not* recognise the voices?'

'I am certain,' I said. 'They sounded like no one I had ever heard before. But the voices were like ghost voices – there was the fog, and the sound came out of the dark. And,' I added truthfully, 'of course I was drunk at the time.'

'Quite so. And you wished to bury the undignified recollection. What exactly brought this scene back to mind tonight?'

'Well,' I said hesitantly, 'some young rascal who jostled me in the crowd the other day reminded me – for no very good reason – of the ghost. And the shadowy figure in the grove made me remember that impudent young man, for he wore a hood too. Though the impudent young man was very much alive, and not ghostly. This shape I just saw in the grove looked more like a female, and like a shade. It might have been the ghost of Kharila. But also, I suppose, it might have been a man – like an Orestes, mad and condemned.'

'Interesting,' said Aristotle. 'So Lysippos' house is haunted by Orestes and Elektra. And now perhaps your Orestes is here? We must rid you of your habit of ghost-seeing, Stephanos. Though the real Orestes came to Delphi. Yet what does this place of Apollo's light have to do with ghosts and shadows and strange figures seen out of the corner of the eye?'

He folded his hands together, matching fingertip to fingertip in a judicious manner.

'A strange position we find ourselves in, Stephanos. Here we are, setting peaceably forth to Delphi to find a missing heiress. We do not find the girl but on our journey we find two corpses and two slaves – ourselves not requiring a set of either. We freeze and fast on the cold heights, and then are entertained royally in Diokles' house, reading manuscripts and going on pleasant expeditions. The corpse we saw last upon Oidipous' crossroads appears to be transported to Kirrha, a silver image is murdered and buried, and a young nobleman is singing for hemi-obols outside a brothel. Now Orestes is in the mix too. The heiress seems to have disappeared into thin air – and where is her guardian? Look, I have just received this letter – it was delayed on the road, and sent to the wrong house.'

He handed me a tablet with a message on it, in a square precise writing that I recognised:

Lysippos not at home, nor Timotheos. Hegeso very ill. Daughter also missing. Have told no one else. Will write again.

Theophrastos

'What does he mean – *daughter* also missing?' I asked. 'He must have got matters mixed up. He thinks that Anthia is Lysippos' daughter, not his niece.'

'Oh, no, Theophrastos *never* gets confused about details. If he says "daughter", he means exactly that. Myrrhine – Lysippos' daughter, the one they call the mad girl – must have disappeared too. But I have hopes – sad hopes, if one can say that – of seeing Lysippos and Timotheos soon.'

'You do? Where?'

'In Delphi, of course. Why not? Everyone else seems to come here. We should start looking for them tomorrow. Let us try to find your Kharila-person again. Why should she – or he – or it – not come to the grove at dawn as well as in the evening? It is, unfortunately, most probable that we shall find her (or him or it) to be some well-known beggar of the district.'

XIV

The Hanged Girl

Aristotle and I went out together very early in the morning for a walk to the sacred spring. And the strange figure was there – but we were a trifle late, for the hooded visitant had just received whatever food somebody had offered, and was going off with the basket. A water-jar was upon her head. So it was – obviously – a woman. She saw us and quickened her pace, muttering impatiently. I thought I caught the words:

> '"And I myself bear water from the spring; I, without share in holy feast or dance,"'

though I could hear only what came drifting over the shoulder of this second Kharila, whose face I could not see.

'That's not a ghost, at all events,' said Aristotle. 'She has taken water, and probably a gift of bread.' He started to follow the retreating figure, but it was going uphill at a very good pace. Before we could pursue the hooded woman, we were interrupted by the advent of two of Aristotle's friends, anxious to introduce him to other citizens. This sort of thing was always happening in Delphi – Aristotle running into people he knew. It was a great nuisance, when we were trying to follow a secret case.

Aristotle, always polite, was unusually charming even for him. He suddenly became most affable, even gregarious. Forgetting all about the 'ghost' which had aroused his attention earlier, he was delighted to accept invitations to various meeting-places and homes. I was of course also invited, and quite enjoyed the morning, although I wished we had been able to follow the strange woman. On the other hand, we heard a great deal of news – some interesting, some not; some news of Athens, but more of local matters.

At last I thought I could see into my friend's purpose, for we heard something to the point. In the middle of chatter about somebody's great-uncle's swollen leg, one of our new acquaintances asked if we knew Lysippos the silversmith of Athens and had heard of his sad affliction.

'He is grieving, poor man, for the death of his son,' our informant explained. 'He has just come, in the care of his brother Timotheos. Quite broken-hearted he is, they say, and in a daze. I mean Lysippos is. His brother is mostly in a daze, an absent-minded man, a philosopher. But now Timotheos takes charge, Lysippos is so cut up.'

'How did his son die?' Aristotle asked.

'Straton – that's the son you know, and the apple of his eye – was killed, it seems – slaughtered and left by the roadside. Brigands, most likely. Dreadful! Lysippos found out about it a few days ago, while he was on his way here. So sad! He was on his way to the consecration festival. When good Lysippos left Athens he did not know he was on his way to a burial.'

'Lysippos is here in Delphi now?' I asked in some surprise.

'Yes. Delayed by the horrid discovery and the burial rites. The funeral was in some tiny village in the region where the boy met his death. Hardly enough of a body left to bury, they say – the crows and so on. I suppose later they'll take the remains back to Athens. Of course there must be an investigation first. There seems to have been an outbreak of crimes and robberies on the road.'

'The authorities must look to it,' said someone else sternly. 'The roads must be kept free and safe for all pilgrims coming to Delphi.'

'Of course it is quite safe really,' said another Delphic sage soothingly. He evidently did not wish to dwell on any discomforts or dangers menacing travellers to his sacred city. 'People don't even have to come by road. Consider the sea journey – quite charming in spring and summer. Most of the roads are excellent, and entertainment easily found. Why, fathers of families bring their children.'

The conversation turned upon the duty of authorities of all regions to maintain the roads to Delphi, and the historic well-attested benefits of making the journey to revere or consult Apollo. It was easy to see why, while living in Delphi, we had heard nothing of a disturbing nature. Even the discovery of the corpse of Ammonios had not been bruited about. The intimidation of travellers is not in the interest of Delphi's citizens. The sad fortune of

Lysippos' son was mentioned again, as something that had happened in a far region, and indicating the advisability of travelling in a party.

'Very sad, most distressing,' said Aristotle, who had looked suitably shocked and sorrowful. I had taken my cue from him, and tried to look as if this 'news' were new to me also. 'Such a shock,' Aristotle continued. 'Poor Lysippos, it is only right that I should pay a visit of condolence.'

As soon as we could, we got away from these friends and betook ourselves to the house where we now knew Lysippos and Timotheos were staying. Their host, an ancestral friend of the family of Lysippos' father, had been deprived after the most recent and terrible Sacred War of all rights related to the functioning of the Oracle, and of most other political rights. He had been lucky enough not to lose his home. This man was not displeased to see Aristotle. Cultivating the famous Makedonian might prove a first step to his own reinstatement. At any rate, he welcomed us cordially. We were admitted, and directed to a pleasant courtyard, Lysippos' host explaining loudly that Lysippos needed peace and quiet, but that he (the Delphian) was glad to see us as Lysippos wanted rousing. To these contradictory statements Aristotle gave cordial assent.

We found Lysippos and Timotheos sitting side by side on a bench in the inner courtyard, with a magnificent view of the Shining Ones behind and above them. It was a shock to see Lysippos – he who had been so handsome and in such good spirits on the night of the Anthesteria festival. Even when I had last seen him, when he was hurried and harassed by the mysterious disappearance of his niece, he had still looked strong and handsome. Now there were great circles under his eyes, his cheeks were gathered in, and a multitude of lines had appeared under the eyes and about the mouth. Lysippos' hair seemed unwashed and unkempt, and so did his big rippling beard – not very brown now, but predominantly grey, not even silver any more. Indeed, as he stroked his beard in a weary and unmeaning gesture, the contrast between the shining bracelet that he wore on his right arm and the dull grey hair was almost painful.

'My poor Lysippos! I have just been told . . .' said Aristotle. 'No, do not get up – do not disturb yourself.'

'Dear friend,' said Lysippos to Aristotle, raising his sad eyes, 'it is good to see the face of a friend from my own city. Sit with us a while. Yes, you see me in deep sorrow – dreadful, incurable trouble. My poor Straton!'

'Yes, a dreadful trouble,' said Timotheos. 'But do not let it bear you down into the earth, my brother. Take something to eat, I beg.' With awkward kindness Timotheos reached his skinny silver-hooped right arm along the bench and patted his brother's shoulder. Timotheos too looked altered. He also appeared very tired. Sorrow had hollowed out his thin cheeks even more, so that the bones stood out in ridges. His eyes were red-rimmed, and his hair looked thinner and more wispy. As usual, he appeared a trifle out of place, hesitant and ungraceful on any occasion of social meeting. Yet his strong brother was so much afflicted that he seemed to need Timotheos to take the lead and to look after him. Lysippos answered with grateful meekness, 'Yes, I will take something now, brother, if you say so,' and a slave was soon summoned.

'There now,' said Timotheos, 'he suffered for lack of eating. You have done him good already.' Like an anxious nurse Timotheos watched Lysippos take his soup and bread and well-watered wine. Aristotle and I waited too, dismissing Lysippos' apologies for his rudeness, and talking of the benefit derived from nourishment. Having eaten a little, Lysippos subsided into inactivity again.

'You know of Straton's dreadful death,' said Timotheos after a pause. 'We must not talk too much about it before *him* –' nodding at his brother. 'It upsets him, and little wonder. His tears have fallen like spring rain, until he has no more left to shed. And our poor Straton did not even have a good funeral.'

'It was a very poor funeral, alas!' said Lysippos tremulously. 'Nobody there – not like Athens. No family but myself. I couldn't even hire a big ceremony. Poor lad! I buried him with his bracelet on, and a silver pin I had with me, and my pottery cup – but there was nothing splendid. In Athens I shall put up a monument – a big monument with a carving on it. We can bring his bones back to Athens later. Nobody shall say any more of our family lie in unmarked graves. But I couldn't help it, could I?'

'No, no,' said Timotheos, reassuringly. 'You did everything you could – and what had to be done. Even I, Straton's uncle, was not there at the time – for I, in my foolish restlessness, and without help, had already gone off at last to search for Anthia myself.' He looked reproachfully at Aristotle.

'You had some suspicions yourself, perhaps, that you did not wish to share?'

'I had begun to suspect Ammonios,' said Timotheos

slowly, 'when I found he had left Athens. Though I see now this may be absurd. After all, Ammonios is a widower, and well-born and rich, so he might have wished to offer for our heiress. I left Athens and went on ahead of my brother, so that I could visit a known associate of Ammonios on the road towards Delphi. I did not want to trouble my brother Lysippos with my suspicions until we were certain.'

'Very good of you, brother,' said Lysippos, smiling feebly.

'This man – Ammonios' friend – is a very low person indeed. A connection of Pataikos, another somewhat unsavoury personage. At least I think so; perhaps my standards are too high. The home of this cousin of Pataikos is well enough, and as a landowner he indulges in country sports when he can. But he uses his ancestral home – most disgusting! – as a brothel and a school for brothel workers.'

'Most improper,' I murmured my assent. 'What did this man say?'

'He said he had seen Ammonios, who stayed secretly overnight and took medicine. Ammonios was in a bad temper, it seems. Said he was on the way to Delphi, on the track of a prostitute slave he wanted to get back. But you realise, as Ammonios had been travelling on his own, he cannot have been the Abductor. So that attempt – my pitiful attempt at tracking down an enemy to our family – came to nothing. I returned to Lysippos who was behind me on the road, and found that Straton was dead. Imagine our distress! But you cannot imagine it. We didn't know what to do. And we had heard nothing from you all this while.' Timotheos looked reproachfully at Aristotle.

Aristotle bowed his head. 'I have indeed been worse than useless. I shall always regret it. I have not helped you, despite my good will. I am deeply sorry,' he continued, raising his head and looking at them earnestly. He spoke very sadly. 'I have failed you both – failed you most profoundly. I can see no way of atoning.'

Lysippos raised a shaky hand. 'Do not reproach my good friend Aristotle. Alas! If he, the wisest man in Athens, could do nothing, what could any of us do? The gods are against us. I thought it dreadful when my niece had gone, had disappeared – but this is far worse.

"When of the house a man dies, what great grief!
A woman does not matter."

The hope of my house and my line is departed. Our shining prospects were shadowed by the death of my poor Gorgias, and are now completely eclipsed, and for ever. Such a flourishing family as we once were! My father Demodikos had three sons, and I had two. And now I have none. Ai! Ai!' He began to weep, softly, a few painful tears starting up from the fountain which had flowed so long as to be almost dried up.

We sat in silence about him, commiserating.

'And now,' said Timotheos, 'we hardly know where to turn, to do justice on the murderer. For there is some debate about exactly *where* the murder of Straton took place, whether in Attika or Boiotia. And no one knows whom to accuse of the murder or even whether the murderer is of Attika or Boiotia, one or many, a traveller, a foreigner or a local brigand. And we have not found Anthia! What can we do! We do not know where she is –

or if she is still alive, or a virgin. Dark riddles, beyond the wit of man –'

'Perhaps if you ask –' I began eagerly, thinking of Kallirrhoe, but Aristotle frowned at me and hastily took up my speech himself.

'What my friend Stephanos means to say – though he is a trifle quick to offer advice to his elders – is that perhaps you should beg an answer of Delphic Apollo. Gain an interview with the Pythia and consult the Oracle. Matters beyond the wit of men are not beyond the gods. You are in the one place where hard questions can be answered.'

'Yes, very true,' said Timotheos. 'I urged my poor brother to come to Delphi, as this was the direction in which Anthia was supposed to have been taken – but also because Delphi is good for body and mind. Look above us at those shining mountains! It would be too bitter for my poor brother to return to Athens. But, as you say, the Oracle. Yet we who have come suddenly can hardly expect an opportunity for an interview with the Pythia.'

'True,' said Lysippos sadly. 'Our host here cannot act as proxenos and as host of Delphi. Would that he could! My poor brother's daughter. Ai! Ai! In my grief for poor Straton, I yet feel responsible for Anthia – and so helpless. We cannot even find a way to the Oracle.'

'Do not trouble yourself over details,' said Aristotle. 'I can arrange an interview for both of you even at such short notice. I shall send word to you today or tomorrow. The next propitious day is two days hence. Let us hope you can consult the Oracle at that time – the same time as myself.'

'Hope?' said Lysippos, smiling pitifully. 'You are

speaking to one to whom *hope* is a stranger. My hopes are dead.'

'Poor man, poor man,' said Timotheos, accompanying us to the gate. 'All that he says is so terribly true. Who can console him? Yet I think if he could lay his sorrowful questions before Apollo his mind might be comforted. And even a philosopher cannot disdain the Oracle. Did not Sokrates himself consult the Pythia? And what she told him was true.'

'So I remember,' said Aristotle.

'My unfortunate brother of course is no philosopher. He has never understood the truth. Poor fellow. He has set his mind on particulars, material things, mere shadows and shows of the real. If he had learned, as Plato says, to love the Good, he would know that what happens – or seems to happen – in this shadowy cave is not of importance. He sets his heart on that which passes away, on mortal flesh subject to decay.'

'He is greatly to be pitied.'

'Yes,' Timotheos sighed. 'Even I am more man than philosopher. I cannot detach myself from the sorrows of my kindred. And if I had children, I should know better what *he* feels. Thank you for your kindness.'

We walked away. I still felt the weight of Lysippos' sorrow pressing upon me like a darkness in the air. Even the Shining Ones did not seem so high or so beautiful as before. What Aristotle had admitted was true. We had done nothing to help. If only it were possible to go back in time, to the first day of the Anthesteria, when Anthia was safely in her uncle's house, and Kallirrhoe with her, and Straton was alive and cheerful – and Ammonios too. Everybody as they were.

'Aristotle,' I said suddenly. 'You didn't tell Lysippos and Timotheos about Kallirrhoe. That might have pleased them. Should they not interview Anthia's slave-girl? And shouldn't you have asked them about Myrrhine, Lysippos' daughter? Theophrastos said she was missing.'

'Kallirrhoe would be no consolation to them,' said Aristotle. '*She* doesn't know where Anthia is. There is no good news to report. I shall wait. And it is ill done to bring more sorrows to a house of sorrow. I hope I did not do Lysippos harm this morning.'

'By talking to him? Surely not. They were glad to see you. But – Myrrhine?'

'Who knows?' Aristotle replied. 'If they did not mention her, neither should I. Families are entitled to their own secrets. If Lysippos and Timotheos have sorrows that are now public knowledge, that does not mean that they want *everything* known and discussed.'

'Ah, yes,' I said. 'I suppose the girl went completely mad and has been privately locked away somewhere. Unhinged totally by her cousin Anthia's disappearance and then the death of her brother Straton. Most likely. She was said to be mad anyway, I remember.'

'It seems as if everybody is going mad,' said Aristotle. 'Including Polemon and Glaukon – and you, with your ghost-seeing. And not least myself. I will have to use what friendship, money and influence can do to arrange *four* interviews with the Pythia in two days' time – madness! Glaukon – Polemon – and now Lysippos and Timotheos. As well as our own consultations, which are already settled.'

'Why do you want us all to go on the same day?' I asked.

'We Athenians –' Aristotle the *metoikos*, never to be a true Athenian, gave a grin in which self-mockery predominated – 'we must surely remain united. Shoulder to shoulder, like comrades in arms, or what would the Spartans say of us?'

'Is that really all? You seem determined that all of these men should consult the Oracle along with us.'

'Well, Stephanos, consider the nature of the Oracle, and its traditions. Would you not say that going to the Oracle is not only taking advantage of divine favour, but also a kind of test?'

I could not make too much of this, though I ruminated on it. Exactly how he managed it I do not know, but Aristotle did arrange, through Diokles, four other consultations with the Oracle. I believe that some other pilgrims had to be persuaded with substantial presents to relinquish their turn and await another propitious day. Diokles certainly went about the business very effectively, and without abating any of his usual kind cheerfulness.

'Poor Diokles,' said Aristotle to me, 'in what difficulties has he been enmeshed through having us as guests. Housing extra slaves – providing extra interviews with the Oracle – all at short notice. I hope it may not be worse. I must invite him and his family to visit me for the Festival of Athena, or the Great Dionysia. Now, let us look for your ghostly Kharila again. We saw her the second time, but where exactly did you see her on the first occasion?'

We were on our way to the Kastalian spring, just at dawn, the morning after the day on which we had seen Lysippos; it was the day before we were all to consult the

Oracle. I was so acutely aware of our visit to the Pythia the next morning, and anxiously wondering how to phrase my question, that I was no longer interested in the strange hooded person of the grove. Aristotle's interest was, however, unextinguished. However restless he seemed at times, the philosopher did not readily relinquish any subject once he had taken it up.

'Just there,' I said, pointing. The grove was still dusky, partly sheltered from the first beams of day by the powerful mountain. 'Just there where – Great Lord Apollo! She's killed herself!'

We both hastened, looking with horror at the dark shape that swung from the bough of an old gnarled tree. It was like the shapes that swing in the trees in the Anthesteria, yet too large to be one of those toys. It was the shape of a girl, wearing a girl's long white garment, and she was apparently suspended by the neck, dangling from the tree with her feet above the earth. The corpse moved restlessly, twitching to and fro in the dawn breeze.

'No!' said Aristotle, as I was rushing towards the swinging body of the girl. 'Wait!' He drew me after him into the shadows of the grove. It was very still; I could hear the whisper of leaves and the murmur of water from the spring – and also the sound of footsteps.

The person approached – the thin someone with a cloak of dark stuff and dark hood or wrap over the head. She – if it were she – came by the grove near to the spot where we were standing, and was about to pass under the very tree of death when she saw the hanged shape. The Kharila-figure wavered and twirled in the dawn wind. There was a gasp – and then a piercing cry.

'Ai! Ai!' screamed a high voice that left no doubt that

this was a woman. Yet she was courageous, for from her cloak somewhere she took a knife and began frantically to cut at the rope. But then she stared at the body of the wretched creature, and dropping her knife, screamed again.

'By the gods, I am accursed! Are we all to be accursed? I have seen my own death!' So the stranger exclaimed. She bent and picked up her knife with a shaking hand. Then, making no further attempt to help the swinging victim but abandoning the hanged girl, the woman took flight, and ran off through the trees and up the hill as if Pan had frightened her.

Aristotle lost no time in rushing over to the body on the tree. He got there just before I did, and with one wrench at the partly cut rope freed the poor dangling body and laid it on the ground. He bent over the wretched figure. And then, to my surprise, Aristotle laughed aloud. With horror I heard him laugh at the pitiful sight. But then I started laughing too, from sheer relief. For now I too saw that this girl who had died by hanging was no woman or child, but simply a carven image. The figure was really smaller than that of a grown person – it was the robe that made it look as large as a mortal girl. The figure was carved of wood; that is, the head and top part of the torso were made of hollow pieces of light-coloured wood, carved into shape and fitted together, front and back. Arms and hands were also of wood, while most of the 'body' was made of straw tied in a bunch to the wooden bust. The hands were carved carelessly, as if the woodworker had lost interest, and the arms were stick-like. Face and head were more attentively rendered.

The image was not particularly amusing, not at all like a toy, though that was what the stick-like arm reminded me of. Around one wooden arm there was even a tiny loop of silver.

But the eyes were sightless – not just naturally so, as of course the eyes of all statues lack real seeing. These eyes were made to look wide and bulging and staring in death. The mouth was drawn in the horrid smile of death and the tendons could be seen in the neck, with a bulge of wooden puffiness in the carved neck and throat, as if the rope had caused swelling. The hair was carved quite carefully in front, but a few strands of horsehair had also been added with some kind of gum, plaited and twisted over the carven hair in a kind of grim playfulness.

'Do you notice anything about the face?' Aristotle asked.

'It's horrible,' I said.

'Yes, but does it *remind* you of anything – anyone?' He covered up the lower half of the face. 'It looks a bit like Lysippos,' I said hesitantly. Aristotle raised the image off the ground so it seemed to sit up. I was suddenly reminded of Straton discovered in his grave. There was a resemblance.

'It *is* like Lysippos – and like Straton too,' I said uncertainly. 'But this figure is certainly meant to represent a girl.'

'We must hide this – this thing.' Aristotle wrenched away the straw 'body'. Taking the wooden parts of the figure, with particular care of the head, he wound the white robe of the 'hanging girl' carefully around them. Then he hid the whole bundle under some dead leaves and branches in the deepest part of a nearby thicket. 'We will come back for this later,' he announced. 'But now, we must follow her!'

It has taken longer to describe the hanged image than it did to see it, or even to dismantle and hide it. Although the shadowy girl certainly had the advantage of us, we followed not long after. We set out on the same path, running, and were rewarded with the sight of her, speeding up the hill beside the sanctuary.

'After her!' said Aristotle. And on we went. The girl travelled quickly along the road by the temple precincts, then at the top turned to the left, westward. Once, she looked back and saw us, gave an exclamation and redoubled her pace. The next time she looked we were ready for her and had hidden ourselves. The way was uphill and very steep – all this running and pursuing was not as easy as it sounds. Aristotle wheezed and clutched his side, and my shoulder started to ache again. Once Aristotle stumbled on a tree root, and stopped to rub his leg and curse. Finally, as an old man, he had to pause for breath. In fact, we both did.

'She must be – native – of this place?' I suggested, between breaths.

'Or resident – a while,' Aristotle agreed. 'No one – new to Delphi – could run about – mountain – like this.'

We had to go more slowly by the time we got to the Stadion, and could just see the girl disappear around some of the rocks that made the deep base of one of the points of the Shining Ones. The girl sped swiftly along the border where the rocks rose solidly and massively out of the ground.

'Think,' panted Aristotle, 'she will leave – track for us. Wisest – not to follow – too closely.'

We continued the chase by following our quarry's footprints. This also sounds easier than it was, for the base of the crag was still in shadow, even though the sun had arisen over the valley and the birds wheeled delightedly in the new day. Hills, green and grey, were brightening in the light, and below us Delphi itself was touched with cheerful morning. Yet here we were, again on the heights, going around the flank of a mountain.

We looked constantly for the light track of feet in the earth. The ground was fortunately still wet with the dew upon it, and prints often showed. At one point the fleeing stranger had evidently clambered some of the bare rock and taken a drier and more difficult path. But we caught the sign of a damp footprint and fresh earth on the stone, and went on along the rocks. It was still and quiet during this chase. Occasionally we could hear the sound of goats' hooves on stone, or the hawk's cry, and the call of the birds. It struck me that I didn't know exactly *why* we were pursuing this unfortunate unknown young woman. She must already have been frightened enough.

At last, Aristotle said 'Hush!' though I had not been saying anything. Then, through the damp air I thought I could hear something. The sound was not very loud in comparison with the noise of birds whose songs echoed among the mountains, or with the subdued but clear sound of water running from some limestone channel. I listened more carefully, and caught again the other sound, a faint murmur. Voices.

We looked about us: bare rock, empty slope, save for a few pine trees below. 'There.' Aristotle was gesturing with his eyes rather than whispering. I followed the direction and saw the outline of a natural cave where earth and rock met. The entrance had been partly overgrown with bushes, but when one looked intently it became evident that extra bushes and brushwood had been piled up at the gap.

We crept close to the grey mouth of rock. Silence. The scream of a bird of prey far above us. Silence again. Then the faint murmur once more – certainly from within. A voice. A man's voice, gruff, then rising. The murmuring voices of two women. Silence.

'Now,' whispered Aristotle. Then, standing at the entrance of the cave he gave voice aloud and cried, 'Let us in, children of Athens! We also are of Athens, and your friends!'

A new kind of silence – as of shocked people holding their breath. 'Let us in, young man, or at least speak to us,' said Aristotle.

The brush and bushes opened, and a young woman appeared.

XV

The Elektra of the Cave

I gazed in astonishment at this girl, who must have been the person we were following. But she astonished me even further by spitting, quite forcefully. She did not spit exactly upon us, but around the threshold and in our general direction.

'Go away!' she said – much as my young brother said 'Go away, Goblins!' during the Anthesteria at the end of the Night of the Ghosts.

'Ai!' I said. 'Stop that, you!'

'She is only guarding against evil spirits and enemy forces,' said Aristotle. 'But we are not spirits, child, nor are we in any way hostile. No need for apotropaic spitting.'

The girl looked up at him. It was oddly easy for us to look at her, for she was not veiled. She had cast off her cloak and her head and face were bare, though she was still wearing the robe of dark stuff – brown homespun it appeared on closer inspection. Her face was browned by the sun and wind; although she had made an attempt to do her hair up like a well-born woman, it was tumbling about her face. The black elf-locks about her forehead, combined with the piercing effect of large dark eyes and scowling strongly marked black eyebrows, gave her something of the look of a malign enchantress of the wilds.

'Who *are* you?' I said with more force than politeness. But Aristotle was ahead of me, for he said smoothly,

'Myrrhine, daughter of Lysippos of Athens, I am Aristotle of Athens, and I wish to speak to you.' He peered into the cave. 'And to your brother, also.'

'To *Straton*?' I said, alarmed. If Straton were inside the cave, then the world was ghostly and frightening indeed.

'Straton? Indeed not!' The girl Myrrhine gave a shrill laugh. 'Straton is as dead as mutton – dead as last year's sacrifices down below.' She nodded in the direction of Delphi, now invisible to us. 'How do you know I have a brother here?' She turned to Aristotle. 'I have heard of you. The philosopher. You wise man of Athens – or wherever in Makedonia you come from. You and your friend, who is not so wise – how do you know I'm not cohabiting with someone who took my eye? We're strange beggar folk who live in a cave. Why do you wish to trouble us?'

'I know,' said Aristotle gently, 'that he who is with you is your brother. Your brother Gorgias. And the reason you keep aloof must be knowledge of blood-guilt.'

'Blood-guilt – so *that* is why you wish to associate with us. Of course. Come in then, sir.' She made an irreverent bow, but did not move aside to admit us. 'You know all. You are a philosopher, perhaps a seer. A peripatetic chresmologue, a golden-tongued wanderer. Are you, O chresmologue, not afraid of blood-pollution? Ah, no, I forget, you two are murderers too. How very pleasant – like a meeting in a guild, a council of masters of the same trade. Do you bear up, or do you find yourself going mad under it? Being murderers, I mean.'

'You're afraid for your life,' said Aristotle. 'But you need not be. Trust us, and pray to Apollo.'

'Apollo? Pray to Loxias? The prophet in ambush, the speaker of obscure oracles. Loxias the twister. The talkative Wolf-god. He has undone us – and what will he do to help us? No – the gods have given us over to danger and madness, to destroy us.'

'Please, lady, let us help and comfort you,' said Aristotle. 'Your cousin also must be in need of help.'

'Oh, yes – all the family, in fact. Demodikos begat an unhappy line. Come in if you must. It will attract less attention to our fine house than your standing outside. But

"Hush, hush, tread softly, light-sandalled,
Do not murmur, do not make any noise,
Step within – but away, keep away from his bed."'

She drew aside. We stepped into the cave, which at first seemed as dark as a womb or tomb. It took my eyes some time before they could see by the little light which filtered through the entry and through some distant crevice high in the living rock. The walls were fairly dry, but there was a pervasive smell of damp earth. On the rough earthen floor, sprinkled with leaves and dead fern, were a few poor possessions – a cloak, a sheepskin, a water-jar broken at the rim and some cups – unglazed and lumpy, the kind that potters throw away.

At length I could see in the further corner of the cave a man stretched out on a pile of leaves and covered with a cloak. Aristotle moved quietly towards this man and stood looking down on him. I followed. The face was partly obscured by matted hair and an unkempt dark beard. The skin, though recently acquainted with sun and wind, was pallid and covered with sweat. The eyes were blue-circled. Yet this was evidently a man in the flower of youth, though worn by misfortune and illness. Also, this face with the dark hair and well-marked eyebrows was astonishingly like that of Myrrhine, and like Lysippos too.

Gently Aristotle put a hand on the sweating brow and dirty hair. Someone else, someone sitting beside the bed, veiled, holding a cracked water-jar, stirred.

'Let him be!' the unknown woman said sharply.

The man stirred. 'Now you have awakened him,' said Myrrhine. 'What a pity! You will kill him if you drive sleep from his eyes. If he could only stop dreaming – both sleeping and waking – and get some proper rest!'

The man under the cloak mumbled, stirred restlessly, and then suddenly sat up, waving his arms wildly. There was a silver bracelet about one thin sunburnt arm.

'O gods! I can see them again! They're coming – they will have me! With faces like dogs. With bloody eyes! Leave me alone!' He flailed away at us, and Myrrhine rushed to him. Aristotle withdrew to the other side of the cave, and I too. I was affronted at being so addressed and described. In Athens, I thought, people were more civil, but on this journey people had been throwing insults at me – and even spit.

'*Now* I hope you are satisfied!' Myrrhine said to us bitterly. 'There, there, brother. It's all right. There are no demons here – it is all a vision. I'm holding you. I won't let them get you.'

'Dead!' screamed the man, rocking back and forth. 'They have taken me – he has hold of me and will throw me into Tartaros. He wants me to come to Hades with him! Let go!' And with great strength he thrust his sister from him and rolled to and fro in his agony until he fell back panting.

'You see?' said Myrrhine to us. 'Patience, brother, nobody threatens you.' Taking some raw sheep-wool she poured some water and dampened the wool in one of the lumpy cups. Her cloak slipped up and bared her arms; though her hands were brown, her upper arms were whiter than her face. She wore no jewellery of any kind. I thought she looked like a witch. But tenderly she began to wash her brother's face, speaking soothingly as if to a child.

'There, there! Don't worry, you're not going to Hades. You're not. Or if you do, I'll go with you, and we'll keep them all off. Now get some sleep. You know I need you. Where would I be without you?'

He became calmer under her ministrations, and rested again, soon falling asleep.

'So,' said Myrrhine to the other watcher, 'just keep bathing his head a little, very gently, and he should be well enough for a while.'

Her female assistant turned to the task. Myrrhine sighed, and tears stood in her eyes. Aristotle looked attentively at this other woman who sat by the sick man's bed.

'Her face is stained with the weather, and by hard living and tears,' Aristotle said softly but audibly. 'The daughter of Pherekrates was not born for such a rough life. Yet, Anthia, you must be glad to have found refuge among your own kin.'

Myrrhine surprised me by breaking into laughter. 'Oh, yes, such a refuge, such fine kin. What a delightful family altogether –' her voice was quelled by her own tempestuous unhappy laughter. Aristotle, most surprisingly, shook her, quite roughly.

'Stop that. Bear up, girl – if you endure, the end of these troubles will come.'

She wiped her eyes and her laughter ceased. She drew herself up rather nobly, despite her dishevelled appearance.

'Oh, yes, the end will come. Death comes to all – eventually.

> "Nothing there is so terrible in story,
> No piteous suffering nor god-sent mischance,
> But poor mankind may bear it."

But other than death I can imagine no end for us. How can we carry this load? One cannot put an end to being a murderer!'

'But yes,' said Aristotle, 'one can. There is compensation – purgation of blood-guilt –'

'Or execution by the law,' added Myrrhine brightly. 'You know all about the law, O Aristotle. But you too suffer – so one would suppose – though you bear it very well, you and your friend. You go to Delphi very happily, even in the sacred precincts, as if nothing had happened. That makes the curse upon you much worse, though you have not yet felt the touch of the gods' little finger. Oh, they will make you pay! But my brother sees gorgons and demons and Hades in his dreams and in his waking. You will see the same, at least when you come to die, for there is blood-guilt upon you –'

'There is *not*!' I said indignantly. 'We never killed anybody! Who told you we did? I'll prosecute him for evil-speaking. He will have to pay me compensation, and my city, for such horrible –'

'Fine talk!' she said with contempt. 'You cannot prosecute either my brother or myself, for what we say is true. We needed no one to *inform* us. We know. We saw you – all three of us. We *saw* you on the crossroads, bending over the body of Ammonios, after killing him with a boar-spear through the body. Oh, that was excellent. You need not imagine we bear you any particular grudge for the deed. Ammonios was no good friend to us. I suppose you had your reasons.'

Aristotle smiled and sat down on a pile of leaves. 'Daughter, we would ask your hospitality. Will you give us a drink of water?'

She said nothing, but poured water into one of the badly shaped cups and gave it to him. The scene became more ordinary, somehow. I wondered at Aristotle, for my first desire was to run away from this place – away from the raging madman on the bed and from the dangerous madwoman who accused us of murder. I thought bitterly of my desire to know important people – which had led me to this gathering of ill-dressed and smelly persons, murderous and mad, in a place as earthy as my grave. The cave seemed tight, and I felt trapped.

'We can hardly expect,' said Aristotle, 'to convince you of our innocence in that matter. You have circumstances on your side, and you strongly desire that others should be as guilty as yourselves. Yet you were curious as to who else was on the highway, even as you yourselves were fleeing, and wished to remain hidden – since the killing of Straton. You thus chose to go by hill paths, or into the mountains, while keeping an eye on the road. From what vantage point did you see us on that fatal crossroads?'

She laughed without mirth. 'From one of the ruined watchtowers above, where we had spent the night. We heard horses and peered out. We saw you two handling a big boar-spear, and we could see too that you had stuck it into someone.'

'Dear, dear! Pity you didn't wake up earlier – you could have seen the actual murder.'

'Yes, they saw us. And they followed us after that!' I broke in. 'It was *your* face I saw once, as we made our way on the mountain track to Delphi. Peering down at us – you malicious and indelicate girl! Though I thought then you were a boy. And I do believe –' (the thought had just struck me) 'that you tried to kill us on that mountain! The shower of stones, the displaced path! That was you!'

She quailed a little before my indignation. 'Yes,' she said. 'Perhaps it wasn't a very good action. Please understand, we were not trying to *kill* you – just to make you go away. We thought, Gorgias and I, that you might be pursuing us, and we knew you were murderers, after all. We wished just to – to discourage you.'

'But you *laughed*,' I said, still with my grievance. 'You laughed when I fell down.'

'But you weren't much hurt, were you? Moving the stones on the little bridge – that was Gorgias' idea, but I helped. After that, you did go more slowly, and we went ahead of you – we were so relieved. We didn't see you again.'

'But I did see you again. I saw you the day of the consecration, in Delphi. By the sanctuary, dressed as a boy. Impudent and shameless!'

'Yes,' she admitted, with only a slight blush. 'My brother was tired and ill – though not as ill as he is now – and I wanted to hear the news. I didn't go into the sanctuary precincts of course – how could I dare that? But I wanted to find out who you were. And I did, too. I caught sight of you before in Delphi. You were both very conspicuous, going about with that beautiful boy. The celebrated Aristotle of Athens! And his friend Stephanos, son of Nikiarkhos. I nearly laughed in your face.'

'Well,' said Aristotle, 'now we know so much, all of us, it is a pity for each of us not to know more. But you have a more interesting story than ourselves, I do believe. There is always something interesting about fratricide. How long has Gorgias been like this? I am of the tribe of Asklepios, and may be of use.'

Now the girl sat down and poured herself a drink of water. Her hand shook slightly.

'He has been "like this", as you call it, for four days. Since we got to Delphi and found this cave. Before that, we were escaping from our home, you see, and plotting revenge. After we killed Straton, we came upon my cousin Anthia wandering about the wilds, very distressed.'

'You killed Straton!' I exclaimed in triumphant horror. 'So – we have found the murderers!'

Myrrhine ignored me.

'Someone – Anthia says she doesn't know who – abducted her from her father's house, and was taking her to Delphi. Well, my brother Gorgias thought we should go on to Delphi, and perhaps take vengeance on Anthia's Abductor. His mind was full of vengeance then, having just taken vengeance on Straton. Besides, he had dreams, for many months, about Apollo, and thought that at Delphi we might find the help of the god. So we came here. Of course we had been in hiding and didn't want to go among people. And we were blood-guilty, so it was not fair to bring pollution into the houses. I found this place. It's not too bad.' She looked around at the cave, thoughtfully.

'It seemed a good idea at the time. I thought we might rest and recover our strength and think what to do. But, as soon as he had leisure to rest and was no longer moving about or going somewhere, Gorgias began to sink in his spirits. He fell ill, with a low fever. He is strong, so I was not too worried at first. But in his fever the dreams became much worse, so he was frightened of sleep. Since the night of the dedication of the new Temple of Apollo, my brother has had restless dreams and bad visions, even when waking. Sometimes he is quiet, but he has often been raving as you have heard. "Nor do I despise/Tending a brother with a sister's hand", as Elektra says in Euripides' play. And Anthia helps of course,' she added as an afterthought.

'So,' said Aristotle, 'you – O maiden-who-becomes-Elektra-from-time-to-time – have been looking after your brother. You have been begging for food by the grove, like a more successful Kharila – until today you saw that image, as of yourself, and were frightened away.'

'Yes,' she said defiantly. 'We sold some things, but now I – we – live by begging. There are worthy people of the town, and one good widow in particular has been giving me cabbages and bread and some very good cheese. I took water up from Kastalia, thinking it might be more beneficial to my brother than the water here. But that image! Myself hanging and shaking in the breeze!'

The strange girl shuddered. 'I am accurst. It is a sign. I am cursed like my wretched family. The image of the hanged girl was sent to warn me of evils to come. My brother will die, and I shall be driven to kill myself. I see it now.' She gazed into dark futurity, her face bleakly resigned, but she was shivering.

'Let us not borrow ill of the future. It is a bad lender, often promising what never appears – evil as much as good,' said Aristotle. 'But let us go back in time. *How* did you and your brother kill Straton? It was a deed of vengeance, you say – but how exactly?'

'It *was* a deed of vengeance. My brother Straton had tried to compass Gorgias' death. Almost all our lives, you see, it was Straton who was the favourite child of the family. Gorgias was the elder son, but he was rather slow as an infant, and his father never cared very much for him. As for me, I was sickly as a baby and my father and mother even discussed disposing of me before the naming. Perhaps I should never have been allowed to live.' She sighed.

'But Straton was *very* much beloved. He was beautiful, you see. And he was a singer, too – everyone noticed him. My father would always cross Gorgias to please his darling. Poor Gorgias found life at home so difficult that when he was grown he went off as a soldier. My father had, of course, taught him the family trade – or tried to – but he was always so angry with Gorgias' mistakes. He said Gorgias was no good at the silver business, that he was but a second Timotheos. So Gorgias grew to hate the making of silver. While I – I should have liked it, for I like working with my hands, and I know the designs.' She brightened a little. 'When I was a very little girl, I used to watch them working in the shop. They would let me take part sometimes. I know how it's done. I have thought sometimes I would like to be the wife of someone in the common way of trade as a silversmith. As long as my husband did not beat me, and I could have some share in the work – and have children – then I could be content.'

'But you can't get married *now*,' I said unkindly, before I had thought. She was a strange girl. My harsh words brought the sombre look back to her face.

'No. I have been long unwed. I suppose now the blood-guilt means I shall not be marriageable, not ever. Anyway, once Gorgias was far off, Straton began to dream of taking the family business and the inheritance all to himself. If both brothers lived, you know, the inheritance would have to be divided equally between them, as Athenian law has it. So it was with my father and uncles; two brothers prospered while Timotheos did not labour but spent his money and left the rest of his share in Lysippos' hands. To draw on without trouble. But Straton never liked sharing anything with Gorgias.'

'How was he going to prevent it?'

'Chance favoured him. Gorgias ran off to war, and Straton could hope he'd die in battle. And his wishes nearly came true, for Gorgias was wounded and also taken captive in battle against the Persians. But he recovered from his wound (or almost), and made an escape; he came westward, sending a letter ahead to tell the family he was coming home to Attika on a ship that would put in at the harbour of Laurion. If he had been coming to Peiraieus it would have been more difficult for Straton to carry out his plan. Straton intercepted this letter, and my father never saw it.'

'Did you know about it?'

'I saw Straton destroying tablets and a token, and I accused him of hiding something to do with Gorgias – but he only laughed. I told my father and uncle, but they said I had dreams, and was mad on the subject of my brother who was lost in the wars. I had no proof, you see, and I had not actually read what was on the tablets. Now I know what Gorgias has told me, that he did write a letter, I believe it was that epistle I saw being destroyed.

'So Straton knew Gorgias was to arrive and on what ship. Straton watched the ship arrive, we surmise, saw the disembarkation, and followed his brother. Before Gorgias could start on the way home, Straton waylaid him and offered him – as from his father – oil for his wounds and an ass on which to ride. He pretended they were going to see Father at one of his mines close by. Straton took him to a convenient spot nearby in an abandoned mine working, where they stopped for food and wine. Then Straton strangled his brother, and flung his body into an empty mine shaft. Of course he thought he had killed Gorgias.' Myrrhine sighed deeply.

'I suspected something bad was in the wind – I am very quick to gather anything that concerns Gorgias. Straton was too anxious for a while, and then much too pleased and cocky. But I could do nothing. Nothing I said was believed, and I had grown wary of saying much, for by that time the rumour had begun to go about, even outside the family, that I was mad. And I knew nothing in detail – just understood from Straton's strange behaviour. Not long after that we received a letter saying that Gorgias was missing after a big battle, and must be presumed dead. That was official enough. So we went into mourning, and I certainly believed he was dead. By one cause or other.'

'Then Gorgias returned secretly,' said Aristotle.

'Gorgias returned secretly,' Myrrhine confirmed, 'after waiting until he was thoroughly recovered. After Pherekrates' death he sought me alone, not trusting any of the others.'

'Ah, yes,' said Aristotle, 'Gorgias was lucky. I take it the mine shaft was shallow, after all. So he arrived on that misty night – the Night of the Ghosts – and spoke to you; he was standing outside the wall. (Your "Orestes" made that second set of footprints, Stephanos.) So – then you and your brother decided on revenge?'

'Yes. We decided to take revenge on Straton, and kill him. When Anthia was abducted, we thought it was Straton's doing. In the hurly-burly at home I found a chance to slip away and join Gorgias as arranged. We followed Straton, for quite a long way –'

'We know of that journey,' I interrupted, pleased at discovering something for myself. 'Your brother stopped at a farm and asked for food and water for you both. "He came snooping . . . a tall young rascal",' I quoted, remembering. 'And you were chased away by an ill-tempered farmer with a dog, weren't you?'

'Yes, truly – a most unpleasant person. We were so thirsty and tired! Though I don't know how you know about that. Perhaps it wasn't a good thing to go among people. We tried to go in disguise. My brother carried a couple of hides, at first, as a shoemaker, and I dressed as a man-slave, his apprentice. Later, in Delphi and Kirrha, I dressed in Gorgias' clothes. We wanted to leave no traces. But when we had to part with the skins for money we stopped being shoemakers. On the road, we followed Straton, quite cleverly, and met him at last – by the side of the road, near a hill with a big oak tree on it. He was looking down the road as if he were expecting somebody, but of course he wasn't expecting to meet *us*. He was truly surprised!'

'And far from pleased,' suggested Aristotle.

'And far from pleased, naturally, at finding Gorgias was still alive. But Straton was always foolhardy. He didn't think of Gorgias as dangerous to him, just a nuisance. He drew us back a bit from the roadside while we conversed. When we were children, Straton could always order Gorgias to do things. He'd get his way by taunts if all else failed. Now he laughed at Gorgias, calling him a failure in dying and in living. Then Gorgias' blood was up and he deliberately did what he had said he would do. With my encouragement – for I was by his side – he struck Straton with a knife with the full intention to kill him, as he had sworn. Straton fell down, and the life seemed to go out of him all at once. Then we fled away.'

'Yes, of course you would have done,' said Aristotle. 'I quite understand. But you came back soon, did you not?'

'I am not sure how you know that. But it is true. After several stadia we turned back, impelled by pity and custom to bury our brother. We returned in trepidation to that hill, as you can imagine. The body wasn't where we left it. Straton could not have died all at once, for he had crawled somehow further up the hill to the oak tree. I suppose the life wasn't out of him just after the blow, and he had crawled away to get help and water, and died. But one look at his face told us he was perfectly dead this time.'

'You're sure?' said Aristotle. 'He seems to have had wonderful powers of recuperation.'

'Oh, yes, he was *very* dead, by then. Gorgias must have struck more times and harder than we could remember.' She shook a little at the memory. 'There was a lot of blood. We carried out the burial ritual as well as we could in the circumstances – even the prayers. Then we went on. Next day we met Anthia.'

'So that's how it was, then,' said Aristotle. 'May I see the knife that did the deed?'

'Here.' Myrrhine went across the cave and came back with a small bright object in her hand. I flinched from her. A madwoman and a murderess with a knife in her hand is not an encouraging sight. But she gave it calmly enough to Aristotle.

'This is the blood-guilty weapon. I'm afraid it smells of onions. After the murder we cleaned it. And then, as we had no other knife with us – such things are not to be found in the wilds for the asking – I'm afraid I must admit we used it for cooking. It seems horrible enough now, but the killing seemed all right at the time. We were very excited then – happy, even drunk in a strange fashion. We felt like – oh, it's difficult to explain – bigger than life. Like people in a play. And when you have defied the largest laws of gods and men, why worry about smaller ones? It was too terrible to think of a member of the family never able to cross the Styx, and insulted for ever by having no burial, so that we put right at last, for the honour of the family. But we didn't regret our deed, even then. The misery at the heart came afterwards.'

Aristotle fingered the knife, gingerly, and peered at it. He tried out the edge on a piece of stone, looked at the instrument again, and smelt it.

'Onions – and some fish,' he pronounced. 'Where do you get your fish? Kirrha, of course. And you paid for it by selling your bracelet, Myrrhine. I think I know the shop where it lies. You could get it back. Anthia, daughter of Pherekrates, what is *your* story? I suppose you don't know what happened to the slave-girl Kallirrhoe?'

Anthia left her sleeping patient, and came forward to join us. Now she stood up, you could see she was elegantly shaped, a tall girl, taller than Myrrhine. Cave-dwelling did not suit her for she had to stoop when she walked. Her hair was golden, and her eyes were blue. Though her face was tired and her mouth drooped in a pout, Anthia was undeniably pretty. She also seemed – thank the gods – sane (at least one of them was).

'I know nothing about the slave-girl,' the daughter of Pherekrates said in a clear well-bred voice. 'At least, I don't know where she is now. All I know is I got her to change clothes with me in the litter, after I was abducted. And I left her in my place to act as me. I don't know exactly what the Abductor had in mind for me. If it was a forced marriage – why, perhaps he has married a slave, unwittingly, by now. And *that* would serve him right.'

'Who was the Abductor?' Aristotle asked patiently.

'I don't know. How should I? I'm not in the habit of meeting men, aside from my own close kindred, whatever may be the custom in some families . . .' She looked, rather scornfully, at the bare-faced and ill-clad Myrrhine.

'You're sure the Abductor wasn't one of your own kindred? Was it Straton?'

'Well – I haven't talked with Straton, not since we were both small children. Last year I saw him from a window and heard him talking to my father, and I also caught sight of him in the Dionysos Procession. So I know Straton was tall and well shaped. The Abductor was somebody different, that I am sure of. His body was shaped differently, and not graceful. Still, I thought Straton was there at one point, when there were a number of voices. But it's all so confused. I was frightened, and I had been sick too –'

'Yes, we know,' I said hastily.

'Though I did try to see who it was, and so did Kallirrhoe.'

'Did he sing, this Abductor?' asked Aristotle.

'*Sing?* I can't remember. The slaves sang a bit. The Abductor – at least the man who was the leader of the party – had no voice for singing. Though perhaps he was disguising his voice. Rather a high voice it was, and hoarse. Not at all like my cousin's voice. But it may be that the Abductor who accompanied us was merely some creature of Straton's.'

'Why do you think that Straton might have been the real Abductor?'

She frowned. 'How can I know that? But I ask – why did the man who carried out the abduction not try to look upon me and talk to me, at least, if it were true that he wished for me? Was he working for Straton? But I can see no reason why Straton couldn't have married me anyway. His father could arrange it, and my cousin would have been the obvious choice. My nearest male relative, and I am an heiress.' She thrust out her lower lip and hitched up her shoulders. 'I wouldn't have minded marrying my cousin. He was *very* good-looking.'

Anthia cast a frightened, yet obstinate glance at Myrrhine. 'However,' she went on, 'if he was a bad man, maybe it's just as well we didn't marry. These two say Straton tried to murder his brother, which is not a nice thing to think. But I don't really in my heart think the Abductor – the man who was with us when we were forced to travel in the litter – was Straton.'

'Hmm,' said Aristotle, thoughtfully, fitting the tips of his fingers together.

'Can't you do something, sir, to make it right? I've heard of you. They say you are clever. And I don't like living in a cave. I wish we could go home – oh, how I want to go home!'

She burst into tears, and dried her eyes on her veil. Aristotle sat and thought. Suddenly, there was a rustle from the bed. Gorgias was sitting up.

'It's all right,' he said weakly. 'I'm not seeing – er – *them*. Myrrhine, my sister, have these men come to kill us?'

'No,' I said shortly.

'I wonder,' Gorgias said in a dreaming tone, 'if they will execute us. Mightn't it be better for us to kill ourselves?'

Anthia started to wail.

'He *will* talk like that – and she does, also, sometimes. I don't want to *die*! I'd rather even marry someone disagreeable and old than die! And if they both commit suicide and I do not, what will become of me?'

'We are all going to die eventually,' said Aristotle. 'But

there is no reason why any of you three should die now. True, counsel to kill a man – bouleusis of homicide – is a serious charge, and if you, Gorgias and Myrrhine, were convicted of counselling and plotting someone's death, the penalty would be death.'

Anthia started to cry again. The other two remained mute.

'But I think,' said Aristotle, 'that is not exactly what you did, for you have been living in a sort of dream. The sufferings the gods have already sent you are a sufficient payment. Meanwhile – if you *will* go about the country before winter is fairly over, and will sit about weeping in damp caves, you may harm your health. But I believe I can help you.' He stood up. 'Myrrhine, at dusk we will bring some food and good wine to you at the point where the path here runs above the Stadion. Remain concealed, at least for another day. But – you say you have water here? You would all be the better for a bath, if you can heat a little warm water. Wash in the day, in sunny hours. Not in the evening when the chill is on the air. Keep the patient warm, and feed him a little at a time. I shall send some medicine as well as the food.'

'Oh, the doctor calls,' said Myrrhine. 'How very good of him.'

'It is,' said Aristotle, smiling. 'My father was a physician. Myrrhine, you only injure your brother by alarming him. As a sick-nurse, Elektra has her deficiencies. You read a great deal, and Gorgias too. It is not common for a girl to know how to read in this way – I take it Gorgias taught you, Myrrhine, when you were younger? You and Gorgias are both fond of plays – a family characteristic. The drama is a very great thing, but don't try to imitate it, as if you were characters in a fiction. That's not what tragedy is for.

'Do try to think of something other than the Furies and gorgons and so on. Go out tomorrow. I hope you will go out, and Anthia too, if the sun shines and you can emerge unobserved. When you go, look upon all the plants and birds and name them. Order your minds. And pray to Apollo, for he is able to help you. Think of light and healing.'

'Phantom and illusion,' said Gorgias. 'The shadows of the imitations of things, flickering on cave walls.'

'No,' said Aristotle. 'Come out of the cave into the sun. Daylight and health are not illusions. However miserable we may be at times, we must remember that. And – what was I going to say? Oh, yes. I think I can banish one trouble from your minds. You are innocent of brother-killing, though your intention was evil. *That*–' he pointed to their knife – 'did not do the deed. I saw the corpse. Whatever you may have intended, you are not actually the murderers. I also swear solemnly by Zeus and Apollo, and as on the tomb of my mother and my father, that Stephanos and I are both guiltless of the death of Ammonios.

'Farewell. Tomorrow I go to the Oracle of Apollo. And therefrom I hope much regarding your deliverance. Keep your secrets and your hidden life until all can be revealed. I will see you on the morrow or the day after, I trust the gods.'

He turned to the mouth of the cave and we left, clearing the brushwood cautiously away from the entrance and leaving the three behind us in their darkness. Aristotle walked so swiftly back on the mountain path that I had much to do to keep up with him. He seemed new-inspired. His reddish hair shone with light in the midday sun, but there was something fell about his countenance.

'Those poor young people,' he said to me at last, after keeping silence for a long space. 'And I too can quote poetry upon occasion.'

He lifted up his voice suddenly in the great lines spoken by the chorus in the *Orestes* of Euripides:

'"Dark Eumenides, wide-winged above us
Soaring in free space of clear arching sky,
  Avenging injustice, blood-guilt avenging,
  Hear me and my cry
  Imploring, imploring:
Forgive the sad son of great Agamemnon,
Forgetting the mania, the cruelty of madness –"'

His voice reverberated among the strong rocks, and echoed from Parnassos itself.

'What a wonderful speech!' I exclaimed. Aristotle paused in his recitation.

'Yes. You remember, Menelaos in that play says that Grief is a dreaded deity: "For terrible is that goddess, but we have a cure for her." That's the best thing Menelaos ever says in the play. After that, Euripides makes him into a butcher. A great mistake. That bungling by Euripides damages the entire drama. Why should a king not be a gentleman? But these are the great lines.' And he started again, crying out like an actor, 'Dark Eumenides, wide-winged above us,' while the dark-winged hawks soared and hunted in the sky between the peaks.

XVI

The Oracle of Apollo

Next morning's dawn brought us the day appointed, when we were to visit the Oracle, to speak to the Pythia, to Apollo himself. We had arisen very early to take the purifying bath in the Kastalian waters and make prayers, as is right, and to don ceremonial garments. Then we went out fasting into Delphi. Diokles, who was with us, was anxious that all should go properly. The Pythia herself at the same time would have been taking the ceremonial bath in the waters of Kastalia, and purifying herself at the temple hearth. The morning was clouded, the air warm and still.

We went up the road through the sanctuary – pilgrims now indeed. Holy fear started to come upon me, so that I could scarcely notice the beautiful things around me. Aristotle seemed restless; he kept glancing backwards. We took our places in the throng outside the temple. Visitors, each one with his special host, awaited their turn with moderate patience. We were all dressed in our clean white garments of purest wool, and went with washed hair, so the general effect was pleasant.

'I hope these others come,' said Diokles. 'They cannot consult the Pythia save through me and at the time arranged.'

'I hope so, too,' said Aristotle, glancing back again. 'Ah – here is one.' Polemon joined us. This man must have undergone careful purification after the defilement of contact with Ammonios' corpse in order to be capable of entering the sacred precinct. But here he was, washed, cleansed and dressed in white.

'Well,' observed Aristotle genially, 'now you are respectable, my good Polemon, and look much more like the son of a good family.' Indeed, Polemon looked much better than he had as a street singer. His face was pale, however, and worn, and his eyes looked weary.

'You left us somewhat abruptly in Kirrha,' Aristotle went on in the same easy tone. 'Dare I guess the reason? In that – er – particular house we entered you saw a person who could identify you?'

Polemon left off being pale as an awkward blush rose in his neck and face. 'It is true,' he admitted. 'That girl – Tita – the Egyptian. I knew her from Ammonios' house and from his – you know, the other establishment in Peiraieus. That Egyptian girl would know me by name. I didn't want to be known by name to anybody in Kirrha. Those people in that bad house, and the men outside – the ones throwing coins – would mock me. It would disgrace my family. And I still had to worry about . . . about the body of you-know-who,' he ended in a whisper.

'Very nice-minded,' said Aristotle. 'Allow me to make you known to our proxenos.' Polemon, introduced, made proper acknowledgements to Diokles, and took his place with us.

The air was loud with the sound of bleating goats, and as we came closer to the temple we could hear the slaughter and catch the first scent of the rich temple smell, the reek of blood and burning fat, with odour of myrrh and flaming laurel.

'What must I say to the Pythia?' Polemon enquired. 'And what form exactly should my question take?'

'You must ask the question simply,' said Diokles. 'It should be in one sentence, if possible. It is customary and most correct to ask if it is better *to do* or *not to do* something-or-other. Do *not* engage in oratory or rhetorical speech in speaking with Apollo. Remember, it is he whom you really address, not the Pythia who utters the speeches he sends her.'

'The Pythia herself is not a Sibyl, then?' said a man in front of us; he belonged to another party and his own proxenos frowned. This man was the little bow-legged fellow whom I had already seen begging his sponsor to help him ask Apollo for children. His Delphian had done his best, obviously, in getting him here, but this pilgrim seemed ill-instructed.

'No,' said Diokles, 'the Pythia is not a seeress in herself. She becomes inspired only when she takes her seat on the tripod, and at no other time. The present Pythia is a very ordinary woman, the widow of a stonemason of Delphi. All our female prophets of Apollo who officiate in the *adyton* are respectable matrons, past child-bearing age – that is the only requirement.'

'There is no – no special sign upon her?' asked the persistent little man.

'No. In fact, my wife knows the Pythia we are to see today. A good widow, the mother of a family. She makes fine cheese, and lives with her eldest grandson. She's like anybody else. But when she sits in the tripod with pure heart and pure body and Apollo speaks through her, then she is not herself, but his voice.'

'Shall we be able to understand her?'

'Oh, yes. The last one mumbled a good deal, having lost her teeth, but this one speaks out very clearly.'

By this time we were nearing the great altar outside the temple where we must first offer the sacred cake. Aristotle kept twisting his head round to look back.

'I don't see them,' he said – 'but no! I am wrong. There they are at last.'

Lysippos and Timotheos came into view, a trifle breathless from having hurried up the hill and along the Sacred Way.

'He's not very well,' whispered Timotheos to Aristotle, 'but I persuaded him to come. It was good of you to send Diokles' slave to us to conduct us to the purification.'

'Not at all,' said Aristotle. 'I was anxious that you should not miss this sacred opportunity.'

The grieving brothers joined our group. Lysippos looked too weary and dispirited to take much notice of what was going on around him. It was strange to see Timotheos as the more energetic and bustling of the two.

Our goats, which Diokles had kept together for us near the temple, now joined us; they were bleating in chorus, reminding me of the flocks Aristotle and I had seen and heard on the hillsides during our memorable journey. The sacred cakes Diokles had kept in a little bag, and he now passed one to each of us. We had already paid for them – they were very expensive. Where was Glaukon?

'I'm afraid we must give up the last member of our party,' said Diokles, vexed. 'We must make our sacrifices soon.' Already we were coming near the altar, where the priests purified us again with the last lustrations before we made our offering. The air was milky and close. A few drops of rain began to fall, then thought better of it and stopped.

'I'm sorry,' said an awkward voice, and Glaukon came towards us. 'Couldn't see you at first. And it was hard to pass through this crowd.'

Glaukon was the least neatly attired of all of us, and was frankly – and unpleasantly – sweating with his hurry and the warm air. The hem of his cloak was muddy. Had he come all the way up from Kirrha this very morning? Diokles looked at him ruefully; folk who present themselves to the god are supposed to be especially clean. Our good proxenos removed Glaukon's soiled cloak and tried to straighten his white garment – attentions which Glaukon received without noticing. His eyes were vacant, as if he were thinking of something far away, whereas his freckles, staringly visible, looked sharp and knowing, like little eyes. When Diokles gave him his cake, Glaukon nearly dropped it from his inattentive hands.

'Now,' said Diokles. 'Don't keep the priest waiting.'

We received our purification from the sacred water, and offered our cakes. My hand had crumbs on it, and I had to remember not to lick them off. Then we went into the temple, and came to the inner hearth, leading our sacrifices. One of the priests began sprinkling the goats – a tense moment. For before the moment of sacrifice the animal must tremble in token of acquiescence, otherwise it would not be acceptable, and the would-be questioner could not make his sacrifice to Apollo nor consult the Pythia that day. I watched eagerly, but my beast shook soon enough, and then its throat was cut. The great stone of the altar was rich with blood, and red blood streamed down its marble sides. Glaukon mopped his brow and Diokles frowned at him.

Glaukon's own goat, which came next, shivered very violently almost at once, and was soon dispatched. They had more trouble with Aristotle's goat, which was stubborn; the priests kept sprinkling for a long time before it made the sign. After that the sacrifices of Lysippos and Timotheos and Polemon were offered without trouble.

'Come,' said Diokles, and conducted us away from the altar and the hearth of eternal sacred fire of pine and laurel. Smoke and the smell of roasting meat wafted about the temple and swirled around the head of the great chryselephantine statue. It promised good meals for the inhabitants of Delphi that day. The odour was almost overpowering. I had not expected that I would feel hungry when I went to consult the Oracle, but that was the effect upon me.

We went, in orderly fashion, through the temple by the side aisle, past the great shining statue of Apollo of Delphi. Apollo the Musician, Apollo the Healer, Apollo Quick-to-help. We came to the back of the temple, the west side, and stood at the top of some shallow steps. My heartbeat quickened.

We had to wait for a small space as the previous questioner had not yet finished. At last he emerged. It was the little bow-legged man; he looked excited.

'I must sacrifice to Zeus,' he burst out, as soon as he saw us. 'And I must go with my wife to Hera at Argos and we must make sacrifices and offer our hair. Then all will be well – isn't it *wonderful*!'

His sponsor tried to hush him, and Diokles looked slightly scandalised at this chatter.

'But it's important,' said the little man. '*Children!* I must go home and tell my wife!'

He left, and we descended the shallow stair that led down into the earth. 'Now,' said our proxenos, 'think pure thoughts and speak well-omened words.' The room we came to was small and dark, a confined waiting-chamber lit by one lamp. A dim daylight fought its way in from above. The smell of burnt offering was above us now and far away, and far away also were the sounds of the world. The scent of damp earth and a strange slightly sweet gaseous smell mingled with the odour of fresh laurel leaves in our nostrils. Somewhere there was a trickling sound as of melting snow running off down the mountain in some hidden stream.

'Think of all who have been here before us,' said Aristotle in a low but clear voice. 'Sokrates – Oidipous – Kalonodas Korax.'

I shivered.

'You go first,' said Aristotle, pushing Polemon and Glaukon gently before him into the anteroom to the sacred *adyton*. They went. We could see into this anteroom, and even a little into the covered inner room beyond, and we could hear almost everything that went on. After the introduction of the younger man there was a short silence, and then Polemon asked:

'Is it better that I take the body of a – my relative – back to Athens in the manner I have chosen, or that I give him a funeral by fire, where he now lies?'

An attendant priest repeated the question. A pause. Then a low-spoken answer, in a woman's voice.

'It is better that you commit his remains to a funeral pyre, and with prayers. Take the ashes home with you in a plain jar. Do not spend money on fine monuments for him, but spread a table for Plouton and give to the gods, and to the poor of your city.'

Polemon said no more – rightly – and the next questioner was Glaukon. When introduced, he cleared his throat twice. He seemed to have difficulty in getting his question out.

'Is it – is it better that I sacrifice to Zeus or to Apollo or the other gods to be delivered of ill consequences for a – for a rash action? A *very* rash action,' he added earnestly, as if the words were being forced from him.

The answer took longer to come this time, but it was quite clear:

'The consequences have come and are still to come. What is just cannot be averted, but all is not ill with you. Silver and gold are not your friends. It is best to sacrifice to Zeus Basileus and to Apollo, with the sacrifice of a whole ox and a distribution of meat to the citizens.'

Polemon and Glaukon came out of the antechamber of the *adyton*, looking awed and thoughtful. Then it was the turn of Aristotle and myself, and we passed into the other room.

This anteroom was a narrow semicircle looking into the *adyton*, a very small circular room, like a cave, with a recess at the back. We had not descended very far, but this place seemed the absolute centre of the earth. In it stood the Omphalos, the navel stone, reminding us that we stood upon the middle of the world. Beside it was the golden statue of the god. The slight but hauntingly sweet smell was more noticeable here, and the bubbling of water more audible. In the centre of the *adyton*, presumably directly above the sacred chasm, was the Pythia. She was seated in the bronze three-legged pot, as one might sit on a raised chair. It was the sacred tripod itself. Her face when she was seated was on a level with ours as we stood before her. The priest who would repeat our question or interpret what she said stood just behind her.

We could see the Pythia quite clearly, for her veil was drawn back from her face, showing her hair, as a young maiden arranges it when she sits at ease in her family home. Her dress was also the simple dress of a young girl. Yet it was no virgin girl, no youthful maiden upon whom we gazed, but a woman past fifty years. Her skin was old and faded, and there were deep wrinkles about her eyes and mouth; her hair, so neatly arranged, was streaked with grey. Her face was, however, tranquil, the face of one who has lived a blameless life, who has known toil and leisure in fresh air, and has taken a harvest of good years. I had never met her before, and yet she seemed to remind me of somebody. The clear brown eyes that looked unwaveringly upon us, as a woman never looks usually upon a man, were wide open, large and surprisingly youthful in that elderly face. I felt abashed under that searching, unblinking gaze, for this woman seated on the sacred tripod saw us with the eyes of Apollo himself.

Aristotle pushed me forward, signalling that I, although the younger, should ask my question first. Proxenos Diokles announced my name.

'Stephanos, son of Nikiarkhos of Athens.'

My throat contracted and my mouth went dry. Suddenly, my hungry stomach gave a most enormous rumble, so loud that I knew that the Pythia herself must have heard. I was wretchedly ashamed – I could not look at Aristotle, nor at any of those around me, but blushed and looked at the sacred Navel Stone. I saw the Pythia's hand, the wrinkled work-seamed hand holding the branch of laurel, tremble slightly.

'Address your question,' Diokles prompted me, in a resigned tone.

'Is it better for me to marry soon? And should I marry into the family I have just met?' I blundered. Diokles repeated my question, with a frown, for this was not exactly as I had given it to him before. Earlier, I had said I wished to ask if I should marry the daughter of Kallimakhos. I thought that this was the question I wanted to ask – but my real question came out differently. In fact it was two questions, which was against the rules.

The Pythia gave a low sound, like the beginning of a laugh. Then she spoke to me – and I found myself compelled to look up and meet her gaze. The priest repeated her words:

'Stephanos of Athens, it is best that you do as your father before you.'

That was all she said to me. I waited for more, but she appeared to feel that she had spoken enough; or rather, Apollo had nothing more to add.

Then it was Aristotle's turn. He stepped forward, and Diokles was about to introduce him, but before the philosopher's name could be told he was recognised by the god through the woman seated on the tripod:

'O Aristotle, philosopher of Athens, yet not of that city, I know you. In Athens you were not born, in Athens you shall not die, but where the water turns round. The trees of the East shall wither but the trees of the West shall flourish. You will beget and begin a line, yet your offspring will be unable to do you funereal service. Knowing much, you yet know only a little – but that you also know. You have a strange purpose in coming here. Do not think to put the gods to work for your own purposes, for their ends are greater than yours. Yet if your heart be not impure, ask your question.'

'O Apollo,' said Aristotle, 'is it best, and best for me and for others, that I should set free the newest slaves of my household?'

The Pythia did not wait for his question to be repeated, but spoke directly to him:

'They are not in your household now, but in that of another, and should never be slaves in your house. They belong to no man, but you must pay for their freedom. Unbind them though they be not yours to unbind. Keep them, and mischief will follow. Sacrifice to the gods and pray for the prosperity of those whom you make free.'

'May I ask another question?' said Aristotle eagerly, to his proxenos. Again the Pythia responded to him without intermediary.

'Question me no more, wise man, for there are those without to whom I must speak, though I had rather keep silence. The god bids me speak. The air smells strange and foul.'

Her eyes looked beyond us, as if tired of seeing us. Our interview was over. We left the small room. The Pythia gazed after us at the entrance, her head moving uneasily from side to side, anxiously, as if our interview had been but a holiday interval before some important labour.

The place felt frightening, full of holy power – very gracious but in some manner most dangerous also. I was shaken by the experience of being so close to the god, and even Aristotle seemed deeply agitated, his usual cheerful calm almost struck away.

'Now!' he said to Lysippos and Timotheos who waited outside the door. Diokles took them by the arm to guide them into the anteroom to the *adyton.* Before their feet had touched the threshold of the anteroom, there was a rumble of thunder, far overhead in the skies above the temple. We who were underground, with the weight of the temple above us, felt its sound and violence in the earth itself. I wondered at first if this were an earthquake.

'No!' Lysippos cried out suddenly. 'No – I cannot!' He and Timotheos abruptly turned and ran back through the waiting-chamber and up the shallow flight of steps.

XVII

The Murderer

'After them!' cried Aristotle. We ran out of the holy place. Lysippos and Timotheos rushed in an impious manner through the temple. With Diokles following, Aristotle and I hurried along in scarcely more religious a fashion, though the crowds prevented our going with utmost speed. We went past the altar, through the haze of smoke of laurel and meat and myrrh, to the outer gate, the eastern entry to the temple. Ahead of us we saw Lysippos and Timotheos shoving their way through the throngs by the doorway and then turning to the less crowded part of the sanctuary, past the row of tripods towards the Leskhe of the Knidians. There they took the path that led to an upper gate in the sanctuary wall.

We followed as quickly as we were able – myself and Aristotle, with Diokles just behind, and Polemon and Glaukon, who had already been on their way out of the temple when they caught sight of us, bringing up the rear. Once outside the sanctuary gate, the two who seemed to be fleeing stopped and turned to face us, Lysippos, pale and breathless, leaning on his brother's arm.

'Now we know!' Aristotle said to me as we went along the path just below the Knidian club house. But I knew nothing. 'Lysippos looks ill,' I said. The thunder growled and rattled among the mountains. We had slowed to an ordinary walking pace as the brothers seemed to be waiting now for us to catch up with them. Passing through the gate we came up to Lysippos and Timotheos, where they stood on a path leading to the base of the western crag of the Shining Ones.

'You know, don't you,' said Aristotle, 'that planning or counselling a murder is as bad as murder itself? By law, bouleusis of homicide carries the same guilt as committing the deed. The one who causes it to be done is guilty, though his fingers never come near the corpse.'

It was Timotheos who spoke, ignoring Aristotle's last strange remarks.

'There is nothing to be alarmed at, gentlemen. My brother was not feeling well. He often has the headache in thunderous weather, and he has never liked close rooms. Today he was taken also with trouble in breathing, and pains in his chest. You know he is not very well – all this sorrow.' He looked down at Lysippos, who was leaning against him. 'The effort was too much. A sad mistake it was to bring him here – he was not capable of the long day's ceremony. *Most* unfortunate. Our apologies to your – our – proxenos. But you must forgive us, please. And now if someone would help us to the house, we should be grateful!'

Aristotle replied, but his manner and tone did not match those of Timotheos. Aristotle sounded more like the god speaking through the Pythia. Looking the two men in the face unwaveringly he gave utterance in measured speech:

'Your hopes are dead, but not your children – save one. For you, O Lysippos, were cursed with a son too obedient, yet disobedient. Fly, O Lysippos and Timotheos. Murder itself, and also compassing and plotting murder, are great crimes. Make your escape to other lands, and save yourselves – if the gods will allow it.'

Lysippos suddenly broke away from his brother's arm, and, sobbing, started a feeble run up the hill path. Timotheos followed and grasped his arm again. Lysippos turned and faced us. I can remember now how he looked, how pathetic, as he stood above me on a rock in the path, white-faced, with sudden tears streaming down even to his beautiful beard.

'Straton!' he cried. 'My son Straton! Ai! The gods carry vengeance for blood-guilt!' He looked beseechingly at the cloud-darkened sky, which answered only with a pitiless rumble of thunder. The echo of the thunder hung over the gorge. Knowledge had taken me by surprise, but I realised the full meaning of the strange scene then. Lysippos – he was the murderer of his own son! He had killed a son, a young man in the pride of his age. It seemed too horrible and unnatural to contemplate. And I had polluted myself by being in his presence.

'Save yourself from blood-guiltiness!' said Aristotle.

'I have shed no blood,' said Lysippos, gathering up his courage in defiance. '*I* am not a murderer.'

'You know,' said Aristotle. 'Yes, you know full well that your mind was murderous and foul. Bouleusis of homicide is the same thing as homicide. Your own deed has returned upon you!'

'Ai! What have I done?' sobbed Lysippos, hiding his face with his hands.

'You have plotted the murder of an Athenian. You have connived at poisoning. You have compassed the abduction of an Athenian citizen's daughter.' Aristotle stared ruthlessly at Lysippos. 'You know well enough what you have done.'

'Yes – yes. It all went wrong, it all went wrong!' exclaimed Lysippos, waving his hands in the air. His face was ashen and his beard was matted with damp drops.

'Alas!' said Timotheos, tearing his own wispy hair. A few drops of rain had begun to fall sluggishly, spattering earth and rocks. Rain dropped on Timotheos' hair and face so one was not sure which were tears and which were drops sent from the heavens. He had let go of his brother's arm in horror, though he still stood beside him. Now Timotheos moved a few steps up the path, above and away from the distressing figure of Lysippos. Lysippos covered his face with his hands and stood there, shivering.

'Ai! What grief is here? My brother a murderer!' Timotheos cried out in anguish, gazing at the sobbing figure. 'He has been unsettled in his wits, gentlemen. On him – and on me – have pity. Justice, I know, directs you to stone him where he stands. The gods have driven him mad long ago. He killed Straton – his own son! And I . . . I had some hint in his ravings since this illness, but did not understand all. But now, though he did not dare to face the Pythia, the gods have driven him to confess. And he *has* confessed – alas! – though he deny it the next minute. You have all heard him. What will happen to our miserable family? Oh, it were better he should die – he, a murderer!'

'No,' said Aristotle, judiciously. 'Lysippos is not exactly a murderer. Certainly not the murderer of Straton. *You* are.'

Lysippos uncovered his face and turned to look at his brother and then at us.

'Is that true? Is it certain?' he said wonderingly, like a man wakening out of sleep. 'I thought . . . I suspected . . . Are you sure?'

'Look at your brother and see,' said Aristotle.

We all looked at Timotheos. He laughed wildly as the thunder shower broke around us.

'You conceited idiot!' he shouted at Lysippos. '*I* am not fool enough to confess before witnesses!'

'I shall kill you!' said Lysippos, as if given strength by the fresh rain. He grappled feebly with Timotheos. The one standing on higher ground had the advantage and Lysippos was brusquely pushed down upon the muddy ground. Timotheos stood above him, with a strange smile on his face. He made no effort to help the fallen Lysippos. I think it was this action of Timotheos against his brother, to whom he had been acting with such apparent kindness a short time before, which made everyone present certain that Aristotle's accusation was true.

'Stone him!' said Glaukon. Seizing a large pebble he flung it at Timotheos.

'No, no! Don't do that!' Aristotle cried, but Timotheos did not wait to hear the result of this argument. Immediately he turned and began to run up the path, towards the Shining Cliff. In a cluster we came after. The sharp rain hid him for a moment. Then it ceased as abruptly as it had begun; a bright gleam of sunshine appeared, though the thunder growled still over the gorge.

The end of the rain shower showed us Timotheos unbelievably climbing the crag. He had gone up the path and the lower reaches of strewn rocks, and was now on the Shining Cliff itself. The place was so steep that only a goat could approach it with confidence. Yet Timotheos, taking strange power from his danger, went about climbing quite well. He shook off his sandals and threw off his sodden cloak – we found it, drenched and heavy, on a rock. With his khiton clinging about his body and steaming, he managed the next distance, working his way eastwards, away from the temple sanctuary.

'The gods have made him mad!' said Diokles, dropping out of the chase. Aristotle and I followed Timotheos still, albeit cautiously. We had made our way up the path, and now began to climb the sharp face. I found here a foothold, there a foothold.

'Timotheos,' gasped Aristotle, who was going four-footed just behind me. 'There is no escape here. This is folly!'

There was no reply from the fleeing Timotheos. Yet, seeing us climbing so awkwardly and unwilling to go further, he paused. He took the time to slip off his khiton. His damp naked body, white where the clothes usually covered it, shone in the spring sun like ivory. On he went, climbing up Parnassos.

'Wait!' Aristotle pleaded. 'I promise you a safe return to Athens, if you will stand trial. Take the path of justice. Do not give way to fear!'

Timotheos went a few feet more, and gained a better footing; he stood above us, glaring down. Suddenly, he seized a pebble and threw it at Aristotle. The stone missile missed its target – but only just.

'Aristotle! Aristotle of Makedon gives good advice. Take that, you smug rhetorician! You teacher of the earthy ways of plants and animals, you Makedonian collector of straws! *You* – a great philosopher! Do not you wish you were?' Teasingly he threw another stone. 'Look at you crouching and flinching. Movement of animals, shall we call it? I tell you, I am a better man than you! And a better philosopher! For I follow Plato, and look to the heavenly world, the realm of the Forms. Purity is mine, and divine law, not the crawling of crabs and the rhetoric of the market-place. You a philosopher! You have betrayed Plato. The divine realm is not for you. You are afraid of the heights.'

'Even if – if all you say is true,' Aristotle gasped, clinging to the mountain side, 'come to Athens and plead your cause. Seek Justice! Does not Plato honour Justice?'

Timotheos smiled grimly. 'Tell me, base pseudo-philosopher from a Makedonian hamlet – what *is* Justice?'

He did not wait for our reply, but went on, and we too crawled a little way further. I could no longer look down with ease, and I felt afraid for Aristotle, an old man on this treacherous height. Timotheos did not seem to be an old man, but went naked and full of energy, like a youth.

'Go back!' I commanded Aristotle. 'Do not try to go any further. I will go to him – and I will do him no harm.' I crawled on, only stopping to frown at Aristotle and see that he obeyed me. It was madness for him to risk his life so. And he did stop, clinging four-square to his own bit of Parnassos. But he did not go back.

Timotheos reached a narrow ledge above the chasm between the Shining Ones, with steep rock above and below. He stood up again. I crawled a bit further towards him.

'Come back, please,' I requested. But he paid no attention to me.

'Tell me, what is Justice?' he demanded again, looking scornfully down at where Aristotle was spread-eagled against the rock. 'Look at yourself, mighty philosopher! And look at those down there!' He pointed to the gaping crowd which had gathered below us. Seen from this distance, the men, open-mouthed, were small.

'Little, stupid men!' Timotheos waved his right hand scornfully. 'My brothers sought to cheat me out of my inheritance – was that Justice? And I was so much better than they, for they worked on silver with their hands – mere mechanics. But *I* worked with my mind. I am a midwife of the spirit, true descendant of Sokrates and Plato. Yet *I* was despised. Was that Justice?

'But I was cleverer than they. And I would have taken all their wealth – all that they so patiently gathered – in the end. Then with that heap of silver I could have founded my own Academy. For I was patient too, as well as clever. I would have taken all, O Makedonian, if you had not interfered.'

'Did you kill Straton?' Aristotle yelled up at Timotheos from his precarious position. 'I accuse you –'

'Yes – I did. I certainly got rid of Straton, that foolish swaggering youth. You, curiosity-monger – since you are itching to know, I will tell you. And it was I who killed that fat pig by the crossroads. Stuck him like an old boar with a spear I borrowed for that purpose. I have deceived you all finely until now, haven't I?'

'Very finely,' Aristotle said, in as soothing a tone as he

could manage while shouting carefully from his patch of mountain.

'And I tell you, man of Stageira, that it was my brother who was a coward, and flinched and ran from the Pythia. Not I. I would have gone through with the whole, Oracle or no. For I defy you all. All of you, people of Athens and Delphi alike, or wanderers to these shores. Small men asking for trash – gold and wives and whelps and houses. Small men of material mind, begging their cheating images. The empty-handed gods that you adore!'

'Oh, be careful!' I warned, the words torn from me involuntarily at this blasphemy. And then again, 'Oh, be *careful*!' I cried. For I saw that the place Timotheos was standing on was slippery with rain. In his exalted fury the naked man had forgotten to move cautiously, but was swinging his white body about and almost dancing on his bare toes. The slippery rock gleamed in the sun.

'Look! I speak and the sun comes out!' Timotheos spoke mockingly. 'The earthquake falls on the sacred temple, thunder resounds over the pilgrims' heads, but the murderer speaks the truth and the sun appears!' Certainly, the clouds had faded. The sunlight aimed its shaft over the gorge, falling on the rock and on the temple and on the Tholos of Athena Pronaia, much as I had first seen it.

'Apollo, the pot-thief, the foolish god!' said Timotheos, chuckling to himself. The sun shone dazzlingly upon water drops and pools of rain and on the smooth limestone ledges. And I think the sun was in Timotheos' eyes and in his understanding, for he took a step on nothing, planted his right foot on the unsolid air. His left foot slipped on the shining rock before he could regain his balance and return.

'Loxias!' he shouted, and fell into the narrow gorge between the Shining Ones, almost at the point where the Spring of Kastalia gushes forth. We held our breath in horror, and heard one long wordless scream and the body of Timotheos striking the sides as he went. Then there was a faint crash and a smaller echo and silence. An eagle screamed above.

We were all amazed by that sudden fall. The little crowd below remained standing open-mouthed, gazing at empty air. I was not happy, for I had been nearest Timotheos, and his misadventure made me dizzy. I realised I would have to go back the way I had come. I crawled backwards, like a crab, along the sharp wet rock, with the sun in my eyes, until I reached Aristotle and we could help each other. Very slowly we went, until at last we reached a rock-fall which offered better footing, and could walk to the path and safety.

The scene below looked much as it had done when we first attempted the Shining Cliff – save for the absence of Timotheos, now eclipsed for ever. There were a few more spectators. Lysippos still sat huddled on a stone, weeping.

Aristotle touched the man on the shoulder.

'You must go,' he said. 'Your brother is certainly dead, but you must not stay.'

'What you say is true.' Lysippos raised his face. 'Have pity on me, good people. I wish to speak alone to these men of my own city – to Polemon and Glaukon and Stephanos and Aristotle.'

The audience, though they had expected more, were kind enough to retire. They had certainly taken a good view of an important event. Some of the bolder spirits among them now suggested going to look for the body of Timotheos. Men of Delphi should be sent for, labourers who knew the rocky place. Someone grimly suggested fetching a door, and ropes.

When our little group was alone with the bereaved Lysippos, he sat as if yet powerless to move, facing us as we stood in a ring about him.

'I shed no blood,' he said. 'But it is true that I planned and counselled a murder. I had wished at one stroke to rid myself of a rival, and to disinherit and destroy my own brother's daughter. What madness the gods put upon me I know not – that I should do such things! But the way seemed plain before me until the deed retorted upon my own head. Most terribly – my son, my Straton!'

'But you have another son,' said Aristotle gently. 'I tell you, through the mercy of the gods he lives. Gorgias is alive.'

Lysippos shook his head, and the tears welled once again in his eyes.

'Gorgias? Most strange . . . you say so? Gorgias whom I thought dead still breathes and walks upon the earth? A miracle without meaning. A poor exchange! Gorgias has been dead to me for such a long time. And he was *never* the son that Straton was. Gorgias was not important to me. Without Straton, I am nothing.'

'But,' said Aristotle, 'the inheritance must be kept for your living children. Should you go to Athens and face trial for your wrongdoing, your children might suffer severely. There might be sentence of exile for you, and certainly a fine or confiscation. Yet – is it right that we should all keep silence? Especially the man whom you injured most of those still living, who is Glaukon here.

For you did try your best to compass Glaukon's death, did you not?'

Lysippos nodded mutely.

'And you contrived the abduction of your brother's daughter – an act that seems to me almost worse than murder itself. Fortunately she lives and is well, under the care of Gorgias. But you sent an unsuspecting girl who depended on you – your brother's orphan daughter, a sacred charge – into an alarming experience of very real danger.'

'Yes,' whimpered Lysippos softly. 'Yes – but you don't understand. It was all part of a plan –'

'I understand the plan,' said Aristotle. 'And it does you no credit at all. Now, is it right that you should enjoy at home the fruits of your two brothers' deaths, as if nothing had happened? And was your heart entirely guiltless of the death of Ammonios? Did you not connive at poisoning – in your own house?'

'Well,' said Lysippos slowly, 'it seems so long ago now. It wasn't my idea. And Ammonios didn't die then, you know. Big fellow. Very hard man to kill, Ammonios.'

'Not your idea,' said Aristotle. 'True – some of the ideas came from Straton, did they not?'

'Yes,' admitted Lysippos. 'Straton suggested the abduction plan. *He* didn't like Ammonios – told me that Ammonios had lewd thoughts about Anthia. And I saw for myself that was true.'

'You told me the same thing,' said Glaukon. 'Said you feared Ammonios' lasciviousness was not under proper control, and that he would make an attempt on your niece.'

'Yes, I did tell you that,' agreed Lysippos.

'So you planned to murder Ammonios,' said Aristotle. 'But is there not a still worse element in your plan regarding Anthia? Anthia was to be "abducted" by your arrangement.'

'It was Straton's idea.'

'Very well then. You and Straton planned the abduction. And Straton was to find the Abductor and Anthia. You must thank the gods that Anthia was not sexually molested and was not killed. Was it not the plan, O Lysippos, was it not the terrible plan that Straton in a fit of righteous indignation should kill both the Abductor and Anthia – as if she were a partner in his crime? Or did you merely intend to disinherit Anthia by rejecting her as a lascivious wanton who had run away with a man?'

'Well, we thought of that . . .' said Lysippos.

'But decided that to kill Anthia offered the straighter way to Pherekrates' wealth?'

Lysippos looked mournfully at the ground. 'I don't know – I have nothing to tell you. What Straton may have thought of was his own affair. I told him I didn't need to know everything.'

There was a moment's horrified silence. Then Lysippos lifted up his head again. 'From what you yourself have said,' he remarked, 'Anthia lives and is well. So there is no homicide, nor anything else to answer for in that case. Except she had a little unexpected journey.' He laughed, a melancholy and discordant sound.

'Alas!' said Aristotle. 'You made a beautiful image of your beloved Straton, but you and Straton did each other no good at all.'

He sighed, and Lysippos sighed too. He lost his defiant look and tears began to drip from his eyes.

'Well, now,' said Aristotle, 'tell me, Lysippos, what is just? How should we treat your case? Your brother Timotheos, guilty of deeper crimes even than your own, is already disposed of. What is Justice, then, for you?'

Lysippos smiled without mirth. 'You heard my brother. Oh, he was strange. In the last few days I have come to fear him greatly. But I still repeat his question. What is Justice? Some of his words are true. I *am* ill. I have suffered from lack of breath, and strange pains.'

'Hmm,' said Aristotle. 'Men in such bad case do not go running to relieve their pain.'

'No,' said Lysippos, blushing a little. 'It was not true just now, when fear gave me a strength not truly mine. But now, gentlemen, see how I tremble, how wildly my heart beats! I am dizzy and there is a rushing in my ears. I swear most solemnly that I believe in my heart I am soon to go on the dark road, and must face the justice of the King of Hades, if such there be. I appeal to you.'

He spread out his trembling hands, palm upward, towards us. 'I ask you, for my children's sake if not for mine, do not torment me any more. Who would profit in bringing more disgrace upon us or our city? I have no desire to return to Athens, even if I could do so in all propriety. My house is desolate to me without my son. Let me go. Let me go *now* – away from Delphi, away from Attika. My son Gorgias, if he is truly in being, can deal with my brother's funeral. Let me sail to one of the farther islands. There I will spend my last days. My children will be blest, as far as the gods and you permit, with their inheritance and something of the name of honour.' He looked at us pleadingly.

'Will you allow this?' Aristotle asked the others. They

nodded, but Glaukon said, 'Yet, if he should return to Athens –?'

'I promise I will not,' said Lysippos wearily. 'If you wish, write out a short description of the case and I will sign it. It could then stand in evidence against me, were I to return to Athens. Return? You don't know what you are saying. Athens! I am sick of the very name of the city.'

'Let me talk to him alone,' said Aristotle. We moved away, while the two conferred. Their conversation was not long.

'Lysippos is well enough to walk now,' said Aristotle, returning. 'But he will need help. Polemon – for the honour of Athens and the safety of this man's wretched children, I beg it of you. Will you assist him on the journey to Kirrha and see him on board a ship that will take him away? A ship leaves for Naxos shortly. It is a great deal to ask of you, Polemon, but someone strong and honourable – and competent – must see Lysippos into exile.'

'But Lysippos cannot take the regular ship to Naxos,' I protested. 'He would bring blood-guilt to all the passengers and crew. And you and I are polluted now, having been so close to him and to Timotheos this hour.'

'Oh. True. A nuisance. Certainly, the passengers to Naxos would be terribly upset if they found out. Lysippos must charter his own boat, and give extra money to the crew at the end of the journey for purification. Oh, and he must leave some money to cover the purification of all four of us, and Diokles, our ever-unfortunate host.'

'He won't have much money left,' Glaukon objected.

'Lysippos has great resources. He can send to Athens from the-god-knows-where and get some more money.

But haste is necessary. Fetch a mule, Polemon, and ride down to Kirrha as fast as you can without making Lysippos ill. Do not leave him, and make sure he goes aboard. Ah! Here is Korydon. Excellent, he can run some errands for us.'

The young man had just come up to us, very eagerly, his face shining with excitement.

'I heard you were here,' he said. 'Did you see it all? Was that villain who died the Abductor? Kallirrhoe will be so pleased. How I wish I had been with you when he dropped off the mountain! To think I missed it!'

'Korydon,' said Aristotle, 'do you go and bring me fresh writing tablets from Diokles' house – and bring also some clean clothes for this man, Lysippos, from the house of his own guest-friend, and all the money that Lysippos has in the house.'

'Trusting a slave with my money?' said Lysippos indignantly. Nobody attended to him.

'Where is that?' said Korydon, quite amiably, considering that his position as our attendant never held any particular charms for him.

Aristotle gave directions. 'Lysippos had better not go back there,' he added. 'They may be bringing back the dead body of his brother to that house. He is too unwell at the moment for such an encounter.'

'I don't think they'll find the corpse so soon,' said Korydon with some relish. 'And it won't be a proper body when they do, probably more like a mush. When they do find the thing, it will be too polluted to take into a house. They'll have to set it up in a shed, or an unused yard or field. *Everyone*'s talking about it. They say that the Athenian man confessed to murder and then was thrown off the rock by the god Apollo into a place so narrow they may not find him at all. He may end where he lies now, like one buried in a cave.'

'A cave? Dear me,' said Aristotle. 'I nearly forgot. Let us go, Stephanos, we still have much to do today. Polemon, please to take care of Lysippos and send him on his voyage. Korydon will bring his possessions to you.'

Polemon began to lead the tremulous Lysippos on the southward path down to the town and the Sacred Way. Glaukon still stood where he had been, looking askance at Lysippos and nodding thoughtfully to himself, the freckles as plain on his pale face as bronze coins on a marble slab. Beside him stood Korydon, not disposed to hurry when he could linger and gaze up, open-mouthed, at the Shining Cliff. Plainly he regretted not having been a spectator of the calamitous incident.

'Please, Korydon, my lad, hurry,' said Aristotle, as he turned toward the western path. 'I would do it all myself, but I have to deliver some children from a cave.'

'Can we do that yet?' I said. 'Don't we need to purify ourselves? We have been in company with the blood-guilty. And anybody who touches us shares in the curse until we are cleansed of it.'

'The bother! You are right, of course. We must get some ritual purification in a hurry. I don't want Elektra shut up longer than need be. And I pray Orestes may be healed of his madness – or, at least, somewhat better.'

Glaukon and Korydon looked at him as if he were the madman. But Aristotle had no chance to explain further just then. For a stocky, plainly-clad man with a very red face had come lunging up the path. After brushing by Lysippos, of whom he took no notice, he burst among us.

A strong odour of farmyard, particularly of pigs, accompanied him.

'You, boy! Impudent rascal! I'll deal with you later – but take this on account!' The stranger gave Korydon a great box on the ear, so that the boy jumped back and cried out.

'And now,' said the red-faced newcomer, 'what I want to know is: *who* stole my slave? Whose slave are you now, boy?'

Korydon obstinately shut his mouth and turned away, but Glaukon, puzzled, pointed at Aristotle.

'Ah!' The stranger rounded on Aristotle and went up to him, taking him by the shoulders and shaking him. 'Hear me, all of you! I complain against this man for slave-theft! A valuable slave, too! The villain! I'll have justice on him, or I'm not a Boiotian!'

'Ha, ha!' Korydon's laugh was disdainful. 'Now you have acquired blood-guilt too, farmer, and you will have to await purification. You could do with it!'

XVIII

Justice and an Abductor

The rest of that long day was largely taken up with cleansing rituals. Diokles, naturally, was not best pleased. Even his hospitality and good nature suffered under the strain.

'You have brought blood-guilt to the house – and to the whole of Delphi,' he said with vigorous reproach to Aristotle. 'And to the holy temple itself, in its rededication. You made me the proxenos of a killer! You let a murderer take his crime within our temple – even to the holiest place!'

'Ah,' said Aristotle. 'I deeply regret what has occurred. But you must see, the approach to the Pythia was a test – *the* test. If the men were willing to undertake it, logically it would seem that they were not the killers, whatever other crime they might have committed.'

'What a shame for Delphi! How could you do it?'

'Not a shame upon Delphi,' said Aristotle eagerly. 'A glory, rather. The Delphians must show how the power of

Apollo was displayed this day, how a murderer was found out by the purity of the temple, and how Apollo brought the blasphemer to his death. Think about it. Many will come to Delphi just to look up at the site where Timotheos fell.'

Much later, on the evening of that same day, Aristotle sat in a room in Diokles' house surrounded by a very mixed party of friends. Diokles could not be there, as he had gone to a meeting with other dignitaries to discuss the situation.

The corpse had been recovered – thanks chiefly to the intrepidity of someone's slave, a man who had once worked in the mines. The body of Timotheos was sadly battered: 'every bone broken', some reported. The corpse had not been improved by being dragged out of the crevasse with ropes and hooks. It now reposed outside Delphi. The civic authorities wished to discuss the pollution of Kastalia, and how to keep news of the striking event from having the wrong effect on future pilgrims. It seemed likely they would take the line suggested by Aristotle, which was in fact what they did in the end. Historical records of the rededication, however, make no mention of Timotheos and his ending.

A series of short thunderstorms had died away, leaving clear cool weather behind. A small fire burned in a brazier in Diokles' comfortable room and beside it sat Aristotle, in the best chair, drinking wine and looking thoroughly satisfied at having a group to address, like a small class – save that there were women present. (It was also unusual in that more than one of the class was a criminal – in deed or in intention.)

The philosopher beamed on the children he had

rescued from their cave – later than he had intended, for he had first to pacify the odoriferous Boiotian and urge him to wait for their common purification. Aristotle had then brought Myrrhine and Gorgias and Anthia from the depths of their cave out into the light, and then down from the mountain back into the world. We all – including the Boiotian – underwent cleansing lustrations together. The farmer was anxious to claim the return of Korydon, or a price for his boy. This matter took a while, as the farmer, even after he became placable, was a bargainer who disliked being hurried. He should have taken the first offer, for Aristotle beat him down with the argument that Korydon was not really a slave at all but the captive of pirates. The man had to content himself with only a few charitable obols, to which was added the value of his dog. After settling this matter, Aristotle suggested dinner for all. Diokles' wife, so we heard from Kallirrhoe, had been in a great taking at having to feed so many.

After dinner, Glaukon came to see us, at Aristotle's request. Polemon was still shepherding Lysippos into exile. Anthia had modestly retired to the women's quarters and remained there, but Myrrhine, perhaps recklessly feeling that her maidenly reputation was for ever lost, had insisted upon coming in with Gorgias to hear our discussion. She sat quietly in a corner with her face veiled. Kallirrhoe and Korydon, with the freedom of household creatures, sat upon the floor, looking more like favourite good children than obedient slaves. Kallirrhoe's big Persian eyes glowed. She had now assumed the headdress of a lady, but her short hair in its curling ringlets escaped to shine darkly in the lamplight. Korydon, looking proud and – unbelievably – more handsome than ever, pressed close to Kallirrhoe and held her hand from time to time when he thought we were not looking.

Aristotle smiled upon them all, and then his look became grave. 'I know it is hard,' he said abruptly, 'to talk about what evil has befallen people we know, and what evil they have done, particularly as one family among us is most painfully affected. But no one is the happier for knowing only part of the truth.'

'I want to know the whole,' said Gorgias, who was pale and sat wrapped up in a blanket as he still felt the cold. But he looked a great deal more like a man and a citizen than the restless shadow we had seen before. 'I must know – what did Straton do? Why was Ammonios killed? And how guilty is my father?'

'Who was the Abductor?' asked Kallirrhoe. 'Anthia wants to know, too. She said to me before dinner, "Find out from them who was the stupid Abductor."'

There was an uneasy pause, and someone coughed.

'Well,' said Aristotle, 'I can answer all those questions, if you allow me to describe my own experience of the case from the beginning – where it began for *me*, that is to say. Every story should have a beginning, a middle and an end, but where to start is often a puzzle. The real beginning goes back years ago, but this will serve.

'The beginning of this story – our story – as *I* knew it was the abduction of Anthia. It seemed obvious at the outset that some man abducted Anthia, Pherekrates' heiress, in the hopes that her family would permit a marriage. Thus, the Abductor would come into great wealth. Yet it was a hazardous undertaking. Timotheos hinted to me that the Abductor might be Straton. But *why*? Straton was a natural choice as Anthia's husband, despite any earlier arrangements between Pherekrates and Polemon's father. Lysippos called upon my services in pursuing the Abductor and making a bargain with him. I fell into that trap. Though I wondered, even as I left the city, whether Lysippos wanted me to investigate, or whether the plan was forced on him by the instigation of the civic-minded and law-abiding Kleiophoros. Efforts to speed our departure actually retarded it. Supplying such horsemen as Stephanos and myself with steeds would be a good method of causing delay. I began to wonder if Lysippos wanted me out of Athens for some reason. Were we pursuing nothing at all?'

'But a man with a litter was indeed heard of,' I said, 'and *then* we found the body of Straton.'

'Exactly. Stephanos and I in our travels discovered the body of Straton. This was indubitably murder. And murder of an unusual kind. You remember, Stephanos, how the body looked.'

'Hideous,' I said, recalling that stinking flesh, that wobbling head. 'With a wound in front and in back.'

'Actually, there were *three* wounds. I suggested to you the speech of Patroklos, the man thrice killed. "You are the third to kill me." But – *three* killers? Was it a group acting in concert? Hardly, for the wounds were made at different times. One, the shallower cut where the blood had dried, had been made earlier than the blows which inflicted actual death. There was some swelling and bruising, and, in short, the normal symptoms of the reaction of a living body to a cut. A cut from an ordinary knife, used otherwise to cut onions and so on. The other two wounds were much more important, inflicted by a stronger and sharper implement. It was harder to tell which of those two blows had caused death – the blow to the chest or the stab in the back.'

The rest of us, no physicians, blenched a little – all but Korydon who was so happy with Kallirrhoe that he would have not been troubled by the images of any number of painfully slain corpses.

'The most telling circumstance of Straton's death,' I said, proud of my own deduction, 'was the proper burial. Very odd. Murderers don't usually perform pious funerals for their victims. So it looked as if Straton had been killed by a member of his family. And that proved to be right in the end, although those who performed the rites, Gorgias and Myrrhine, only *thought* they had killed him. The burial did lead me to suspect Anthia herself.'

'Anthia a murderess!' said Kallirrhoe, laughing. 'I will tell her you thought that. She will not be pleased.'

'I got no further substantial help in the matter of the disappearance of Anthia,' Aristotle continued, 'until with the aid of Korydon, whom we met on the way, Stephanos and I eventually found Kallirrhoe. Once we met Kallirrhoe, we knew more of the abduction – which was a very peculiar affair. No attempt at sexual assault had taken place. The accounts given separately, first by Kallirrhoe and later by Anthia, confirmed each other in every important respect.

'Polemon was a further complicating factor. He turned up on the road, because he was going to Delphi. He was not far away when Ammonios was killed, which is how he became responsible almost at once for the corpse of Ammonios. I expect that Polemon lost his money at the brothel belonging to Ammonios' disreputable acquaintance not far from the Split. So, there was Polemon, a recurrent element. And he ran away with suspicious abruptness from the house in Kirrha – yet really out of modesty, not guilt. Anthia had formerly been promised to him, but Polemon was not guilty of abduction. It was not fear of Kallirrhoe's identifying him as the Abductor that drove young Polemon from the house in Kirrha, but aversion to Egyptian Tita's identifying him by name and bringing him into visible disrepute at a difficult time. In his other behaviour Polemon was driven by a very natural piety towards Ammonios, and a desire to save his body and reputation from injury.'

'Our lives would have been so much easier,' I remarked, 'if Ammonios had stayed in Athens and not become a corpse – dressed up as a pedlar – at Oidipous' crossroads. *We* might easily have been suspected of this murder.'

'We might indeed. The villagers still suspect us,' said Aristotle. 'Well, on the road I had already begun to wonder about the unknown but recurrent perfume-seller. Was this pedlar perhaps the real Abductor? That would mean that the man who walked with the litter was merely in his pay. Then we found Ammonios dead – but what was to be gained by killing him? Were the murders the work of the same person? It seemed probable that everything was connected.'

'The Silent Dinner, that's what connects things,' I said. 'It was too much of a coincidence that almost all of the party who met at Lysippos' house for the Silent Dinner appear to be involved in this strange affair.'

'I believe the murderer or murderers invited me to the Silent Dinner in order to woo me into playing their game,' Aristotle elaborated. 'Something else happened on the same evening, on the Night of the Ghosts. Stephanos –

whom incidentally I must thank most warmly for saving my life this afternoon –'

'No, no,' I protested.

'Yes, yes. I don't think I could have got down that slippery rock by myself. Stephanos at last told me of a peculiar conversation he had overheard near the grounds of Lysippos' house just after the Silent Dinner. Once I knew of this conversation, I saw it was most likely that Gorgias, the supposedly deceased son of Lysippos, had returned – like Orestes – and spoken to his sister. The man who returned – this unknown Orestes – spoke of vengeance. *He* was a likely candidate for the role of murderer of Straton.'

'You guessed aright,' said Gorgias. 'I first spoke to Myrrhine on the Night of the Ghosts. Straton had tried to kill me earlier – I had reason for vengeance. You thought that I was the Abductor?'

'An Avenger could have been the Abductor – in theory. But would an Avenger have been so secretive, so cool? An overwrought Orestes-type would have killed Straton at once. Rape and mayhem would abound. But everything we knew of the Abductor spoke of a deliberate person – the opposite of Gorgias. Quite unlike an Orestes. A secretive, cautious man. Now consider the case of Glaukon.'

We all turned to stare at Glaukon, who shifted in his seat and was taken by a fit of coughing.

'Yes, Glaukon. We came upon him in Kirrha. He told us he had arrived by a certain ship. A simple and ascertainable lie: so he had really come by the land route. And he laid stress on his *recent* arrival. That realistic touch about the seasickness, eh, Glaukon? But he had presumably been in or near Kirrha for some little while.'

'Perhaps I did not tell you all my business. But – anyone can go to the port for any number of reasons,' Glaukon said defensively. His voice was rising.

'Ah-h!' Kallirrhoe's eyes flashed. 'I recognise that voice now! So – you vile and ugly man! *You* were the Abductor!' Kallirrhoe rose and glared at Glaukon.

'So!' she said. 'If you are the Abductor, you are the one responsible for selling me to Haimon in Kirrha! To live in that disgraceful place. *You* did this!'

Glaukon's whey-face looked even paler in contrast to Kallirrhoe's flaming cheeks. She seemed to grow taller in her wrath, her black hair curling like snakes about her head. And then – to our great surprise – she brought her open hand down with a smart sound, upon first one side of Glaukon's face, and then the other.

Slap! Slap! The sound resounded through the room. Glaukon yelped. The rest of us did nothing. But we were more stirred when Korydon came swiftly to the back of Glaukon's chair, rising behind Kallirrhoe like a sun behind the moon.

'Dog! Son of a bitch!' In one clean gesture, the young man wrapped his hands around the throat of the unfortunate silversmith, who uttered only a faint gurgle. Glaukon's goggling eyes stared out at us in alarm. Then the handsome youth, maintaining his grasp and raising his victim upright, moved quickly to the front of Glaukon's chair, where he had more room to deal with the flopping body of his opponent. Still grasping his victim firmly by the throat, Korydon seemed to lift Glaukon bodily into the air by that handle. Glaukon could not even gurgle. He flailed his arms in the air, wildly at first and with increasing feebleness. His goggling eyes stared at us and seemed to be about to pop out.

'I will have the heart out of your body,' Korydon announced to his silent opponent. Then, his hands still firmly clenched around the unlovely freckled throat, Korydon thumped Glaukon, like a doll of straw or wood, repeatedly upon the floor. I recalled that Korydon had once strangled a dog.

Glaukon's face was turning a delicate spring-sky blue when Aristotle and I at last jumped to the rescue. We had much ado to separate Korydon from his prey. I held the boy, with some difficulty (because of my bad shoulder) twisting his arms behind his back. Aristotle and Gorgias laid Glaukon down upon a bench. Slowly he gasped in new air, and his freckles came back to a face now the colour of mushrooms at dawn.

'Korydon, do behave as if you were not a ruffian,' Aristotle said repressively, before turning to Glaukon. He stood over the hapless silversmith and gazed sternly down upon him.

'Korydon is wrong – perhaps – but I am not really sorry for you,' Aristotle said to him severely. 'Kallirrhoe is quite right. You, O foolish Glaukon, might face some interesting legal penalties for abducting her, for there is reason to believe she is well-born and should not have been enslaved. To say nothing of penalties regarding Anthia. Such an outrage!'

'What about this assault – this outrage – against me?' Glaukon gasped and coughed. He eyed Korydon with malevolence. 'Your slave – as he *is* a slave, nothing more – merits the death penalty for attacking me.'

'Glaukon, if you try to bring charges, I promise you, we shall all say that you fell against a table and blamed it on the slave,' said Aristotle. The rest of us nodded in agreement. 'You may be glad,' Aristotle continued, 'ill-advised and greedy as you have been, to escape with a whole skin after *two* such outrageous abductions. If we choose to bring charges, you are subject to severe penalties. Be glad that radishes are not yet in season! And you owe *me* the money paid to Haimon of Kirrha for Kallirrhoe's redemption.'

'All right,' said Glaukon hoarsely; the man was readily cowed. 'I only sold the slave-girl because things went so terribly wrong, and I lost Anthia. At least I didn't *kill* this girl. I didn't kill anyone!'

'That doesn't mean you cannot be killed,' Korydon muttered through clenched teeth.

'Oh, do sit down,' said Aristotle. 'Of course, Kallirrhoe is right. Glaukon is the Abductor. In fact, Glaukon was always a strong contender for the role,' Aristotle continued, sitting down again. 'The young girls captive in the litter, having no acquaintance with any man, could identify no one. But what they said told us that this Abductor was cautious and efficient. Consider Glaukon's character. He is a cautious man. Now, what would make Glaukon, an efficient man of business, take such a risk? He is not naturally rash, not hot-blooded. Why antagonise so dreadfully such a formerly dangerous rival – and new friend – as Lysippos? What, I asked myself, would make Glaukon do such an insane thing as abducting Anthia? Why, the expectation of a reward from his wealthy superior in his own trade. Glaukon would have abducted Anthia *if Lysippos asked it of him*. I take it, Glaukon, that was what happened?'

'Well, yes,' said Glaukon. He nodded. 'That's how it all came about.' His pale eyes moved nervously under the sandy lashes, as he looked quickly at the rest of us to see how we took this revelation. 'I – it wasn't all my fault. Not at all. I'll explain.' Here he sat cautiously upright and took a sip of wine and water.

'You see, Lysippos knew that the mines of Laurion are running thin, and he worried about this. I knew it too, naturally. But my contract this year was for a part that was better than his. Lysippos also saw that the capture of the silver treasure in the East may make life more difficult for us: the value of the product of our mines will sink. We are, however, encouraged by the *ateleia*, which diminishes our tax risk and permits us to keep more of what we do make than a potter or producer of oil can do. And we not only extract the metal, but create fine things. Many of Lykourgos' taxes fall chiefly on foreign merchants of the *Emporion*, so there might be more demand and better prices for our own Athenian craftsmanship – for well-wrought objects in silver.'

'Very far-seeing,' said Aristotle, nodding.

'Lysippos was – is – an expert man of business. He argued, shrewdly, that any new influx of silver would bring into request and repute more ingenious and elegant workmen. He suggested that he and I become partners. If we combined we could not only handle the business but also take over some other shops, and stabilise trade. His surviving brother Timotheos was useless, he said, and he needed someone in whom he could have confidence.

'I had already offered – for a consideration – to drop the lawsuit against Pherekrates' estate. Lysippos said it was Pherekrates who had caused any former trouble between us, and now in compensation for my claim, and over and beyond it, Lysippos promised me Pherekrates' daughter in marriage. All enmity at an end. I would be the heir of Pherekrates, and a partner.'

'But Pherekrates had promised Anthia to *Polemon*,' I argued, speaking up for the absent ephebe.

'Yes – Lysippos told me Polemon thought he was betrothed to Anthia, but that arrangement was really ended by Anthia's father's death. Lysippos said, too, that his son Straton also thought he should marry her. But Lysippos said Straton had enough anyway, and the business needed an experienced man. Lysippos confided to me also that he was troubled by Ammonios. Ammonios had lately begun to speculate in silver, and was endeavouring to get in on a mine contract.'

'But why would Ammonios, whose money was all in brothel-keeping, want suddenly to go in for silver mining?' I asked. 'I've learned you need a number of slaves for mining, and if you have to rent them from somebody else, your profits are much less. And you have other costs too, like imported wood for pit-props.'

'That's so,' said Glaukon. 'Lysippos thought – and I agreed – that Ammonios was partly interested just because he was getting richer, and being in silver would have meant he could get rid of war-tax. As well as associating with some very wealthy and influential people in a more respectable line of business than his own. Lykourgos and his friends are so keen on public morality, they are not likely to favour over-much a man who is not in a reputable way. Lysippos thought that when Ammonios realised that he couldn't get a contract for mining, he would then be full of resentment. He'd think there was a conspiracy against him. But Ammonios could get his own back by taking Anthia against her guardian's will – bringing on a marriage which would give him Pherekrates' share of the wealth and the business also. Ammonios already took a lewd interest in Anthia; he had been heard talking of her to other men.'

'That's not untrue,' I agreed, remembering.

'A girl's reputation can be so easily injured! Having made Anthia cheap, Ammonios might put himself forward as the only man willing to take her. So – Lysippos told me I must abduct the girl if I wanted to make *sure* of marrying her myself. Lysippos said he would be happiest once Anthia was spirited out of Athens.'

'Delphi was Lysippos' idea, then?' I asked. 'I suppose Lysippos promised he would make Straton see reason.'

'Yes,' Glaukon replied. 'Lysippos said Straton would take some while to pacify. But once married was always married. As her husband, I would get Anthia's inheritance. Lysippos promised to induce *you*, O Aristotle, to go in pursuit of us. That way we would have a disinterested witness who could give evidence that I had gone off with Anthia, but also that she had been unharmed.'

'So!' said Aristotle. 'I see you had gone into many details. And I suppose you committed this rash act with full regard for provisions – a nice watertight litter, the slaves, food and firepot and so on. And a good knife too, O Glaukon?' Glaukon blenched and shifted in his chair.

'I fully recognise,' continued Aristotle, 'that according to your plan I was no more than another utensil. Doubtless my respectable old age and my Makedonian influence made me useful.'

'Yes, and you could be a mediator to clap up a marriage bargain. Later when trouble died down, Anthia and I (now married) would return to Athens, and I would get hold of Pherekrates' share and go openly into partnership with Lysippos. That was the plan.'

'Not exactly . . .' said Aristotle. 'That was *your* idea of the plan. Did you not have any doubts, any compunction, about taking such a course? Frankly, undertaking such a wrong course?'

'No,' said Glaukon simply. His freckles dimmed themselves in a slight flush, but he maintained his composure. 'Alexander pursues the Persians to take their silver and sack their treasure cities. So why should not I be daring and take some treasure of my own? It seemed safe enough. After all, Lysippos was Anthia's *guardian*. In law. And Lysippos gave her to me. Everyone would countenance the marriage later. Meanwhile, I took an oath not to take Anthia as Hymen bids, nor to let Eros stir me, nor even to look upon her face until the wedding. This was proper for her, and safest also for me – in case anything went wrong. Lysippos and I planned the abduction together.'

'Most horrible!' said Gorgias. 'My own father to plan the abduction of his niece! I can hardly believe it. And you are a proper villain!' He threw off his blanket and stood up, weak as he still was, and stalked over to Glaukon, who shrank a little in his chair.

'*I* didn't do anything,' protested Glaukon to this new adversary. 'I did nothing except take the girl away. It's all Lysippos' fault, really it is. I have been very hard done by. And it's much harder work than you realise, all this abducting. Particularly when you have to keep yourself hidden from the girl, and you don't know who might come up and say "What have you got shut up in there?" I didn't have a happy moment on the road. And when I found the heiress – not being privy to the secret – had taken matters into her own hands and escaped, leaving only the slave-girl –'

'*Only!*' said Korydon, indignant.

'Why, I was in despair. I knew everything had gone wrong – but I didn't know quite *how* wrong.'

'The fool!' exclaimed Gorgias bitterly. He was unable to strike Glaukon as he evidently wished, for he wobbled on his feet; Myrrhine took hold of her brother and guided him back to his chair. Ignoring his shamefaced protests, she wrapped the blanket round him once more.

'So,' said Aristotle, gazing severely at Glaukon. 'A rash act – as you admitted to the Oracle, and as the Pythia confirmed. Silver and gold are *not* better friends than virtue. You nearly planned your own death. As for Lysippos – thinking he could use *me* in that manner! Well,' he caught himself, 'the poor man is undoubtedly very ill.'

'But no! Lysippos did not intend to use you exactly in that way,' I protested. 'What Lysippos told Glaukon was not his real plan, was it?'

'Good, Stephanos. You've been thinking to some purpose. No, indeed, that was *not* Lysippos' real plan,' said Aristotle. 'Lysippos did mean to use me as a witness, I am sure. But as a witness to something else – to Straton's *justified* killing of Glaukon. The penalty for seduction is *the death of the seducer*, if a male relation of the girl catches him in the act. Straton was to have caught up with Glaukon and Anthia. He would murder Glaukon, just before or just as I came along. (Our departure,

Stephanos, had to be timed aright, delayed a little so that we would not catch up with the abduction party too soon.) Then, with loud outcry, Straton would explain to me as witness his full justification for killing Glaukon. Most likely he was to kill the girl – his own cousin – too.'

'No! How dreadful!' exclaimed Kallirrhoe. 'I don't know how I can tell Anthia that.'

'He might have killed you too,' said Korydon. 'All because this shrivelling spotty-faced coward is such an imbecile.' He glowered at Glaukon.

'Anthia would be an awkward residue once the plan had gone that far,' Aristotle commented. 'Once her reputation had been ruined – Anthia being taken with a lover and that lover righteously slain – she would hardly be marriageable. Her money would never go to a husband. But she would still be inconvenient while alive. And how to keep her absolutely quiet about the truth of her seduction? I believe that the stress on Glaukon's not seeing Anthia, let alone touching her, was partly to leave some latitude for safety in case the plan did not work. It was no good risking the family honour *unless Glaukon died.* The irony of maintaining the family honour in reality, by permitting the murdered man no enjoyment from his "seduction", would have appealed most strongly to Straton. In fact, the stress upon Glaukon's secrecy indicates to me that Straton himself may have wished to be the first and last man the poor girl was ever to know. After killing Glaukon he could quickly deflower her and then kill her, just before I got there to hear this tale of sad necessity, dishonoured womanhood, and disgraceful lovers caught in the act. Anthia was right to feel endangered – although the danger did not come from the

Abductor. Or at least not from the official Abductor, which was Glaukon's role. The moving spirit behind the abduction was Straton.'

'Oh, no!' said Myrrhine. 'My brother plotting so against everyone – against poor little Anthia too. It is too terrible to believe!' Tears came to her eyes. I realised I had never seen this strange wild girl actually shed tears before.

'I'm sorry, my daughter,' said Aristotle. 'This last was mere speculation. I may have gone too far. But the plan for doing away with Glaukon I have had from Lysippos' own mouth in our short conversation today. Your brother's arrogance and greed stimulated your father to evil deeds. Lysippos and Straton were in a manner abductors of each other. For they took each other secretly away to an evil place.'

XIX

Silver, Gold and Virtue

There was a short silence while the company meditated on the ways in which this melancholy moral truth bore upon their own history. Glaukon seemed especially struck by the fact that his own death was included in his friend's grand design.

'Lysippos did not succeed, the gods be thanked!' said Glaukon devoutly. 'Nor Straton either.'

'No, or you would have been very cold meat by this time,' said Korydon, with little friendship for the unhappy silversmith. 'Poor Anthia! What a fortunate escape!'

'It wasn't mere fortune,' said Aristotle. 'Straton's nature came into it. He had more things than one on his mind. You remember, Kallirrhoe, telling me that you thought at one point the Abductor met a friend; they sat and talked on the hill by the oak tree.'

Kallirrhoe nodded solemnly. 'Anthia will tell you the same,' she said.

'Anthia did say something similar. When I asked if the

Abductor were Straton, she said she thought not, but added, vaguely, "I thought he was there at one point." Reconstructing the history from fragments of evidence, I saw that Straton did meet Glaukon when the latter was busy abducting. At the hill with the oak tree. Perhaps by prearrangement? The two men sent the slaves away so they could talk. What did Straton say to you, Glaukon?'

'Well . . .' Glaukon was deeply uncomfortable. 'We did meet by prearrangement. Lysippos had described to me the place with the sacred oak and said there would be a messenger for me, and I should wait there. Straton caught up with me shortly before I got to that place, and we went there together. He told me most emphatically that I must not harm the girl, or see her – and he would permit us to go on. He even gave me some money. He seemed perfectly convincing. We had some problems with the slaves, and he helped beat them. Straton managed to worm – I mean, I told him *almost* all I had been ordered to do. But I kept my own plans as dark as I could. I mean, I just pretended I was doing Lysippos a favour, and did not touch on Anthia's inheritance, or my marriage. Straton said he would meet us again in Delphi. He seemed quite light-hearted.'

'Yes. Just as I thought,' said Aristotle triumphantly. 'Fortunately for everybody in this room, Straton did *not* carry out his father's instructions. Not perfectly. Had he been obedient to Lysippos, he would have killed you, Glaukon, at once. He postponed the deed. After all, Glaukon travelling slowly with a litter would be easy to overtake again. No, Straton was more eager to do something else before he undertook what would have to be a very *public* murder. First he had to meet the messenger from home who would look for him by the oak tree. And then he knew he would have a little private murdering to do in some out-of-the-way place, which it would be better to get over before enacting his role of the injured kinsman and killing the Abductor. He needed to get rid of Ammonios.'

'Why does Ammonios get dragged into this family story?' I asked. 'Just because of his ambition to be one of the Silver Men?'

'Yes, in a way. I'm afraid what Aiskhylos in *The Persians* calls our Athenian "treasure in the earth" has very mixed effects on the human mind. A silver contract would help Ammonios a good deal. He wanted to be accepted by Lysippos' family and associates, and he may seriously have thought he could marry Anthia.'

'Well, after all,' I admitted, 'I suppose, even if he were a loose-liver, he was a widower, and rich, and thus eligible. But I can see why Straton might not have cared for this idea.'

'Ah, now.' Aristotle leaned back. 'Cast your mind back to the night of the Silent Dinner, Stephanos – and Glaukon too, for you were both there. Remember how intently Straton looked at Ammonios – and how Ammonios became ill. After Ammonios was found murdered, I began to think about the man and his illness. Stephanos helped me there.'

'I did?'

'A remark made by you on the way home from the Silent Dinner came back to me. You know you were . . . we both were . . . ah . . .'

'Drunk,' I said shortly.

'Quite. And you had lost your sandal. You said,

"Someone's *poisoned* my foot." Now, people say odd things when under the effect of wine – but what brought the idea of *poison* to your mind? Were you thinking without knowing it? The Silent Dinner would offer the ideal opportunity to poison someone. As each man has his own separate food and wine, there is little danger of getting the wrong victim. And none at all of killing off your whole dinner party, which casts such a blight on an evening. The victim's first symptoms will be set down to the expected drunkenness.

'Now, what happens next? Ammonios is sick – recovers – and leaves Athens, in disguise. Why? Let us see if matters fit together. Suppose Ammonios was – or thought he had been – poisoned at the dinner? Likely he suspects exactly who his enemy is. Ammonios leaves Athens in disguise, for safety's sake. He goes as a perfume-seller, and thus he can easily carry with him the remedies and antidotes he needs. Ammonios was still suffering from indigestion when he met his end: that bottle of gripe water we found was only one-third full. The unguents and perfumes he carried also make acceptable and practical gifts useful to his business connections with brothel-keeping "friends".

'Ammonios stays the first night with a friend near Eleusis. The next night, we don't know. But the night after that he stayed with a friend living near the Split, not too far from the village where we met the wedding party. Polemon knew of Ammonios' low connections, and took advantage of them. Timotheos also knew that Ammonios would often visit a pretty "unsavoury" friend, a connection of Pataikos, living not far from the Oidipous crossroads, in the Daulis direction. Timotheos himself let this information drop when we were talking with him and Lysippos in Delphi. That was one mistake Timotheos made perhaps, letting us know that information.'

'So my uncle Timotheos wanted to kill Ammonios,' said Gorgias. 'Did both Straton and Lysippos want to poison Ammonios?'

'The attempt at poisoning Ammonios at the Silent Dinner was, we will surmise, Straton's very own brilliant idea. Not part of Lysippos' main plan. Ammonios had teased and taunted the young man when he had taken Straton's own mistress, the flute-girl, and put her in his brothel. And Ammonios had been too interested in Anthia. Once in league with his father to kill Glaukon, Straton evidently felt free to take whatever life he wished. Straton, however, was always careless – he was actually not a good killer, but repeatedly ineffectual. And in poisoning he was inexperienced – so he gave too small a dose of the poison to Ammonios, who was a large man.'

'Was my uncle Timotheos party to that plot too?' Gorgias asked.

'I think it was, rather, a vexation to Timotheos, and made him the more certain that he needed to get rid of Straton. The poisoning attempt had made Ammonios an enemy of the whole family. In order to enjoy the family wealth in security, Timotheos needed to feel that all enemies were out of the way. Ammonios might accuse the surviving members of the family of trying to kill him, even when Straton was gone. So it would be beneficial to Timotheos, and much tidier, to have Ammonios dead.'

'Ammonios was not stupid, which made him more dangerous,' I mused.

'True. Ammonios was a shrewd man – not like some' – with a glance at Glaukon. 'When Ammonios met you, O Glaukon, he realised that Straton was involved in a very complex abduction scheme. And Ammonios learned from you of the meeting point of the oak-tree hill. He now knew that Straton was embroiled in a delicate trick which he would not wish to go wrong – and which obviously had already gone wrong through the escape of Anthia. Straton was now alone and could be thrown off balance, so Ammonios took the opportunity to find and confront him. I think he was planning to throw Straton into confusion when they met by telling him in sympathetic tones of the escape of Anthia from the litter. Ammonios set off – back along the road – first providing himself with your excellent knife, Glaukon. Timotheos later returned that knife to Ammonios, and I hid it to save Ammonios' reputation – but I should better have returned it to *you*.'

'No!' cried Glaukon. 'I did no murder!'

'Very well. You merely provided a useful weapon, in a good knife. Ammonios could trust you to have nothing but the best. Thus armed, Ammonios was fortunate enough to find his enemy in a weakened state, nursing himself after the fight with Gorgias, who had earlier attacked Straton, stabbed him and knocked him down, leaving him prostrate and briefly unconscious. When Ammonios encountered Straton, words would have been exchanged. It seems most likely that Ammonios taunted him with the news that Anthia had escaped. The upshot was that Ammonios could easily get rid of this weakened and confused enemy. He gave him more than recompense for the poisoning attempt on the Night of the Ghosts; he certainly intended to make a ghost of Straton.'

'But then Ammonios would have wished to get away? So fast that he didn't make sure Straton was dead?'

'I think he was interrupted by the advent of another person at that busy hill of the sacred oak. The false "perfume-seller" bustled off, hearing or seeing somebody else coming. Straton was still alive – though dying – when this other person came on the scene. All along, Straton had been unaware of the source of his greatest danger.'

'And that was Timotheos? His own uncle? My uncle –' Gorgias' voice trembled. 'Why did *they* hate each other?'

'Timotheos and Straton did not hate *each other*. Straton thought of Timotheos as an ally. Had they not worked together to get rid of that brother whom Straton despised? Straton would never imagine that his uncle did not regard him highly. We know better, Stephanos. The destruction of the image of the silver singer in Delphi shows how insanely Timotheos hated the boy who was so doted on. Hated him even after his death, and rejoiced in that death. The ruination of that statue was a mocking signal from the killer.'

'So Timotheos became the killer of Straton – or rather his third killer, as Hektor was to Patroklos,' I said.

'Yes. The meeting at the hill of the sacred oak was not coincidence: Timotheos had learned of that meeting point. Perhaps Straton was even expecting supplies and news from his uncle's messenger or his uncle himself. By the time Timotheos got there, however, Straton was already prostrated by Ammonios' blow, and dying slowly. Not, I believe, in such a bad way as not to be able to speak – or whisper, rather. Timotheos would have been much enlightened by what his nephew had to impart about Gorgias, Glaukon, the heiress and Ammonios. Even though Straton would have died anyway – within a couple of hours at the utmost – from the blow Ammonios had dealt him, Timotheos was taking no chances. He sent his nephew to Hades by the most rapid route.'

'And why,' I asked, 'did Timotheos follow Ammonios? Speaking of rapid routes, how *did* Timotheos get about so rapidly? So that he could be killing on the Oidipous crossroads shortly after he left Athens?'

'Ah, but Timotheos left Athens almost as soon as we did, Stephanos, and lost no time on the road. Even so, he must have gone by a slightly longer route; needing to ensure that he didn't bump into us, he went a different way. I believe Timotheos may have been riding to Peiraieus when you and I, Stephanos, were first trying to manage our horses. Going that way of course he remained ignorant about Gorgias and Myrrhine who were a little ahead of ourselves along the road. At the port, Timotheos could then take a boat a short distance westward to near Eleusis – though he would have to pay well for travelling in the dark. He could then travel fairly quickly along the northward road. Timotheos wanted to make sure of intercepting Straton.'

'Of course,' I admitted. 'The meeting point at the hill was not really so far from Eleusis as to be difficult to attain, even if it was in the wilds. We just took a long time to get there.' A thought struck me. 'Why – all these killings of Straton must have gone on while we were being entertained at Smikrenes' farm!'

'Exactly. It was easy for Timotheos to calculate on catching up with Straton. The young man he planned to kill would be easy to find because he was waiting at a prearranged meeting-place for a messenger from home.

But events had taken new turns. From what Timotheos learned from Straton before he gave him the final deadly blow, he realised he had to go after Ammonios. Ammonios was now a deadly enemy of the family, and he knew far too much. So Timotheos now set out in pursuit of him.'

'How did Timotheos proceed so quickly on a long road?' asked Glaukon.

'It is a tiresome distance. And Timotheos missed seeing us or Gorgias' party – luckily – because I believe he was taking another track. I believe Timotheos shortened the wearisome hill travel and the winding road by crossing the isthmus and taking a ship, landing at a point along the coast of eastern Boiotia. He could then travel on horseback straight up into the hills towards the famous crossroads. He knew the fake "perfume-seller" had a friend there. It was most likely that Ammonios would stay with his friends to recover his health, and Timotheos hoped to waylay him. As for his own wanderings, if anyone needed an explanation Timotheos could always say that he had been in search of Anthia. As you and I, Stephanos, were going on the normal road, Timotheos as a good concerned uncle could claim that he had to cover the other route in trying to rescue his niece. Now, we know Timotheos knew of the location of this country manor house that was also a brothel – though he didn't know Polemon was in it at the time, losing his money.'

'But the boar-spear?'

'Country folk keep weapons in their halls or in some convenient place during the season. The simplest answer is that Timotheos went into the house itself and was able to filch one of their own boar-spears. He could give one of the manor slaves a message saying someone was coming who would wish to speak to Ammonios. That would stimulate Ammonios into leaving the house in order to evade the visitor – and thus running into an ambush. Timotheos waited for Ammonios on that lonely road just before dawn, and was able to kill him very thoroughly.'

'Perhaps,' I wondered aloud, 'it amused him to do it that way – a sort of joke about pig-sticking. The manner of this killing might fasten suspicion on one of the boar hunters.'

'Maybe,' said Glaukon, 'Timotheos hoped the killing would look like a hunting accident.'

'I suppose if there were an enquiry somebody could question the house-owner and his slaves,' I mused. 'But there is no one who will want to carry on a prosecution. The results would be so bad for the repute of Ammonios and all his relations. And Straton's and Timotheos' family don't want to know any more. So we will never discover all the details, will we? But Ammonios' death was obviously no accident. Most deliberate murder. We knew that when we saw the body.'

'We have actual *proof* that it was deliberate murder,' said Aristotle decidedly. 'The killer of Ammonios left in his bag of perfumes *the* knife – the one that had been used by him in killing Straton. The really lethal knife, not the onion-cutting one. You remember, I hid that big knife at the site of the murder. The blood on it was dry, so it had been used for a killing, but not recently. What I didn't then know was that Timotheos was – with deliberate irony – returning what he thought was Ammonios' own murderous knife to him. If Ammonios' corpse were to be discovered with that knife in his possessions, Ammonios would become known as the killer – the only killer – of Straton. He was certainly *one* of the killers.'

'So, you're saying,' said Myrrhine, 'that the real plan of my uncle Timotheos was the killing of Straton, and that Ammonios was just an extra problem. But why did Uncle Timotheos want to kill Straton? And why so much action – such energy? It seems so unlike him. He was always a dreamy man, a philosopher.'

'Because once he deciphered Lysippos' truly wonderful and wicked secret design, Timotheos realised he had the perfect opportunity to rid himself of Straton and take the family wealth entirely into his own control.'

'But,' protested Gorgias, 'Timotheos was unworldly – he was never interested in wealth.'

'No,' said Aristotle, 'he didn't seem interested in it. Perhaps he himself thought he was not concerned with it. But there came a time when there were enough great riches at stake to arouse his attention. The real question is "to whose interest?" Who profited? There was one missing element in all this puzzle, someone not mentioned so far, yet someone there all the time.

'You see, we were so taken up with one heiress – Anthia – that we did not think of another young woman who in certain circumstances would be an heiress too.'

'*Myrrhine!*' cried Kallirrhoe, as one who successfully works out a puzzle.

'I?' said Myrrhine. 'But I am nobody – and quite unmarriageable.'

'Not at all, O Myrrhine, daughter of Lysippos. One brother was (supposedly) already dead. If your other brother were to die, unmarried and without issue, that would make you an heiress on the occasion of the death of your father. True, you were not very marriageable.

Timotheos and Straton had seen to that, with well-placed rumours of your madness.'

'It is not just rumour,' said Myrrhine. 'I am curst with ill humour. Men do not please me. And when I heard of the death of Gorgias, and felt that Straton had something to do with it, that drove me nigh mad.'

'I did not think of you, Myrrhine, until Stephanos repeated to me the Orestes-conversation that he heard after the Silent Dinner. Then I saw that you and your brother Gorgias, returned, could be dangerous – *you* could be the murderers of Straton and even of Ammonios. But if you were not the killers, then you yourselves were threatened. Once I caught a glimpse of you in Delphi going about your Kharila-like activities I recognised your importance. And I knew that Gorgias' life was in danger if his uncle ever caught him.'

'We saw Lysippos and Timotheos in Delphi,' I remembered. 'You suspected them, didn't you, Aristotle? That's why you wouldn't tell them anything, including where Kallirrhoe was.'

'Yes. Shortly before we first talked with Gorgias and Myrrhine, we saw Lysippos in Delphi. You recall how they looked, Stephanos? Lysippos, ill and terrified, with his attentive brother hovering over him. Timotheos was wondering when would be the best time for Lysippos to die – and if he would do it naturally, or would require unsolicited assistance. Lysippos, you remember, Stephanos, would take food only in our presence, when he felt safer.'

'But surely,' said Gorgias, 'Myrrhine's life was in danger just as much as mine. That is shown by the dreadful image of the hanged girl. She told me about that.'

'That image comes into my nightmares,' said Myrrhine. 'It was *me*! – hanging by the neck and swaying in the breeze.'

'The image – yes, that was interesting. It was meant to frighten an unhappy girl who came upon it alone, in the shadows of dawn. Timotheos understood from his conversation with the wounded Straton that Gorgias was still alive, that Myrrhine had run away from home to join him, and that both were somewhere in Delphi. He was on the track of Myrrhine. But Timotheos overdid things. The image of the hanged girl was the final clarification. It had to be made by someone who had skill and some training in carving. Such training Timotheos had once received. The thing was made hollow, like a mould for a statue. It lacked the elegant touches of Lysippos' own work, yet there was a family resemblance. In all senses, for it was made by someone who knew *you*, Myrrhine. The only people who could know you personally were members of your own family. And there was that crowning touch, the unmistakable object, or token.'

'I knew it! The silver bracelet!' I exclaimed.

'Yes. Someone had to know Myrrhine very well, to know about the silver bracelet and include it on the doll-like image. It was a family symbol – each member wore one. And who would be more likely to have silver wire with him than a silversmith? The object was to frighten you, Myrrhine. If you did not commit suicide, you would flee from Delphi, a mad and unprotected woman. Then Timotheos could dispose of Gorgias, who had been inconsiderate enough to come to life again. As far as everyone but Myrrhine was concerned, Gorgias had died long ago: that would be the safest of the murders. And

Timotheos would no longer have to rely on Straton, who had proved sadly inefficient.'

'Straton was never really good at business of any kind,' said Gorgias.

'If Myrrhine died, Gorgias and Straton both being dead, then Timotheos would inherit everything. And if Myrrhine were to live on as an heiress – but a woman whom nobody else would marry – Timotheos could very neatly and respectably and openly lay hands on *all* the wealth. He would take pity on the poor mad creature, do his family duty, and marry her. He would control all.'

Aristotle sighed. 'It was a family crime. As in so many dramas. Dreadful deeds seem more terrible and pitiful when they are committed by natural friends. Yet are not greed, envy, jealousy, hatred and desire – the strongest emotions – stirred within the family? And great loyalties too.'

Aristotle nodded at Myrrhine and Gorgias. 'You need to shed the murderous habits of your family, my children. But, for your consolation, it is the truth that the blow that Gorgias struck, although it must have made Straton feel unwell, did not kill him. Ammonios later struck Straton a shrewd blow with the sharp-pointed knife. It punctured the lung – blood came out frothy, mixed with air. There were a few signs of that kind of frothy blood on Ammonios' tunic. You remember, Stephanos? Ammonios did not wait to see if Straton were dead. He would have died in several hours' time, but he wasn't allowed to linger. Ammonios meant to commit murder, but Timotheos fully achieved it.'

'This is an explanation which fits all the facts,' Gorgias

said with a sigh. 'The murderer of Ammonios, as well as of Straton, was assuredly my uncle Timotheos.'

'Timotheos announced it himself, in his boasting before he fell off the cliff,' I reminded them.

'True,' said Aristotle. 'But the logic of the case tells us as much. We can work it out with our own minds. And Timotheos had this one great advantage: no one was ever frightened of him. He was seen – by Straton and everyone else – as an ineffectual dreamer.'

'But – why?' asked Gorgias. 'Timotheos was so unworldly. Why did he – of all men – want so much money that he was trying to rid himself of all other heirs?'

'He had his own great dream. He wanted to found a school, another Akademeia, with himself as head. It didn't matter if in the process he had to kill most of his family – and Glaukon, and ultimately and unexpectedly Ammonios to boot. Timotheos was not attached to particulars.'

'The gods be praised, I have escaped,' said Glaukon devoutly. 'So then, after killing Ammonios, he rejoined Lysippos, who was already on the road to Delphi?'

'Yes – and Lysippos suffered a horrible shock when he found Straton had been killed. Timotheos, who had been off "searching" for Anthia, as Lysippos thought, brought his brother to Delphi, where he could keep him under his eye while he waited to catch the others. Glaukon very wisely kept away from Delphi, in Kirrha.'

'But why –' I began, but was fated not to finish my question. For our door was flung open by a stranger.

'My friends, at last I find you!' cried this person. He paid no heed to Aristotle but gazed raptly at Korydon and Kallirrhoe sitting on the floor.

This intruder was a man in early middle age; there was

a bald spot in the middle of his head, and his brown hair, streaked with early grey, curled about his neck and ears in something of a foreign fashion. He seemed prosperous; he wore a gold pin to fasten his cloak.

'Korydon! Kallirrhoe!' he cried. 'I have come to rescue you from bondage!'

Korydon and Kallirrhoe leaped to their feet.

'Theron!' they shouted, and rushed to him, embracing and kissing him, and hanging about his neck.

'I have looked for you so long, my children,' he said, taking each by a hand. Tears stood in his eyes. 'Thanks be to the gods! I am not a slave any more. I will redeem you, and you shall be slaves no longer – never while I live.'

Aristotle rose and went forward to greet the visitor.

'Theron of Halikarnassos,' he said earnestly. 'You are welcome – heartily. I fear that at present I am welcoming you to another man's house. Would that it were my own roof. But I should be honoured if you would sit and take wine with me.'

'Who is this old man?' Theron demanded suspiciously of Korydon. 'Is this your master?'

'Well, yes,' said Korydon laughing. 'But legally only from this afternoon.'

Theron frowned. '*Legally*, you should be no man's slave. But I will pay this person whatever he asks – though I hope we shall come to some reasonable arrangement. What is his name?'

'This is Aristotle, the great teacher at the Lykeion of Athens,' I said.

'The philosopher? Yes, I have heard of him. Though,' said Theron in a low voice to Korydon, 'I have no reason to believe that your philosophers are less keen to bargain than other men. I thought he had been bigger,' he added, looking appraisingly at Aristotle. 'Come, sir,' he continued, 'it is a long story, but I am the friend of both these people. They are well-born, and the victims of war and mischance. Let us come to some agreement.'

'It is disgraceful,' muttered Glaukon, 'the way these foreigners behave. So rude. One ought not to burst into a party uninvited and then begin business at this hour.'

'Oh yes, Theron should,' said Aristotle. 'But he has anticipated me. I meant to tell you at the end of my narrative, Korydon and Kallirrhoe – I was trying to lead up to it. You are both free. The Pythia told me that I must pay for you both, which I now have done. And she said that I should set you free. And so I do now. There!' He went up to them and took the iron collar from Korydon's neck. He then kissed them both, very solemnly. 'You *are* free – as you were free-born. So, O Theron,' he turned to the visitor, 'there is nothing left for you to do but be our friend and take wine with us.'

'By Artemis!' Theron was taken aback. 'I hope you treated them properly. Are you both well?'

'Oh, yes,' said Kallirrhoe. 'He is a *good* old man, Theron. And I have had many adventures since I saw you . . .' Theron groaned slightly. 'But I am quite well. I was in a – I mean, they cut off my hair, but it will soon grow. And I am still a virgin!'

'Not for long,' said Korydon firmly. 'We wish to be married very soon, Theron. Can you not arrange it? You see, we are far from our parents. And how did you find us?'

'Not so fast!' Theron smiled for the first time. 'I will take advantage of the kind invitation, and explain.' He sat down and accepted a cup of wine. Having made libation, he looked, a long look, at the golden-haired youth and the dark-haired girl next to him. Then, with a polite effort, he transferred his attention to Aristotle.

'I am honoured. You must pardon my discourtesy – the day has gone so rapidly, and much has happened. Last night I found this – in Kirrha.' He produced a gold bracelet.

'Kallirrhoe's gold bracelet. We have heard of it,' said Aristotle. 'Haimon must have sold it very recently. I swear it wasn't in the shops in Kirrha when I was there looking for bracelets. Perhaps Haimon thinks of selling up and removing very soon.'

'We have heard the tale of this pair's lives, O Theron, and hence something of you,' I said, 'until the point when you disappeared from their sight. So when you saw the bracelet in a shop in Kirrha, you knew Kallirrhoe must be near?'

'Yes,' said Kallirrhoe, reaching for it. 'How wonderful! Anthia's family let me keep it but *they* – the persons you know of, in the bad house in the port – took it from me.' With Korydon's help, she put it on her slender wrist, and they both admired it.

'I knew the work at once,' said Theron, 'and went in search of the seller. Then I heard tales of a girl as lovely as Aphrodite, who had been in Kirrha – you know where. I came hither following the maiden, who had been bought and taken away to Delphi. And then I heard also of a young man, as handsome as Apollo, though only a slave. I was sure it was Korydon. But Aristotle was not the man Korydon served first, and how you both came here is perhaps better told on another occasion, when my head is clear enough to understand it.'

'But what happened to *you*, Theron?' asked Korydon.

'Well . . .' Theron rested his back against the wall, 'I do not mind relating – but I fear I disturb this distinguished company? You were talking of something else?'

'They've finished all that,' said Korydon. 'Go on.'

'Do,' said Aristotle. 'You are a brave man, as I know from your exploits in the burning city. I am eager to hear of your fortune.'

'The rest is not as exciting as what went before. When we three were parted – in distressing and sordid circumstances which I need not specify – I was, ah – in effect, and not to put a fine cloak on it, sold to a merchant of Korinthos. (I wish I could have the law on that high-handed naval man who brought us to such a pass!) This Korinthian was a goldsmith. He never made a better bargain. For I was a better worker in silver and gold than he. My labours brought wealth into his boxes, and he was happy. I say "was", for this goldsmith is not a man of this world any longer. He had suffered some years from the cough, and died less than a year after I entered his service. In his will he bequeathed me my freedom, so I bear him no grudge. After that, his wife, poor thing, was at her wits' end to keep the business going. And with her family's agreement (there was only an uncle) she married me. I consented, for how else was I to keep in the trade? My former master's wife never alluded to her previous authority, and was a meek little person enough, and clever with accounts. I hoped for children from this union, but it was not to be. She died in pregnancy of some kind of fever in the stomach and blood.

'Her death left me with a business in Korinthos, though her uncle has a share in it. So here I am, as you see, prosperous once more – though not nearly as rich as I was in Halikarnassos. The men of Ionia value fine things more than the people here. And trade is bad generally, since the wars, though improving. I saved my money to rescue these young people, and I am certainly able to pay for their freedom. I insist. And I have a home, though as I have no wife there is no proper women's quarters. It would not be suitable for Kallirrhoe, a free woman of noble birth. We must think about this.'

'Ah,' said Aristotle. 'I think I may see a way to settle it. But about yourself, Theron – are you going to consider marriage again?'

'Probably,' said Theron. 'A man needs children – or where's the satisfaction of his wealth? Boys are ever-charming, but barren. Yet I should need a good dowry with a wife. And I would prefer a woman who knows something of the business. I have to do most of the skilled work on my own; I am anxious to improve the bronze statuary. It's not a very grand way of living – I couldn't afford to marry a woman of noble life, accustomed to idleness –'

'Wait,' said Aristotle. 'Suppose I could point out to you a girl of good education, a member of the family of a silversmith, with some knowledge of the business? Her reputation has been unjustly tainted in her own city, but she is intelligent and virtuous. Her brother, who loves her, would see to her welfare and would provide a dowry. Mind you, even if you were not fond of her, you would have to promise on oath not to ill-treat her, nor to abuse her, nor even to beat her as men do their wives.'

'*I?*' said Theron. 'I have never ill-treated anyone in my life, as far as I know, free or slave. I cannot imagine abusing the wife who shared my roof. And I would not beat anyone.'

He smiled again, and I realised that his face looked kind.

'You mean myself, O Aristotle,' said Myrrhine, speaking out of her shadowy corner. 'It is a good idea, I think. I too by now have heard Kallirrhoe's tale, and know of this man. And it is best for me that I marry.'

'No!' said Gorgias. He jumped up, casting aside his wrapping of blanket once again. 'Don't listen to them, Myrrhine! Why should you be forced into a miserable marriage with this foreign man? You have a brother who loves you and will always take care of you. You must live in my house.'

'Dear Gorgias,' said Myrrhine, laying her hand on his. 'Life has been hard on us. And it will not be easy now. You must make your way in Athens, and retrieve the honour our father and uncle have lost. You will have to work hard, and you must marry as soon as you can. A woman with a good dowry. A doleful sister huddled peevishly by the hearth is a burden to any man's home – and still more to his wife. My presence in Athens, a city I care for no longer, would be no help to you. It is true that my reputation is clouded by the rumours of madness set going by unkind relatives – and by our own expedition to Delphi, too. I insist this gentleman named Theron to whom I have been proposed must hear all about it. Then, if he will have me, let me marry this man and go to Korinthos. I can be of use to him; I would like to have something to do.'

'You both agree then,' said Aristotle. 'At least provisionally?'

'Yes,' said Theron. 'If she has knowledge of the business, that is excellent.'

'Good,' said Aristotle. 'Then, Gorgias and Myrrhine, you should go back to Athens as soon as possible after Gorgias has seen to the necessary funeral. When the rites pertaining to the deaths in your family have been performed, and the wonder has died away, let Theron come to Athens, take up the dowry, and marry Myrrhine. They will go to Korinthos. I will do my best to see that Athenian objections to an Athenian woman's marrying a foreign man are waived – and will also try to assure Theron of honourable standing in Korinthos, even as a *metoikos*. Your sister is right, Gorgias. Meanwhile, let Korydon and Kallirrhoe accompany you to Athens as your guests. They will marry from your house; Theron and I will pay for the wedding. Let them live after as man and wife in your home – Lysippos' house. A big empty house it is now, with only Hegeso within it, fading away.

'As for this young pair who have had so many adventures – I will set enquiries going to try to find their kinsmen in Ionia. Perhaps they will be able to return. Korydon should, however, learn a useful trade or occupation soon, for it is doubtful that his future state will be as luxurious as the condition in which he began life.

'Now,' said Aristotle, extending his hands expansively to the group. 'Do you all agree to that?'

'Yes,' said Gorgias and Myrrhine and Theron and Korydon and Kallirrhoe.

'What about Anthia?' asked Gorgias.

'What about Polemon?' I enquired.

'What about *me*?' said Glaukon.

'Polemon may try for Anthia through the proper

channels – he must ask her cousin Gorgias, now her practical guardian in place of the absent Lysippos. As for you, Glaukon, you seem to have forfeited all claim through your disgraceful behaviour –'

'Anthia wouldn't have you, you snivelling Abductor, not if you dressed her in gold,' said Kallirrhoe with emphasis.

'Quite. So with Timotheos' and Straton's fearful examples before your eyes, you, Glaukon, may meditate upon how to act properly henceforward, and be glad that Justice did not catch up with you. For had Straton executed his plan, you would have deserved your fate. Attend to your business, and make it honest. As for Stephanos and myself, we must return to Athens, for I too have left my business too long. Anthia will return home with her cousins, and I think Polemon need not despair of that marriage – if he does not prefer older men, or Egyptian girls. Polemon has performed good service in conducting Lysippos off our Delphian stage. He must also see to the funeral of Ammonios, and carry his ashes back in a plain box, as the Oracle said. It is always best to do as the Oracle says. I'm going to bed. Good-night.'

XX

Aristotle's Poetics

Aristotle and I did set out for Athens soon, with Glaukon accompanying us. On this journey, we did not have to climb among the ridges and skulk about the hills. As we came up the mountain road, I looked back at Delphi, remembering all that had happened there, and saw once more the clear-shining new temple, and the thin column of smoke above it, rising from the eternal hearth.

We were all three on foot, unembarrassed by horses, guilty knowledge, or secret-heiress-keeping litters. Glaukon, it transpired, had long ago seen to the destruction of the litter and had hidden its remains, and one of his first actions in Kirrha had been to send on a long journey the slaves who had been his assistants. Now Glaukon had to carry his own pack on the road; when he once ventured to complain, Aristotle sharply reminded him of the money he owed for Kallirrhoe, who had not been his to sell.

One might think we would have had many things to

talk about, considering the matters that had occupied us all recently. The end of these things was still unfolding. Lysippos had sailed. Timotheos' funeral (an obscure business) was to take place the day after our own departure from Delphi. The Delphic authorities were still discussing – and arguing about – how to treat the events. And one of the two missing horses – the ones which Aristotle and I had deliberately lost – had been found, and claimed by Gorgias.

Yet we did not speak of these things – or not very much. Glaukon was not in the best of spirits. Happily, after several days of brisk walking, we were able to bid him farewell. For Aristotle and I were to stay at least one night at the house of the farmer Smikrenes, and Theophrastos was to meet us there.

Our visit was Aristotle's idea. I was a little surprised at his desiring – or daring – to be the guest of the bad-humoured farmer. I had feared for the safety of the messenger Aristotle had hired to send word ahead with the request that Smikrenes be our host. But Aristotle had pointed out that we might need somewhere to stay in that region, and that if we brought gifts (and the messenger had already been commissioned to deliver a skin of wine), then Smikrenes might be appeased.

And it was so. Smikrenes seemed much more cheerful than I remembered him. He met us at his gate; his weather-beaten face wore a smile instead of a frown, and much of the earth had been washed off it. He wore a clean khiton and smelt a good deal pleasanter than of old – though the dungheap by the door still gave off a healthy odour. Surprisingly, it had increased rather than diminished, despite the present season being the dunging-time.

'Come in,' said Smikrenes, flinging his gate open so vigorously that he caught Aristotle smartly on the shoulder. He insisted upon our having something to eat right away; we sat outside his door and were treated to wine and food – there were cakes of fine flat bread, very good, and I thought I recognised Philomela's handiwork. I realised she must be nearby, if out of view.

Humbly we spread our gifts before Smikrenes, begging him to accept a few trifles for friendship's sake. We had brought some cloth of Delphian weave, and two small statues of Apollo. And for the girl, a pretty ilex box with a bronze clasp, containing sweet incense and some laurel leaves of Delphi. As we spread the things out in the dooryard, I thought I caught a glimpse of Philomela hiding behind the house door as it stood ajar.

'Of course,' I said, 'I know your daughter is excellent in weaving, but we believed a piece of the foreign cloth might please her. And the larger piece you could wear, or use as a floor covering, or a spread for the bed.'

'Well, now,' Smikrenes said, feeling the cloth with his earth-stained fingers. 'I don't mind if I do. I could stand that. As for the girl, she has enough to wear as it is. She can have the box, though – I've no time for such fripperies, d'ye see. And she weaves well enough, herself, as you kindly say. Oh, yes, she's a good one to work. She is minding the new brood of chicks now' – with a warning glance at the door.

After this gracious acceptance of our gifts, conversation fell into silence and was renewed only by Aristotle's industrious talk about weather and crops. After the meal, Smikrenes had work to do, so Aristotle and I went for a walk by ourselves. My mind was still running on the matters connected with Delphi and the extraordinary events of our journey.

'Aristotle,' I said. 'When I told you of the Orestes-conversation, you thought the speakers were Myrrhine and her brother rather than Anthia and her brother Demodikos. As both brothers were supposed to be dead, either alternative was improbable enough. But what made you decide it was those two?'

'Ah – you will see if you think about it. Anthia can hardly have known her brother. And the family of Lysippos were all of a literary turn, but the family of Pherekrates were not. You didn't tell me about that conversation, incidentally, until after our return from Kirrha. So you confirmed my suspicions about the interesting possibilities of a silver bracelet I saw in a dusty shop. Tarnished, but remarkably like the silver armband worn by Lysippos, Timotheos and Straton. When we met Lysippos and Timotheos, they both wore their bracelets, and Straton had taken his to his grave. So I deducted some other member of the family was nearby, and had sold the bracelet. Presumably either Myrrhine or Gorgias.'

'So you expected the Kharila ghost to be Myrrhine? I see.'

'I certainly wasn't surprised. And do you remember the image of the hanged girl? She had a silver loop on her arm. But Myrrhine wore no such thing when we saw her in the cave. Thus I asked her, idly, if she had bought fish in Kirrha. She must have sold some object to raise the money to buy things, fish included. I also deduced that Timotheos had not spoken to her or approached her in Delphi, or he would have noticed that her bracelet was gone. I also thought he could not have gone to Kirrha as yet. He would be likely to see the bracelet, and would certainly recognise the family work.'

Aristotle frowned, and looked thoughtful. 'By the time we went to the cave, I had already met Lysippos and Timotheos in Delphi. When we sat there in the courtyard I told them I deeply regretted having failed them. I was speaking most earnestly – though in veiled language. For I *had* indeed failed them. I did nothing to prevent or arrest their grievous fall from all virtue and decency. I fell in with their bad arrangements at the outset. Had I seen enough, and had I intervened, I might have prevented all this murder. It *should* have been prevented, Stephanos. I believe Lysippos, at least, could have been deterred from taking his bad course. The name of the dead is sacred, but truth more sacred still: I cannot speak well of Straton or Timotheos. Yet I might have saved them from terrible evil, if I had been wise. I feel old, sometimes, and not wise at all. "You know only a little, but that you also know," said the Pythia.'

'But you do know a lot,' I said comfortingly. 'And who could suspect that members of the same family should hate each other so?'

'Yes, there was great hatred there. Do you know what I find the most shocking thing – the most dreadful image in the whole affair?'

'The body of Straton,' I said, remembering dead Straton spitting out his coin. 'That was terrible.'

'No. The mutilated statue.'

'I had once thought it might have been Myrrhine – she was in Delphi near the temple site. A strange girl going about like a man. Really mad – she's frightening.'

'No . . . no. Myrrhine will be all right when she has something to do other than grieve. She would not assault the statue! Why, she would never go into the temple precincts while she was so painfully aware of being polluted by the murder of Straton. Blood-guilt weighed on her. It could only be Timotheos.'

'Blasphemy! To spoil the god's property. And such hatred, even beyond the grave! For he knew that Straton was dead.'

'Hatred so deep it included a desire to erase the beauty that had been as if it never was. The silver and ivory image – very fine – was the work of Lysippos, whom he hated, and of whom he was jealous. It showed Lysippos' love for his son. In wantonness – in sheer hubris – malignant Timotheos ruined the silver singer. As if he could erase the memory of Straton. Timotheos, you see, once had ambitions to be a poet and singer, as well as a philosopher. He was jealous of Apollo himself – another Marsyas. Or like Thamyris who challenged the Muses and was blinded by them.'

'Catching the murderer by arranging the visit to the Oracle was very clever. But it seems dangerous to set the gods to work like that. And how did you know it would work? Particularly as the murderer was so hardened against the laws of gods and men as to dare to enter, polluted, the sacred precincts.'

'Of course, I didn't *know* it would work,' Aristotle admitted. 'But it was the only thing I could do quickly, and it seemed a pity not to use the opportunity of having those four men together. And what could we do? We were weavers of straw among these Silver Men. I did not know everything. I did not know the exact degrees of guilt or innocence of any. But I thought it most likely that men would reveal themselves in that encounter, as in no other, and that anyone conscious of the guilt of murder might crack – or could be made to crack.'

'The whole process is so solemn and holy. It would wear upon the stoutest heart.'

'Exactly. When we were in the waiting-chamber, I reminded them all, you remember, of the notable story of Kalonodas Korax, the murderer identified by the Pythia. What man with Greek blood in him could confront the Pythia with unaltered face and voice, with such guilt on his mind?'

'But it was Lysippos who cried out and fled.'

'Lysippos cried out. And he fled. But who else fled? Who controlled and directed Lysippos? The two brothers had both had the chance to sweat in fear in the chamber beside the *adyton*. Both were guilty – in different degrees. Timotheos could have held Lysippos back, but they both darted off as if they were running a race. Lysippos broke, but Timotheos, for all his pride, cracked a little. I must say, I thought it all went rather well – though I could not have expected anything as helpful as the thunderstorm. What a piece of luck!'

'If it was luck,' I said dubiously. 'Aristotle, I've been thinking of the Oracle's words to me – and to you, too. She said some curious things about you. What do they mean?'

'I've wondered, too,' he acknowledged. 'Her sayings run in my mind more than they should. "The trees of the East and West"? I'm not sure. And I shall not die in Athens, but "where the water turns round". Does that mean death by drowning? A wet departure, you must admit. But,' he added more cheerfully, 'she promised I should beget and found a line – that means a son. And my sons will not be there to conduct my funeral – but perhaps they will be great travellers.'

'I was told to do as my father did before me,' I said. 'He died before he was fifty – and lost a great deal of money before he died. I don't want to do that.'

'Ah, but consider the question,' said Aristotle. 'The answer belongs in its proper context. You asked if you should marry soon – *and* into a family you have just met. (You certainly seem to have forsaken Kallimakhos' daughter, by the way.) Now what do question and answer together indicate?'

'The answer doesn't seem particularly helpful,' I said. 'But I'm sure she means I should marry. And – stay! – my father married when he was young. He married a good-looking healthy woman who brought some land into the family.'

'So,' said Aristotle encouragingly. 'There was land. Does that suggest anything to you?'

He let his gaze wander over the landscape around us, and I too looked about. The shadows of the day's end were beginning to creep eastwards. Before me was a field, the good soil carefully ploughed and tended, the fresh green shoots bending softly in the light evening breeze. Beyond, on the hill slope the olive trees whispered, and beside these were the vines, clinging to their neat wooden props and throwing out new tendrils. Below on the hill, on the other side of the house, was the grove with the shrine of Pan. I could hear the lowing of a cow. On the breeze was wafted the smell of earth and animals and fresh air, and also the good smell of burning holm-oak; the charcoal burner had been at work somewhere not far away. How sweet these things seemed against the background of harsh silver in which we had been forced to work. Silver had shone everywhere, with a hard glow, with argent distance and coldness. The gentle earth, the grass, the trees, were warm and fresh.

'This land is very fine,' I said. 'And if wishing were all, I should like to marry the daughter of Smikrenes. After all, she is of respectable birth and good behaviour – even though I have seen her, which is not proper. But I cannot be sorry for that. For she is good to look upon, and sweet-tempered. We know that she works well – indeed I think she works over-much, and I would like to give her a happier life. But you will think me foolish. The land would be of great value to me. If I married her, I should be bringing some land into the family, as my father did before me – though in a distant country deme, one must admit.'

'Well. Yes. There you are,' said Aristotle.

'But,' I said sadly, 'we have seen what happens when men begin to covet heiresses. I do not wish to be like Glaukon – still less like Timotheos. I do not want to let greed take possession of me.'

'I am glad you have said that, Stephanos. You are a good man. You deserve the prize of life. Yes, you must acknowledge what your desires are, and then control them by reason. You are not like Glaukon, willing to do underhand things for a bargain. Still less like Timotheos. He pretended to despise what he really desired, and that makes great misery.

'Do you know what made me suspect him above the others? That fine talk about Plato, when we left the courtyard in Delphi. He used the opportunity to boast and to despise his unhappy brother. What would Sokrates have said? I think Timotheos even deceived himself, which is a great evil to the soul. Know Thyself. And have a just estimate of yourself, too. You are a healthy young man, and a good man, and well-born. You would make a good husband. Go tomorrow morning to Smikrenes, and make an honourable offer. State frankly what you have to offer, and what your debts and difficulties are. Allow the man to consider your case on its merits. After all, he has no son – and he is getting older. Some day his daughter should marry, and he must have help in the farming.'

I breathed deeply of the fresh air, and felt encouraged. Happiness began, like the tendrils of the young vine, to twine and curl within me. I realised suddenly that I had not known much happiness in the last three years, not since my father had died.

'A family is always important,' said Aristotle.

'Families are important,' I agreed, 'as recent events have shown us. But not always happy, are they? Like Agamemnon's ill-starred family. Do you know, Aristotle, I've been thinking: the events of these last weeks would make a wonderful tragedy – or epic, even.'

'Do you think so?' Aristotle paused to consider. 'You may be right, in some respects. But where would our part be then, yours and mine? For we saw only piecemeal, and were not the central characters.'

'Ah,' I said, laughing, 'but *you* are essential. You were the Avenger.'

'But I was powerless to prevent any ill. More like a messenger who comes on stage to tell a king his city has fallen. And what kind of drama could it be, this disarray that we have lived through? For we could hardly call it a comedy, yet there was much comic about it –'

'Yes,' I said, remembering. '"Kleobis" and "Biton", for instance.'

'And then there is the odd story of Kallirrhoe and Korydon, which is certainly not a comedy, yet for them not tragic. Their story distracted us at times from the central plot of Lysippos' family. An episode. What epic or dramatic writer of worth would ever deal with the loves of two unimportant – if attractive – young people who pass through many illogical vicissitudes? Now, Lysippos' and Timotheos' story has logical unity, certainly. Cause and effect – though with a certain dash of chance, of the kind not uncommon in Tragedy. But which of these men is our central figure, our hero?'

'Straton?' I thought. 'No, surely, it is obvious. It must be Timotheos.'

'Must be? What is the point? The passing of a thoroughly bad man from good to bad fortune satisfies the feelings of an audience. For no one who loves mankind and respects social law would wish it otherwise. So too with the reward of the good. We may call this "philanthropic justice". But the discovery and rightful death of a bad man is not the stuff of true tragedy. It does not stir pity and fear. The protagonist of a tragedy ought to be a man somewhat like our own selves – or ourselves as we think we are – but really better in some ways. A man who falls not through gross villainy but through making some fatal mistake.'

'Well,' I persisted, 'could not Lysippos be our protagonist? He is not a thorough-going evildoer. Your description applies to him.'

'But he is hardly eminent, either in rank or personal qualities. Besides, although he made mistakes enough, he was ineffectual. He *planned* a murder, but did not *do* it. All that family went in for action but didn't perform very well. Timotheos was the best of the lot, in that respect. In life we wish murderous deeds averted. In drama we like violence. What should we think of a character who planned a desperate act, but muddled it?'

'Very well,' I said, 'we have no satisfactory protagonist. Yet you must admit there were enough bloody deeds. And we have had plenty of peripeteia and many discoveries. I *did* feel pity and fear sometimes – as when we uncovered the corpse of Straton. And what could be more stirring than seeing a man in pride of heart walk off a cliff?'

'Yes,' said Aristotle. 'We were moved, because we were there. And we had been Timotheos' friends. It would be hard to make an audience share our feelings. They would feel something more like satisfaction "Ah! There he goes! Serves him right!" That sort of thing isn't found in good literature.'

'But what about the *Odyssey*?' I asked. 'There you have different endings for good and bad characters. And nobody could call the *Odyssey* a shabby work!'

He laughed. 'You think you have me there, Stephanos of Athens. But the *Odyssey* is a tale of wonders. It is not a tragedy, and you see at once how difficult it would be to make a play of it. The sort of ending you describe, where the good are rewarded and the bad punished, belongs more properly to comedy, which is not intended to arouse pity and fear. Instead of grand actions we have petty squabbles, family bickering, silly mistakes and everyday life . . . or the imitation of it, rather. Two or three families in a country village is the very thing to work on – as we see in a play like *The Akharnians* or some modern comedies. But once murder comes in at the door, Comedy flies out of the window. How could an author handle such a mixture – and what would be the meaning of it?'

'I cannot agree with you altogether,' I said stubbornly, 'though I don't know why, exactly. But I still think the story we have lived through could make something interesting. Even with no protagonist, and with mixed effects, and philanthropic justice at the end. Though some of it might seem unconvincing.'

'As for improbabilities, an author can use them skilfully; I admit they exist in the world. As Agathon said, "it is likely that unlikely things should happen". One would rather have a probable impossibility than an improbable possibility. But if the story – or stories – in which we have been actors or spectators were to be told, the problem remains still – *how* to tell it. It would not be easy to make a drama, without spoiling those very surprises and reversals which have so much impressed us.'

'I see what you mean,' I said. 'The audience would not see the action as we did – sideways, and piecemeal, and not knowing what was true and what wasn't.'

'Not a tragedy – and not precisely a comedy, as we have seen. There is, however,' said Aristotle, looking into the distance and stroking his beard, 'an art for which we have no name yet – a lower art than the true poetic. This can be seen in Sophron's comic sketches and Plato's dialogues, where characters talk of whatever occurs to them, in ordinary language (more or less) without metre, and while they are eating or drinking or walking about. If this art were to develop itself further, as we know Epic and Tragedy have developed, then we might have a new form which could accommodate you. And I will concede this is possible. Literature is in the process of becoming. When I think of what Tragedy became in a very short time – developing from goat-song to the plays of Sophokles – I am amazed. And who knows whether new forms will appear? Sometimes, Stephanos, I feel sad – now, this really *is* foolish – at the thought of all the epics and plays and poems that will be written in years and years to come, after my death, when I will not be able to read them. I wish I could believe that for the virtuous philosophers in Hades, libraries would be provided.'

'O virtuous philosopher!' I said. 'You told the girl Myrrhine not to abuse works like the plays of Euripides. You said that is not what Tragedy is for. But what is all this *for* – Epic and Drama and maybe other kinds yet to be born – that you should wish still to have it even in Hades?'

Aristotle looked serious. 'You have me there. I do not entirely know. For purging of fear and pity may not be all we want or need. But our host will be expecting us. I wonder when Theophrastos will arrive? I should not imagine the good Smikrenes is interested in literary matters.'

Smikrenes certainly was not, but we had another conversation about crops, in which I took a larger part than before. Next morning, fortified by Aristotle's encouragement, I sought Smikrenes and nervously broached to him the subject of marriage with his daughter. He did not foam at the mouth nor chase me away with execrations, as I had half expected.

Smikrenes did not altogether approve of me – he said frankly he disliked fine Athenian youths, who read philosophy and did not know barley from pigs' tails. I showed, however, that I did know something of farming, and almost approached his good graces. He insisted that the son of a certain neighbour would be preferable to myself, and that this lad had been almost promised to Philomela – but then was forced to recollect that he had quarrelled with the neighbour very bitterly last winter, in a disagreement which ended in the argument of Smikrenes' winter boot being brought into forceful opposition to the neighbour's backside. (I wondered where young Menandros was.)

Smikrenes then admitted he was getting no younger, and had found the work increasingly difficult. Philomela deserved a good home, and he wanted grandchildren. The central issue was evidently decided, but certain details were still in the unsatisfactory half-moulded state they often have when a new plan is formed. Still, it seemed likeliest that I should marry Philomela in the next year, and take her to Athens. If I still rented out the farm near Athens, I could afford to offer Smikrenes some slaves to help in his work. Eventually a son of mine would take over Smikrenes' holding. Meanwhile, part of the yield could be mine, part Smikrenes'; we were still haggling, though not acrimoniously, over the dowry.

After leaving Smikrenes, I went quickly past the house, where I knew Philomela was hidden (she had taken care to act most correctly during our visit). I thought, however, I could see her standing beside one of the windows. I smiled in that direction and waved my hand, and she waved back before she thought.

I went in front of the house, to find Aristotle and tell him of my success. He was at the gate, with a tall awkward man, whom I recognised.

'Stephanos, look, here is Theophrastos!' Aristotle was evidently happy to see him. 'He came as punctually as anyone could wish. Now at last I shall have news of the Lykeion.'

'Of course I came. I said I would,' said Aristotle's chief assistant, in his precise way. Theophrastos looked at me very solemnly during greetings, as if he disapproved of me; I think he may have done, but cannot be sure, as that was his manner with everyone.

'Why did you not reply to my letter?' he asked Aristotle.

'I'm so sorry. I forgot,' said Aristotle, really contrite. 'But a great deal has happened which I must tell you about later. Now I am starving for news of the Lykeion. How did –'

'Wait.' Theophrastos dug into his travelling bag. 'I have some letters for you, and accounts. I paid the lamp-oil man. We had better trade with another. Then, this letter is from Hegesinous. Rude. I had to reprimand his son. Idle lad. But there is a more serious difficulty with another student – young Parmenion. From Rhodos, you remember.'

'Oh, yes, the nephew of Philotas and son of Arkhander. Grandson of Alexander's great general Parmenion. He may have a career in the army yet, though the child once thought of being a physician, and then of becoming a rhetorician. He always seemed bright enough. What's the matter with the boy?'

'He's fallen into a bad state of mind. Very bad. If he gets any worse, one of us will have to take him all the way back to Kos or Rhodos. I hope you are coming back soon.'

'Tomorrow, dear friend. Don't worry. Dear me, more

young people and their troubles,' Aristotle grumbled, but it wasn't serious grumbling. 'Did Parmenion send a letter, then? I see you have another one for me.'

'No – I forgot. This last one is from your wife. I called at your home to say you were coming, and was given this from her. In her own hand.'

Aristotle snatched at the tablets, and turned eagerly to the letter from Pythias, paying little attention to the lamp-oil man or to the offended and offensive parent. He opened the tablets and read rapidly. Then he amazed us both by flinging all the letters into the air, as he waved both arms in a gesture of jubilation.

'The gods be praised! Stephanos, the Oracle was right. Theophrastos, what news you bring! My wife has written to say that she is with child again, at last. She wants me to be with her – she has been a little unwell. Herpyllis, my mother's favourite slave, has come to stay in our house; Pythias is fond of Herpyllis, and she is an excellent nurse. But I cannot wait an hour longer – we must go back to Athens at once! Pythias and I must share this joy together.'

And so we did go back at once, or almost, as soon as we could pack up our few possessions and give effusive thanks to Smikrenes. Our host, relieved to see us go (he was still not used to guests) came out to the gate and detained us long in farewells.

'And look at this place,' he said to me. 'You won't see a finer bit of soil. Look at that dung-heap – magnificent, isn't he? I've kept him going for years. Tickles up the vines, that does, a good bit of dung. Here are some cakes for you – Philomela's baked them – and some of our own cheese.' He pressed the delicacies, rather squashed together, into my hands.

'I don't recall when I've enjoyed myself so much,' he continued. 'We must have another twist at our bargain, you and I. Mind you, I don't say "yes" to the whole contract yet – but I don't say "no", neither. Come back soon. And your friend, too. I must get used to company. After all, why shouldn't a man love his fellow-men? 'Tis only natural.'

'That's right,' I agreed.

'Why, only look at the sheep – and the bees and other beasts. They stick together, so it's only natural,' he repeated, enjoying his philosophy and leaning upon the handle of his hoe. Then he looked beyond us, along the path to the shrine, and his face contracted. A tremendous scowl crept darkly over his forehead, like a thunderstorm moving across the sky.

'Who *are* those coming to the sacrifice?' he asked angrily. Catching up his hoe and holding it like a lance, he moved off at full speed towards the offenders, bellowing like a bull escaped from a barn. The little procession – a city wife, her children, a young man and three slaves – fled with astonished cries, dropping pots, pans and cushions in their wake.

Aristotle and I burst out laughing. Theophrastos looked from us to Smikrenes and back again, thoughtfully.

'An irascible man,' he said. 'Yes. I see.'

The interruption gave us the opportunity of moving away at last from Smikrenes' gate, and, shouting our last farewells from the road, we went on our way.

'I shall have a son,' said Aristotle joyfully. He put his arm about my shoulders in a brief embrace. 'And you, Stephanos, shall marry. You shall be wived within the year, with a fine bride, and after wedding and bedding her you too shall have children, as your father did before you. The Oracle is wise in all things.' Then he turned to Theophrastos, and they began a conversation.

I had leisure to meditate as I walked along. Already the events of the past few weeks were fading from my memory, distanced, like a play seen a while ago. The Silver Men seemed remote. My own life now felt more real – and prospects were fair. Almost without noticing it, I began to hum, and the song was 'Love came knocking at my door'. The sun shone, and new anemones bloomed in the ditches and on thymy banks. The lark sang clearly overhead, and troops of black-backed swallows flew high against the dome of the sky. It was true spring.

ARISTOTLE DETECTIVE

Athens 332 BC – a city uneasy under the sway of the Macedonian Alexander the Great, now fighing the King of Persia for control of the East. In this time of fresh ambition and furtive discontent, an eminent citizen is brutally murdered.

Young Philemon, an exile formerly guilty of manslaughter, is accused of the bizarre homicide. In his absence his cousin and nearest male reative, 23-year-old Stephanos, must conduct Philemon's defence and attempt to clear his family's name of this bloody murder.

Stephanos seeks help from Aristotle, his former teacher . . . and Aristotle turns Detective.

'Why did no one think of this before?'
– The Times

'Wit in a first novel is rare enough, and when allied to the skilful unravelling of a murder story set in Ancient Athens it makes us doubly grateful for *Aristotle Detective*'
– Daily Telegraph

'Eminently enjoyable'
– Colin Dexter

ARISTOTLE AND THE SECRETS OF LIFE

It is summer, 330 BC. The Macedonian Alexander the Great has conquered Asia Minor but now his armies are far from Athens, and those who support Athenian independence are beginning to chafe and plot against him. Foreigners, like Aristotle, and those suspected of befriending foreigners, such as Stephanos, are threatened. A series of threats persuade these two that they will be best served by quitting the mainland for a while. They both find suitable excuses: Aristotle has to transport a sick student home to Rhodos, while Stephanos must find a relative of his bride-to-be Philomela to clear up an inheritance dispute.

With a varied cast of travellers they set sail across the Aegean to the sacred isle of Delos, to Mykonos and beyond to the coast of Asia Minor. There they will soon be embroiled in investigating conspiracy and murder. But first they must survive life on the high seas where storms and piracy honour no man, least of all the greatest philosopher who has ever lived.